Blackbeard

A TALE OF VILLAINY AND MURDER
IN COLONIAL AMERICA

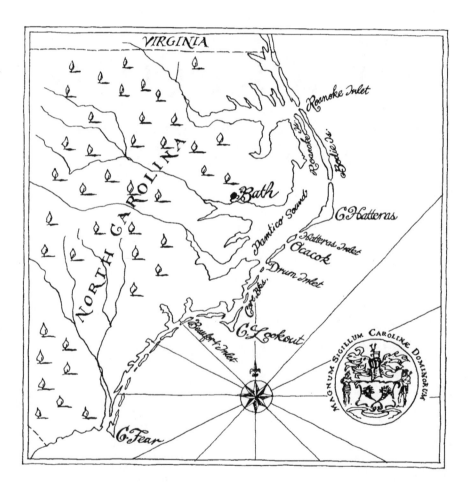

Blackbeard

A TALE OF VILLAINY AND MURDER IN COLONIAL AMERICA

Margaret Hoffman

Coastal Plains Publishing Company
Raleigh, North Carolina

Published in Raleigh, North Carolina
by Coastal Plains Publishing Company

Coastal Plains Publishing Company
3l16-27 Dockside Circle
Raleigh, NC 27613
(919) 788-9539

Printed in the United States of America

Library of Congress catalog card number: 81-69261

ISBN 0-9607300-1-X

To Phil Masters
and the dive team that discovered the Queen Anne's Revenge

Contents

Acknowledgments

Pirates, and especially Blackbeard, have always been a subject of intense fascination. But it was not until the discovery of Blackbeard's flagship, the *Queen Anne's Revenge*, that there has been a resurgence of interest in Blackbeard unprecedented in America's history.

It is to Phil Masters of *Intersal* and the dive team that discovered the *Queen Anne's Revenge*, that I owe the publication of this book. It is not everyday that an author's ship, literally, comes in.

Blackbeard's forty-gun flagship, the *Queen Anne's Revenge*, was the most powerful pirate vessel to ever sail in American waters. It was one of Blackbeard's flotilla of four vessels which blockaded Charleston harbor for a week in May of 1718, finally sinking off Beaufort Inlet, North Carolina (in those days named Topsail Inlet) a month later. The sinking of the ship is described in full in Chapter Three of this novel.

I would like to thank all those people who have been involved in the *Blackbeard Project* from its inception. The project began in the early 1980s, when nautical archaeologist David Moore, then a graduate student at East Carolina University, researched the Blackbeard story. He wrote a report suggesting that a search effort be mounted. But it wasn't until 1986 when Richard Lawrence, the North Carolina state underwater archaeologist, brought this report to the attention of Phil Masters, that the discovery of the ship began. Phil started his own archive investigation and put together a proposal for the recovery of the *Queen Anne's Revenge*. He obtained a state permit, incorporated under the name of *Intersal* and began the search for the lost pirate ship in 1988.

In 1996, after years of frustration, *Intersal* hired Mike Daniel, who specializes in locating lost historic sites, as director of operations. It was Mike's interpretation of Phil's research that made the difference. On November 21 of 1996, one day shy of the exact day that Blackbeard was killed in 1718, *Intersal* discovered the *Queen Anne's Revenge*.

Aware of the historical significance of the pirate ship, *Intersal* agreed in talks with North Carolina chief archaeologist Steve Claggert that everything recovered should remain as an intact collection, never to be sold. The non-profit *Maritime Research Institute* was incorporated, with Mike Daniel as president, to work in cooperation with the North Carolina Department of Cultural Resources, Division of Archives and History (headed by Jeffrey Crow) to excavate the site and conserve the recovered artifacts. The *North Carolina Maritime Museum* in Beaufort, represented by David Moore, the archaeologist who started it all, is responsible for curating the collection. To this day, over 300 artifacts have been discovered including cannon, a ship's bell and a blunderbuss or small gun.

When the discovery of the *Queen Anne's Revenge* was announced in March of 1997, it triggered an avalanche of worldwide interest in piracy in general, and Blackbeard, in particular. My book, which was researched and written in the years 1976 to 1981, obtained interest from a publisher, Robin Sumner Asbury, who had the foresight, independence and initiative to take on its publication.

My gratitude is given to the North Carolina Department of Archives for the paraphrased quotes from the letters published in the Colonial Records of North Carolina, William L. Saunders, editor. These quotes appear on pages 264-265. I would also like to thank the Virginia Historical Society in Richmond, Virginia for the paraphrased quotes from the Lee-Ludwell papers on page 235.

In addition to the above people and organizations, there are others who have helped in one small way or another throughout the years to bring this book to publication: Marjorie and Julian Hoffman of Danville, Virginia, my parents, who originally sent me a newspaper article on Blackbeard in 1976; Robert E. Lee, who wrote an authoritative historical text on Blackbeard entitled, *Blackbeard the Pirate*; Mike Everette of Raleigh, North Carolina; Rick Allen of Nautilus Productions located in Fayetteville, North Carolina; Greg Davis of DKI International Video Productions in Morehead City, North Carolina; Josephine Hookway of the Bath Historical Commission in North Carolina; Professor William Hardy of the University of North Carolina at Chapel Hill; Peter Guzzardi of Chapel Hill, North Carolina; J.W. Hester of Chapel Hill, North Carolina; the North Carolina Department of Tourism; Dick Andert of Atlanta, Georgia; Nancy Lewis of Winston Salem, North Carolina; the Sinbad Privateering School of Beaufort, North Carolina; the crews of the following tall ships—the *Providence* of Rhode Island, the *Bounty* of Fall River, Massachusetts, and the *Barbra Negre* of Savannah, Georgia; Mel Fisher of Sebastian, Florida; Ben Cherry of Plymouth, North Carolina, impersonator of Blackbeard; and Glenn Mayes of Greensboro, North Carolina; John Headen of Graham, North Carolina; David Dickieson of Washington, D.C.; Nina Graybill of Washington, D.C.; Samuel Rael of Atlanta, Georgia; John Headen of Graham, North Carolina; Randall Cash of Danville, Virginia; and Bonnie Ross Cooper of Danville, Virginia.

To all of you—a toast to the pirate's life!

Margaret Hoffman
Raleigh, North Carolina
June 13, 1998

Introduction

In 1716 off the coast of Nassau, Edward Teach, otherwise known as Blackbeard, raised his Jolly Roger. That was almost three centuries ago, and still his name lives on. His depredations have produced a legend that have made him, along with Captain Kidd, the best known pirate of all time.

For only two years, before his death in 1718, Blackbeard was to wreak havoc on Atlantic coastal shipping. His beard, wrote Daniel Defoe, "like a frightful meteor, covered his whole face, and frightened America more than any comet that has appeared there for a long time."

The entire coast was to bear witness to the daredevil deeds of this tall, enormously strong, wild and brave sea rover. Charleston, South Carolina stood by helplessly as Blackbeard blockaded her harbor with his flotilla of four pirate vessels and held the town for ransom. Later Charleston would have her revenge on the pirate by hanging his shipmate, Major Stede Bonnet, at White Point. Blackbeard so frightened Virginia that her governor sent warships to capture him.

Blackbeard's name can be found in the archives of Great Britain as well as those of Pennsylvania, Virginia, North Carolina and South Carolina. The Gulf of Florida became his favorite sea lane to the Spanish Main. Legends of Blackbeard's buried treasure linger in Georgia where enthusiasts still hunt his pieces of eight at Blackbeard's Island. Numerous places have been named after him in North Carolina—Blackbeard's Point in Bath, Teach's Hole at Ocracoke Inlet, and Teach's Oak near Oriental. His skull was reputed to have been fashioned into a punch bowl which once graced the tables of Raleigh's Tavern in Williamsburg, Virginia.

But no one site is more famous for Blackbeard's nefarious activities than historic Bath on the mouth of the Pamlico River. There the pirate lived out his remaining months. It was in Bath that Blackbeard became associated with Governor Charles Eden of North Carolina. This association especially shocked Englishmen of the era who held their governors, as representatives of the king, in high regard.

To all appearances, the governor and the pirate had a close friendship. But there were those who held the opinion that the two had other connections as well, namely business ones. Some said the governor and the pirate found the profits of illegal trading alluring. Others swore the two were involved in piracy. However, no one guessed that the pirate and the governor were involved in one of the major crimes of the century...a crime that would send two colonies to war and foreshadow the American Revolution.

This novel begins in Bath in 1718 during the "Golden Age of Piracy" when the boldest and most notorious sea rovers infested the coastal waters of the English colonies. It is based on a true story. Although certain fictional elements have been added, the characters can be found in the Virginia and North Carolina Colonial Records and the actual events have been told in the sequence in which they occurred in history.

—Such a Day, Rum all out; —Our Company somewhat sober; —a damn'd Confusion amongst us!—Rogues a plotting; —great Talk of Separation. —So I look'd sharp for a Prize; —such a Day took one, with a great deal of Liquor on board, so kept the Company hot, damn'd hot, then all Things went well again.

—From Blackbeard's Journal

Rogues a' Plotting

It was a good day for a hanging.

Governor Charles Eden glanced out the open window of a house he and his council members had rented to view the hanging. There was not a cloud in the sky. The thought crossed his mind that this should indeed please the rabble below who would not take kindly to a chance thundershower spoiling their entertainment.

It was early, but already the crowd had begun to gather in the common below the window. The attraction they so eagerly awaited was the hanging of three relatively unknown pirates. The pirates, hands cuffed behind them, had already been dragged onto the scaffold and were standing in a line and gazing apprehensively at their fate—a gibbet from which dangled three nooses. Dressed in black, the executioner began fiddling with the nooses.

"Some more champagne, perhaps?" one of the councilmen asked.

Eden shook his head.

Elegant in his cravat of lace with square ends, Eden gazed down at the crowd once again and wondered what they saw in these hangings. Ever since his birth in 1673 in London he had been taken to executions, from the Grand Stands at Tyburn Fair to this rented house in Bath, North Carolina. The thought struck him that the whole scene was rather macabre. However, he would be surprised to know that the other gentlemen he was seated with considered the whole situation as natural as eating breakfast, which, by the way, they were enjoying on this sunny, spring morning as they gazed down at the pirates.

"I dare say you haven't touched your eggs," one of Eden's council members said, glancing at his plate.

"I don't care for breakfast." Eden pushed aside his plate. The whole situation was having an adverse effect on his digestion.

"It shouldn't be long now," said the spokesman of the group.

Eden nodded, took out a gold watch on a chain from his breast pocket and flipped it open: nine-twenty.

The crowd was growing larger with each passing minute. Indeed, it was so large now it was beginning to jam the common. Eden sighed in relief. He had counted on a large crowd for the hanging. Public floggings and water duckings rarely brought so many people.

Below, the provost marshal began to cry out, "One John Silias, one Archibald Duck, and one Jeremiah Harriott—ordered by the Court of Vice-Admiralty to be hanged, drawn and quartered for the crime of piracy on the high seas on this third day of June in the year of our Lord, seventeen hundred and eighteen."

The grim-lipped provost marshal then stepped aside.

Eden noted, with a sort of curious satisfaction, that the crowd of onlookers below were waiting with various kinds of delight. Some were intrigued with the gibbet from which the men were to be hanged, others by the sharpened blades that would be used for the quartering of the pirates.

Eden, on the other hand, took no more than a passing interest in the hanging. Instead, he adjusted the spyglass in his hand and applied it to his eye. He was obviously searching for someone as he surveyed the area—firstly, the Pamlico River to the south, where sloops, schooners and brigantines loaded goods bound for the mother country; then the stores, where the red men (Pamlico, Machapunga, Coree and Tuscorara) traded furs and deerskins for rum and guns; and lastly, the town's dirt streets where the razorback hogs rooted for acorns, hickory nuts and chinquapins.

Not at all satisfied with what he saw, Eden returned the spyglass to his lap and sighed in discontent.

"He's not here?" one of the council members asked.

Eden shook his head.

Fashionably dressed, Charles Eden looked the portrait of a genteel nobleman. In fact, it was often said of Eden that he was quite charming and maintained a captivating address. But his face betrayed a somewhat roguish smile and in later years, he was referred to as "a strange unaccountable man."

Rising from his chair and turning his back to his council members, Eden crossed the room. Turning once more to face the men, he spoke with the confidence of a man who was accustomed to having his own way. His voice was firm, well-modulated and authoritative. "I trust," he said, without a hint of hesitation, "that the syndicate is with me."

The spokesman of the group saw fit to partake of another sip of champagne before answering. "Most assuredly, Governor, the syndicate will back you...as long as, I might add, your stratagem involves a quantity of money."

Still certain that he had the upper hand, Eden took a pipe from his breast pocket, filled it with tobacco from a small box on the table and lit it. "Twelve million pesos worth of Spanish silver is quite a goodly sum," he remarked.

The councilmen nodded in agreement.

Eden flicked open his watch again—nine twenty-five. Then he recrossed the room and gazed fixedly out the window.

Below, a whole crowd of rough, raucous people had gathered—their total concern, the pirates. Eden smiled. A hanging was the perfect diversion for his plan. Not one person would be paying the slightest attention to him.

The crowd cheered.

Onto the platform below stepped the executioner, followed by the chaplain reading from the Bible.

At this moment, there was a good deal of laughter and shouting and stomping of feet.

"Time's come," the executioner said to the pirates, and he smiled with easy joviality.

Gazing on the pirates, Eden reached the sudden realization that he, or any of the other members present, if found out, could suffer the same fate as those poor prisoners below. For what were they planning now, if it wasn't piracy?

"I don't like it," Tobias Knight said. He was obviously having second thoughts. "What if we're found out?"

Eden, taking a puff on his pipe, frowned. His collector of customs and judge of the colony was a thin, meager-looking man with large, black eyes. He was suffering from a cold, his nose dripping at such an incredible pace that it was necessary to hold a handkerchief in front of it during the entire course of the meeting. His constant coughing irritated Eden to no end.

Nervous even at the best of times, Knight looked an utter wreck as he gazed at the condemned men and thought of his own possible fate.

"We must consider the fact that the plate fleet has never been captured by an Englishman before."

"Knight is correct," the spokesman remarked. "Governor, you know as well as I that the Spanish guard their treasure ships with utmost security. They have whole armadas of warships for the plate fleet's protection—the Windward Armada, the South Seas Armada, the *Tierra Firme* Flota and the New Spain Flota. To succeed in capturing a plate fleet would demand an amazing amount of audacity and risk. It would be the major crime of the century."

"The idea's quite extraordinary!" Knight said.

"Almost preposterous!" another council member exclaimed.

"Incredible!" the spokesman said.

Eden, who had not expected any obstacles so late in his plans, sensed this sudden hesitation was costing him all his headway. "Perhaps," he said, suddenly whirling around on his heels, "I should take my business elsewhere."

The councilmen glanced at each other uneasily. "Not so fast," the spokesman said. "We were only commenting on Knight's opinion."

For the moment the men dispensed with Knight as they would an unwanted thought.

They preferred to turn their minds to the silver until one of the four suddenly become aware that the chanting from the crowd below had ceased.

Rising from his chair and crossing to the window, one of the councilmen, arms drawn behind his back, made the abrupt pronouncement, "The hanging's about to begin."

Charles Eden, after calmly shaking the contents of his pipe into a small container, joined him at the window.

The crowd seemed to be holding its breath in mass unison. Everyone watched intently as the first pirate was brought before the noose. The pirate's face was expressionless as the executioner put the rope around his neck.

Crowd won't like that, Eden thought. He's not suffering enough.

And indeed, as if in confirmation of his thoughts, an old woman screamed, "Make him cry out."

The executioner ignored the woman.

With a grimace, Eden turned away from the window. Wasn't the crime these people committed against their fellow human beings worse than the crime of piracy on the high seas?

The question was food for thought, and Charles Eden, who had hardly consumed anything all morning, digested this idea briefly. However, the chiming from the belfry across the way brought him back to his present situation. "It's nine-thirty," he pronounced.

"He's not here yet," one of the council members remarked.

"He'll be here," Eden said. "You can count on that."

"Have you the letter?"

Eden, now reaching into his breast pocket, took out an envelope. Unsealing it with care, he opened it to reveal a rough-looking piece of parchment. Crested with the coat of arms of King Philip of Spain, the letter was not more than two paragraphs long, written in small, precise calligraphy.

Curiously, the three councilmen looked at the parchment. Then the spokesman withdrew his spectacles from his waistcoat pocket and placed them on his nose. He squinted. "I warrant it's very prettily writ, Governor," he said, "but hardly readable to an Englishman."

Eden drew in on his pipe. "As I informed you, Gentlemen, the letter was found on board a prize, *Madre de Dios*, captain, Alonso de Pales, taken in March. It was found hid in the captain's log. A seaman brought it here."

"For a stiff price, no doubt," Knight said, raising an eyebrow.

Eden gave his councilor a sharp glance. The man was certainly contrary today. Perhaps his cold was adding to his sour disposition. "It was quite a stiff price, if you must know, Mr. Knight," Eden continued. "But well worth it. The letter is a *real orden* of King Philip of Spain—an exceedingly important document."

"Exceedingly," the spokesman said, fingering the paper.

Eden quickly withdrew the contents of the envelope from the spokesman's grasp. Studying it for a moment, he added proudly, "This letter, gentlemen, is priceless. It tells of a secret ship, the *San Rosario*. This ship, and this ship alone, will be carrying the silver. No guard ships will be accompanying her. No armada. Nothing."

Breaths held in eager anticipation, the four gentlemen gazed at the paper in reverence.

Below in the common, with equal reverence, the crowd gazed at the executioner.

Eden placed the letter on a table and returned to the window again. He watched the executioner tighten the noose around the pirate's neck.

In no more than a fraction of a second, the first pirate was allowed to drop.

In this process of hanging, drawing and quartering, the pirates would not be hanged in the normal way. The drop was not that lengthy. Instead, the first pirate was allowed to dangle from the rope only long enough to entertain the crowd by a convulsive dance in mid-air.

"That don't count," the executioner said, and the crowd broke into riotous laughter.

Eden felt his stomach turn over.

Knight looked out the window. "One mistake, and we'll end up with a noose at our neck."

"There won't be any mistakes," Eden said. Descended from the lineage of an English nobleman, Charles Eden had always been successful at everything in his life. He saw no reason to fail at this.

Looking at Charles Eden, one might quickly formulate the opinion he had been born to win. His tall, muscular physique and vast wealth indicated this. Charles was one of the ancient and distinguished Edens of the English family seated in the County Palatine of Durham. He held the title of landgrave, although most Bath citizens ignored it.

In fact, Eden's rise to power was due only in part to his heritage. One doesn't advance in governmental positions without a little manipulating, a little back-stabbing, a few tough tactics. At heart, he was not against moving his superiors up and competitors out to get ahead. If that meant a little illegal behavior at times, he was not against that either. It was the price one paid to get ahead.

But Charles Eden was also a man who could start a project and carry it through. Not bothered by humanity, he would start this enterprise or that, draw it up on a sheet of paper and say, "Do this and see you damn well do it properly." Charles Eden did things; other men only talked about doing them.

Most people are guided by an internal code of ethics. Charles Eden was not. He had no principles.

His behavior, instead of being bounded by principles, was limited to what it could do for Charles Eden. Pride was his motive. That pride of his took part in what looked like generous impulses, and he would sometimes secretly scoff at himself for the actions he took. He thought himself superior to others. "Look at me, look at what I can do," his eyes seemed to say. But he was dangerously dependent on others to reinforce his superiority. If he fell in the eyes of others—he was desolate.

Charles Eden laughed at the world. He stood outside of it and he watched its goings-on with scorn. And law? What was that to Eden? Looking down on the proceedings below, he would have said he was above it.

Standing now at the window, feet planted firmly beneath him, he watched the first pirate.

The crowd, eyes also riveted on the pirate, pressed in closer to the scaffold.

Eden looked away from the scaffold. With a cursory glance, he searched the crowd.

"He's due," the spokesman said.

Eden flipped open the lid of his watch to catch the time again.

"Perhaps it's too much of a risk for him now," Knight said.

Eden, already impatient, lost his temper with the man. His voice rose in intensity as he shouted, "Even if someone were to recognize him—a highly unlikely assumption, I might add—do you suppose for one instant they would take their eyes off the drawing? Well, do you?"

Dumbfounded, Knight could only tremble.

Eden continued. "I suppose you'd rather some dark alleyway, some seedy grog shop where someone's sure to expect the worst."

Knight shook his head.

Satisfied that he had silenced the man, Eden once more turned to face the window. He left a rather disconsolate Mr. Knight sniffing softly to himself.

"Have you ever made his acquaintance, Governor?" the spokesman of the group asked.

Eden shook his head.

"Nor I," the spokesman said. "But I've heard tell the merchants in the syndicate have taken quite a liking to him. They enjoy stolen goods at bargain rates. In fact, he's somewhat of a hero amongst them."

"So they say." To the eye, Eden showed no more than a casual interest in his contact. But in his heart, he felt the excitement racing. For months his total being had been consumed by thoughts of the man he was about to meet.

"What's to make him want to join us?" Knight asked. He had recovered from Eden's fit of temper and was regaining his former annoying disposition with an amazing degree of alacrity. "He's the most feared pirate alive. In fact, he's just held Charleston harbor for ransom. The people ran through the town terrorized like mad things when they saw him. Even the king's navy can't stop him."

Another councilman had to agree with Knight. "It's all very well and good, Governor, for you to want him to capture a ship for you. But it's easier said than done. How do you propose to go about it?"

Governor Eden laughed, shrugging this problem aside as inconsequential. Eden looked at Knight. "You say that the king's navy's after him?"

"Yes," Knight said.

"So, Mr. Knight, I merely had the merchants in our syndicate inform the king's navy in a rather roundabout way of a few of his favorite hiding places."

"But they'll capture him!" Knight exclaimed.

Eden burst into laughter. "Capture the most infamous pirate that ever lived! I should think not." After regaining his composure he continued, "He's the bloodthirstiest hound ever to sail. And crewmen—why, he's got four hundred of them! And a larger flotilla than any pirate sailing. They also say he's the cleverest pirate in history. But if he's as clever as they say, he'll surrender first to my protection. That, you see, Mr. Knight, is what I have to offer him—his life for my protection. And if he's anything but a fool, he'll accept it with gratitude."

Knight pressed his lips together and crossed his arms. "I still don't like it."

Eden glared at the man.

Cringing, Knight looked at the spokesman with a helpless gesture.

Obviously trying to save Knight from coming to blows with the governor, the spokesman interrupted the two. "I don't know much about him, Governor. But if we're to be on a working relationship with this criminal, I'd like to know some more."

The spokesman's little diversion worked extraordinarily well. Eden was so sufficiently distracted, he forgot completely about Knight. "Very well," he said. "The man was born in 1680 or thereabouts in Bristol, England. He joined the ships of privateers, then, during Queen Anne's War."

"Bristol's quite a seafaring center," Knight commented. "If I do recall, John and Sebastian Cabot were from Bristol."

Eden gritted his teeth at Knight. He would have liked nothing better than to give the man a blow. Instead, he lit his pipe.

"Do continue," the spokesman said.

Eden nodded.

However, the other councilman broke in. "He socializes freely with wealthy politicians and members of the upper class."

"One questions why they would associate with a pirate," Knight said.

"Money," the councilman responded. "What else?"

"From the rising merchant class, no doubt," the governor added.

"No doubt," sniffed the councilman.

The gentlemen seated here were from the aristocracy. They had inherited their wealth. Although the merchant class had become quite large, there was still a great deal of class consciousness, especially from the upper class who saw itself threatened by an emergent middle class.

"Most likely, he comes from a well-to-do family to move so freely in social circles," the councilman continued.

Eden was visibly moved by that last statement. "Odd. Most of these seamen come from the lower class—beggars, sniveling fellows sponging for bread. As often as not, they haven't a shirt on their back."

The councilman nodded. "Come from a well-to-do family...and a criminal."

"I dare say, I come from a well-to-do family," Eden added, smiling and all the while puffing on his pipe. "And I, too, am a criminal."

"I wouldn't go so far as to say that," Knight said, glancing over his shoulder at the condemned men below.

Eden chose to ignore Knight's comment. "I hear he's quite intelligent."

"Most," the official said. "He reads and writes fluently for he often corresponds by letter to many government officials."

"Hmm," Eden said slowly. He took another puff on his pipe. "They say after the War he joined with Hornigold—the great Hornigold."

"That's correct, Governor," the councilman said. "Hornigold trained him. Hornigold was the fiercest pirate of the lot—save for *him*."

Eden turned to watch the crowd again. Suddenly the governor's eyes fell upon one man in particular. The man was tall, broad-shouldered and robust. His eyebrows were extremely bushy. He was dressed in black outer regalia, a broad hat and knee boots. Unlike many in the crowd who were clean-shaven, he possessed a dark beard. Below his waistcoat, hung a pistol and cutlass.

For a moment their eyes met—the governor's and the ruffian's. And then, so as not to appear too obvious, the ruffian turned away.

Eden turned around to speak, but Knight took the words right out of his mouth.

"He's here."

Eden returned his gaze to the pirate. He could not take his eyes off this legendary figure.

"What might his real name be?" Knight asked.

"Edward Teach," Eden said.

"Teach?" Knight screwed up his nose in distaste. It was evident to everyone present he didn't like the sound of the name.

"Teach," the councilman repeated. "They spell it in numerous ways, some Thatche, some Thach, some Tache, some..."

Eden waved his hand to stifle the man. "That'll do."

Curtailing the conversation, Eden walked across the room and picked up the *real orden* of King Philip of Spain. But before he took his leave, he turned for a moment. Poised at the threshold, letter in hand, Eden whispered, "Gentlemen, say nothing, do nothing, see nothing. Sit where you are, raise no alarm and twelve million pesos worth of Spanish silver is yours."

And then pocketing the *real orden*, Eden walked out of the room and down the stairs to meet the greatest pirate who ever lived, the infamous—Blackbeard.

Blackbeard—
Lord Of The Black Flag

lackbeard saw Governor Eden's figure retreat from the window. Only moments later he noticed the man descending the rickety outdoor steps to the street. Blackbeard studied the man for a few minutes. He looked to be a true gentleman—just how Blackbeard would have liked to look had he been an aristocrat—powdered wig on his head, gold cane in his hand, dressed in a broadcloth waistcoat and silver-buckled shoes.

Most of the people in the crowd did not bear much resemblance to Eden. They were a shabby bunch dressed in cheap serge, frieze or kersey. To make matters worse, they were noisy. The din of their voices was almost deafening. They jeered and laughed and shouted. As the morning wore on and they had their fill of small beer which was being passed around, they uttered rude obscenities. Their children, laughing shrilly, raced in and out among the carriages along the streets.

To add to this uncomfortable atmosphere, it was hot. The few shade trees had long ago been taken by the first arrivals, and as the crowd packed closer and closer together in the stifling heat, the odor of perspiration and stale beer penetrated the air. Flies and gnats buzzed over the crowd.

Blackbeard had to be grateful for all this bedlam. It hid his identity beautifully. No one paid the slightest attention to him. As it was, not many people would recognize him anyway, having been on land while he was at sea, but he did notice a few straggling sailors in the area who might have had a run-in with him. As he pulled his slouch hat tighter over his head, he was thankful Eden had suggested this as a meeting place.

"Shouldn't he long now before the drawing," said an old woman with a scabby nose. She was talking to a scrawny little man, her husband, standing next to her, and Blackbeard wondered if her nose might fall off at any instant. He guessed she had obtained her wobbly nose due to the habit of eating too much undercooked pork, a common condition among lower-class North Carolinians.

The man didn't answer her. Instead, he took a swig of beer, swirling it around his month with his tongue. Blackbeard could watch the course of the beer down the man's throat as his Adam's apple bobbed up and then down. After watching the man, Blackbeard allowed his attention to wander to the scaffold.

The crowd grew quiet as the provost marshal, dressed in a dark suit, stepped to the forefront of the scaffold. Hurling his fists to the high heavens, he spoke in fierce condemnatory words on the subject of piracy. "These are murderous scoundrels that stand here before you. They deserve to die. They would be free had they surrendered to our governor and taken His Majesty's pardon. But they chose not to surrender, preferring to bereave men of their lives and provision for a pastime and diversion. Ah, but they are scoundrels!"

"Here, here," the woman shouted, and the crowd rallied closer to the scaffold.

"See here," the provost marshal continued. He pointed now to the pirates, one dangling in unconscious spasms from the rope, and the two others shivering from fright, even in the sweltering heat. "These pirates come from New Providence and, as you know, New Providence is ruined by the pirates of late. Now North Carolina is fair aswarm with these villains. If no effectual care is taken to suppress these pirates, North Carolina, too, will he overrun with them. Let us take care lest we suffer the same fate as New Providence."

"Let them die," shouted the old woman, so enthusiastically that Blackbeard pulled his waistcoat around him very closely even in the heat and then glanced anxiously through the crowd. He had no wish to change places with those poor pirates on the scaffold whose faces were now caked with dust and whose bodies were already being nibbled by flies. The crowd's viciousness was beginning to unnerve him. It was time for the drawing. Where was Eden, he wondered? He should be here now.

Like clockwork, Blackbeard noticed Eden step into the crowd just as the drawing was about to begin. The governor quickly made his way through the riff-raff.

As Eden approached Blackbeard, the old woman beside the pirate began to speak.

"It's been some time since we had a proper drawing," the woman said, again looking at the scaffold.

"It's been some time since we had anything," her scrawny husband answered. "The last was Goody Howerton's whipping." He remembered the woman naked from the waist up, standing on the scaffold.

"Didn't even give her a full whipping," the woman said, also obviously dissatisfied with the way punishments were being handed out in Bath.

The man took a swig of beer. "She had a nice front though. It's been years agone since I seen a nice front."

The old woman, whose own breasts were wrinkled and sagging, pressed her lips together and gave her husband a nasty glare.

Blackbeard allowed his eyes to stray to the drawing. It was a particularly grisly affair and he knew he would be better off not watching it, but there was something that drew his eye as it drew the crowds.

"Get on with it," someone in the crowd shouted. "Cut him down."

The crowd, which was now experiencing an elevated sense of existence, clapped.

Blackbeard noticed the executioner, a big man with large muscles, did not listen to the crowd, but instead, took his time. He had done drawings many times in the past and knew the ritual to be followed. He flexed his muscles as if in anticipation of the heavy work he would be performing. Then he cut down the first pirate whose body was still spasmodically jerking on the end of the rope. Very smoothly, he removed the rope from around the culprit's head. Quickly stripping the pirate, he shoved him onto a stone block. After plucking a hair from his head, he tested the knife. Satisfied that it was sharp, he raised it above the hanged man's body.

The crowd cheered.

Blackbeard watched as a look of extreme enlightenment spread across the executioner's face. Obviously, the crowd's cheers seemed to reinforce the idea that the executioner was indispensable in his services to God and his country, for now, in one determined swing, the executioner, sharing the crowd's zeal, lowered the sharpened blade and sliced off the prisoner's penis and testicles.

"Make him cry out," the old woman shouted, although the pirate was unconscious.

The executioner, totally absorbed in his duties, ignored her. He ripped out the pirate's belly and entrails. Finally the body was cut into quarters. The other condemned men, witnessing this scene, let forth a series of bloodcurdling screams which served to create more enthusiasm in the crowd.

Blackbeard shivered. He would kill himself before they took him like that. But he was careful to conceal his reactions and he stomped and shouted and ranted with the throng of Bath citizens.

In a moment he saw the governor more than a few feet from him. All the while Blackbeard had been observing the drawing and quartering, Eden had been staring at Blackbeard.

Blackbeard returned the stare. He studied the man he had chosen to surrender to. The governor bore some resemblance to himself. Eden was of the same muscular build and height as Blackbeard, but what he lacked were the dramatic flourishes—the bushy, black beard, the cutlass and pistols, the cordovan boots. Instead, clean shaven, dressed in a brocaded waistcoat and a cocked hat that had recently become the fashion of the wealthy, Governor Eden looked no different from any other gentleman he had met. But give him a few months at sea, a ration of biscuit and dried beans, and he would have that same swarthy complexion and leaner build which characterized Blackbeard's appearance.

Under any other conditions, perhaps Blackbeard would have put up a good fight for his freedom. But the last several weeks had been something of a nightmare. Sudden skirmishes with the Royal Navy had left him wondering whether he had a spy in the midst of his crew. Certainly, the navy had gained an unusual amount of information concerning his hiding places. These frequent battles had made up his mind for him. He would take the pardon. If the governor expected a favor in return for his life, he was more than willing to comply.

It was quite a good thing for the governor that Blackbeard never suspected him of purposefully maneuvering the pirate into surrendering. What might have happened to Eden if he had come under Blackbeard's suspicion, can only be imagined. Perhaps be would have ended his life here and now in some particularly gruesome way at the hands of the pirate. But as it was, Blackbeard gazed at the man with trusting curiosity.

The two continued to eye each other—the one a gentleman, the other a ruffian. Then, with a flourish of movement beginning with a nod and ending with his hand retrieving the *real orden* from his waistcoat pocket,

Eden placed the precious letter in Blackbeard's palm. For a moment they touched. Then they parted.

It was said later by those councilmen who viewed the little rendezvous from the clapboard house above, that Blackbeard waited a few moments before reading the paper. He spent that time watching the hanging.

Only after the second condemned prisoner had been hanged, drawn and quartered, did Blackbeard take the letter from his palm and scrutinize it. He examined it basically to see if it was genuine. Seemingly satisfied with King Philip of Spain's signature, he slipped the letter into his waistcoat pocket.

Blackbeard was well aware of King Philip's unstable situation. It had been sixty, maybe seventy years, since Spain had sailed a yearly armada. Since then, only one fleet had made the voyage every five years—poor pickings for the pirates who hoped to attack some straggling ship that could not keep pace with the others.

The reason for this slowdown in the ships was that for years Spain had imported all of her commodities, relying on her treasure to pay her debts. She had mortgaged shipments of the plate for years in advance to foreign bankers. Now King Philip V was hopelessly in debt, with no money to finance on armada. So, sometimes he sent out lone ships with treasure unguarded by an armada. Blackbeard had heard about the secret ships that King Philip sometimes sent to Spain. But never in all his days of cruising had he come upon one. Now he literally had King Philip's treasure in the palm of his hand. His heart, in joyous expectation of the twelve million pesos worth of Spanish silver, beat rapidly.

So absorbed was Blackbeard in the thoughts of the silver, that he hardly noticed the seafarer watching him from a distance.

For some reason, unknown even to himself, the seafarer had taken his eyes off the hanging. It was just by chance that his eyes came to alight on the governor and Blackbeard at the very moment the exchange of the *real orden* took place. The seafarer was filled with curiosity as to the nature of this exchange. Why, he asked himself, with good cause, would the governor of North Carolina have any dealings with such a ruffian?

Out of curiosity, the seafarer made his way through the crowd and approached Blackbeard.

Blackbeard did not take his eyes off the hanging for a good two minutes. When he did, he found himself looking down on a scrawny little man dressed in a brown cap and a suit of coarse frieze. Obviously a sailor, the man had scars along his neck of the type commonly obtained from keelhauling or being dragged right under the keel of a ship so that the points of encrusted shells had lacerated him. Blackbeard found it rather amazing that the man had survived the punishment. He hoped the seafarer hadn't recognized him.

"Good morrow, mate," the seafarer said. "It's a fine day for a hanging, if I do say so myself."

Because the seafarer did not address him by name, Blackbeard hoped he hadn't been recognized. He answered the seafarer only with a nod.

The seafarer continued his inquiry. "You're a stranger to these parts, are you, mate?"

"Aye," Blackbeard said. What the devil did the man want, he wondered?

"From whence come you?"

"Providence." Blackbeard eyed the seafarer who was gap toothed and dirty from weeks at sea.

"Come lately, I'd imagine," the seafarer said.

"Aye."

Edging closer to Blackbeard, the seafarer whispered in a soft, little voice, "Now what would they call you?"

Blackbeard said nothing. All he wanted was to be away from this little man, from the crowd, from Bath, from North Carolina, even from the continent. However, he could not just run out. It would cause too much suspicion.

Up front, on the scaffold the third pirate was being hanged. Eyes closed, lips trembling, tongue out, he waited for the noose. Blackbeard watched the pirate, hoping the seafarer would do the same.

But instead, now visibly discouraged by the unresponsive answers to his questions, the seafarer gave full vent to his impatience. "Well, Mr. Tew..." he began.

"That's not my name," Blackbeard interrupted. He continued to stare ahead. The crowd was cheering now and he joined in.

The seafarer gave Blackbeard a sidelong glance. "It's little I care," he huffily replied. "It's the name of a pirate of my acquaintance. And from the looks of you, I'd say you were a sea dog."

Blackbeard still did not satisfy the man with an answer. Instead, he moved up to get a better view of the hanging. The seafarer pressed ahead also, jostling the old woman beside him.

The woman gave the seafarer a nasty glare. "Who do you think you are?" she asked. "Pushing ahead of everyone?"

The seafarer apologized and tipped his hat, but it did not seem to remove the woman's sour disposition.

Blackbeard resumed the conversation with the seafarer. "And you," he said. "As like as not, you're a sea dog, yourself."

Highly affronted, the man was quick to defend himself. "A privateer, I am. No scurvy sea dog, and you may lay to that."

Blackbeard smirked in reply. The fact was he could have disagreed with the sailor on this technicality. In reality, there was no difference between a privateer and a pirate, for indeed, they both intercepted Spanish shipping, only a privateer did so during wartime by receiving a commission from His Majesty and so was not declared a common criminal. But he declined to argue with the man. Indeed, he was well aware of the hypocrisy of his fellow human beings.

This last bit of conversation seemed to have aged Blackbeard considerably. For the first time the seafarer noticed the weather-worn face, the crow's feet around the eyes. But he continued to address Blackbeard just at the time when the third pirate was being drawn. "I warrant the pirate Hornigold will take the pardon," he said.

"Aye," Blackbeard said, still staring ahead at the bloodthirsty ritual.

"And Vane?"

"I've heard tell he'll most likely go on the account."

"And thee?"

The devil plague the little man, Blackbeard thought. He was all too inquisitive. However, he did not trouble to answer, instead, cheering again with the crowd.

When the drawing was over and the crowd began to disband to their carriages, Blackbeard turned to go, but found the seafarer still standing next to him. Why was the man still here? He watched the man's hands fidgeting in his pockets and feet tapping impatiently on the ground.

But Blackbeard didn't have long to wait for an answer to his question because the seafarer drew nearer to Blackbeard now, and after glancing first at the governor, and then at the pirate, spoke in a hushed whisper. "What was that paper?" he asked.

Blackbeard whirled around on his heels. It suddenly hit him the seafarer had seen his little rendezvous. Reacting quickly, he grabbed the short man roughly by the waistcoat. And in a tactic that had never failed him yet, his beard bristled and his eyes suddenly caught fire as if the sulfur and brimstone of all hell would burst forth. Then in a gruff, terrifying voice that grew deeper with each word, he whispered, "Blood and wounds! Look you scurvy wretch, breathe one word of that matter and I'll run my sword through thy guts. How, impudent rascal, dare you speak to the face of Blackbeard the pirate? Be off before I blow thy brains out, damn you!"

The seafarer, staring wide-eyed in dismay, felt his throat promptly go bone-dry.

Treachery at Topsail Inlet

Blackbeard later contended, in private conversation, that the seafarer never opened his mouth again. The little man became, in fact, the butt of many of Blackbeard's jokes for days to come. At sea, Blackbeard's shipmates gave the seafarer the alias, "Lock Jaw," and they never failed upon speaking his name to burst into riotous laughter.

Had they known, however, that they would be the next victims of Blackbeard's prankish stunts, perhaps they wouldn't have poked such fun at the seafarer. The evidence, of course, was there, but they failed to notice it.

For two mornings, instead of taking his usual round of rum, Blackbeard had spent his time ceaselessly pacing the deck of his ship, the *Queen Anne's Revenge*—his eyebrows knit in thought, hands behind his back. He was considering taking the pardon, but surrendering meant disbanding his fleet. Scattering his men would not leave enough loot for everyone—especially himself.

Completely befallen to the evils of alcohol, however, Blackbeard's men overlooked their captain's change of mood and began striking up a song.

Blackbeard suddenly ceased pacing. Mood changed, hackles risen, he walked to the bulwarks of his vessel and put a speaking trumpet to his lips. He called to his first mate, Israel Hands, who was on another ship following them, the *Adventure*. Blackbeard's flotilla consisted of the *Revenge, Queen Anne's Revenge, Adventure*, and a smaller sloop.

"Hands," he shouted. "Your captain would be wanting to talk with you. Oblige me by coming aboard the *Queen Anne's Revenge!*"

Most people would think Blackbeard an extremely hard-hearted human being to play such a dirty trick on his mates as he now had in mind. But the fact of the matter was Blackbeard had enormous compassion for his fellow human beings. This compassion, even in the best of times, occasionally got him into trouble. There was one instance when he refused to murder one of his mates who had attacked him after a card game in which Blackbeard was the winner. This cutthroat pirate took a swipe at him with a butcher knife when Blackbeard's back was turned. For this oversight, Blackbeard lacked a piece of his ear.

Surprisingly, Blackbeard was a very moral person. He never harmed a woman, always honored promises and bargains, and could be counted on to help in disasters.

But as fate would have it, Blackbeard had not been destined to live a moral life. He had chosen to join the ships of privateers during Queen Anne's War, and Destiny had rewarded him with a smack in the face. After the war, when he returned home, he found he could not find employment. Most people considered privateers the scum of the earth, no better than murderers or felons.

So in desperation, he chose the only career open to him—piracy. It was not a particularly likable career. He was surrounded by hardened criminals—rapists, thieves, murderers—men who would just as soon slit his throat as look him in the eye. They knew nothing of morals or good or compassion. All they knew was survival.

Blackbeard was a survivor. If circumstances had proven otherwise, perhaps he would have been a truly outstanding human being—a judge or even a governor. But as it was, he could do nothing but play his role as best he could. Indeed, he was extremely cunning and crafty and intelligent, and it wasn't long before he proved himself the leader of his mates.

Blackbeard found himself trapped in a situation beyond his control. In this case, he only did what he had to do. He played his role to the hilt.

As for taking the pardon, he knew full well that once he settled down, there was still a good possibility he might not find employment. Of course, there was the Spanish silver on the horizon, but he was too knowledgeable of accidental circumstances to count on that. However, he was determined to have enough money to survive and live out his days in Bath Town.

Blackbeard watched his first mate lower a small dory from the *Adventure* into the water and subsequently a rope ladder. The two had steered, reefed and roped together, fought battles together, drunk together. No other man aboard ship could be trusted as much as Hands. Together from the first, together to the last—that was the way it would be between the two.

So Blackbeard waited in hopeful expectation as Hands climbed down the ladder and jumped into the dory. After rowing to his captain's flagship, Hands climbed on topside.

Blackbeard clasped his friend's hand warmly.

Hands returned the shake. Something, the first mate thought, was in the wind. He could tell by the twinkle in his captain's eye, the slightly upturned curl of lip. All ears now, he listened as Blackbeard placed his right arm about his shoulder and took him aside.

"Now, then, me hearty," Blackbeard said, his voice gruff and deep, his lips not more than a hairsbreadth from Hand's left ear, "I seen many a man o' fortune what's starving to death. Tell me, where's all Vane's men now? Hell if I know. And Hornigold's? Why most of 'ems aboard here and glad to be—been begging and stealing before that. Aye, I seen a sight o' poor seamen starving and cutting throats, by the powers."

Hands nodded in agreement. If anyone knew life as the bottom rung of the ladder, it was Hands. Suffering from scurvy, belly distended from malnutrition, he had been found by Blackbeard, at death's doorstep in London.

"Now listen," Blackbeard continued. "I'm not to go without, not me, no sir. I'm planning to live easy, never deny myself nothing my heart desires—sleep on goosedown and eat dainties all my days. You gets my drift?"

Hands nodded with pleasure. He counted himself fortunate to be Blackbeard's first mate.

"Aye," Blackbeard said, his voice alluring in its harshness. "Now, you know as well as I, Hands, the booty we have aboard ain't near enough to make us men o' leisure, leastways, if we gets our rightful share-outs. Do I make myself clear?"

Hands smiled. "As clear as noonday, Captain."

Blackbeard, suddenly straightening up and taking his arm from Hands' shoulder, beamed. "Then suppose we talk." Blackbeard led Hands into his cabin.

It was no small thing the two discussed in the cabin that day. In about an hour's time, Hands emerged from Blackbeard's cabin in anticipation. He embarked on his dory once again, and waving in secret acknowledgment to Blackbeard, returned to the *Adventure*.

When Hands was safely aboard ship, Blackbeard gave the orders for the ships to set a course towards Topsail Inlet. Then signaling to

Hands in the assurance of the foreplanned event, he turned to sense the wind. It had shifted to a northerly direction and Blackbeard shouted through his trumpet in a commanding voice for his ship to change direction.

"Ready about!" he cried.

He watched the men loosen the sails. Again he shouted through his trumpet, "Helm alee!"

Blackbeard heard the familiar sound of sails flapping against the masts, and then a man in the foreyards cried, "She luffs."

The ship bore up gallantly and dashing directly through the sea, threw up foam into the very eye of the wind. Then she yielded gracefully to the wind and fell off on a starboard tack.

"She's on a broad reach," shouted one of the crew who had just grabbed the yards.

Blackbeard nodded. "Keep a good full," he yelled.

Bellying with wind, the sails flapped once, and then the ship moved calmly through the water towards the inlet.

Blackbeard was giving commands when a portly little man, dressed in a bright waistcoat and a gentleman's wig, appeared from a hatch below deck and approached Blackbeard.

"Good morrow, Captain Teach," the man said.

Blackbeard turned around to face Major Stede Bonnet. "Why, if it isn't my brethren of the coast, hisself," he addressed the major. "I see you've come up topside."

Blackbeard looked at Major Bonnet for a moment. He turned around quickly to avoid breaking into guffaws at this roly-poly little man who considered himself a pirate.

Like many other gentlemen, Major Bonnet had a secret wish to be a pirate. Unfortunately, he was ill-fitted for the job. Why Major Bonnet had even considered piracy was a mystery to Blackbeard. The man had come from a good family, owned a substantial amount of land in Barbados, was well-educated and had served in the King's Guards. This did not necessarily disqualify him from being a pirate. But Major Bonnet had been foolish enough to actually purchase a ship and hire hands from his own funds, an unheard-of thing, for everyone was aware pirates stole their ships. Bonnet gave his chief reason for becoming a pirate—his wife—who was a shrew and nagged him. So he had departed one evening in his ship, the *Revenge*, without even saying goodbye to Mrs. Bonnet.

Gazing once more at Major Bonnet, Captain Teach thought the man must surely suffer from some disorder of the mind.

"Captain," said Major Bonnet, who now stood side by side with Blackbeard, "we're on a port tack, or I'm mistook."

"I'm afraid you're mistook, Major," Captain Teach said. "T'is a starboard tack we're on."

"Aha, I see," said Major Bonnet who did not really see at all. Poor Major Bonnet was not well acquainted with maritime affairs.

"We steer a course for Topsail Inlet," Blackbeard said, trying to change the subject and make light of Major Bonnet's all too apparent ignorance.

"By the deep six, Captain," shouted the crewmen taking the soundings.

"Captain," Major Bonnet said. His voice had suddenly become quite plaintive.

"Yes," Blackbeard said, rather distractedly. Shouldn't be long now, he thought, imagining the escapade Hands and he had planned.

"I was just wondering," Major Bonnet began.

There was a soft, little whining voice in Blackbeard's ear. Bonnet, who had once again interrupted Blackbeard's train of thought, became the focus of the pirate's attention. "Come, come Major Bonnet, sir," Blackbeard said. "Speak up. It makes me rightly agitated to see a man jabbering his jaw and saying not a word."

Trembling at Blackbeard and yet obviously disturbed enough to continue his conversation, Major Bonnet cleared his throat. It was quite clear that the man had been thinking of what he was about to say for quite awhile now. That he had gotten up the nerve to say it at perhaps the most inopportune moment for Blackbeard was unfortunate indeed for him. "Well," Major Bonnet said, wringing his hands, "am I not commander of the *Revenge*?" He looked longingly out to the sea where his own dear ship was peacefully sailing behind him—having been robbed of his captainship and become part of Blackbeard's flotilla.

"That you are," Blackbeard said, also looking out to the *Revenge*.

"Then why, pray tell, is Lieutenant Richards in command of my ship?"

Blackbeard, totally distracted from his thoughts, turned to face Bonnet. The man certainly had picked a hell of a time to air his grievances.

"I would fain have my ship," Major Bonnet demanded. He stomped his foot to emphasize the point.

Blackbeard, realizing that he must do something to calm the man down, took him aside and put his arm around Major Bonnet's shoulder in a gesture of comradeship. "Major," he said in a comforting voice, "of course, you are captain of your ship. Why captain you are and captain you will always be. You can count on that."

"But I feel a prisoner aboard this ship," Major Bonnet protested. Mindful of the impression he was making, Blackbeard suddenly looked quite forlorn and downcast. "A prisoner!" he declared in surprise. "Why, Major Bonnet, what do you take me for?"

The pitiful condition to which he had reduced Blackbeard, made Major Bonnet think twice before pushing the subject harder. "Well I..." he began.

"Wouldn't you be cuffed and in chains if'n you were a prisoner?" Blackbeard said.

Bonnet looked puzzled. Blackbeard did have a point there.

"No, Major. No prisoner you are, but a guest aboard my ship. It's because I thinks gold pieces of you, gold pieces, that I have given the cares of your post to Lieutenant Richards, All for you, Major Bonnet. So you can decline the post of captain and live easy. It's only proper a man o' leisure like yourself should not be obliged to perform the fatiguing duties a sea voyage demands."

Bonnet had never been good at hiding his feelings. He looked at Blackbeard in a questioning manner, not quite able to make up his mind. Was this cunning scalawag telling him the truth? However, when he went to the stern quarter of the *Queen Anne's Revenge* and looked at his own beloved ship, which was now following Captain Teach's along with the *Adventure*, he could contain himself no longer. Now beside himself with grief, he took from his breast pocket a handkerchief, and into it wailed, "I am confounded with shame. Oh, Lord, I would gladly leave off this way of living, being fully tired of it. Oh, I would I were in Spain or Portugal. If there I might be undiscovered and spend the rest of my days in these countries, thus never having to face another Englishman again. Otherwise, I shall have to stay with these filthy sea dogs as long as I live—a fate worse than death. Oh, if I could be spared the shame of staying aboard this ship, I would separate all my limbs from my body, only reserving the use of my tongue to call continually on and pray to the Lord."

These words may have served to relieve Major Bonnet's dismal state of mind. However, in his efforts to bewail his own fortune, Bonnet had completely infuriated those sea dogs of whom he had spoken. Assailed with such disparaging remarks, one of the crew bounded to his feet, grabbed his sword and lunged at the major. Thrusting the sword right before the major's lips, he shouted so loudly his voice was heard in the neighboring ships. "I'll separate thy limbs from thy body, I will, and feed them to the maws of sharks!"

Heaven only knew what he had done, thought Major Bonnet. He trembled with fear.

"Avast, you miserable sea dogs!" Blackbeard suddenly walked to the stern of the ship where the two stood—the sailor, eyes gleaming wickedly, and Major Bonnet, hiding his head in his hands.

"Captain," the sailor exclaimed, "the men like Major Bonnet none the better for his behavior. I swear they'd be wishing to throw him overboard."

"By the mark three," shouted the sailor who was taking the soundings.

"Blast you, leave off the major," Blackbeard threatened, planting his feet firmly on the deck. "Or I'll set thy arms to the foreyards and tan thy hide!"

"Aye, aye, Captain," he said. He slunk away in fear.

The seaman had barely returned to his former position when the leadsman shouted, "Captain, she's by the mark two! Headed straight for the bar, she is! She'll run aground!"

Before Blackbeard could answer, there was a crash and the sound of wood rending. The sailors barely had time to scurry down the ratlines before the main mast had broken and all the stays parted.

All hell broke loose on the ship.

To make matters worse, Major Bonnet let forth such an earsplitting shriek, it almost shattered Blackbeard's eardrums. Then Major Bonnet waved his arms frantically and wailed in dismay. "By God in heaven, we're sinking!"

"Foundering," Blackbeard corrected.

Technical language was the least of Major Bonnet's worries at the moment. In utter agony, the distraught Bonnet cried, "We're doomed!"

Blackbeard smiled in amusement at Major Bonnet. Such a lack of bravery was indeed rare in a man.

Then, averting his attention to more important matters, Blackbeard placed his speaking trumpet to his lips and, in the voice of an experienced and concerned sea captain, called to Israel Hands, "We've run aground. Warp her out. Throw a line now and double-quick!"

On cue, Hands, who had been waiting for such a call, threw his lines of his own ship across to the *Queen Anne's Revenge*. But his efforts were to no avail. In a moment there was another crack from the *Adventure*.

She, too, was now stuck in the sand. As the moment occasioned, Hands' face took on an extreme expression of bewilderment.

Major Bonnet ran back and forth across the deck, waving his arms in mid-air and staring wide-eyed at the *Adventure*. This was all too much for him. He had been rendered totally speechless.

Assured now that Major Bonnet had suffered enough trauma for one day, Blackbeard calmly patted Bonnet's shoulder. He assumed a contrived look of sorrow and utter hopelessness. "Now if this ain't a fine mess, eh, me hearty?" he asked Bonnet.

Bonnet, whose powers of speech still had not been fully restored, could only nod in agreement.

"Aye, we're in a bad way," Blackbeard said. "Ship wrecked and the king's navy dead on our tails. It's a dirty piece of luck, it is. Aye, Blackbeard the pirate has no luck, not I." Blackbeard paused, sniffing sadly to himself.

Blackbeard's pause was just long enough for Bonnet to contemplate Blackbeard's sad lot in life. What a wretched life this man must have had! What untold sorrows he must have suffered! He felt a pang so strong it wrenched his very heartstrings.

"Yes," Blackbeard continued, "I reckon we'll have to take the pardon which comes hard, you see, for an old sea dog like me."

Take the pardon, questioned Bonnet to himself?

Blackbeard waited for a moment.

Bonnet's face broke into a broad smile.

Obviously, Major Bonnet had had his fill of piracy. In fact, there was nothing he would have liked better at this moment than to take the pardon. "Aye, Major Bonnet said, his speech now fully restored.

In a good-natured way, Blackbeard put his arm round Major Bonnet's shoulder. Bonnet looked in askance at the pirate he had hithto regarded as a crafty villain.

"Aye," Blackbeard said, interrupting Bonnet's thoughts. "The king's navy's upon us, I've no doubt o' that, Major Bonnet. And without our ship, now where would we be? Why, they'd take us faster than you can say Jack Robinson, Major, and you may lay to that. Our best course is to surrender to Governor Eden."

"Aye," Major Bonnet agreed.

"Major Bonnet, you're a man as can be trusted by my account," Captain Teach declared.

"I should hope so." Major Bonnet carefully eyed Blackbeard.

"Yes," Blackbeard said. "A gentleman o' honor you are. I could see that clear the first I laid eyes on you. I said to myself I did, Captain Teach, that's a true gentleman, Major Bonnet—a man to be fully trusted."

"Yes," Major Bonnet agreed.

"Now, Major, I admires a man o' his word, so I'm going to prove to you how much I trusts you."

"And how will you do that, sir?"

"By gum," Blackbeard said, "by giving you full command of your ship, the *Revenge*."

"But it's the only remaining ship!" Major Bonnet uttered in surprise.

"Right you are, Major Bonnet. But I trusts you to sail the ship to Bath and back again. In the meanwhile, the crew and I will take the dories to Bath Town to surrender."

Words couldn't express how overwhelmed Bonnet was with Blackbeard's benevolence. Oh, how could he not have trusted this man? In contrition at his former thoughts, Bonnet lowered his head in shame. "Sir, you are most kind. But my crew and I do not need the *Revenge*. We shall take the smaller sloop to Bath Town. To be sure, we would not leave you without a ship to defend yourself against the king's navy."

Blackbeard smiled broadly. "That's mighty kind of you, Major Bonnet, mighty kind. Bless your heart, you are a man o' honor. Now I'm thinking of another idea as well."

"And what's that?" the major asked.

"Now, if'n I heard tell correctly it seems to me war is threatening again between the Quadruple Alliance and Spain. Why, you could get a commission to go to Saint Thomas and fly the colors of King George, you could."

Bonnet smiled. This was just what he wanted...a chance to restore his respectability. Oh, to be a gentleman again! He was quite elated. "In the meanwhile," Major Bonnet said, "you and your crew can fit out the *Revenge* to sail to Saint Thomas. I'll make haste to return, you can count on that."

"Do that, Major Bonnet. Just you do that."

It was with complete devotion that Major Bonnet now eyed Blackbeard.

Blackbeard smiled as he watched the little man disappear down the hatch to collect his belongings. Indeed, thought Blackbeard, his plan had been executed with amazing cunning. He watched as Major Bonnet, waving, doffed his hat and departed.

It was easy enough to transfer all the goods to the *Adventure*. The transference took little more than an hour to complete. Nevertheless, there was time enough for some of the crew to guess what their captain was up to. Huddling together in a group and eyeing Blackbeard, they came to the obvious conclusion he was about to rob poor Major Bonnet. Those that were going to share in this loot thought it necessary to take things into their own hands. One swarthy pirate stepped forward and proclaimed, "Captain, the crew's gotten wind of your plan and a villainous plan it is—your wanting to nail what is another's loot."

"Well now," Blackbeard began. He had not expected any protests on the men's part.

"It's not seamanly behavior, nohow," said the crew member, who had been opting for a change in captainship of the *Adventure*. It need hardly be mentioned he considered himself, Timothy Robbins, the most likely candidate to succeed Blackbeard. "The crew's dissatisfied," he continued. "They don't value bullying a belaying pin. This crew has its rights such as other crews."

In a thunderous voice, Blackbeard shouted, "So, you're protesting, are you? And how many of you are protesting?"

Twenty-four of the men raised their hands.

"Yes, there's them that defies you," Robbins said.

"You dare to cross the great Blackbeard!" thundered Captain Teach whose barbaric threats usually had the effect of silencing any opposition. "Why, there's never a man that's crossed the great Blackbeard and lived to see a day afterwards."

The men shrunk back in fear.

"I shall have thy livers for dinner, ye swabs," Teach shouted.

"We was merely protesting," a crew member muttered.

Blackbeard's face became red with anger. Indeed, the furnaces of hell seemed to be raging in its depths. "Protesting!" he yelled. "A mutiny, more like."

"No mutiny, Captain." Robbins was now reduced to trembling. His sword at his hand was suddenly little consolation. For what could a sword do against the infernal powers of the devil, himself?

Blackbeard waited for no more explanations but drew forth his cutlass. More furious than ever, his voice filled the air with satanic curses. "Oh, blood and thunder!" he yelled. "Oh, hell and damnation! Oh, glimble!" he continued, so angry he could not even make sense.

The men had no idea what "Oh, glimble!" meant, but they were certain it must be something worse than death itself.

"You'll pay for this," Blackbeard shouted. "So you're outs with your grievances, are you? But I'm still your captain. And you'll do what I say until the time comes when another takes my place." Then he immediately ordered a small boat to be dropped over the side.

"Into the dory!" Teach shouted. "All of you miserable sea dogs."

Eyes already moist with tears, lips trembling, the men looked at their captain in fear.

"Straightaway!" Blackbeard yelled.

The men scrambled into the boat and it was lowered into the water.

"But Captain," pleaded one of the men, looking at the only land, "that island's a maroon island, to be sure. If ever there was an island to perish on, that's one. Without bird nor beast nor herb for sustenance." He broke into tears.

"Then perish ye will!" Captain Teach said, heedless of the man's pleas.

And in a grand finale, he cut the ropes to the boat.

"Get the ship underway," Teach shouted to the others, as the rising tide loosened the *Adventure* from the sand bar. Unlike the *Queen Anne's Revenge*, she was undamaged. "Stand by to loose the topsails."

Two days later, in blissful ignorance of his fate, Major Bonnet returned to find twenty-five marooned men on an island and his ship, the *Revenge*, robbed of all its loot. Vowing to search the seven seas to take his revenge on his adversary, careful not to get his feet wet as he stepped onto the deck of the *Revenge*, Major Stede Bonnet gathered up his men to sail the North American coast.

On the other hand, beaming cheerfully and now quite a wealthy man, Blackbeard entered Bath Town harbor to take the "gracious pardon" of His Majesty's Royal Proclamation and to swear to settle down in Bath and never go a'pirating again.

Some said he did settle down for a time and establish a quiet, respectable life. He bought a home at Plum Point. He had quite a few friends whom he lavishly entertained; and Blackbeard often boasted that there was not a home in North Carolina where he could not be invited for dinner.

But others reported he had dealings with unsavory characters and that he met with known smugglers at a tavern in Bath. Still others said he pirated small trading vessels along the Outer Banks. And there were even a few who said that when Blackbeard met with the governor of North Carolina, Charles Eden, to take the pardon, that the two planned the largest piracy in Blackbeard's career—the capture of the Spanish plate.

Two Conspirators Talk

The night Blackbeard chose to take the pardon was extremely dismal. Low hanging cumulonimbus clouds swept the sky. It is recorded that the "lunar coronae was marked with chromatic peripheries." Outside wind blew, rain drizzled.

On this dark night, a figure of a man could be dimly discerned. He was dressed in a long coat of bright silk, gaudy knee breeches, and low shoes with large buckles. Three pistols hung in his belt. He was occupied, at present, in steering a small dory across Bath Creek to Governor Charles Eden's plantation home on the opposite bank. Those who had chosen to look outside might well wonder why on a night of such extreme weather when visibility was almost impossible, a man in his right mind would venture to steer a boat across a creek. Surely, they would conclude his visit to Eden's home wasn't social. They might even formulate the opinion, as he docked his boat and glanced cautiously over his shoulder so see if someone were watching, that his purpose was even—clandestine.

Charles Eden had no need to guess as to the nature of this visit. It had been previously planned by him. Poised at one of the upstairs windows, his face in the shadow of flickering candles, he stared through the drizzling rain as far as his eye could detect. In sudden recognition of a familiar sight, his eyes alighted on Blackbeard. He sighed. He could not have asked for a better-timed arrival.

In acknowledgment of their foreplanned bargain, he took from his pocket, the pardon. Then, anticipating the pirate's arrival at the appointed hour, he walked to his desk.

Grasping a quill in his right hand, Charles Eden added his signature to the pardon with a flourish of bold, black ink. Immediately, impressions of other papers he had signed in his lifetime flooded his mind.

There were the orders for public whippings of naked women whose only crimes had been birthing bastard children; and reprieves for the men who had fathered those children. There were papers for the tar and feathering of men who spoke out against the king; and levies for minute fines for men who had murdered their blackamoor slaves. There were pardons for men who had enough money to pay for their crimes and writs for decent, hard-working men to be clapped in jail because they had no money to grease palms.

The papers only confirmed Charles Eden's opinion of the law. It was a mockery of justice and morality. Although day-in, day-out, he continued to sign the papers as he had always done, never voicing his opinion, in his heart, Charles Eden held the government under His Majesty, the king of England, in contempt.

Putting the pardon in his breast pocket and blowing out the candles, Eden now descended the stairs in a mild flurry of excitement. The thought of his first true meeting with this adversary of the king thrilled him.

The lights flickering in the windows upstairs, and then in those down below were the signal to Blackbeard that the governor had seen him. He knocked on the door, just loud enough to be heard, and then waited patiently until the massive piece of wood swung open and he stood face to face with Governor Charles Eden.

They studied each other for a moment until a slight noise broke the silence and caused Blackbeard to look uneasily over his shoulder. The pirate moved not a muscle, said not a word.

It was obvious to Eden that the man still suspected him of some plot against his person. But that was to be expected of a man who had been hunted half his life.

"It's only the wind rising," the governor said. "Won't you come in?"

Blackbeard smiled in a somewhat sarcastic manner. "Are you saying, Governor, that you, a representative of the king, will have the company of a pirate?"

Eden took Blackbeard's hat. "No man is a pirate unless his contemporaries call him so."

Blackbeard, whimsically eyeing the governor, entered the house. "Aye, so you'd be thinking of Sir Francis Drake, would you?" he asked.

Eden nodded. Drake had been a privateer for Queen Elizabeth but his actions had been no different from any other pirate. He robbed, murdered, raped. But the fact that he had plundered in the name of the queen made all the difference in the world. She knighted him. Eden saw this action only as another hypocrisy of England's government.

Reading Eden's thoughts, Blackbeard smiled. He already liked the man.

In a better frame of mind than before, Blackbeard followed Eden into a superbly furnished room of Turkish carpets, Russian leather chairs, and bound volumes of gold engraved books.

Eden stirred the coals in the fireplace with a poker.

"The fire and brimstone of hell," Eden said, smiling at Blackbeard and then returning the poker to its rightful place beside the fire. "I hear they call you the devil, himself," he added, trying to make light conversation.

"Some do," Blackbeard answered, still somewhat amazed at his luxurious surroundings. "Aye, some do."

Eden lit a silver candlestick above the fireplace. He had thought to offer the pirate some Kill Devil, New England rum so powerful it was said to kill the devil himself, but on second thought due to Blackbeard's numerous associations with the devil, Eden favored some Irish whisky which he poured from a decanter into a glass.

Blackbeard accepted the whisky with gratitude. Put at ease by Eden's charm and good manners, he seated himself in one of the leather chairs.

Seeing that Blackbeard was comfortable, Eden decided to waste no more time with social amenities. Instead, he withdrew the paper from his waistcoat pocket and handed it to the pirate. "Your pardon," he said.

Unbelieving at first and then just stunned, Blackbeard took the pardon. Tears welled up in his eyes. For years all he had wanted was a respectable life—a chance to walk the streets of a town without fear of being jailed or stabbed and left to die in some Godforsaken alleyway. Now, in one instant, he had been forgiven for all his crimes. It was all too easy after the suffering he had been through. He downed his glass of whisky to force back the tears. Then he revered the paper in silence.

The silence was broken by Eden. "The *real orden?*"

Blackbeard smiled. In full understanding of their foreplanned bargain, he withdrew from his breast pocket the *real orden* of King Philip of Spain. He handed it to Eden. His part of the bargain was sealed. "They tell me you'd be wanting to capture this ship," Blackbeard said.

Eden confirmed Blackbeard's question with a nod. Then taking a pipe from a table beside him, he filled it with tobacco. "Since you are said to be the best of the lot, I felt compelled to call on your services," he said.

Blackbeard could not help but burst into fits of laughter. This was all too much. "Well, now if that don't top it all," he said. "Here I am, done taken the pardon, taken it from you, Governor, to live in Bath Town as a proper man o' means in his retirement and the governor, hisself, wishes me to pirate."

"Indeed, I do."

Blackbeard regarded the governor with curiosity. Then leaning forward in his chair, he asked, "What if I say no, Governor?"

The question did not seem to bother Eden. He remained relaxed but alert, confident but wary, sharp but charming. "I wouldn't do that if I were you."

Blackbeard turned his glass in his hand as if turning around thoughts in his mind. Then examining the glass more carefully, he said, "Now treasure voyages are ticklish work, Governor, and even more so when they're kept secret. My way of looking at it is, it's life or death and a close run."

The governor, ever amiable, and yet more emphatic this time, stated his case. "Listen," he said. "We have a bargain. You were quite downhearted when you came to me—on your knees, in fact. You'd have hanged if I hadn't given you the pardon."

Blackbeard knew he was in no position to argue with the man. "Well, tit for tat," he said. "You saved Blackbeard from swinging, you did, so I'll get your treasure, so be it."

The two men smiled at each other. The precedent thus set could now be faithfully executed.

Eden was indeed quite pleased with the results. With a nod and a smile, he rose from his chair. A little more lighthearted, a little more charming, he clapped Blackbeard warmly on the shoulder and then offered him another drink. Blackbeard accepted and soon fell in with Eden's mood.

"I'm glad you see things my way," the governor said. "It makes everything so much easier, wouldn't you agree?" The question was for Eden rhetorical, and he gave little recognition to Blackbeard's reaction to it. For a moment he seemingly succumbed to a private world. Finally, he spoke. "You'll give me the maps to get the treasure by, of course, and you'll capture the ship. Also, you'll drop your pirating for a while and your stealing from the traders in Bath. That's for suspicion's sake. And I'll divide the treasure with you man for a man."

Such a bargain was indeed benevolent of the governor. Blackbeard smiled, then finished off his whisky with a gulp. "Handsomer, I couldn't hope to get, Governor," he said.

"Good." Eden refilled the pirate's glass. However, his voice conveyed a little more tautness, a little more harshness, as he stressed the seriousness of their venture. It was necessary that the pirate know he would not be indulged any mistakes. As Eden turned to hand the pirate his drink, he warned, "Now you hear me and hear me well. If you cross me, I'll engage to drop you in irons and take you home to England for a trial. You can't sail your ship here unless it's under my protection with a proper certificate of registration. You'll get that. And, in the name of heaven, these are the last words you'll hear from me on this subject. If you ever so much as tell anyone of this conspiracy I'll put a bullet in your back when next I meet you."

Blackbeard downed his drink. He was well aware of the importance of this venture. The governor was telling him the recourse available should the pirate betray him. Blackbeard had known that recourse even before the governor had spoken, so he nodded in agreement.

Eden paused to sip his drink. With his mind racing ahead to picture details of the plan, he asked, "What is the usual route of the plate fleet?"

Blackbeard walked to a small table opposite where a map was laid out. His forefinger traced a line across the map. "Now then, I'll put it to you straight, Governor. Years agone the Spanish had two armadas. This map here shows their passage. The New Spain Flota bound for Mexico sails in May or June, she does. She reaches Veracruz before the northerners start in October. Woods and waters in the vicinity of the Virgin Islands, then she passes along the northern coast of Puerto Rico and Hispañola. From there she sails to Veracruz whither is held a fair for two to six weeks. Here also are the treasures from the Manila galleons sailing from the Orient. From Veracruz the New Spain Flota, well, she sails back to Havana where she then rendezvous with the *Tierra Firme* Flota."

Having perused the map with care, Charles Eden relaxed in his chair. His train of thought returned to the second fleet. A momentary pause gave him time to fill his clay pipe with tobacco and light it. "And the *Tierra Firme* Flota?" he asked.

"You'll be thinking of the second fleet, then," Blackbeard said. "She sails in convoy with the galleons in March. Victuals in the Canaries. Then makes her landfall in Trinidad and Tobago, passes amidst the Galleon Passage, then sails for Cabo de la Vela, and last of all, Cartegena and Porto Bello. But just before that time the Pacific Armada of the South Seas has brought the plate from Peru to Cartegena. Now that's when the Spaniards hold their fairs. And then the *Tierra Firme* Armada and the Galleons sail back to Havana amidst the Yucatan Channel. Here they join the New Spain Armada. They both set sail for Spain, in the month of February or thereabouts, following a northerly route amidst the Straits of Florida further north to Carolina."

"Carolina?" Eden's eyes suddenly lit up at the thought of the ships sailing past his colony.

"Aye," Blackbeard said, smiling. "Then they head for His Majesty's crown colony of Virginia and next veer easterly. But this year, if this one ship sets sail, I believe it'll be different, Governor."

"Different?" Eden asked. A difference in the Spaniards' plans might well brook some special contrivance on his part.

"Aye. I'll stake my life on it, Governor, the ship will not set sail at the usual time."

"But, why?"

"The galleons don't sail regularly anymore. Too many sea dogs skulk the West Indies. The Spanish waters are a den of mutinous dogs that lollop at ease waiting for booty."

Eden looked puzzled. He hadn't counted on this. He gulped down his whisky. "Then how will we find out the route of the ship or her passage?"

"Never you mind, Governor." Blackbeard smiled. "I have my ways o' finding out things. Aye, you picked the proper man for the job, Governor, that you did. Ah, yes, Governor, you'll bless your stars you were the first that found me."

Eden stared at Blackbeard. He couldn't believe his luck.

Blackbeard returned the stare.

Then the two men broke into a smile at the same moment.

"I think I'll take another drink," Eden said, rising from his chair.

"Well, seeing as how you're pouring yourself another, I'll make so free as to do likewise." Blackbeard grinned. "You can pour me a dram along o' you."

Eden walked to the decanter and poured some more whisky into the glasses. He handed one to Blackbeard.

They both pressed their glasses together.

"I propose we drink a toast," Eden said. "To the greatest pirate that ever lived."

"Nay, contrarywise." Blackbeard waved his mug in mid-air. "To the most respectable man in His Majesty's colonies—the governor of North Carolina."

Blackbeard chuckled.

Eden laughed.

Neither drank.

"Then, sir," Eden said, "to a most remarkable companionship."

They both finished off the whisky in one gulp.

There was a silence so profound they could hear each other breathing.

Blackbeard broke the silence by pouring himself another drink, and in a ruff, grumbling voice said, "Here's to you, Governor. You know as well as I you could have treated me like any other ill-looked sea dog. Had me strung up on Gallows Road."

"And leave off the conspiracy!" the governor commented. "Not likely!"

Blackbeard cleared his throat. "Now I'm asking you polite-like, hoping you won't take no offense by my words now, Governor, but why should a governor, the most respectable man in His Majesty's colonies undertake such a criminal venture?"

"I wish to be a pirate."

Blackbeard stared at Eden. The man was unbelievable. He burst into laughter. "Blood and thunder! Now that's a laugh. Forgive me, Governor, but you a pirate! You with a top knot of periwigged hair and a waistcoat of the finest Bretagne linen. You a pirate! Hah!" And then shaking his head in wonder he muttered to himself, "Fancy that! The Governor, hisself, wishes to be a pirate."

Eden stared at Blackbeard. "Indeed I do," he said, without the least bit of cynicism in his voice.

"Now I asks you, me hearty, who do you know does not wish to be a pirate? Ah, them that wishes, wishes for a grand old time, a fling at that. Adventure on the high seas, wine, women, mirth, song, riches beyond measure. But them that's been pirates, they know better. They know the hard lot of it, Governor. They was took to the sea hired out by the queen's own navy to serve as privateers to fight the Spanish. But did England appreciate it? No. Not two coppers. For when wartime was over and she had no need of hands, she told them to find employment elsewhere. And tell me, Governor, where's a poor sea dog to find employment? No man of respectability hires a scurvy tar. So what do they do? Plunder ships, that's what they does." Blackbeard drank another gulp of whisky.

Blackbeard's words hit Eden with a blow. The governor had never wanted for anything. What was his own life but a cut and dried affair? What risks or adventures did it have? Life for men such as Blackbeard, who lived on the edge, was vastly more adventurous.

"Now," Blackbeard continued, "there's those that has their pardon, thanks to you, Governor. I'm not like the most. The most goes for rum and a good fling and then its back to sea again with only the shirts on their backs. But that's not the course I plan to lay, not me. I puts it away and once back from cruising I can set up a gentleman in earnest—start a new life, buy me a house, get me a wife—all proper—like a refined man o' means. I'll become a respectable gentleman. Fancy that. A respectable gentleman. Perchance given time, I might even become a..."

"Yes," Eden said, leaning forward in his chair.

"A governor."

"So you'd be thinking of being the governor." Eden burst into laughter.

"Aye," Blackbeard suddenly grabbed Eden's periwig and walking cane and leaping from his chair, began prancing about the room. When he had tired himself out, he sat down.

They both laughed.

"Fancy that," Blackbeard said, catching his breath. "Yes, a governor who wishes to be a pirate and a pirate who wishes to be a governor. A fine lot we are."

"I reckon we are," Eden added in agreement. "A fine lot."

Just as spontaneously as the laughing had begun, it ceased. Quite solemnly the two men finished off what liquor they had left. It was no small thing they had agreed upon.

A Meeting
With the Free-Trader

After receiving the pardon on Wednesday of the following week,
Blackbeard took his evening meal at a tavern or ordinary off Front
Street—*The Lion And The Unicorn*.

That, in itself, was not unusual.

The Lion And The Unicorn's main bill of fare was its steak and kidney pie prepared in a flaky pastry with plenty of hot gravy. It just so
happened that Blackbeard was quite fond of steak and kidney pie. He
liked it. Very much, in fact.

Blackbeard always ate his steak and kidney pie in very small bites
so that he could get the full flavor of the kidney.

Another thing he liked about *The Lion And The Unicorn* was its
atmosphere. Situated right on the wharf off Front Street, it reminded him
of his seafaring days. It was a well-known hang-out for sailors who
swapped their tales freely amidst the clatter of the kettles, spits, pots and
gridirons and the high strung notes of a fiddle. As they talked, the tobacco smoke from the long, clay pipes they puffed on circulated constantly through the air. The more they talked, the more they drank from
pipes of Madeira wine, tankards of Barbados rum, drams of peach brandy,
and flagons of cherry stout.

The Lion And The Unicorn was frequented by Blackbeard for other
reasons as well—namely, the women of disreputable character. They
walked among the customers freely, with painted faces, bared bosoms,
and certainly, for Colonial America, with a phenomenal amount of ankle
thrust forward. The tavern keeper kept a private hotel upstairs and many

of his customers, hungry for other sensual delights, found their appetites more than satisfied on the upper floor.

It was Blackbeard's custom when he visited *The Lion And The Unicorn* to take his evening meal in a corner window seat and there, watch the ladies work the tavern. He took great pleasure in the ladies—even more so than the steak and kidney pie.

Numbered also amongst the pleasures of the tavern were the gaming tables. His weakness for gambling had become quite evident in only his first week in Bath. He would often put down, say one hundred pounds or so at either whist, ombre or lanquinet.

Fortunes could be lost or made at *The Lion And The Unicorn*. It was a heady place and the stakes were unusually high—one hundred pounds at the tables for the dedicated, fifty or so for those of a little less courage who still wanted to make their mark in society, and twenty-five for those who considered a concession to the wheel of fortune measurable in some degree of moderation. Because of its high stakes, the tavern drew also another class of people—wealthy merchants who had a taste for the low life.

On this particular Wednesday, Blackbeard did not come to *The Lion And The Unicorn* for its steak and kidney pie. Nor for its atmosphere. Nor for its women. He was not in the mood for these things. The fact was he had business matters here.

It should be mentioned that *The Lion And The Unicorn* was famous for one other thing—it was associated with members of the criminal class, and even more so with a specific member of the criminal class—namely, smugglers.

Gambling was in full swing as Blackbeard sat down to his dinner. Be that as it may, he could not bring himself to bet this evening. Instead, munching on his pieces of kidney, interspersed with gulps of small beer, he remained impervious to the rattle of dice across the hardwood tables and the click of billiard balls being hit by sticks. He waved away one hopeful contender. To others, he gave evasive responses.

But one opponent could not be so easily disposed of. He was a well-built man with a flushed visage which could most likely be attributed to his predisposition to alcoholic beverages of which he freely indulged. Brandishing a mug of ale in one hand and a pack of cards in the other, he took a seat beside Blackbeard, who in recent days, had become his drinking and betting companion. Not a member of the syndicate, he was, nonetheless, one of the wealthy individuals of the upper class who secretly objected to the English trade laws and considered it smart, profitable and proper to trade with the pirates. On the side, he had quite a lucrative business in stolen merchandise. Noticing that Blackbeard was not quite himself and trying to humor him, he made a remark to that effect, not failing to mention his jolly disposition in his pirating days.

References to his pirating days made Blackbeard uneasy and when the gentleman made this remark, the pirate lowered his head and pressed his lips together in frustration. He was trying as best he could to establish himself as a respected man about town—building a home; associating with the aristocracy; looking into new business ventures—all perfectly legal. This pardon had given him the one chance he needed to live a moral, upright life and to be a respected citizen of Bath. He had made a promise to himself this conspiracy with Eden would be the last of his pirating and he meant to stick to that promise. He was determined not to spoil his chance. "I go by the name of Captain Edward Teach," Blackbeard forced himself to remark during the course of the conversation. "You can address me as such." He hoped the gentleman would remember that in days to come.

This retort, when it was made, was obviously taken by the gentleman as a joke, although Blackbeard was serious when he said it. The gentleman winked at Blackbeard as if the two shared some dark, unfathomable secret. The fact of the matter was he thought Blackbeard was just putting up a front after taking the pardon. Snapping his fingers at the bartender, he ordered two drinks that were immediately brought on a pewter tray. He proposed a toast and after downing a whisky in satisfaction, he returned his glass to the table. "Once a pirate, always a pirate," he said, and he gave Blackbeard one of those chummy pats on the shoulder that elicit feelings of warmth, brotherhood and good cheer. He had a bluff, jolly way of speaking and he was one of the most popular people in the tavern.

In many ways, the merchant was like many other people who frequented this tavern. He enjoyed Blackbeard—his stories, his gambling. But most of all he enjoyed the pirate's merchandise. He would have been adverse to any changes. Blackbeard's move towards becoming respectable was in direct opposition to his welfare.

Of course, he, like the others present, felt these new actions taken by Blackbeard toward establishing himself as a citizen were just part of a good front. But just in case the pirate got any ideas into his head about making a change in life, he felt he should warn him.

Of course, he would never pirate. Far from it. He had a good standing in Bath. A wealthy merchant and planter, enjoying the respect of the entire community, he would be the first to speak out against the barbarities of crime and piracy. But if one indirectly profited from the pirates, well, what harm was there in that?

So, at one point, while making light conversation and jokingly patting Blackbeard warmly on the shoulder, the merchant laid his cards down on the table and spoke. "Now, then," he said, tweaking the pirate on the cheek, "it would be far better for a pirate such as yourself, not just you, but any pirate, mind you, to keep up his pirating. Not just for our sake but for his sake as well." He winked at Blackbeard. "Why, once the traders this pirate robbed got wind he wasn't a'pirating anymore, they might think he lost his guff. They'd think maybe they could settle old scores with this pirate. Believe me, I say this friend to friend, man to man," he said, interrupting this monologue to wink in a harmless manner even though his sentence didn't sound innocuous. "Yes, there's many a poor seaman t'would like to put a knife in a pirate's back, and no mistake."

As the bartender was later to recall, Blackbeard chatted amiably with the merchant that evening until a particular man shouldered his way through the bar. The man was tall and lanky. He had a thin, wiry neck, and a face narrow between the ears and across the brow. His complexion was the color of mahogany, darkened, the bartender guessed, by strong weather conditions due to service at sea. He sat down at one of the tables— a rough hewn board laid upon trestles—and ordered a drink.

At first sight of the man, Blackbeard excused himself from the company of the merchant who had reassured himself through plenty of drink and joking that Blackbeard had not made any major changes in life.

Blackbeard took a seat beside the man.

For awhile, Blackbeard and the man talked of inconsequential matters. The man was Thadius Taylor, a mariner. He ordered some dinner and then some beer. Sometime thereafter he asked about the girls, mentioning he'd like to "give one a flourish." Blackbeard pointed out one in particular. She was an especially attractive creature with a low-bodiced chintz gown that purposefully showed off her assets. During the course of the sailor's dinner, the girl winked often at Blackbeard, and in awhile she approached the two and offered her services.

"The girl's a hurricane. She'd burst the caulking in a ship, the wench," Blackbeard commented.

When the girl bent down, the sailor could smell her strong perfume wafting through the air. As she did so, she lovingly placed an arm on Blackbeard's shoulder and whispered provocatively in the pirate's ear. But he refused her offer, giving her a pat on her behind and a gold guinea which she bit between her teeth to test its value.

When the conversation stopped of its own accord and the sailor, full now on beef and beer, leaned back in his chair to take a sip on an after-dinner drink and exhale tobacco smoke into the room, Blackbeard got down to business.

A chocolate pot, a wooden frother and a wooden trencher had been placed between the two. Blackbeard pushed them aside to get a clearer view of his companion.

The pirate pulled his chair in toward the sailor and lowered his voice to a whisper. "Taylor," he said, in all seriousness.

"Aye."

"I heard tell you'd be running the Acts." "Running the Acts" meant running the blockade on the Navigation Acts of the 1660s which put heavy import and export duties on goods.

Slowly, Taylor drew in on his pipe. He fixed his eyes carefully before him, not looking at Blackbeard as though afraid to show any emotion. "I might be," he answered. Taylor was a smuggler and smugglers could not be too careful in this day and time.

"Well, now," Blackbeard continued, swallowing hard with the knowledge that he wasn't going to get anywhere with the man unless he used a stronger persuasion. "Your captain has a mighty agreeable way with him, particularly in drink, your captain does. Now we'll put it for argument's sake that your captain has a patch on his eye and we'll put it, if you like, that eye's the left one."

Taylor lifted his brow.

"Aye, well I told you," Blackbeard said. "Now I heard tell you'd be running the Acts from your captain."

Obviously, the last bit of information had cleared Blackbeard from any suspicion on the sailor's part because he answered with a nod. "Then you heard right," he said.

For a moment the two very quickly resumed a normal conversation while a tavern wench filled their glasses. When she had finished, she hurried off behind a serving area to pour herself a nip or two from the derelict bottle.

When she was out of sight, the men continued their previous conversation.

This time, however, the sailor felt a bit uncomfortable under Blackbeard's scrutiny. Those half-smiling eyes had a look of devilry and bemusement in them.

But Taylor hadn't long to wait to discover the reason for this look. Blackbeard doused the light in a pewter candlestick with his forefinger.

Taylor drew his breath in between his teeth. To his surprise, Blackbeard's forefinger showed no traces of being singed. Taylor leaned forward in his wainscot chair. "They told me of thee," he whispered. "What they say is true. It's the devil, himself, sits beside me."

"Aye," Blackbeard said, smiling at his little joke. "Aye," he continued, "Hornigold, his old self, was feared o' me. Feared he was, to be sure. They was the roughest crew afloat, proud to sail the Jolly Roger, was Hornigold's crew."

"Aye," Taylor agreed. "The devil would have been feared to meet with the likes of them."

Blackbeard leaned closer to Taylor, his hot breath near Taylor's face. His eyes had a wicked gleam in them. "Yes, the most feared pirate alive, I am. Why, only two weeks since I took a Portuguese mulatto off the Virginia capes. Now this mulatto, he had not offended me. But do you know what I did to him?"

Taylor shook his head.

Blackbeard's eyes fired with excitement. "I sliced off his lips and had my cook fry them up, that is what I did to him. And then, by thunder, I made the Portuguese captain eat his lips."

Taylor gasped.

"But the next was the worst," Blackbeard said. "Next I shot him dead in the bladder for the reason I ordered him to smack his lips, but he had none left to smack."

A more horrible form of punishment for falling into the clutches of Blackbeard's crew could not be imagined by Taylor. His left eye began to twitch uncontrollably. He reached for his drink to steady himself.

"Yes," Blackbeard said. "I'm not a boasting man, but you can see how well I keep company in this tavern."

Taylor studied at the customers in the tavern, the rich merchants with gilded canes, bending over the gaming tables; the sailors, diffusing an odor of alcohol and black tobacco leaf. He nodded.

"Now," Blackbeard said, "you sir, are the man I want."

"What would a free-booter be wanting with a free-trader?" Taylor asked.

Blackbeard smiled. The two men stared at each other, one a pirate, the other a smuggler.

"A trading with Virginia, perhaps?" Taylor asked.

Blackbeard shook his head.

Taylor eyed Blackbeard then with a touch of quizzicality in his lifted eyebrows.

"We'll talk square like old shipmates, then. Your ship, she moors here, does she not?" Blackbeard asked.

"Aye," Taylor said. "She's a stiff vessel."

"The *Bachelor's Delight*, is she not?"

"The very one. The *Bachelor's Delight*." Taylor wondered what Blackbeard wanted with his ship, and he shot his companion a sidelong glance to indicate his suspiciousness. "Burden, six hundred tons."

"How many murdering pieces?" Blackbeard asked.

"Twenty-two."

"And hands?"

"One hundred and forty."

"What colors?"

"English."

"She has a broker, no doubt?" Blackbeard asked.

It was the custom for smuggling ships to be backed by rich and well-known merchants whose names were usually kept secret. The ships themselves were fitted out under pretense of legitimate business.

Taylor stared at Blackbeard. What was in the wind he had, as yet, no idea. "She has a broker," he said. "She's fitted out from New York. Laden with glass, china and paper Sunday last. She'll go a round." Taylor's curiosity was growing, and at this point, he leaned closer to Blackbeard. This was all small talk to him. "She weighs anchor in a fortnight," he said.

"Whither is she bound?"

"On a trading passage to *Tierra Firme*."

Blackbeard's eyes lit up.

The fact that Blackbeard was suddenly very interested since the ship was on its way to the Spanish Main served to arouse Taylor too. He thought he was getting somewhere now with the man so he gave out some more information. "She'll get her boot tops in Tortuga," he said.

"Then I takes it, she'll steer her course through the Windward Passage," Blackbeard said.

"Aye."

"Where's she's bound?" Blackbeard asked.

"Porto Bello."

"Good then. That's exactly what I wanted to hear, mate," Blackbeard said.

Taylor could contain himself no longer. He was bursting with curiosity. What was it this man wanted, he wondered? He clenched his fist and struck it on the table. "All ports are closed shop. Is it tobacco you want to ship?"

"Nay," Blackbeard said.

Taylor pursed his lips. "Then what?" he demanded.

Blackbeard smiled and leaned back in his chair. "I want to know of a galleon."

Taylor could not hide his disappointment. His eyelids drooped sadly. Then recovering somewhat, he snapped in a cross manner, "A galleon."

"Aye," Blackbeard wasn't at all disturbed by Taylor's reaction. "The *San Rosario*. Whence she sets sail."

Taylor leaned closer, tentatively probing for some more information. "And..." he whispered.

"And what passage she steers," Blackbeard said.

Taylor had had enough of this game with Blackbeard. In defiance of the man, his jaw suddenly became rigidly set. And then finally all his reserve burst forth. "Well, blast it," he said. "Why do you want to know?"

However, Blackbeard did not trouble to answer. Instead, he gave Taylor a forbidding look.

Taylor's face lit up. He had been guessing all along that the ship was one Blackbeard wished to capture and he let it be known.

"A prize, eh?" he asked.

Blackbeard seemed determined to confide nothing more.

Intuitively, Taylor sensed the ship was a prize. "Then what's the plunder?" he demanded.

But Blackbeard would have no more of this sailor's incessant questioning. Leaning forward in his chair, he whispered, his mouth no more than a hairsbreadth from Taylor's ear. "I'm warning you mate. Do not meddle. You heard that from my own lips, you did. Meddle and you'll fare the worse, you can count on that."

Taylor gritted his teeth in a fit of stifled rage. "Fifteen hundred pounds I'll get then," he said.

"That's your share," Blackbeard agreed.

Taylor leaned back and stared at Blackbeard. He was surprised. Fifteen hundred pounds was a large sum of money for such a small bit of information. That ship must be worth quite a lot. Then he shook his head in amazement and took another drink. This was too good to be true. "Fifteen hundred pounds is to my liking, mate," he said in amazement. "Damn me, it's done, and you may lay to that."

Taylor smiled then, and clapped Blackbeard warmly on the shoulder.

Blackbeard relaxed somewhat. However, his eyes still held a serious look as he gave out his instructions to Taylor. "Now, then, this is what you'll do. You'll sail with the *Bachelor's Delight*, and you'll slip off the ship when she comes to the harbor, and you'll find your way to the town. Then you'll learn of the *San Rosario*'s route and departure, and you'll return to your ship."

"Aye," Taylor said.

"Now," Blackbeard continued, "you'll live hard, and you'll speak little and you'll drink no more whisky, 'til I give the word, do you understand?"

"Aye." Taylor seemed satisfied.

Blackbeard leaned back.

The bargain, agreeable to both of them, was sealed with a toast.

But Blackbeard knew one could not be too sure of anyone. Just to make certain that everything was perfectly understood, he added, "And I'm warning you now mate—do not breach my faith."

"And why not, may I ask?"

From the depths of Blackbeard's fierce frame, the answer came in a growl. "The reason being that I would wring your sea calf's head from your body with these hands, I would."

Taylor was appalled at the severity of Blackbeard's statement. For a moment he had forgotten to whom he was talking. "A gold chain or a wooden leg, I'll stand by thee," he said aghast, his left eye twitching nervously.

"Right then," Blackbeard said. "Make good speed."

"Aye, that I will," Taylor answered.

When he had finished eating, Blackbeard left the tavern. Outside, the fog rolled in from the river, heavy and thick. A cat's paw, as the sailors termed a light, delicate breeze, stirred the air. The only sound was the water lapping against the ship's hulls. Blackbeard wandered through the streets of Bath past Willis' Wharf, then Scott's Wharf, then Marsh's Wharf. He peered into the darkness. The fog was so dense, he could see no more than two feet in front of him. The street lanterns did not help the visibility.

Suddenly, he heard footsteps behind him. He turned, but all that met his eyes was the black shroud of a North Carolina evening.

Fearing that perhaps he was being followed, he lengthened his stride. The footsteps quickened. Thump. First one hit the street. Thump. Then the other hit. With some apprehension, Blackbeard ventured down Beaufort Street.

By the loudness of the footsteps, the pursuer was gaining on him. In what seemed like hours, but was only a matter of seconds, Blackbeard let his hand slide beneath his waistcoat to his pistol. Beside the white-washed paling of a clapboard house, he stopped. Then he turned around and drew his pistol. The figure appeared out of the fog. Cloaked in black broadcloth, an unknown face stared at him. Just as suddenly, he heard a sound behind him. He whirled around. Staring at him was the face of Governor Eden.

Blackbeard breathed an audible sigh of relief as the pistol dropped to his side.

"It's done?" Eden asked.

"Done," Blackbeard said. His pistol, though, still trembled uncontrollably.

Both men now stood beside him. Blackbeard placed the pistol back beneath his waistcoat.

"When does she set sail?" Eden asked.

"In a fortnight," Blackbeard said.

"Where's she bound?"

"Porto Bello."

"Good then." Eden's expression turned into a leer. Was this man really the fierce Blackbeard? His hands were still trembling. He could not help but reply, "Your hand rattles like a dead man's bones."

Blackbeard could sense that Eden thought him a coward. Straightening to a ramrod posture, he insolently shot back, "Damn you, I scorn your thoughts."

Eden's face, however, did not flinch. He looked Blackbeard up and down, measuring him with those dark, penetrating eyes. "The infamous Blackbeard," he said, sliding a friendly arm across the pirate's shoulder, "a sneaking puppy."

However, as the three of them walked off together, Blackbeard between the two dark clad men, Eden could not help wondering if the pirate was all he had been cracked up to be.

And inside Blackbeard's waistcoat pocket, the hand still trembled.

A Pirate Meets A Lady

In the days to come Charles Eden observed Blackbeard's goings-on in Bath with mixed emotions—half whimsy, half dread.

The pirate's efforts to become a respectable gentleman of Bath were nothing short of amusing. Just to see him strut forth from the barbershop on Carteret street still clothed in his usual pirate garb, with his hair and beard in a cloud of powder, would send Eden into fits of laughter. Or to watch the pirate hurry from the tailor on Front Street, gold cane in hand, gloved in white silk and still carrying his tremendous cutlass would make Eden burst into guffaws. Or even more hilarious to Eden were the pirate's unpredictable satanic curses uttered in the best of company at small dinner parties.

But Blackbeard's adjustments to Bath weren't hilarious to him. Sometimes, yearning for the pirate's life, he would take himself into fits of depression that would worry Eden. During these times the pirate would consume large quantities of intoxicating beverages. Then strutting forth from his lodging, he would wander to the waterfront community of Bath— those dirty, twisted streets filled with charwomen, sailors hoping to pay rent, beggars living on two pence a day, and ladies prepared to shed their clothes for a guinea an hour. There in some small, confined room filled with roaches and tobacco smoke, Eden would find the pirate, hours later, bedded down with one or sometimes even two ladies of the night. Or, Eden might discover him in a tavern reminiscing over his seafaring days and gambling away fortunes at the gaming tables. These searches for the pirate, late at night and in the worst part of town, opened up a seamy side of life to Eden. When these searches ended, Eden would pick the pirate up, pour cupfuls of coffee down his massive frame, and, once the gin and ale had dissipated, would carry him home again, the pirate all the while muttering about his days at sea and how he wanted to "go on the account."

The subtle effect these alcoholic binges and jaunts had on Eden were at first not felt too deeply by the governor. But lately, Eden would awaken in the middle of the night, startled by his own nightmares. Jumping out of bed, he would dash to the window. There, he would take the spyglass from the windowsill and apply it to his eye to make certain the pirate's ship was still in the harbor. Only when he saw the flag of the *Adventure* waving in the night wind, would Eden return to his bed for a fitful sleep.

Eden found himself losing more and more sleep until one day at the end of June when the two were taking an afternoon stroll together along the wharves of Bath. They had just stopped beside a newly arrived ship from England, and Eden was about to introduce the pirate to the ship's captain when Blackbeard happened to catch sight of a lovely young lady. The pirate couldn't take his eyes off her. She had chestnut hair, a perfect nose and eyes that were widely set. She wore a white-frilled dress and apron and carried the tiniest of white parasols. Eden, suddenly unable to get Blackbeard's attention at any cost, realized that perhaps his inclination for introductions had been misdirected.

The girl was Mary Ormond, the daughter of a wealthy Bath planter, and for every two men who looked at the girl one was smitten by her. Even Eden, who had vowed to live a bachelor's life after his first wife, Penelope Golland, had died in 1716, had been taken by Mary and was one of her regular beaus. Eden even toyed with the idea of falling in love with the girl. And well he might. Nothing half so charming, so gay, so lovely had ever found its way to Bath Town. She had an excellent figure, strong spirit and an expression old for a girl of almost sixteen, being calm, yet adventurous.

Eden could well see why Blackbeard was taken with the girl. She was respectability at its height, a lady if ever there was one, and with all the proper credentials—a background of wealth and English ancestry from London which she still now and then visited. What a stroke of luck, thought Eden, to run into Mary standing only ten yards away—charming, extraordinarily beautiful, heiress to an estate and, most of all, eligible. For what, asked Eden of himself, could keep a man at home better than a wife? He must see to it that Blackbeard gained the girl's acquaintance.

It would be unfair to say that the governor did not feel some pain in parting with Mary Ormond. No other women in Bath aroused his desires as much as lovely young Miss Ormond. He was fully aware that such a woman as Mary comes along only once in a man's lifetime. On the other hand, during Blackbeard's entire stay in Bath, the governor had never on any single occasion seen the pirate so captivated. Eden, now watching Blackbeard longingly eye the girl from a distance, came to the painfully regretful, yet inevitable conclusion that he must relinquish Mary. In all truth, the Spanish plate carried more weight in Eden's mind than a wife. So without further ado, Charles Eden did the only sensible thing. Poised now at the wharf, pipe in hand, gold cane gleaming in the afternoon sun, he took Blackbeard aside and nodding at Mary, spoke. "I don't believe you've had the pleasure of meeting that lovely young lady. I insist that you do."

Blackbeard, for the life of him, could not disagree.

Now there are those men who because of circumstance or tremendous vitality, experience more of life's amorous pursuits than the average human being. These men are unusually virile. More often than not their bodies are sinewed with brute strength and muscle. Furthermore, their language is often offensive to the ear because they have discovered that laying aside all culture, even the most refined ladies are, if truth be told, animals. These men are the male ego personified. These are men of the world. Blackbeard was one of these men.

At heart, an experienced woman will recognize such a man immediately as able to satisfy the innermost cravings of her body, and her eyes inevitably in the course of her conversation will stray to the instrument of that man's power with fleeting and yet longing glances. But the more inexperienced woman, still virgin, will sense this man as a destructive force, totally foreign to her nature, uninformed, uncultured, valueless and more bluntly—a beast. Her instincts suppressed through culture, she will ignore this man in favor of the more refined man of means. So Mary, when confronted with the two men, shot the pirate only a passing glance, preferring to concentrate all her attention instead on her beau, Charles Eden.

Pink cheeked and glowing-eyed, she greeted the man. "Governor Eden," she remarked. "How good to see you again." Just now she gave Eden such a winsome smile coupled with a flurry of fluttering eyelashes that he almost regretted his decision to introduce her to the pirate.

Obviously, thought Blackbeard, Mary was completely taken with the governor, for her blood rose and her cheeks flushed as she threw him admiring glances.

Mary and her father had come to the wharf early this afternoon to collect some packages from the ship just arrived in Bath. Governor Eden had no idea what was in the packages, but he surmised by the care given them by Mary that, no doubt, they were the latest fashions from London. Mary had a weakness for clothes. Both she and her father were fully loaded with the packages, and Eden offered to relieve them of their burden while they talked.

Mary graciously declined. "Father's rather late for an appointment," she explained. "And we must be on our way. I hope we'll be seeing you at the house this evening," she added.

Mary noticed that the governor's face took on an extremely stunned expression and she couldn't possibly imagine what she had said to upset him.

"This evening?" Eden asked.

"Yes. Our dinner engagement." She hoped Eden hadn't forgotten.

Mary could not remember when she had seen Eden look so downhearted. His eyelids lowered. His mouth turned down. Tapping himself with his palm on his head, he answered. "How silly of me. Forgive me, Mary, but it completely slipped my mind."

Mary raised her eyebrows.

Eden shook his head. "You'll have to forgive me. I've made other arrangements."

"I see," Mary said, a bit taken aback. It was rare that a man refused her, and she did not know quite how to react to the situation. This was most unusual and needed more looking into. "Well," she continued, "I suppose we'll be seeing you another time."

Eden said nothing.

Mary pressed her lips together firmly. What had come over the man? Only yesterday he had told her he would give her the moon, and now here he was ignoring her. In her young and yet womanly body came the first flutterings of loves gained and lost, passion and sorrow, happiness and tears. It was altogether a too uncomfortable feeling to continue for too long a time and she suddenly blurted out, "I told my father we'd only be here a short while so we'd best be on our way."

Eden's eyes had a startled look.

Indeed, the governor was stunned. He had thought to introduce Blackbeard to Mary and now here she was about to leave, without so much as even a passing nod to the pirate.

But Eden was saved by a train of thought blurted out suddenly by Blackbeard which took him as much by surprise as it did Mary.

"I'd set no limits on what a lady considers a short time or not, as the case were," the pirate said.

Mary thought that statement uncommonly rude. For the first time since their meeting, she noticed this newcomer in their midst. Giving him a glance, she assumed that contrived look of disgust perfected over the years for such as pirates.

"Meaning no harm to you, though," Blackbeard quickly apologized, realizing he had said the wrong thing.

The pirate shuffled about for a moment, obviously embarrassed. His association with the opposite sex was limited to barmaids and wenches. He had no idea what to say to this delicate, high strung breed of the female gender—the lady.

Mary, however, had no clue as to Blackbeard's thoughts nor did she care to know them for that matter, and she sniffed disparagingly at the pirate. Then she stuck her little pink nose into the air.

It was such a perfect nose though, that Blackbeard could not help but admire it even though the lady was surly.

This sudden exchange of words and looks by the pirate and Mary had allowed Eden just the time he needed to formulate another strategy, and now with considerable finesse, he made quite a gentlemanly proposal. "Why not allow us to see you home, Mary," he said. "That way your father need not rush so to his business appointment."

Mary regarded this proposal as an opportunity to continue her relationship with Eden, and now aglow with a new radiance, she readily agreed. Her father, too, who had hitherto regarded this conversation as only a waste of time and had given intermittent glances at his watch to show this, was also ebullient. He thrust the packages into the two men's arms and bid his daughter a fond farewell.

The three watched him strut jubilantly off for his appointment.

When the man had completely disappeared, Charles Eden turned to face Mary once again. He was all politeness and charm. "I don't believe that you've had the pleasure of meeting my companion."

The idea of meeting Blackbeard was obviously distasteful to Mary for she sniffed again, but she couldn't by social standards flatly refuse Eden's polite manners so she replied, "Why no." Her voice though, sounded reluctant.

"Split my sides, now she ain't met me," Blackbeard remarked with renewed confidence.

Mary looked shocked. This man was certainly vulgarity to its limits.

Eden politely gestured at Mary. "Mary Ormond, I'd like you to make the acquaintance of Captain Edward Teach."

Mary gazed on the man with all the disgust of a king looking on a cat. Then her face turned a livid scarlet. "Captain Edward Teach?" she repeated as much to herself as to the men present.

Blackbeard bowed. "Pleased to be making your acquaintance, madam," he said, bowing graciously as the governor had done. He would have kissed her hand, but she did not offer it.

Mary's eyes opened wide as if with sudden enlightenment. She knew who this man was. Those delicate tiny lips curled with anger. She seemed quite put out. She turned to face Eden. "Sir, this man is none other than Blackbeard the pirate—a scoundrel of the most common sort. Charles Eden, I'll have you know I don't think highly of pirates. Reformed or not, they're the most abominable riffraff ever to disgrace the earth. What's more," she now said, turning to face Blackbeard, "what's more, Mr. Blackbeard..."

"Captain Teach," Blackbeard said, correcting her.

"Whatever," Mary continued, unwilling to be interrupted. "I find your presence here highly obnoxious."

Eden's mouth opened in amazement.

Blackbeard cleared his throat. He had never felt so disgraced or wretched in his life. Indeed, Mary had humiliated him as far as it was possible to humiliate a human being. Oh, if only he had never been a pirate, he would be worthy of this beautiful creature! He lowered his eyes in shame. "Madam, you wouldn't think I had a pious mother to look at me, would you?"

"Why no, not in particular," Mary snapped.

"Ah, well, but I had," Blackbeard said remorsefully. "Remarkable pious. And I was a pious, civil boy and could rattle off my catechism that fast." He snapped his finger, then paused to see if Mary's reaction to him would improve.

However, it did not. Instead, she only huffed. "Little good it did you."

"Ah, yes, little good it did me," agreed Blackbeard, now so ill at ease he could hardly think straight. "And here's what come of it. I'm ashamed it has, Miss Ormond. T'was New Providence that put me here—Hornigold and New Providence."

"And I shouldn't wonder," continued the perturbed Mary, "if you sailed with the likes of Hornigold. He's an uncommonly vicious pirate."

All the while Mary and Blackbeard conversed, the young lady's patience had been wearing more and more thin with the pirate. So when there was a lull in the conversation, Mary took the opportunity to take the governor aside and away from hearing distance of Blackbeard. In the course of their brief but intimate conversation, she made it perfectly clear to the governor she wished this obnoxious pirate removed from her presence as soon as possible.

As the two talked, the pirate paced the wharf in a nervous manner. To make matters worse, he lit a pipe. Tobacco smoking was a habit Mary detested and although her father had made a fortune in the leaf, she could never quite accustom herself to its horrid smell. She had been known, on occasion, even to faint from its vapors. So, when the two returned to the wharf, Mary stopped dead in her tracks, opened her purse and withdrew a handkerchief which she immediately put to her nose.

This gave Blackbeard more than ample opportunity to whisper his thoughts. "I swear, Governor, the lady hates my guts."

Downcast, Eden opened his mouth to answer, and then on second thought, closed it. Why couldn't he take advantage of that little conversation with Mary? So when he opened his mouth again, there was a twinkle in his eyes. "On the contrary," he remarked to Blackbeard. "She's quite smitten. Taken a liking to you right away, she has. Why, just now she told me what a fine, handsome man she thought you were."

Blackbeard shook his head and blew out a puff of smoke into the air. "Now if that just ain't like a woman," he remarked.

Suddenly without further ado, Eden spoke in a voice louder than usual. "Captain Teach," he said, addressing the pirate, "the lady has just requested your presence in accompanying her home."

Mary, all thought of the tobacco smoke suddenly lost, whirled around on her heels, her eyes flashing. "Governor," she began, "I..."

But before she could get a word in edgewise, Eden continued. "And Mary, I must take my leave of you."

In utter amazement, Mary stared at Eden. How could he do this to her—leave her with this pirate, this rascal, this horribly rude scoundrel? She stomped her foot. Never in her life had she been so upset. It was almost more than she could bear. "But you told my father..." she began.

"And a foolhardy thing that was indeed," Eden interrupted, taking out his watch from a small pocket on the side of his shirt, and flicking open the cover. He was now obviously involved in the process of examining the time. "You see, Mary, I have a business engagement that slipped my mind completely."

Mary opened her mouth in amazement. "Well, there's no doubt about it. Your mind is slipping today, Charles Eden."

Eden took Mary's retort with quite remarkable good nature. What was meant to draw anger, on the contrary, only served to elicit a smile. Quite pleasantly, he tipped his hat, turned on his heels and walked down the street, smiling and whistling a little tune to himself. He looked, not in the least, remorseful.

Mary watched Eden with such surprise that her tiny pink mouth opened in amazement. When he disappeared, her lips trembled and her eyes became moist with tears.

Blackbeard, on the other hand, was jubilant. He began to talk off his head, this time with the utmost enthusiasm. "Miss Ormond, you were quite a pleasant surprise for the poor old captain. When first I set eyes on you I said to myself, I said, 'hello, well, look ahere, if this ain't luck for the captain to meet a proper lady, and you may lay to that.'"

"I may what?"

"It's an expression what's used by gentlemen o' the sea," Blackbeard explained.

"Hump," Mary said, "gentlemen of the sea—common pirates more like." And her nose immediately took off into the clouds, with that air of disparagement reserved for Blackbeard.

"Now, mam," he said, "I own myself once a pirate, a scoundrel o' the most common sort, put it as you will, I does at that, but this here talk from you is too much."

"Then I suggest you take your leave of me, sir," Mary said, grabbing her packages from the pirate in a fit of stifled rage and then turning on her heels to leave him. She wasn't about to allow a pirate to see her home, let alone the most infamous one of the day.

Now, if Blackbeard had been a common pirate as Mary so clearly suggested, he would have washed his hands of the irate woman at this point. He would, being disturbed beyond the ordinary limits of patience, have left her to fend for herself and seek her own way home. But, at heart, Blackbeard was a gentleman. He couldn't, in all good conscience, let a woman roam alone in the company of the waterfront—a place filled with pickpockets, prostitutes and thieves. He resolved to follow her at a distance, all too far for her to notice, but close enough for him to keep an eye out for her.

Blackbeard's worries were well-founded. A woman alone will always draw eyes. But a woman such as Mary, a woman of such extraordinary beauty and grace, will certainly draw more than eyes.

It just so happened that further ahead of her was a particularly rough bunch of sailors on leave from their London-bound ship. In celebration of their arrival in Bath, they had become fully intoxicated and were singing in boisterous voices:

Where is the trader of London Town?
His gold's on his capstan,
His blood's on the gown.
And it's up and away for Saint Mary's Bay
Where the liquor is good and the lasses are gay.

One belched, reached inside a mud-caked shirt and scratched his chest. Another spat a brown glob of spittle and tobacco onto the wooden planks of the wharf.

When the group caught sight of Mary, bedecked in her finery and frills, it was all too much for them. On their ocean-bound voyage, they hadn't even sighted a pair of legs under a grass skirt.

One of the sailors whistled.

"Hm, I've been wanting a share-out lately, lads," another commented obscenely. "How's about a share o' this wench?"

A round of boisterous laughter filled the air.

Mary chose to ignore the sailors as she walked past them.

But before she knew what had happened, Mary had been grabbed by one of the men.

Eyes wild, fear flailing her, she began to struggle frantically with the sailor.

Suddenly one of the men began removing his cutlass and belt. His belly bulged out of his shirt, obesely. A second drooled over his unshaven face. A third swore profusely. Mary felt the men's hot stares. The thought suddenly crossed her mind that she was about to be violated and she let out an earsplitting shriek.

No one could say Blackbeard was not quick. Mary's scream brought him to her side, eyes flaming, beard bristling, cutlass drawn.

The sailors had to take only one look at him to tell who he was. Their lives suddenly threatened, they shoved the girl aside. One dropped his knife. They took off through the streets of Bath as if they'd seen the devil.

Blackbeard could not contain himself. It was all too hilarious to see six grown men so terrorized at the thought of him. He laughed and then said, half to himself, half to Mary. "Ah, but I've never seen a pack o' fools look more frightened. Did you see how they ran? Frightened to death when they saw me, they were." He turned to Mary. "Madam, I've grappled four before and knocked their heads together, me unarmed. But this takes 'em all, it do!"

Mary could say nothing. She felt that if she did, the tears that were welling inside her would suddenly burst forth. Instead, she mechanically began to brush herself off where the sailors had touched her. Blackbeard watched with some tenderness for a moment, and then, gently he took her hand and stopped her.

"You're none the worse now," he said.

She looked up at him. A moment's pause gave her time to recover and collect herself. As she gathered up her packages and parasol, however, Blackbeard politely took the packages from her.

Mary, thinking she should thank Blackbeard for his help, said, "I'm much obliged to you for that, Mr. Blackbeard."

"T'weren't nothing, madam," Blackbeard said bashfully.

She straightened her dress. Once her composure was fully restored, she returned to her former self. "As I said, I'm obliged, Mr. Blackbeard. But I hope you won't be taking any fool ideas into your head, sir, because of it. I hope that's perfectly clear."

"Yes, madam," Blackbeard said. He stared at the ground for a moment, and then suddenly his eyes shot up to stare at her. "But you needn't be so rough with a man," he said, airing his opinion. "There ain't a particle o' service in it, leastways, as far as I can see."

Mary eyed Blackbeard as she carefully put on a pair of silk gloves. In a better frame of mind than before, she said calmly, "You may see me home, Mr. Blackbeard."

Blackbeard smiled. "You can call me Edward, if you prefer."

"I don't," Mary replied tersely. It was best not to encourage the man.

The two walked to Mary's home in silence. The streets were muddy this time of year in Bath and street urchins ran in and out between the chaises and carriages that passed them. On Carteret Street they stopped in front of a large white house surrounded by a picket fence. This was Mary's town home in Bath, her father having the plantation in the country and this home for business.

"Shall I see you to the door?" Blackbeard asked.

"That will not be necessary," Mary said. She opened the fence latch to walk inside.

Blackbeard spoke up quite briskly. "Before you'd be going, madam..." he began. A moment's pause gave him time to collect himself.

"Yes," Mary said. Now what did he want?

"Before you'd be going..." Blackbeard shuffled about on his feet, "there's something I'd be wanting to ask you."

"Do ask then, Mr. Blackbeard," Mary said, rather impatiently.

"Well," Blackbeard said, bowing his head and speaking in a rather timid voice, "I'd take it kind, mam, if you'd let me call on you, and no mistake."

Mary stared at Blackbeard. He was much too burly, much too muscular, much too crude for her. No, it was out of the question. "I think not," she said.

He couldn't just let this woman walk up to her door and out of his life. He must see her again. Blackbeard shuffled about some more. "Now I'm no gentleman, mam, I know, leastways, I'm not like the governor, there," Blackbeard said. "And you're a proper lady, all grand and fancy, but I'm back from cruising, planning to set up as a gentleman in earnest and I'm proper now, see, and in time, well, I'll be a gentleman as your governor here is now."

"Mr. Blackbeard," Mary said, with all certainty, "I'd sooner die than have a pirate call on me."

Blackbeard cleared his throat. "Well, mam, I must say you're a lady what's spoke up free."

Mary lowered her parasol and closed it. "Good day, Mr. Blackbeard," she said.

Blackbeard tipped his hat. "Good day, madam."

But as he looked at this woman entering her house, this vision of white walking gracefully to the front door he was not in the least bit shaken by her words. He was determined to have her and if that was what she wanted—a respectable man—then that was what he would become. In all his life he had never wanted anything so much as he had wanted Mary. He would prove to her he wasn't what she thought—a common pirate.

Blackbeard turned away from the house. He had fallen in love.

A Den of Infamous Scoundrels

If ever a man loved God and country, it was Alexander Spotswood. Governor of Virginia, he came from an old Scottish family and was a keen churchman. His broad face was well colored, clean shaven and plump—common to portraits of the Georgian era.

Spotswood had served in the army from his childhood and had a war wound. It was his outstanding military background that influenced Queen Anne in appointing him to serve her interest in the colony. A stalwart defender of the crown, he had arrived in Virginia in 1710, cocksure and prescient.

Uncertainty, toleration, hesitation, he disliked. Imagination, he trusted little. His duty in life he found very clear and other people's clearer and he discouraged people when they thought for themselves. The habit seemed to him quite dangerous. Rather, he encouraged people to support the existing order of things, especially the British Empire and the Anglican Church. In any quarrel he endeavored to destroy those who rashly sought to drag His Majesty's flag in the dust.

In his judgment, he had seen dangerous times—rebellions—Cary's and Bacon's to name a few. Radical governments were being installed everywhere and proprietary governments such as the one in North Carolina were not much better. It was clear things were going to rack and ruin.

Spotswood saw in the pirates, his universe reeling. Just the mention of the word free-booter brought sweat to his brow and a flush to his cheeks. He was convinced the future of his country lay in extermination of the rascals. He therefore went about suppressing piracy in the colonies in such a vigilant fashion that there were those who wondered what he hoped to accomplish by his mission. To search out pirates and smugglers he had employed two war ships from the Royal Navy, the *Pearl* and the *Lyme*. In recent years Spotswood had become known in the colonies as "the pirate hunter."

To say that Spotswood only hunted pirates would be unfair. There was no species of bird nor beast he did not destroy with equal enjoyment. For this he used a musket and his faithful setter. Rover was never far from his master's feet and Spotswood when referring to the dog, used the collective pronoun "we." "We must eat now, Rover," he would say, or, "We must take our afternoon walk," he would mention, patting the dog on the head as he fastened its leash. Actually, the two were not too dissimilar, for if any strange thing approached the dog it would bark and show its teeth just as Spotswood would, overstating his opinion to the point of being belligerent.

At the moment, the dog was madly racing about the governor's great room on the second floor, yelping excitedly. Spotswood, in the same room, peered out the window. The cause of the dog's arousal were two strangers who at the moment were descending from their carriage on Scotland Street and walking towards Spotswood's recently completed mansion, a distinct Georgian structure with a stately cupola. It was fortified by castellated walls in the forecourts.

Spotswood's momentary surprise at this unexpected arrival passed, however, and he scrutinized the gentlemen carefully. The setter stopped yelping, too, when Spotswood patted him lightly on the head. The dog settled down unobtrusively on his master's feet. Spotswood made a slight movement and trod on him. The setter yelped.

"Damn!" Spotswood said.

Surprised and hurt, the setter leaped up, retreated from his master and then considering the thought that he had not been unjustly treated, approached again cautiously wagging his tail. He had scarcely reached Spotswood's feet when the door was opened and the footman announced the two gentlemen's arrival.

"Colonel Maurice Moore, Esquire," said the footman in livery. "Edward Moseley, Esquire."

The setter gave two short barks, one for each guest, and bounded to his feet to sniff out the two visitors. With a slow movement of the tail, he smelled at the gentlemen's legs.

Spotswood was the type of man who never forgot a face and now upon closer inspection, he immediately recognized the two men. The taller, Edward Moseley, was North Carolina's ablest lawyer, once speaker of the Lower House of the General Assembly, now plotting for the governorship. The shorter was Maurice Moore, member of the North Carolina Council, senior justice of the General Court and collector of customs, son of Governor James Moore of South Carolina. Both were members of Governor Eden's administration.

A fillip of Spotswood's finger brought the setter immediately to the governor's heels.

Spotswood extended his hand to the two men and then after greeting them with the usual "so pleased to see you again," motioned for the two to be seated among the sixteen leather chairs. Spotswood took a seat under a looking glass with the arms of the colony engraved on it.

The dog joined his master, settling himself in comfortably at his feet, and Spotswood, patting the dog gently on the head, made the comment, "We're housebroken."

The gentlemen, a little unsure whether Spotswood's reference was to the dog, himself, or both, but mindful of their impression on the governor, said nothing.

Spotswood took a gold snuff box from the pocket of his waistcoat, flicked open the cover, dipped some snuff, and wondered what in the devil had occasioned these two men to come to Williamsburg.

If Governor Charles Eden of North Carolina had any knowledge of what these gentlemen were up to he would have been most distressed, to put it mildly. One does not make such extensive, drawn-out plans as Eden for the capture of the Spanish plate to have them completely disrupted by a few councilmen.

Governor Charles Eden would have done well to have had more contact with his neighbor to the north. But one cannot actually blame him for ignoring Spotswood. His colony, a proprietary government, was not very similar to Virginia's crown colony, and the two men had little in common.

Governor Spotswood, curious already as to the reason for this visit, took the initiative of beginning the conversation. "Now then, what may I do for you two gentlemen?"

Edward Moseley, who had been counting on just such a remark, quickly replied, "It is not a question of what you may do for us, Governor, but what we may do for you."

"Indeed," Spotswood said, so loudly that he caused the setter, which had just settled down to an afternoon sleep, to start.

Spotswood raised an eyebrow. He was very much surprised to know that a North Carolinian could do anything for a Virginian. This he would have to hear about. He looked on North Carolina as an orphan child of the king—always in want of something, poor, disorganized, underfed and underclothed.

Edward Moseley, certain now that he had Spotswood's undivided attention, began again. "We have heard, Governor Spotswood, through numerous sources that you take a great interest in the pirates off our coast."

At the word "pirate" Spotswood's ears pricked up, much as his dog's did in an afternoon hunt. "So much so," Spotswood said, "that I have warships patrolling the area—the *Pearl* and the *Lyme*."

"We had heard," Moseley continued, smiling secretly to himself and twisting a whitened mustache just above his lips, "that you also have made certain inquiries into the whereabouts of a most notorious pirate. May we continue?"

"Please be so good as to do so, sir," Spotswood said, inquisitive but trying not to appear so. He wished these gentlemen would say what they had to say and be done with it. Indeed, patience was an attribute the Lord had overlooked when making Alexander Spotswood.

"This pirate's a most unscrupulous sea dog—Blackbeard," Moseley said, and he waited for the name to have the desired effect.

At the very mention of the name which represented everything foreign to the governor's nature, Spotswood's eyes flashed, his face flushed, his mouth opened and his lips quivered. "Blackbeard!" he cried.

The setter, convinced now that there was no possibility of getting an afternoon's nap, sat up and began to pant, his tongue hanging out similarly to Spotswood's.

No doubt about it—the pirate Blackbeard was an outrage to Spotswood. What disrespect for English trade he had—blockading Charleston harbor! What total disregard for colonialism—having black slaves serving aboard his ships as free sailors! God wished man to behave in an orderly fashion, wished him not to question or argue. England was the best of all possible worlds, that was clear. But in these days men openly encouraged piracy, openly advocated that the king taxed unfairly. It was Spotswood's sacred duty as an Englishman to exterminate Blackbeard. And in the name of the crown, he would!

"Blackbeard's most unscrupulous!" Spotswood continued, the name whirling around in his brain until every blood vessel on his face and neck was swelled to bursting. "I declare the man's no mor'n a common criminal. His conduct's unsailorly, ungentlemanly and downright un-English!" Spotswood paused for a moment and then continued, "Gentlemen, you know I regard the subject of piracy as hateful. God forbid what the world is coming to. We must preserve the English nation at all costs," he said.

"By Jove, you're right," Moseley said, just at the moment when a young servant, unheralded even by a timid knock on the door, walked in with a tea tray. Spotswood always took his tea every afternoon at four o'clock. No matter that it impaired his daily duties. Tea was served punctually in fragile china cups to the gentlemen by the servant who promptly left after pouring.

Spotswood sat with his dog between his legs, the king's arms engraved on his mirrors, his law books arranged properly on their shelves in the great room, and sipped. He took great comfort in his afternoon tea—an English custom which he never, on any occasion, missed.

After drinking the entire cup and putting it aside, he paused to collect his thoughts. The hunter instinct in him came out again. In hot pursuit he leaned forward in his chair. "I suppose you know of Blackbeard's whereabouts."

Edward Moseley, a master at the art of negotiating, took from his pocket a pipe which he proceeded to light with the efficiency of a habitual smoker. He drew in on his pipe and then exhaled the smoke easily into the room. For only a moment, he watched the glass sconces, chandeliers, and candles in the room twinkle. Then he continued, this time with a cunning smile on his face. "Most assuredly we do know his whereabouts, Governor," Moseley said. "He is now about the inlets of North Carolina under the protection of Governor Eden. He has taken the pardon."

"Oh!" Spotswood gasped. This was quite a different story. One couldn't pursue a pirate if he had taken the pardon. That would be against the law. And Spotswood was certainly law-abiding. The governor was definitely disappointed. His whole bearing had a dejected look to it.

Despite this information, Moseley was not about to let his previous conversation come to a standstill. Still exuberant, he continued, "But by no means, Governor, should that disappoint you."

"Oh?" Spotswood asked, in an entirely different tone of voice.

"No," Moseley said. "For we suspect, Governor, that the pirate is not in retirement at all, but on the contrary, in the process of committing a crime!"

The effect of this last statement was immediate. Spotswood's face glowed with renewed radiance. If Blackbeard was still pirating after taking the pardon he could be captured, tried and executed. But Spotswood would have to have evidence to that effect. "Indeed," he said, sitting quite upright in his chair. "And how can that be?"

Moseley wasted no time in withdrawing an envelope from his shirt, an envelope which he was careful to unfold with utmost diligence. "We have at our disposal a letter that has been written by Blackbeard to Governor Eden."

A furrow formed between Governor Spotswood's eyes. What the devil was Blackbeard doing writing to the governor? "May I examine that?" Spotswood asked.

"Be my guest," Moseley answered, smiling in a twisted, devious fashion as he thrust the paper at Spotswood.

Spotswood looked at the paper carefully. Disbelief, surprise and shock in varying orders spread over his face. His neck grew conspicuously redder, and his eyes, offended at what they saw, stabbed when he looked up. Although there was no specific information, the letter clearly indicated some collusion between the two. For a common man to be in cahoots with a pirate was bad enough. But for a governor to stoop so low was beyond his imagining. Oh, these were dangerous times! And Governor Eden was a dangerous man!

"Yes," Moseley said, as if reading Spotswood's thoughts. "If truth be told, we fear the good governor is in league with this pirate. It is a sad day, indeed." He twisted his mustache.

Governor Spotswood said nothing. But the whites of his eyes became filled with blood.

Edward Moseley began once again to refill his pipe. He finished with a gesture of pushing the tobacco in tightly. Then stressing his point, he continued, "I'll make it a point to say, sir, North Carolina is fast becoming a refuge for buccaneers and pirates."

"Undoubtedly so," Spotswood agreed. He had always had a condescending attitude toward North Carolina and this only confirmed his opinion.

"Most proprietary governments are being overrun by these pirates — of which, I hardly need add, North Carolina is one," Moseley said. "I am sure you are fully aware of the pirates' takeover in New Providence."

"I assure you, sir, I am," Spotswood said, with renewed vehemence. He shook his head. "A most scandalous affair, if I do say so myself. But, fortunately for us all, New Providence was recently overtaken by the Crown to rid the island of these vile villains."

Colonel Moore broke in with a sentiment designed to flatter Spotswood. "Virginia, a crown colony, may be justly esteemed the happy retreat of all true Britons and churchmen."

Spotswood smiled and patted his powdered wig. It was nice to hear something good about himself. He gave his undivided attention to Moore.

Colonel Moore suspected it was time to hit Spotswood with what they had been building up to all along. So wasting no more time he remarked, "Mark me, sir, when the king hears the news of Blackbeard's takeover in North Carolina, he'll think it so corrupt he'll have to make it a crown colony." He said the last sentence very smoothly. In North Carolina he was noted for his smooth tongue.

Spotswood was so excited he could hardly sit still. He had been waiting for this moment... a chance for North Carolina to be a crown colony. For who would be governor? Why, Alexander Spotswood, of course. He had seen this sort of thing happen before. For instance, take New Providence. It, too, had been a proprietary government overrun by pirates. And what did the king do? Why, he made it a crown colony. It was certain he would do the same for North Carolina, and Spotswood suspected he would naturally get the governorship. Spotswood was quite elated. He rubbed his hands together with glee.

Just then the setter that had previously been panting at his master's feet, suddenly pricked his ears. He sensed a mouse running through the floorboards of the room opposite and he emitted a low growling sound. Bounding on all fours to the door, he began whimpering and pawing at the obstruction to the next room. It was clear what he wanted.

However, the door was locked and his master ignored him.

His master had his own territory he wished to invade and he, too, leaped to his feet and began pacing the room, deep in thought.

Colonel Moore spoke again. "But we are afraid, Governor, that Blackbeard consorts with others."

"Others?" Spotswood asked. The pacing stopped.

The setter sniffed under the door.

"Yes," Moseley continued. "There seems to be a great deal of intrigue in the government."

Spotswood's eyes lit up and he whirled around on his heels. The whole conversation was becoming more and more interesting by the minute.

"To name one—Tobias Knight, collector of customs," Moore said.

"And?" Spotswood continued.

"We've no more names at present," Moore continued. "But, trust me, there are more—a den of infamous scoundrels."

Spotswood spoke slowly to control his enthusiasm. "Very likely there's a syndicate in existence in North Carolina."

"Why, yes, you might say that," Colonel Moore remarked. "Certainly it's not uncommon—merchants and corrupt governmental officials contriving to get rich off pirate gold."

"I suppose you think of Fletcher," Spotswood said.

"Yes," Colonel Moore agreed.

"And Governor Markham," Spotswood said.

Colonel Moore nodded.

Governor Benjamin Fletcher of New York, upon his arrival in 1694, immediately appointed members of a mercantile aristocracy into his council who found the profits of illegal trading alluring. Fletcher was charged with giving commissions to privateer to notorious pirates like Tew, Hoare, Glover, and Maston, whose destination was the Red Sea. Immunity from arrest was given for presents of gold. Fletcher denied all this, of course, even though people saw the governor openly welcoming Tew to his mansion for a tot of rum and driving in his carriage with the pirate. Fletcher said of this especially sadistic pirate that he was "Not only a man of courage and activity but of the greatest sense and remembrance...of any seaman I had met."

Governor Markham of Pennsylvania also denied dealings with pirates. But everyone knew that he had married his daughter to Captain James Brown, a well-known pirate, and that this couple often associated with the wealthiest and most notable families in New York. When Governor Bass of New Jersey tried to arrest some pirates, Markham proved uncooperative. Moreover, round him there was said to be "evil men who gave the pirates intelligence and carried them off the country in boats."

"Scalawags," Spotswood said, referring to the governors.

"It's said to be the fashion," Colonel Moore answered, waving a gloved hand in the air.

"A foolhardy fashion, gentlemen," Spotswood said. It might have been a fashion to some, but it was deadly earnest to him. Patriotism demanded sacrifices of men; it demanded that they should curb sinful inclinations and desires. "Eden will rue the day he was in league with that mongrel of a sea dog." Spotswood paused before continuing. "Now, from this letter we may assume that Eden and Blackbeard are up to something."

"Yes, we believe they have been working on something for months, something that's very clever," Moseley said.

Spotswood nodded, determination and will fueling him with desire to capture the pirate. "But the information we have is not enough. We must find out more."

Moseley looked at Spotswood. "Blackbeard is a pirate, sir. And pirates are robbers."

"Yes," Spotswood answered. "We might assume they are planning to steal something. But what, gentlemen? And when?"

"That I don't know, sir." Moseley shook his head in bewilderment. He had been considering these same questions for quite some time now, but so far he had come up with nothing.

Spotswood was bitterly disappointed. Eyelids drooping, lips turned down, he remarked, "Well, gentlemen, then I fail to see what we can do about this."

Moseley thought for a moment and finally replied, "Nothing at present, sir."

The setter began a series of relentless whimperings.

Spotswood still ignored the dog, preferring to give his attention to the men. "Now gentlemen, I also fail to see the reason for your bringing me this news. Surely you are not doing this out of the goodness of your hearts."

"I must admit we would like something in return," Moseley said, revealing a cunning smile. "Perhaps your thoughts if you would be so kind."

Spotswood looked puzzled. He did not understand. "My thoughts?" he repeated.

"When North Carolina becomes a crown colony," Moseley said.

Suddenly a look of enlightenment spread across Spotswood's face.

How could he have been so stupid? Of course, that's what these gentlemen wanted—power in a new government in North Carolina. He walked to the door. "Yes, well then, gentlemen, I'll be sure to keep you in mind." He made quick to add, "This has been a most interesting conversation."

"Indeed," Moseley stressed.

The setter, seeing his master head for the door, began to bark.

Only a few feet from the dog now, Spotswood turned to give vent to some pent-up feelings. "I dare say, there's only one thing worse than a pirate," he said.

"And what's that, sir?" Moseley asked.

"A Spaniard," Spotswood said. "A bloody Spaniard." And with those last words, Spotswood opened the door.

The setter leaped out in joyous expectation of the hunt.

Going A Round

In 1718 the Spanish *Guarda La Costa* protected their shipping in South America more diligently than the English warships patrolled the British colonies. If the taxes imposed by Great Britain were viewed as oppressive, her people in the New World were far better off than their southern neighbors, for the *averia* of King Philip were levied so unmercifully that the Spanish subjects were more than willing to be accomplices to a little international intrigue, should they profit from it. As a result, a lively smuggling trade had developed, fostered by the many merchants who greased the palms of corrupt colonial officials to facilitate the entry of foreign shipping into Spanish waters.

For that reason, the *Bachelor's Delight* had managed to sail by the castle of *St. Philip de todo Fierro*, the iron castle which guarded the entrance to Porto Bello, and make its way to a small bay northwest of the town, *la Caldera*, where it moored in four and a half fathoms of water. The shore of this bay was often used by Spanish captains to careen their vessels and the American ship was all but ignored.

Yet, there were many dangers for an outsider in Spanish waters, not the least of which were the crocodiles waddling on the shore, their horrid claws denting the slimy banks. Thadius Taylor shivered as the ugly reptiles sized him up like dowagers with small malignant green eyes set deep under warty brows. Still, he tried to ignore the crocodiles as he slipped off the *Bachelor's Delight* in a longboat and made his way along the rocky shoreline to the town of Porto Bello.

In the early morning, Taylor moored his boat in the jungle just north of the half-moon shaped harbor. He expected to find a ghost town. During the times when the Spanish did not visit Porto Bello for the fairs, the town was virtually empty except for the soldiers and their families unfortunate enough to be garrisoned here. The heat, humidity and lack of wind, augmented by the high mountains surrounding the town, made the climate so unbearable that King Philip had ordered his fairs to last only forty days. Most of the upper classes vowed to leave Porto Bello as soon as they amassed the necessary funds. Every agent hoped to persuade his employer to recall him.

Taylor was amazed to find the streets crowded with people. Several large ships, including a few galleons well over 1500 tons, were docked along the quay. Taylor was surprised. Taylor had not expected galleons at this time of the year for it was hurricane season, a time when ships rarely traveled the coast. The thought crossed his mind that perhaps the Spanish had changed the times of their fair this year due to the frequency of pirate attacks on their shipping.

With all the commotion, the townspeople hardly gave notice to one man. Taylor had managed to disguise himself in Spanish clothes, yet he was still nervous and ill-at-ease in Porto Bello. The penalty for trespassing in a Spanish territory was death by torture. For this reason, he was careful to avoid the castle of St. Jerome which guarded the town, along with another further south, Gloria castle.

He wanted to see if one of the galleons might be the *San Rosario*, but in the early morning light he was gripped by a moment of panic. Keenly conscious of being an outsider, he took a last look at the large ships docked northeast of Gloria castle, and walked away from the center of the town, losing himself in the narrow, dirty streets.

The town was crowded. Merchants sat cross-legged along the streets, calling their wares. Beggars reached out their hands to passers-by. Slaves roamed the streets. The upper-class citizens rode by in carriages.

Unfamiliar sounds rattled Taylor further—the howlings and shrieks of monkeys in the nearby jungle, the rumbles of thunder which, no doubt, would bring on an afternoon storm, and the raucously braying donkeys laden with faggots, chicken coops and strings of red pottery.

Taylor was careful to keep himself out of the path of oncoming vehicles. The last time he had been to Porto Bello, an old man—Portuguese, Gallician or Basque—had been hit by one of those shrieking carriages called *chirones*. The old man had fallen in the street, and beseeching the cross, had died, but not before a garrulous crowd had gathered excitedly, not really concerned with the dying man. A few women had crossed themselves when the man had expired. Once the man was dead, the streets cleared and everyone went about their business.

He came to the east side of the town, which led to the road to Panama, the quarter called *Guinea*. Here Negroes, both slaves and free, had their homes. He passed an area reserved for the prostitutes. It was hard for him to feign disinterest in one young woman—a buxom, mulatto wench, her brown breasts bare underneath a string of beads and a bright flaming petticoat emphasizing the enticing movements of her hips. Seeing Taylor's interest, she stopped him, but Taylor, in broken Spanish, told her he had a girlfriend and walked on.

Taylor's mother had been Spanish and he understood the tongue. It was the innuendoes and puns which he sometimes missed. With his dark hair, he could easily pass for a Spaniard in these foreign waters, as long as he didn't have to involve himself in lengthy conversations.

One couldn't be too careful in Porto Bello, especially with the prostitutes. They would steal a stranger's money at a moment's notice or have their boyfriends do it for them in some dark room after their victim was lured inside. Taylor could not afford to lose any money. Taylor was not a rich man.

He turned around, because if he walked any further he would be in the jungle and on the road to Panama. As he made his way back up the street, he heard behind him the hooves and trappings of horses, so loud it sounded like cavalry. He stepped aside to let pass a mourner's carriage followed by a hearse drawn by two pair of black mares with black plumes. The driver wore funeral livery. The hearse bounded and slammed and rattled over the stones loud enough to wake the dead inside. If not woken, Taylor thought the corpse must surely be dismembered from so much jostling about. The mourners' carriage was empty. Perhaps, thought Taylor, the man was like himself—a stranger here.

The carriage headed toward a large stone church, decently ornamented, considering the small size of the town. But Taylor knew the Spanish always put great emphasis on their churches, for they seemed more concerned with the hereafter than the English. Taylor thought the man was unfortunate, indeed, to die in such a Godforsaken place, despite the ornateness of the church.

Taylor knew one thing—he did not want to die in Porto Bello.

His thoughts made him want to be off in two shakes. But he was already making his way down to the harbor. He braced himself. He must find out about the *San Rosario*. He wondered if the *San Rosario* was one of the Spanish treasure ships. He knew these ships still sailed, but now they only crossed the Atlantic approximately every five years.

Taylor reproached himself for being so frightened. Hadn't he been on numerous smuggling voyages in the past? Hadn't he always gotten away clean? To calm his nerves, he walked up to a small stand and brought some *chica* or beer from an old Indian woman. He tried not to think how this beer was made—from old women masticating maize in their slobbering mouths. Nevertheless, he drank it.

He again heard the sound of a carriage approaching and wondered if the hearse had returned. He perspired profusely. He told himself the sweat was due not to his nerves, but the deep soporific heat and humidity that oppressed Porto Bello throughout the year. Yet, he felt chilled to the bone.

Instead of the empty hearse, he saw two members of the gentry riding in gilded carriages followed by some wealthy hidalgos on jennet horses on their way to the castle, St. Jerome.

He sighed in relief. It was risky being a smuggler. But over the years, Taylor had learned to live with fear. It had become a way of life with him—the nightmares of being suddenly caught, the cold sweats on hot, sunny afternoons when he passed the authorities. Though he continued to free-trade he was always waiting expectantly for that one big chance, the pot of gold at the end of the rainbow, and then he vowed, he would give up all this entirely.

The harbor was crowded with little stalls where Indians sold fish and green sea turtles from the morning hauls. He began to ask a few questions concerning the *San Rosario*. One citizen pointed out a large galleon.

He was about to approach the ship when he heard behind him the slow plodding hoofbeat of beasts of burden. He turned around to see a packtrain of llamas and mules loaded down with bags and chests. The head *arriero* cracked his whip unmercifully on the backs of several Indians as they unloaded the animals, piling seventy pound silver ingots in full view in the street. Each piece was stamped with King Philip's coat-of-arms. The silver lay untouched and unguarded. Taylor figured no one could get very far in the jungle with such a heavy load.

Another crack of a whip brought his attention back to the Indians. Taylor wondered how the Indians, clothed only in wide white breeches, could tolerate such treatment at the hands of their superiors. He had heard the leaves they chewed were coca, a herb so strong it befuddled their brains. Indeed, they seemingly took little notice of the whip, the heat or the strenuous work they were performing.

Although Taylor felt uncomfortable in the midst of this scene, he stayed. He was lucky enough to overhear a most remarkable conversation between the *arriero* and a captain-general.

"*Buenos dias, Señor,*" the *arriero* said.

The captain-general, a tall man with dark hair and a lengthy, oblong, square-jawed face that gave the impression he had been given by nature a single-minded point of view, spoke. "The last of the silver?"

The *arriero* nodded. *"Si, Señor."* He was about to whip another native when the captain-general grabbed the whip from his hand and laid a stroke so heavily on an Indian, it opened the flesh on his back. The captain-general fixed his eyes on the *arriero* as if to say, "that's how it should be done" and returned the whip to the muleteer. The native cringed, but began to work twice as fast. The captain-general smiled. Then his face returned to his usual stony expression. To him, these Indians were of less use than the beasts of burden because they could carry less silver.

"Madre de dios," the *arriero* continued. "Thanks be to the Madonna that this is the last of King Philip's silver. What a hard journey we had— a two week trip to Arica. The llamas lay down on their backs, spat in the face of their drivers and refused to walk until their load was lightened. Huge, flesh-eating birds, condors, carried off the lambs and pigs which we had for food. The packtrain stayed in Lima for several days, then took the overseas route to Callao, an eight-day journey."

The captain-general was unconcerned with the hardships. "They tell me considerable precautions have been taken with the silver."

The *arriero*, always willing to please, and also always willing to put in a good word for himself, threw up his hands in the air.

"Señor, I assure you every precaution imaginable has been taken with the silver to save it from any *banditos*. Certainly, one doesn't transport twelve million pesos worth of silver from Potosí to Spain without the most considerable safeguards."

"I should be curious to know the nature of these precautions," the captain-general said.

"Of course, *Señor*. The Armada of the South Seas accompanied us to Panama City, a voyage that lasted three weeks. Then when we arrived near the Chagres River, instead of traveling overland where we might be attacked by *cimarrons*..."

"Cimarrons?" The captain-general looked puzzled.

"Cimarrons are wild Negroes."

The captain-general nodded. A native of Cadiz, he was unfamiliar with the bands of escaped slaves which roamed the jungles, marauding and looting.

The *arriero* continued. "Instead of traveling overland the treasure was put on barges and transported via the Chagres River to Venta Cruz— a journey of twelve days. Then it was brought hither to Porto Bello."

"You have been most careful," the captain-general said.

"*Si, Señor*," agreed the muleteer. He smiled. "I hope I have relieved some of your anxiety. And now, *adios*." The *arriero* looked pleased. Perhaps he would get a promotion, if the Spaniard put in a good word for him.

The captain-general stood for a moment with his usual stony gaze, staring at the Indian he had whipped.

Thadius Taylor carefully studied the captain-general. From his frozen expression, he did not look at ease. The captain-general turned his back on the muleteer and walked toward a large galleon docked directly behind him.

Curiously, Thadius Taylor followed behind him in the throng of people as the man headed toward the gangplank of a huge ship. Scripted across its stern was the name, *San Rosario*. What luck! The very ship that Blackbeard wanted was in full view. Taylor waited. In a moment the captain-general was approached by another man on a white horse, dressed in the manner of an aristocrat.

"*Buenos dias, Señor Gobernador*," the captain-general said, tipping his hat.

The aristocrat dismounted from his horse. "It is a good load of silver they bring from Potosí," he said. "I haven't seen this much silver in all the time I've been the lieutenant governor of Porto Bello."

"It is a good load," the captain-general answered. He took a deep breath. "But, I am most worried about it."

"What is there to worry about? It is safe here. You see, no one bothers it. It will be loaded on the ships by morning."

"But I am worried when it is in my hands, *amigo*," the captain-general remarked. "*Filibusteros!*"

"Ah, pirates!" the lieutenant governor exclaimed. "But, of course. We have had our share of them in this town. Barbarous, shameful beasts!" The governor was referring to the numerous pirates who had plundered Porto Bello. In 1595, before the town was half built, it was ransacked by Sir Francis Drake who died and was thrown overboard in the harbor. It was taken in 1601 by Captain Parker, again in 1669 by Captain Morgan, who burned its castles to the ground, raped its women, and pillaged its treasure and finally, in 1678 by Captain Croxon.

"The open sea is a place where the silver will become my responsibility, don't you see, *Señor?*" the captain-general said. "Should it be lost while under my management, King Philip will surely have me executed."

"I understand. King Philip does not tolerate mistakes. But, as you know, only a few top officials who are directly connected with the silver know of its passage to Spain."

"But what if an Englishman were to know?" the captain-general argued.

"Impossible. But let's imagine that there are those who know of this plan. They still could not know the passage of the ship or its departure date. Nor that you will be watering at a small island off Carolina." He pointed to a small map posted on a bulletin board directly in front of him. Although the map did not show a passage, the governor traced a clear route with his finger, stopping at the island.

"That is an unusual place to receive fresh supplies," the captain-general remarked, glancing curiously at the map.

The governor nodded. "You'll be leaving Havana October 1. This is hurricane weather. And going up the coast of Florida is very risky. No one expects a shipment of silver to be transported during hurricane weather."

"I am entirely aware of the preposterous schedule," the captain-general said. He nervously bit his lip. He had once been in a hurricane and barely escaped with his life.

"To add to this, no one would suspect an unescorted ship of carrying so many valuables. Foreigners expect our shipment of treasures to be heavily guarded."

"Yes," the captain-general agreed.

The governor waved his hand in the air. "So, you see, one has about as much chance of capturing the silver as one does...well...sailing to the moon."

The captain-general smiled. "*Señor*, you have made me feel at ease. The plan is absolutely foolproof."

The governor mounted his horse. "I am glad I have restored your confidence." He nodded to the captain-general. "*Adios*."

The captain-general waved as he departed.

Thadius Taylor tipped his hat back from his face. He smiled as the natives continued to load the silver onto the street beside the dock. He couldn't believe his good fortune. By God, he was right! Blackbeard was after the Spanish plate.

He waited until the captain-general had disappeared on board the *San Rosario*. Then he reached in his pocket, pulled out a silver coin, examined it and flipped it in the air. Catching the coin, he pocketed it and walked down the street, whistling softly to himself. A large smile broke across his face as all his fears dissipated. Those who noticed him saw a dark-haired man walking through the streets with such a large grin on his face that they wondered what could possibly have made him so happy.

Thadius Taylor had found his pot of gold, or rather, his pot of silver, at the end of the rainbow.

A Lady-Killer
Meets A Lady

C harles Eden, walking briskly along Carteret Street, was busily
      pursuing his daily occupations with the other citizens of Bath.
      The crowd was thick today. The citizens frequented the shops of
the little town with the sweet zeal of an early summer morning. Eden
tipped his hat to passers-by. His mind was thus distracted for a moment
from last night's escapade.

Last night had been windy and wet from a shower. The evening had
left him with a distinctly uncomfortable feeling. After one of his routine
meetings with Blackbeard, which finished later than usual, he strolled
along the streets of Bath, just as he was now doing. He had been careful
to avoid walking beneath the windows of homes where the contents of a
chamber pot might be thrown out. Since this meeting with the pirate had
been only business as usual, it had come as something of a shock to him
to learn he was being followed.

As he sidestepped puddles of water from the rain, he had heard footsteps behind him with an altogether discomforting regularity. Qualmish,
he had lengthened his stride. His pursuer followed suit. Charles Eden
soon discovered his worries were well founded. Turning quickly around
he had caught sight of a man, skirting behind a building. He craned his
neck to see more of the man, but he had disappeared. Another time,
having stopped suddenly to look in a shop window, he was startled to
see the man's reflection definitely outlined in the glass. It was none other
than Edward Moseley's and it was only a few yards away. He had spun
around desperately, but Moseley had vanished into the night.

What kind of skullduggery was Moseley up to? Eden didn't know. But he was sure of one thing—trouble.

Moseley had been easy enough to shake. Eden had merely taken a coach home and Moseley, on foot, had been unable to follow.

He restrained himself from looking at reflections in shop windows today. However, he did catch himself listening for a minute to see if he could distinguish any one pair of footsteps from the others around him. He couldn't.

It was especially crowded outside the premises of a general store on Front Street. After Charles Eden's lonely evening last night in the dampness, the general store was inviting with its warm smell of baking bread. Having some business to attend to here, he opened the door, and the cheery, tinkling sounds of bells heralded his entry. Noticing the sign of the three sugar loaves above his head, he walked inside.

He nodded to the Hassells, a leading family of Bath. The mother, father and daughter were looking over some dry goods and chatting amiably. Eden, with somewhat less politeness than usual, was quick to tip his hat and be on his way, because the daughter, Anne, was the family's one and only unwed child. She had her eye out for every bachelor available and Eden had no wish to give her ideas.

It is a sad fact of life that some women are not endowed with the graces needed for matrimony. Such a woman was Anne—dull-witted, large, ungainly, with an overpowering nose and drab brown hair—seeking everyone and sought after by none. Poor Anne. Her dresses were always too large, even for her somewhat overweight figure. Her father and mother, through great pains, had sent her to William and Mary College in Virginia to be trained in the art of dancing, yet still she managed to tread on the feet of her partners. This clumsiness was not the fault of her dance instructor, but could be attributed, in fact, to her natural uncoordination. Elderly matrons would shake their heads and sigh and go out of their way to be kind to her. What else could they do? And once she had gone, they would shake their heads again and whisper to each other, "Poor Anne, poor, poor Anne."

Her father—a man not noted for warmth and humanity—would set his mouth firmly and refer to her as an "antique virgin." Indeed, Anne was well past her prime. One can not blame her father for wanting heirs to run his plantation, but so far, even with the dearth of women in the colonies, Anne had not succeeded in wedding. Actually, there were so few spinsters in the colonies that William Byrd had once remarked "an old maid or an old bachelor are as scarce among us and reckoned as ominous as a blazing star." Anne was that blazing star.

However, Anne did have one attribute that gained a few suitors calling at her door — the vast wealth she would one day inherit from her father. Yes, Anne was an heiress—an ugly one—but an heiress nonetheless, and that does, indeed, account for something.

Having perused some dry goods with care, Charles Eden, now with a select group of commodities in hand, was considering heading for the door when he, by chance, overheard a conversation of the Hassells.

"Has he fixed the date yet, Anne?" Mrs. Hassell asked in a rather light-hearted manner as Anne bent over a sack of flour on the floor.

Anne tried to appear nonchalant when her mother spoke of marriage. She did not look at the woman, but instead, concentrated on the sack of flour with such intense interest that one who was unfamiliar with her might wonder if she had lost some article of jewelry in the sack. "Has who fixed the date?" Anne asked.

"Why, Mr. Moseley, of course," her mother said. For the life of her, thought Mrs. Hassell, why does she always have to be so evasive? "Mr. Moseley has been courting you for quite some time now, Anne."

Anne blushed. "Mr. Moseley has not set a date, Mother. Not yet."

Across the room Eden's body stiffened. The dry goods that were in his arms were all but forgotten. They were left sitting on the floor. Of the owner, nothing more could be seen. The course of events that succeeded this unusual behavior took place at such a rapid rate that the Hassells were taken quite by surprise.

"Why, Governor," Mrs. Hassell said, turning to find Charles Eden breathing down her neck, "you quite startled me." Aware of his handsome appearance, she immediately took out her fan and began waving it in front of her face to cool herself down.

Charles Eden, bracing himself for the ordeal, took a long look at Anne. And with all pretense of sociability, he forced a smile.

Anne caught her breath. Her overweight figure trembled as she stared longingly into Eden's eyes. Indeed, her reaction was not unusual. It was reported by several prominent members of Bath society that Charles Eden was so handsome that one young thing had been rendered fully speechless when approached by him and another had fainted straightaway when he most charmingly kissed her hand.

"So nice to see you again, Governor," Mr. Hassell said, going through the usual social amenities.

"A pleasure." Eden made another effort at a smile and then fairly jumped at the chance to introduce himself to Anne. "I don't believe I've had the pleasure of meeting your lovely daughter." He mustered forth all the charm he could in the face of such ugliness and gave a low, courteous bow.

Mr. Hassell was taken aback. In all the years he had known Charles Eden, he had never known him to ask about his daughter. What had brought on this sudden change of heart, he wondered? However, Mr. Hassell wasn't one to look a gift horse in the mouth and he continued, pleasantly surprised. "I don't believe you have. This is Anne."

Anne blushed and giggled and, all in all, made a general idiot of herself, but Eden, with firm determination, took her hand and kissed it. "I am charmed, I assure you, madam."

After this little introduction, Anne gave him somewhat of a nod and replied, "Governor Eden."

"Please," Eden said, "I would prefer you call me Charles."

"As you wish—Charles," Anne responded, now blushing so heavily that she found it necessary to look at the floor.

Mr. and Mrs. Hassell watched this little scene with a mixture of curiosity and mild shock. They studied Anne quickly just to make certain they hadn't overlooked something in the last few days, but all they saw was the same Anne they had known for twenty-eight years. They looked at each other and shrugged. Mr. Hassell's eyes returned to his daughter. Perhaps, he thought, she wasn't as bad as he thought. Her face still hurt his eyes but maybe she had something—maybe inner beauty. That must be it. But why question it? What an amazing stroke of luck! Here was another suitor for his daughter's hand in marriage.

Of course, Mr. Hassell could never have guessed the reason for Eden's sudden enchantment with Anne. Eden's interest could be attributed, not just in part, but entirely to Edward Moseley. For Eden was quite aware that all men tell their innermost thoughts and desires to their lovers. Moseley especially had this weakness. He liked to boast of his achievements to members of the opposite sex. Eden merely had to wait until the time was ripe and pry Anne for information. Ah, yes, Eden was struck not by the arrows of love but the arrows of fortune. So much for passion!

"Governor Eden," said Anne's mother, who was moving her daughter in for the kill by nudging her closer to Eden, "I saw you at a dance April last with Mary Ormond."

"Ah, yes," Eden responded, "quite a lovely girl whom, I might add, I'm no longer seeing."

"Do tell," Anne said, her eyes lighting up.

"A shame," Mrs. Hassell added. She seemed perfectly delighted.

"Since then I've been seeing no one," Eden said, with such a long face that for a moment Mr. Hassell took pity on the man.

"No one," Mrs. Hassell repeated. "A pity." She was inwardly so happy she could hardly contain herself. Her enthusiasm manifested itself in a smile.

Eden looked at Anne and thought how extraordinarily well this was all coming off. "Sadly enough, until now no one has been able to captivate me." He gave Anne another one of those long, soulful looks that sent the girl's head spinning.

Mr. Hassell was so shocked he choked and coughed. This was all too much. Here was this young couple gazing into each other's eyes so fixedly that it was getting to the point where it was damn near embarrassing. Trying to think of something to say, he blurted out, "Governor Eden was previously discussing his travels along the coast with me."

The fact that Eden was a traveler seemed to enhance the governor even more. Anne's eyes lit up like fireworks. She exclaimed, "Fancy that! Do tell us of them. The coast must be fascinating."

Eden, in the rather bored and world-weary voice of an experienced traveler, polished his nails on his coat and replied, "I fear it is more so in the expectation than the telling. I have no adventures of my own to report."

Nevertheless, Anne continued to gaze on Eden with admiration. "Adventure or no, it must be utterly fascinating. I, myself, have not traveled much."

"Then you must do so, madam. I have traveled extensively in America and Europe." Eden thought the woman reminded him of a puppy dog waiting to be patted.

"Oh," Anne said, suddenly a bit taken aback. "There are so many dangers in traveling for a young lady."

"I fear it is so," Eden said sadly. "There is the risk of a great deal of savagery in traveling. I once had a major encounter with a pirate in the Red Sea."

"Indeed!" Anne's eyes flashed. "I have been informed these pirates are some of the most horrible beasts in the world, belonging in confinement rather than loose in society."

Eden immediately picked up on the fact that Anne was stimulated by talk about pirates. She was not the only person in Bath Town who was. For awhile now Eden had seen a change coming on in the attitude of the citizens. They didn't like the high taxes, that was certain, and to avoid paying them, they'd buy black market merchandise from the pirates. On the distant horizon, Charles Eden saw a rebellion. It was only a matter of time.

Sometimes when Eden would walk the streets of Bath, he would overhear the people talking about the pirates, their eyes gleaming, their voices enthusiastic just like Anne's. Public opinion, it was plain to see, favored them. Just look at the way they treated Blackbeard—inviting him to their homes for dinner, stopping him on the streets, asking to hear stories about his pirating days, imagining themselves going to sea. On the other hand, they would hardly give so much as a hello to Charles Eden. He would go from their homes with a peculiar wounded look on his face. Sometimes, he would lie awake in the bed at night and make a promise that he would show them all that he was greater than even the great Blackbeard himself.

He watched Anne's reaction now to his tall tale about the Red Sea pirates. Lips parted, eyes open wide, breath drawn inward, she gazed on Eden in a state of rapture as if he were a Greek god. Reveling in all this new-found admiration, Eden smiled, polished his nails once more on his coat, and made a decision to carry out his role of pirate captive to the hilt.

Careful to conceal his high spirits, he continued. "Indeed these pirates are beasts. And I should be delighted to regale you about my encounter. But I feel the delicate ears of the lady present may be offended, for I met with more savagery than I have ever suffered in the American lands. Indeed, it may shock the lady." Eden flashed a wicked gleam in Anne's direction.

This last statement was meant to excite Anne's curiosity with forbidden pleasures. Admittedly, he succeeded remarkably well, because Anne, catching sight of the apple dangling before her eyes, snatched it up with alacrity. "I have read of these pirates," she said. "Do continue."

Mr. Hassell frowned.

"Very well, then." Eden hitched his shoulders, as though he was proceeding not of his own free will, but by Anne's insistence. "We were traveling off the coast on the ship, the *Bauden*, when we were captured. The pirates ranged down on our starboard quarter and soon took our ship."

"I've heard tell these pirates are extremely wicked," remarked Anne, who was now hanging onto Eden's every word. Indeed, she could not hide her excitement.

Anne was not the only one aroused by Eden's account. Mrs. Hassell, too, felt her blood rising, and she looked at Anne sharply when her daughter interrupted Eden. "Do let the man finish his tale," she remarked.

Mr. Hassell picked up on his wife's excitement exceedingly well, and gave Mrs. Hassell a forbidding look.

Eden collected his thoughts. "These pirates live the most debauched life imaginable—wining and wenching and committing the most barbarous atrocities."

"My goodness," Anne said, her blood going to her head.

"What I witnessed was abject savagery." Eden continued to make up this entire tale as he went along. He paused, seeking to contrive some new twist to his story. In only a matter of a few seconds, he had his new line. "I met up with the pirate captain, Henry Avery, a most clever rascal."

"*The* Henry Avery!" Mr. Hassell said, rather surprised. Avery was one of the most well-known pirates of the day.

"The very one," Eden nodded.

Mr. Hassell's jaw dropped in amazement. Damn, this was something. Now even he was excited by Eden's tale.

"The one who captured the Grand Mogul's treasure ship with an enormous gold hoard?" Anne asked. She could not believe her ears.

"Yes," Eden replied, basking in all this glory.

Mr. Hassell shook his head in amazement. "They say he is a most bold and clever man. He is represented in Europe as one who has raised himself above the dignity of a king, having married the Grand Mogul's daughter. A play was writ upon him called, 'The Successful Pirate'."

Mrs. Hassell, in all due respect to her position as a lady, could not let this conversation proceed any further without making the next comment. "I find it quite ironic these pirates are romanticized so." The statement seemed to her quite profound.

"They are indeed marveled at for the audacity of their acts and their cleverness, madam. To be associated with one lends one a certain air of greatness, don't you think?" Indeed, Eden was rather exhilarated by his own tale, for he was enjoying the feeling of being associated with someone of such great notoriety. The fact that he had never met Avery did not bother him in the least.

Mrs. Hassell looked surprised. Although she was stimulated by the talk of pirates, her role as a gentlewoman in Bath society would never allow her to admit it. So she responded with a habitual sniff of disdain. "I think pirates are disgraceful."

"But by their successful robberies they do seem to prove other mortals mere fools," Eden argued.

Mrs. Hassell thought that statement quite odd. She was later to recall it at a testimony in Bath with extreme clarity. In her opinion, it was the type of statement only a criminal would make. Now she merely remarked, "You do speak strangely for a governor."

She also recalled at the trial that Charles Eden smiled after she said this—a strange, twisted smile.

"Whatever do you think motivates them to do such wicked deeds?" Anne asked.

"Believe me, I have no idea," Mrs. Hassell responded, putting herself above such conjectures that might warrant taking the place of a pirate. Then very shrewdly, she addressed Governor Eden.

"Tell us, Governor. If you were one of those criminals what do you think would motivate you?"

"Well, to see if I could do it, of course," Eden said. "And if I could that would indeed prove me more clever than the average mortal."

"How odd!" Mrs. Hassell said. "Just to see if you could pull it off and nothing else?"

"Nothing else, madam," Eden calmly replied.

"Not even the money?" Anne asked. How unbelievable!

"Not even the money. Merely to see if I could pull it off."

Mrs. Hassell noted that Eden smiled again mysteriously. "Well!" Anne's mother said. She was utterly disgusted with Eden, but she could not quite figure out why.

Anne, however, had had enough of this conjecturing on criminal nature, and returned to their former subject of conversation. "This Moslem princess—was she as beautiful as they say?"

Eden shook his head. "Madam, I hate to inform you, but one tends to find myths created around these pirates. She was much older than he, and, after enjoying her handmaidens, he had his way with her. But he didn't marry her. And he threw her handmaidens into the sea. They were drowned."

Bubbles burst, Anne made a long face. "How dreadful!" she said.

Charles Eden, however, was not about to spoil all this admiration he was enjoying. "Dreadful yes. But not as dreadful as the deed he performed while I was aboard ship. May I continue?"

"Please go on," Anne said, who had been hoping for more.

Eden smiled. What a dupe Anne was. The girl would probably believe him if he professed to being the king of England.

His mind racing ahead, he continued, "They had a fellow that disobeyed the rules on board ship. So they put him on a rack and inhumanely disjointed his arms."

"My goodness," Anne said, fluttering her eyelashes.

"But that was not all," Eden continued. "Then they twisted a cord around his forehead which they wrung so hard that his eyes appeared as big as eggs and were ready to fall out."

"Goodness gracious!" Anne was apparently quite flustered.

"But notwithstanding these torments they hung him from his..."

Breathless with anticipation, she exclaimed, "Do continue!"

Eden coughed and then smiled his wickedest smile of all. He had reserved this smile for the climax of his story. "From his private parts, madam, giving him many blows and stripes under that intolerable pain and posture of the body. Afterwards, they cut off his nose and ears and singed his face with burning straws."

"Good heavens!" Anne's mother said. "I really must excuse myself." It should be noted that Mrs. Hassell had been careful to hear the entire tale before leaving. However, much aware of her duty as a lady, she blanched.

"My dear!" said Mr. Hassell, who always took extreme concern at Mrs. Hassell's conditions. Over the years Mrs. Hassell had managed to turn white, faint, and have hysteria, all at the right moments, and even he was not quite certain now when she was faking it and when she was not.

"Your tales are quite remarkable," Mrs. Hassell said, addressing Eden. "I'll see you in the carriage, dear," she said, nodding at Mr. Hassell.

Mr. Hassell looked at Governor Eden. "You must excuse my wife." Although he was quite proud of her ladylike reactions and always reinforced them afterwards in private, he apologized for her. "She is not accustomed to tales of this sort."

"Perchance I was a little rude," Eden appeared quite apologetic.

"Oh, no," Anne said, who showed perfect delight in the tale.

Mr. Hassell reminded himself to say something to his daughter about her reaction.

Eden looked at Mr. Hassell. "Well, I must take my leave of you, sir. But before I do," he said, turning to stare at Anne, "you must give me your word you will let me call on your lovely daughter."

The displeasure on Mr. Hassell's face was suddenly replaced with a smile. He patted Eden amiably on the back. "Callers are entirely Anne's decision." But he was quick to nudge the girl into nodding.

"As you wish," Anne said, suddenly taking out her fan and waving it in front of her face to hide her embarrassment.

Afterwards, Anne and Mr. Hassell joined Mrs. Hassell in the carriage parked directly outside the store. But as the coach was driving off, Anne remarked to her mother that she found Governor Eden most fascinating "in a rough sort of way." It was generally agreed that Anne was in the possession of one of the most valuable of all possessions, a prospect, one much more wealthy and handsome than Edward Moseley.

A Pirate Tells His Story

Mary Ormond had made an indelible impression on Blackbeard. What was it, he sometimes wondered, that so attracted him to her. Was it the cornflower-blue eyes, the chestnut hair? Was it that certain air with which she walked? Was it her saucy tongue and flashing smile? He didn't know. But he did know the image of Mary Ormond in her frilled white dress, standing at her garden gate, would stay in his mind forever. Love, at first sight, had struck him.

Indeed, it must be love, this certain feeling that left him more light-hearted than he had ever imagined. Why else would he feel faint when he heard her name? Why else would he spend the entire morning before a mirror, powdering his hair? And why else would he practice for hours on end, bowing stiffly from the waist to a broom he used to sweep out his lodging place. Why else indeed, if this wasn't budding, frivolous, romantic, awe-inspiring, wonderful, fascinating, enraptured love. Yes, if ever there was a man who was up to his neck in it, it was Blackbeard.

So, words can hardly describe how he felt when one afternoon, strolling through the streets of Bath, he chanced to see the love of his life, Mary Ormond. At first, he stopped dead in his tracks. Then his heart skipped. Finally, he felt as if he might faint—but that would make her think he had a weak constitution. If he called to her, she would think him forward. If he said nothing, she would think he did not care for her. He wrung his hands in a fit of anguish. What was he to do?

Do? Why, he really had to do nothing, for his enchanting angel, the love of his life, had not even noticed him. Indeed, she was in the mundane process of admiring a dress in a shop window, a rather ordinary habit for a young lady of Bath Town, but Blackbeard found this habit of hers intensely interesting. Indeed, anything his love did he found intensely interesting, be it lifting a slender ankle over a mud puddle or giving a charming smile to passers-by. When she proceeded onto the next shop and then to the street corner he followed, worshipping the very ground she walked on.

Mary Ormond, however, was still completely unaware of Blackbeard's presence. In fact, she had no idea the pirate she so detested was following her. She was more concerned with seeing that her newly-bought tabby dress, imported from England and edged with Flanders lace, did not get muddied from the passing vehicles. When she arrived at the street corner, pink-cheeked and sparkling-eyed, she lifted it grace-fully, showing just the slightest tip of ankle (nothing more, for that would have been lewd for a woman of her breeding) and then proceeded across the street.

Since Mary's eyes were cast downwards on her dress, she could hardly have seen the carriage heading down Carteret Street and directly in her path. The horse suddenly reared up on its hind legs just beside her and the carriage screeched to a grinding halt. The fiery-eyed horse, its nostrils flaring, would have surely trampled her when its hooves hit the street again, had not a strong arm swiftly jerked her from behind, and back onto the sidewalk. She whirled around to face the pirate.

Eyes welling with tears, trembling from head to tiny toe, Mary found it was all she could do to open her mouth and utter, "Mr. Blackbeard!"

However, the driver, veins bursting in his forehead, fist hurled to high heavens, found numerous words at his beck and call, all of them curses and all unfit for ladies such as Mary. He got out of his carriage to hurl some of his vexatious words at the woman, but when he saw Blackbeard step forward he changed his mind, and instead, went to calm his horse.

 Mary forgot her prejudice against pirates. "I'm much obliged to you, sir." She looked at her dress. It was completely ruined now for the horse had splattered it when he reared up, but the matter seemed incon-sequential after staring death in the face. She was a very silly girl, she told herself, and she wondered if it took something monumental, such as this accident, to put one's life into perspective.

Blackbeard, as if reading the girl's thoughts, smiled. Then he spoke. "I'm honored to be saving your life, madam. And as long as I have my eye on you, I'll continue to do so."

Mary nodded. She had forgotten herself for a moment. Then, just as suddenly, she found herself. The insight on life vanished from her mind. She returned to her former state of flightiness, reserved for young ladies who are highly bred and highly strung, and with it returned her prejudice. Cautiously, she eyed Blackbeard. And when she looked at her dress, she wore a particularly long face.

As Mary walked down the street, she found herself in the company of Blackbeard whether she asked for it or not, and for the life of her, she could not figure out how to get him to leave.

So thinking of nothing else to do, she decided to strike up a conversation. Remembering how she gained the acquaintance of Blackbeard, and thinking of the only thing the two had in common, she spoke. "Have you had the company of Governor Eden lately?"

"A little," Blackbeard answered.

"That's more than I can say for myself," Mary sniffed huffily. She did not say it aloud, but she was thinking that the governor was a common cad. He certainly had nerve—to court her and then throw her aside like a worn out glove. For three days, her heart had been sore to the breaking point. She, of all women, Mary Ormond, was no longer wanted! For those three days after Eden had dismissed himself from Mary's presence, she had refused to eat, drowning herself in self-pity until on the fourth day her heart hardened and the hunger pains gnawed her so that she could no longer bear it. On the fourth day, she had come to her senses and eaten a seven-course meal and vowed to flirt with every man in town. That, she thought, should show Charles Eden just how little she cared for him. Charles Eden, after all, cared little for her...not like this man walking beside her.

Her thoughts returned now to her companion. Mary felt somewhat puzzled. What a curious man. Here was a common criminal, a butcher of human beings, behaving like the most respectable gentleman in town. It did not make sense. She decided to broach the subject of her thoughts, tactfully, if she could. "Mr. Blackbeard, it takes me quite by surprise that a man of your character should have the calling of a...common...pirate."

"A calling, madam?" Blackbeard smiled half-heartedly and sighed. Then he shrugged his shoulders as if he carried the burdens of the world on them. He had sometimes wondered why his life had ended up the way it had. But life holds strange twists of fate and ironies for some. Certainly, he had no plans to be a pirate. Yet here he was, as she termed him, a common pirate. He could not deny it.

"T'weren't no calling, Miss Ormond, leastways, I wouldn't say it was."

Quite puzzled, Mary looked at him. "Well, then how did you become a pirate?"

It was not Blackbeard's custom to unburden himself to most people. Through all his hardships, he had developed a great amount of self-control. He was a strong, silent man who rarely spoke of his own problems. But lately, all the changes in his life were taking a toll on him. He had become extremely vulnerable. Now he felt a constriction in his heart which comes when relief and sorrow struggle for self-expression. He wanted to get this all off his chest. Having found a companion in Mary, someone who could lend a sympathetic ear, if need be, he began to talk about himself. "T'was such as this, Miss Ormond," he said, taking a pipe from his breast pocket, and then a pouch of tobacco. "When I was a lad, no morn'n six or thereabouts, I'd oft as not pass the dockyards in Bristol, Bristol that's where I'd hail from. T'was at the dockyards I'd hear the sailors speaking of the grand and glorious life they led. And I had a hankering as many o' the lads did in those days to take to sea. So I learned to hand and reef and steer. I was the best o' the bunch, Miss Ormond, and when I was old enough, instead o' going into the law as my father would have me..."

"He wished you to be a lawyer?" The thought that if Blackbeard had not gone to sea, he would have been a lawyer struck Mary as quite odd. A lawyer must have quite a moral obligation to the law, and a pirate was considered completely immoral. She watched Blackbeard fill his pipe with tobacco and thought that she should surely faint from its obnoxious odors. But when Blackbeard exhaled his first puff, she was surprised to discover it did not bother her in the least. She suspected this was due to her fascination with Blackbeard's story, which was in part true, but it was also due to a fascination with Blackbeard which Mary wasn't ready to admit to herself.

"Aye," Blackbeard said. "My father had chosen the profession o' law for me." He knocked his pipe on the side of his hand to loosen some ashes, and putting his mouthpiece against his lips, drew in on the tobacco. After exhaling another puff of smoke, he continued, "But I had no inclination for the law, leastways, t'was the sea that was in my soul, Miss Ormond. So, such as it was, I joined the navy at the onset o' Queen Anne's War. T'was many a lad then that took to sea, many a lad like myself wanting to captain a ship. Just think!" Blackbeard said, now gazing off in the direction of the sea. "What a glorious thing, to captain a ship for your own country—to sail the queen's own flag."

Mary, watching Blackbeard's eyes light up with an inner excitement, felt some of the thrill he must have felt when he joined the navy. She, too, stared in the direction of the river mouth with the afternoon sun glittering off the water, and she couldn't deny a feeling for the romanticism the sea bore. But she turned away from it and when she did, she caught a glimpse of a shadow crossing Blackbeard's face. His expression became grave. When he faced Mary, he had a stabbing look of pain in his eyes. He shook his head, sadly. "But ah, t'was a sad lot for Blackbeard, a sad lot, indeed. My mother, Miss Ormond, predicted the whole, she did, predicted I would end a pirate. And right she was, dear heart, ah, how right she was!" To hold back welling emotions, Blackbeard exhaled on his tobacco pipe and was, for a moment, lost in thought.

Mary felt she should not interrupt. Instead, she waited. She walked side by side with him, nodding to passers-by. After a matter of minutes, he chose to break the silence. "I reckon t'was the war that made me what I am today," Blackbeard explained. He had finished his first round of tobacco and he tipped the ashes out on the ground and then crushed them under the heel of his right boot. Then taking out his pouch again, he continued. "Captain Smollett was in charge of our ship then. I was just a green hand, so's to speak. Smollett, he was a fine seaman if ever there was one, but stiff on discipline. Duty was duty he'd say, and t'was our duty to capture every enemy ship we could. Ah, yes, Smollett had a way with him, he did. He made a fine privateer o' me, Miss Ormond— taught me all there was to know o' battle plans from start to finish. You see, before then I had none o' the appearance of a man what sailed before the mast. T'was an exciting career being a privateer, I don't deny that, and I worked harder than the rest, so in time I was the best o' the lot. I became a captain—ah, yes Captain Edward Teach. T'was the dream of all the lads to command their own ship, but I was one of the few what did. Aye, I had my own ship—*The Queen Anne*—a proud ship she was at that. But this career o' mine, it ended all too soon—all too soon. For in 1713 the war was over and Captain Teach—why, he was out of work." His voice broke.

"But couldn't you have stayed in the navy?" Mary asked.

A group of chaises and carriages rattled past them as they walked, the passengers headed for a day in the country.

"No, I couldn't have stayed in the navy." Blackbeard collected his thoughts and drew in on his pipe. His voice became firm and well-modulated. "The queen let 'em all go, knowing full well what their lot t'would be. Aye, t'was a dirty trick the queen played on us, a sorry piece o' luck it was."

Mary noticed for the first time that his face appeared drawn, his eyes tired.

"As soon as I come off the ship, I seen 'em, Miss Ormond—my shipmates, begging in the streets, sponging for bread—aye, t'was a sight o' poor seamen starving. And them that didn't starve, stole. Ah, yes, I learned soon enough no respectable man would hire a sea dog. They heard what the sailors done in the name o' the queen—murdered, some of 'em, plundered others."

Mary was reminded for a moment that she was speaking to a pirate and her eyes that had softened suddenly grew hard, her posture frigid. But she noticed as she walked that Blackbeard tipped his hat to some gentlemen who were quite respectable, in fact, close friends of her father, and they returned the gesture.

If Blackbeard noticed Mary's change of mood, he did not show it, and continued, his voice low and rumbling and solemn as they walked down Carteret Street. "Yes the long and the short of it, t'was nothing I could do but take to pirating. Me. I joined with Hornigold." The name Hornigold to Blackbeard was obviously of great importance, and he paused after he said it.

Even Mary stood in awe of the name for Hornigold was the most feared pirate of the day, except for Blackbeard. But like other pirates of the era, he had settled down in New Providence where he sailed ships for the governor of that island—Woodes Rogers. To some pirates he was considered a traitor, for often he would capture the very men he had trained, but to Blackbeard the name Hornigold held great significance, perhaps because Hornigold let Blackbeard get closer to him than any other man alive.

"Aye, Benjamin Hornigold." Blackbeard remembered Hornigold's craggy frame, broad shoulders, and blustering laugh. "He was no common man, not Hornigold," Blackbeard said, his voice enthusiastic as he talked, his eyes on fire. "Aye, he could speak Latin by the bucket, and strong, why, an ox was nothing alongside Hornigold. But I seen him do things." His voice broke off again as he thought of the dark side of Hornigold. But Blackbeard did not want to hold back with Mary—he wanted to tell her everything. "Yes, I seen him do things—murder for one. Blackbeard, Miss Ormond, he's never murdered, you can count on that. I come to blows, yes...but murder, that's another story."

Blackbeard waited for Mary to react to his last statement. He knew she would be puzzled, because he was said to be the most feared pirate to sail the seven seas.

She opened her mouth in surprise. "But your reputation!" she uttered.

Blackbeard laughed out loud. It was not a joyous laugh, but mocking and sarcastic. "My reputation, Miss Ormond," he said, "was all Hornigold's doing."

Mary said nothing, but her brow wrinkled and her eyes squinted up in thought.

He waited to see if he could detect anything more in her eyes, but he couldn't. He realized he had just told Mary something he had never told anyone else in his life. She lifted her brows and gave him a sidelong glance.

Well, he should have thought as much. She didn't believe him, that was sure. He let his tobacco smoke circulate slowly through his lungs before he continued. After collecting his thoughts, he spoke again. "Miss Ormond, it was this way, see. Hornigold, he come to me and he says, 'Edward Teach,' he says, 'you've got a fine sense o' the sea. And you've got a fine physique. Now, I'm going to teach you all I know about pirating and you'll be the fiercest of them all.'"

Blackbeard's eyes lit up with an inner excitement. His beard bristled. "By thunder!" he said, shaking his head, and talking. "Hornigold was always as good as his word." He exhaled some more tobacco smoke to calm himself before speaking again. "Hornigold, he taught me how to curse like a parrot, he did. Taught me how to grow my beard and hair to look a fright. Taught me how to put lighted matches in my hair fit to scare the devil, hisself. Trained me a proper pirate, Hornigold did, no bones about it. And sure enough, Miss Ormond," he said, pausing to look at her with a forlorn expression on his face, "one day every man alive was cowering at my feet like lambs, and Hornigold was telling me I was the bloodthirstiest pirate ever to sail the seven seas. And I swear to God," confessed Blackbeard, raising his right hand as if taking an oath, "I ain't ever murdered one living soul."

Mary tilted her face as if to question him and then stared him down. Did he take her for a fool? Hump! This was all a lie just to win her favor.

Blackbeard immediately reacted to Mary's expression. "But, it's true," Blackbeard said, now fiercely desperate that she believe him. There was such a look of utter and fervent intensity in his eyes, it quite startled Mary. He stopped dead in his tracks. "Blackbeard here's a sham, Miss Ormond, a fake."

"But," she protested, "the tales they tell of you! Horrible tales!"

Blackbeard threw his head back and laughed. "Aye, the tales, little lady. Fit to scare the devil, hisself, no doubt. Want to hear how they started? From a bribe, that's right, a bribe. Hornigold done that, too.

Taught me how to bribe a ship's company to spread terrible tales, grue-some stories as to what I'd done. I'll reckon this'll come as a shock to you, but the ships, they all surrender when they see my Jolly Roger—the rumors frighten 'em so."

Mary suddenly burst into laughter. Supposing he was telling the truth. Then this was hilarious. He'd fooled the entire world.

Mary could not stop herself from laughing until Blackbeard took her gently by the arms and turned her to him, a most serious expression now crossing his face. "Aye, it's funny enough, Miss Ormond, by your account—until you seen what I seen happen to pirates. Aye, you hear me, I seen a thing or two at sea, I has. Why, how many tall ships think you now have I seen laid aboard; and how many brisk lads drying in the sun at Execution Dock and all for being pirates?"

Mary looked deep into the man's eyes with a soul-searching gaze. Yes, he could have been lying to her. But, from the intonation in his voice she knew he was telling the truth. His last words had won her.

Blackbeard whispered his next words. "You're the first I've told this to, Miss Ormond." Blackbeard hoped she knew he had taken her into his confidence, because he wanted her as his companion. Secretly, he hoped for more than just a companion, but that would come in time, he told himself.

Mary nodded in understanding. "But you're a pirate no more," she said. "You've settled down in Bath."

"Aye," Blackbeard said. "I am thirty-eight now and back from cruis-ing. But being a respectable man's easier said than done." He shook his head despondently. "Aye, sometimes I thinks it's all in vain."

"I don't see why."

"Aye, Miss Ormond, you wouldn't and little wonder."

For a moment Blackbeard reproached himself for telling the girl his story. For how much could a young girl like Mary really understand? He wondered if he should tell her more. On second thought, perhaps she would understand. "The merchants don't take kindly to me staying in Bath," he remarked.

"I've heard tell the merchants have great respect for you," Mary said, utterly surprised by this remark. She couldn't help but add, "espe-cially the ones that frequent *The Lion And The Unicorn*." She had heard rumors about the secret operations of the tavern from her father.

"Aye," Blackbeard chuckled. Mary had said all this without batting an eyelid. She was smarter than he had given her credit for. And a lot harder than she showed under that soft, feminine skin that had been bred

only to attract men. He paused to light his pipe again, because a sudden
gust of wind had blown it out. Once the cinders were rekindled, he continued walking and talking. "As long as I brings 'em stolen goods to sell
at bargain rates, the merchants respect me. But I'm no longer a'pirating,
Miss Ormond. And this I'll tell you now, and hear me well. If the merchants don't get their merchandise, then they don't get their money and
the people don't get their goods. With taxes such as they are, in time the
colonists will surely starve. And for want o' the pirates, Miss Ormond.
Aye, the people in Bath wants a hero, Miss Ormond—a hero to fight the
king. I'm that hero. I steal from the rich and give to the poor." He raised
his fists to the heavens, scornfully. "But by God in heaven, they're hypo-
crites." He shook his head then, realizing sadly that he had wasted his
energy. "Aye, no good'll come of these merchants, Miss Ormond, I say.
With them, I've seen my slice o' luck, I has already. For they'd hang me
at the gallows, if they'd half a chance now that I ain't a'pirating and you
may lay to that. Aye, they thought me a proper hero—and I t'weren't
nothing, nothing but a man what wants a home and a wife and decent
life—a man what's decent at heart, but what has a talent for being a good
seaman. And that's his only talent. Ah, dear heart, it's a shame, it is, a
crying shame."

"I'm sorry." The pirate did have his troubles, and from the very bottom of Mary's heart, she sympathized.

"Aye," Blackbeard said. "It's a bad lot I've had, a bad lot. And to
make matters worse, there's those what still wants things o' me, Miss
Ormond, the governor for one."

"The governor?" Mary asked. But, what in the world would the governor want with Blackbeard?

"Aye," Blackbeard said, but then suddenly realizing that perhaps he
had said too much, he whispered, "Now you just forgets I said that."

"Very well," Mary said. She had had enough to take in for one day,
as it was. But what she had taken in, pleased her. She was all softness
and smiles. Indeed, the pirate had won Mary over. And although she
would never admit it, she was just as enchanted with Blackbeard as he
with her.

Unconsciously, she offered her hand and the two, walking arm in
arm, continued on down Carteret Street. They said nothing now, so lost
were they in the thoughts of each other, but every now and then they
would look at each other and smile shyly. How handsome he is, she said
to herself, such strong shoulders. How delicate she is, he said to himself,
like a fragile but precious flower. It could have been spring for all they

knew, so loud did the birds chirp on this sunny July afternoon, so bright were the flowers blowing in the breeze. They were like young lovers everywhere, walking hand in hand, sharing secrets—reflective, dreamy, joyful, enchanted—and hopelessly lost to the world. So involved were they in each other that both of them failed to hear the clomp of a peg leg behind them, and it was not until a figure was almost upon them that Blackbeard whirled around in a quick, almost unconscious reaction to danger.

This sudden movement of Blackbeard caught the intruder off guard and was probably what saved Blackbeard from being killed instantly, for the man had been carrying a knife and had meant to stab the pirate in the back. He was a scurvy, bald, little sailor with a wooden leg, who took off as soon as he saw Blackbeard's face, fleeing furtively into the seamy section of Bath from where he had come, his peg leg clomping in regular intervals along the street. Blackbeard would have sped after him if he didn't suddenly feel a sharp pain in his shoulder. He looked at his arm and saw he had been stabbed. It was only a minor cut, a flesh wound at most, but the blood began to trickle down his waistcoat rapidly.

"You've been wounded!" Mary screamed.

"It's just a flesh wound," Blackbeard said.

Mary searched frantically through her belongings for a handkerchief. She finally found one in her bag and removed it. "Here," she said, wrapping the cloth around the wound.

Blackbeard grimaced. "He was a bad un." He shook his head and stared in the direction to which the man had fled. "But there was probably worse that put him on. Aye, he thought he'd have a go at me, he did. I'm sorry he got away clean." He winced as Mary tightened the handkerchief.

"But why in the world would anyone want to stab you?" Mary asked.

Blackbeard looked at the girl and shook his head in the manner of a father trying to explain something to a child. Although she was intelligent, she knew little of the ways of the world. But how could he expect a goddess, a vision of loveliness and eternal bliss, to understand the sordid business of being a pirate. He tried his best to explain. "There's many that wants my neck, Miss Ormond. Now that I'm settled down, they don't think I'm such a threat anymore. No more the great Blackbead, just Captain Teach. So these men, seamen, there's many a seaman that once I robbed, Miss Ormond, they'd think to have a go at me."

Mary watched the blood trickle down his arm. "It must hurt."

"I'm none the worse," Blackbeard said. He lifted his eyes. Mary saw his look, uncannily impressive, unresenting, unangered and dogged. It caused her to drop hers.

"I don't see why you stay—frightened by seamen and merchants as you are," she said.

Blackbeard searched Mary's face. Didn't she know why he was staying? "It's for you I'm staying."

She lifted her eyes, looking at him in wonder.

"Me?" she asked. Why would this huge, burly man, this incredibly handsome gentleman she had once thought a scoundrel and rascal stay in Bath for her?

Suddenly, Mary understood the meaning behind this whole afternoon venture. Her body was again stirring with unexplained passions and desires. She bent her head. She blushed red and white in turns. When she finally looked up, it was to unlatch the gate to her house.

"Miss Ormond, wait," said Blackbeard, calling after her.

She turned back around to him for a moment, now staring intently into his face. She bent her head again, unwilling now to face him and acknowledge these budding, newly-romantic feelings in her soul.

"Miss Ormond," he said, taking her hand. "I want to call on you."

She paused for a moment, then nodded. Fearing she had been too forward, she cast her eyes to the ground.

Blackbeard hardly felt the pain in his shoulder, he was so deliriously full of joy. His color was high; his eyes sparkled. He thought to himself that he must be the happiest man in the world.

A Stratagem to Capture
a Most Notorious Pirate

Alexander Spotswood liked to pass as a great sportsman. He was particularly interested in hunting and was often seen in the fields in the fall with his dog, Rover, taking a good day's sport at wild birds—pheasant and quail. Upon occasion, he took expeditions into the wilds of the American countryside to collect unusual specimens of birds. His sense of triumph at a bird's death was something just short of ecstasy. No less triumphant was his setter, whose passion for collecting birds was equal only to his master's.

That is not to say Alexander Spotswood did not have similar passions for other sports. Far from it. Sport for sport's sake was Spotswood's motto. Horse racing ran a close second to Spotswood's passion for hunting. Today he was down by the rails at Devil's Field, where he sat in a corner so he could watch his horse, Young Fire, through a spyglass. Young Fire was to run a quarter mile. Beside Spotswood sat his niece, Katherine Russell, and at his feet, his setter.

Through his spyglass, he could see his jockey bringing Young Fire from the stables. She was a brown mare with well-placed shoulders, straight hocks, a small head, and a bang tail. She was followed directly by the challenger, Phillip Ludwell's stud, Smoker, a black horse with a rat tail. The two horses briskly trotted past the spectators to the starting line. Spotswood felt his heart leap with anticipation as he watched Young Fire file by. She was one of his proudest possessions, for in her three years, she had never lost a race yet. He expected that at Devil's Field she would have no trouble proving herself a winner also—as did the crowd, who had arranged their carriages in rows so they could watch the course.

As Spotswood was watching his horse, a short, red-haired man, Job Bailey, appeared on the track and placed a speaking trumpet to his mouth. "Ladies and gents," he shouted. "The race is about to start. Place your bets straightaway."

Katherine Russell took a look at Young Fire for a moment, and then handed the spyglass back to Spotswood. "I should like to place a bet on Young Fire," she said. "About a sovereign. I don't like to bet much."

"It'll be about eight to one," Spotswood said.

She nodded.

He took the sovereign from her and then went below to place the bet. Rover, spotting his master leaving for a moment and wondering if it was due to something he had done, went bounding after Spotswood and licked his hand. Spotswood stopped to pat the dog on the head. His faith restored in his master, Rover followed behind as Spotswood continued his walk. The dog's tail wagged joyfully.

Joyfully, that is, until Spotswood passed Phillip Ludwell. They say that animals can sense their master's feelings, and if so, then Rover was not far from wrong in Spotswood's feelings concerning Phillip Ludwell. He commenced to growl and so threateningly show his canines that he caused the man to turn around. Ludwell leveled his gaze at Spotswood and pressed his lips together as if to say, "Shut that dog up before I do something you'll regret." Spotswood, sensing his annoyance, spoke vehemently at the dog to silence him. Rover gave a few stifled growls and then dropped his head to the ground and his tail between his legs. Somewhat despondently, he followed his master. Although he did not show it, Spotswood always took an ecstatic joy in his dog's threatening growls at Ludwell, and when the dog finally caught up with his master, Spotswood rewarded him with a little scratch behind the ear. Yes, Spotswood hated Ludwell.

The feeling was mutual. Ludwell did not care at all for Spotswood. Their antagonistic feelings toward each other had begun several years ago over a little incident involving the land between their adjacent estates. Ludwell had once been deputy auditor of the colony. But Spotswood had suspended him from office when he had discovered that Ludwell had stolen land from the governor's property, a simple procedure of adding another 0 to governmental papers changing his holdings from two thousand to twenty thousand acres. For the embarrassment of being forced from office, Ludwell was determined to get even with Spotswood.

Actually, this race was all Phillip Ludwell's idea. Ludwell knew it was hard for Spotswood to turn down a race—especially a race where he was ninety-nine percent assured of being a winner. Ludwell's stud had lost several of the major races of the season, and Spotswood's mare had a winning record. Spotswood had jumped at the chance of the small competition. He also had put down a large purse on his horse—fifty pounds. He was expecting four hundred back in return when he won. But both men had more at stake here than the purse. Both were playing a game of one-upmanship with the other. And both were determined to win.

Ludwell knew all this, of course. He had deliberately planned the race. Now poised at the rail, his eyebrows jutting forward, an assured smile spreading across his face, he cheered for Smoker. Ludwell's friend, William Blair, also a member of the governor's council and commissary of the Church of England, shook his head in disbelief. He had seen Ludwell take risks before but this was going a bit too far. He stood to lose more than four hundred pounds on Smoker. Blair felt he should at least warn the man of his chances at a loss. Perhaps Ludwell would back down before it was too late.

"The mare's fleet," Blair said, having himself bet on Young Fire. Blair didn't let his emotions run away with him. Although he was not fond of Spotswood, being politically on the side of Ludwell, he was a practical man.

Ludwell only nodded in response to Blair. His face had that confident sense of self-assurance which characterizes a winner. To Ludwell, Blair seemed quite calm as opposed to the crowd that was clapping, cheering and haggling over the race about to begin.

"You'll look a fool if Smoker loses," Blair commented.

"He'll not lose, you can count on that."

Blair raised an eyebrow. Being a representative of the Church of England, he felt a statement like that should only come from God alone. But he did not press Ludwell further for the jockeys had come onto the field.

In pennant-bright silk, the jockeys were brought before the crowd. Ludwell's was weighed first and then Spotswood's. Spotswood's jockey was a new man on the field by the name of Blackstone. He carried a whip in his hands. His eyelids dropped over his shrewd eyes, his upper lip over his lower and he had no hair on his face.

"Ten stone," Job Bailey shouted. "Same as Ludwell's. That's it, then, ladies and gents. Ten stone for the both of them."

Meanwhile, Alexander Spotswood had reached the box where he was to place his niece's bet and found he had to wait in line. He did not like standing here with the rabble, for although these races attracted the aristocrats, they also had more than their share of the lower class. He folded his arms for a moment, raising his eyes above the crowd, a habit of his which tended to lend his figure a look of disdain.

As Spotswood stood with Rover he could not help overhearing a conversation between two men in front of them. He judged from the look of the men's clothes that they were commoners because their shirts were made of coarse cloth and their hair—that is, the one who had some— was not powdered. When one removed his hat, his little bald head gleamed in the afternoon sun. Wiping away the sweat, and replacing his cap on his head, he thrust his hand across his forehead.

"The word's out that Blackbeard's about our capes," the bald-headed man said.

The other cleared his throat and spat in the dust. "A'pirating, is he?"

"So they say. Plundered a merchantman lately—for medicinals."

"For the pox, I warrant." The pox they were referring to was syphilis.

Both men chuckled at his last statement. Blackbeard was known for his prowess with women.

"Whereabouts did it happen?" asked the man with hair.

"Charleston," the bald-headed man answered. He moved up an inch or so, for he was the next in line to place a bet. Then having nothing else to do for a moment, he put his hands in his pocket and shuffled about on his feet. "They say he held the whole town for ransom."

The other drew his breath in between his teeth, then let out a short whistle. "The whole town. Now, that's a villain."

"Mark me, he'll take Virginia's port next, if something isn't done to stop him."

The other nodded his head in agreement. He stepped up to the betting box and slapped down five guineas. "A purse of five says Young Fire's the winner."

Spotswood smiled. He certainly had public support. Young Fire had been in the public's eye all season, and she had quite a list of credits. The bets made him feel more exuberant. But his thoughts returned to the men's conversation. Blackbeard! What a nerve that man had—blockading Charleston harbor! Oh, these were bad and dangerous times! Oh, his beloved England was going to the dogs! Luckily for him the people in his colony still supported the king—most of the people, that is. Most of them knew what greatness lay in their past. Most of them were frightened of new ideas, just like him. Most, too, were dreadfully frightened of the pirates. They would like them all dead. So would the king, for pirating was stopping his trade. Of course, there were those people that had new ideas—those who might, in fact, cause an uprising of the whole population. These people were pirates, rebels, supporting the pirates against the king, and Quakers, not worshipping in the Anglican tradition. It was up to Alexander Spotswood to stop them.

Spotswood had, in fact, been reflecting on Blackbeard ever since Moseley and Moore had last visited him. But he knew he could not hunt the pirate as long as he had taken the pardon. He would have to obtain some solid evidence that Blackbeard was still pirating. Then, and only then, could he take action. Morally that was only correct. And Spotswood was a man of good moral character. It was only that his morals stemmed from habit and tradition rather than from principle and conviction, and that with the right amount of push he just might be forced into an immoral decision based on the acceptance of tradition.

Spotswood's thoughts were interrupted when a voice in the box called out "next." Spotswood stepped up and gave the man in the box a sovereign.

At the same time, the jockeys mounted the two horses. Once on the animal's backs, they gave them a kick to proceed and then rode them to the starting line. There was an increased excitement in the crowd. "Make your bets for the quarter-mile run," shouted Job Bailey through this speaking trumpet. "Last chance, ladies and gents. The race is about to start."

In response to Bailey's announcement, people ran to the box to put down their last coins. Spotswood, relieved that he had finished betting before this new flood of people came to mill about the box, made his way back to the rails. Rover followed after him.

When he passed Ludwell for the second time, the dog began barking and growling with renewed vigor. Spotswood took his leash and restrained him, but not before Ludwell turned to face Spotswood.

"I have heard, sir," Ludwell said, "that you endeavor to force me from the council."

The comment took Spotswood completely by surprise. Ludwell must have found out from one of the other council members that Spotswood had plans to remove him from the council, if he could. The topic had not come into the open as yet. However, Spotswood could not deny the statement because it was true. So instead of answering Ludwell directly, he merely replied with an evasive answer, "Did you, Mr. Ludwell?"

Ludwell's voice grew a little louder at Spotswood's response. The answer obviously had antagonized him. He set his mouth firmly and said, "You will have a hard time of it, sir, let me warn you. The people would just as soon remove you from your position as governor of this colony."

What Ludwell said was, in part, true. A growing faction of people in the colony did not care for Spotswood. But as of yet, they had not openly come out in support of their opinion.

"If I may be so bold," Ludwell continued, "I'll tell you, sir, that the people are making a good many complaints about the rise in taxes. Bleeding the colony dry, you are. Mark me, one day Virginians will take up arms against the crown. There will be open rebellion within the colony."

Spotswood opened his mouth in surprise. Did this man know what he had just said? God! In these days, pitfalls, dangers and snares were everywhere; in these days men went about openly, unabashedly advocating traitorous doctrines. Let them beware, these men. "You sir, are speaking treason against His Majesty, the king," Spotswood replied. "I should have you arrested."

Ludwell smiled calmly. He knew any arrest of a council member opposed to Spotswood would only cause more dissension within the colony. He also knew Spotswood was aware of this. So he only raised an eyebrow in response. His eyes, however, staring directly at Spotswood, seemed to say, "Just you try it."

Spotswood backed off. He had to be careful with this man.

Ludwell continued to smile.

Spotswood gave Ludwell a sharp glance, tugged at his dog's leash and then, turning on his heels, left as Ludwell remarked to Blair, "He's a stiff one."

Suddenly, the voice of Bailey was heard over the crowd. "Ladies and gents," he shouted, "the race is about to start."

Spotswood returned to his seat and settled down again at the side of his niece. He tied the leash of his dog to the rail. The dog crouched down on all fours and then placed his head between his forepaws. He closed his eyes.

Spotswood took up his spyglass and adjusted the focus. He could clearly see the horses. He lifted his eyes for a moment to catch sight of Ludwell, and then lowered them to the horses which were now prancing about briskly at the starting line.

"Now ladies and gents," Bailey shouted, "are you ready?"

A new wave of excitement rose in the crowd and several people, Spotswood included, yelled "Ready," in response. Rover opened one eye at his master's tenseness.

"And go," Bailey yelled, waving a hand. There was the sound of cracking whips and thundering hooves. Suddenly a roar went up from the crowd.

Rover bounded to his feet.

For a moment Spotswood sat quite still, then instinctively, he bent down over the railing as if charging for the finish line of a race.

Rover began to bark excitedly.

Spotswood ignored the dog completely, all his attention focused on Young Fire. "They're off," he shouted. He watched his horse. Young Fire was leading, Smoker following fast. Now urged to their utmost endurance and speed, whipped by the jockeys whose silken suits melted into a blur of color, the horses nearly flew over the ground.

Spotswood's interest increased with each fresh struggle of his horse. He clicked his teeth and beat on the rails. "Go Young Fire. That's a girl. Go. Faster now. Egad! That's my Young Fire!"

Young Fire was gaining steadily on Smoker; first, one length, then two, then three as the crowd's cheers increased and the whips and spurs beat down harder on the hindquarters of the animals. The spectators screamed no less than the two owners of the horses. As the horses charged on, those that had bet on Spotswood's horse screamed even louder, for his was clearly ahead. Spotswood, as he had expected, was close to victory. "My horse, my horse," shouted Spotswood and tears of pure elation sprang into his eyes.

Spotswood's eyes did not leave his horse. He whinnied and neighed; he panted as his animal galloped faster; sweating as much as his mare, he lunged forward and screamed orders until his throat was sore. His face was ablaze with a gleam of victory, his heart racing with enthusiasm. "Go Young Fire," Spotswood shouted. "Faster, Young Fire!"

But just as suddenly as the mare began to increase in speed, she began to slow down, the hooves pounding the earth slower and slower, her legs falling heavier on the ground. Quickly, Smoker began to gain on Young Fire with a remarkable burst of speed. The ground resounded now with his rapid paces as he streaked toward the post, nearing it closer and closer with each second, now neck to neck with Young Fire.

Spotswood never stopped urging. "You can do it, girl," he shouted. "Go now."

But it was no use. There was a groan from the crowd. Those who had bet on Spotswood's horse were going to lose their money.

And at one length ahead, Smoker crossed the finish line and was declared the winner.

Spotswood's mouth opened in amazement. Never in all the years of her racing career had the mare slowed down at the finish line.

But the race was over; he had lost.

The crowd sighed.

Spotswood bowed his head. His whole spirit was numb. Slowly, he put away his glasses and stood up with the crowd. And like a good sportsman, he did not show his heart on the field.

He took the arm of his niece, Katherine Russell, and went to visit the horse in the stalls. Rover followed patiently behind, waiting for his usual pat on the head, which was not forthcoming. He walked slowly behind Spotswood, his head on the ground, his eyes lowered.

Young Fire was in her stall, fretting under the administrations of a groom. She was streaked with sweat and her legs were outstretched. Beside her, putting away the bridle and bits was the jockey, Blackstone.

For a brief moment, Spotswood laid a gloved hand on the mare's lather flecked neck. Young Fire, eyeing him out of her soft brown pupils, tossed her head.

Then Spotswood looked at the jockey. On his lips were the words, "What made you lose like that?"

Although Spotswood did not say anything, thinking the words too harsh to put into effect, the little jockey understood. In a torrent of language, meant to clear himself from any suspicion, he said, "You take my tip—she a queer one, that horse. She has her own mind, she does, slowing down like that. I'd sell her, I would. When they're like that, nothing can be done." And then hanging up the bit and bridle, he continued working.

Spotswood was silent for several moments. No words of harsh invective were hurled from his lips. Instead, all he said was, "My Young Fire was not herself today, that's plain to see. Many a time she's bested Smoker. Odd, her slowing down at the post." He gave the jockey another glance.

"I'm glad you take your losing so lightly," Katherine said. A cultured woman, remarkably mature for her age, she did not appreciate hot tempers in any man.

Spotswood smiled. "I count it no ill fortune," he said, but the tone of his voice was all too sharp. Behind that smile, he was boiling mad. To think that an upstart like Ludwell could turn the tables on him like this was beyond imagining. He had his suspicions too, about that new jockey—Blackstone. But there was no evidence to support them.

It was because of men like Ludwell that England was getting a bad name. Oh, he would show Ludwell and all the rest of them that England was still supreme. And in doing so, he would restore his own self-esteem. He would not wait for any evidence as to Blackbeard's pirating. He could find that later. He would make plans to capture the pirate now. The people would think him a hero for removing such a dreadful threat. They would rally round him like they did when he first came to Williamsburg. And the king, who had been receiving bad reports about him from men like Ludwell and Blair, would be extremely grateful to him for restoring the trade. Perhaps, after hearing the dreadful reports about corruption in the North Carolina government, the king would give him the colony right away. Yes, his universe would once more be restored to harmony when he had captured Blackbeard. No more rebels, no more pirates, no more questioning of the king's laws. It had always seemed when he pleased the people, he displeased the Crown and vice-versa. Now he would please everyone.

"No," Spotswood repeated. "I don't count it an ill-fortune to lose to Mr. Ludwell. Indeed, I intend to beat Mr. Ludwell at another game."

Katherine raised an eyebrow. "I had no idea you and Mr. Ludwell shared any other common interests."

"A slight political game, my dear." Spotswood smiled at Katherine.

"Oh," Katherine said, passing Spotswood a knowing glance.

After tidying her hair and then slipping on her gloves, she gave him her arm. The two, walking away from the stable, seemed to hold each other a little too closely for niece and uncle. Indeed, for months many people had been wondering in the little town of Williamsburg about Katherine's relations with Spotswood. What they both did behind the closed doors of the palace where they lived was a mystery to everyone and speculations ran rampant.

The two entered their carriage, a fashionable coach drawn by four horses and lined with red morocco. The last glimpse anyone had of them that day was of an elegant young lady dressed in the highest fashions of the day. She was wearing an egret, French beads and bobs, and a black patch just above her mouth for piquancy of expression. Spotswood, her companion, was dressed to perfection with a head of curled and powdered hair, and a tiffany whisk underneath his chin. The postillions, wearing livery of blue broadcloth with brass buttons, then closed the carriage door on which was emblazoned Spotswood's coat-of-arms, a boar's head.

As the coach pulled away and a new race began, Blackstone appeared from the stalls. For a moment, he leaned against the side of the building and lit a pipe. He placed the mouthpiece against his lips, and then breathed the smoke through his lungs. He exhaled slowly. He seemed to be waiting for someone.

In a matter of moments, Phillip Ludwell rounded the side of the stalls. Blackstone gave a twisted smile of recognition. Then his shrewd little eyes darted to Ludwell's waistcoat as the councilman pulled a small bag of silver from his pocket.

"You handle your ribbons excellently," Ludwell said, passing the silver to Blackstone.

The jockey took the silver in his dirty hands, reminding himself to count it later. "As you say sir," Blackstone replied, "pull back on the reins as the horses reach the post."

The jockey threw the bag of silver gaily into the air, caught it, and then pocketed it.

Ludwell smiled triumphantly as the jockey then tipped out his tobacco, crushed it below his feet, and walked back inside to tend to the horses.

A Lady Comes Out

When society in Bath gave such a large party as was being given at the home of Mary Ormond, it was usually a special occasion. Tonight was no exception. For Mary Ormond had been sixteen this morning at exactly nine o'clock. Not fourteen, mind you, or even fifteen, but fabulous, wonderful, sweet sixteen. Sweet sixteen because it meant that Mary was no longer a budding rose, but now a full blossom in the flower of womanhood. But most of all, thought Mary's mother who was involved in laying one of the two large tables for dinner, it meant that Mary was at the ripe age to be courted, to be won and finally, to be married. Marriage was what Mrs. Ormond had in mind as she set the silver coasters down at the twenty-four places at the tables.

One could not rush these things, of course, thought Mrs. Ormond. But there was no harm in helping them along. After all, she had met Mr. Ormond at a party very much like the one to be given here this evening. Anyway, she took great delight in giving parties, unlike Mr. Ormond who regarded all this celebrating as so much foolishness. At parties such as this, he found the jokes dull, the guests stiff, and the entertainment—which usually consisted of a string quartet—deadly. It was his custom to make himself quite scarce so that Mrs. Ormond had trouble finding him. When she did locate him, he was either moving a candlestick here, or a punch bowl there, or giving the curtains a poke. This never failed to impress Mrs. Ormond for it was quite out of character for Mr. Ormond to do housework. He hated doing chores and always left them entirely to her and the servants. Obviously, he hated parties more than housework.

After making sure all the flowers were properly arranged, Mrs. Ormond checked the guest list against the table settings. All the guests, of course, had been carefully chosen—that is, excepting one. A look of pain spread over Mrs. Ormond's face when her eyes alighted on that name—Captain Edward Teach. She had added his name to the list at the insistence of her daughter. Captain Teach had a reputation for being a pirate in his former days. But he was reformed, so they said, and Mrs. Ormond couldn't very well deny her daughter on her birthday. Sighing, she put the guest list away and went to greet the first arrivals.

Unlike her mother, Mary Ormond was not so prepared for her guests. Early this afternoon she had rested for an hour, her eyes bathed in astringent lotion, and had then curled her hair. Now after much painting of the face and perfuming of the body, she was finally ready to make her entrance. An exceptional beauty, she really did not need all this primping. However, in the eyes of her guests, as she opened the door and glided to the head of the spiral staircase, it did seem all worthwhile. She was lovely.

Even more than lovely was Mary to one guest in particular—Charles Eden. As she descended the stairs with the full grace of a woman, hair piled on her head, she met his gaze and his heart skipped a beat. Fortunately for Eden, he had managed to slip away from his companion, the very ugly Anne Hassell who was now in the Ormond's dining room where drinks were being served before dinner. As Mary reached the last stair, Eden took her hand and kissed it even before it had been offered.

Coldly, Mary withdrew her hand. She had not seen Eden for several months, had not, in fact, even heard from him, and it was only at her mother's insistence that he had been invited to the party. She gave him the icy stare of a spurned lover. She wondered at the charming smile he gave in return. There was a mesmerism about Charles Eden and a clear, shameless daring which held a fascination. That was what Mary had been attracted to before she knew him. She could see how he could very ruthlessly, smoothly have his way with his associates, even lay a spell over them. She tossed her head. Never again would she be under that spell.

Heedless of her coldness, Charles Eden took Mary's arm and offered to escort her to the garden. Mary, who could not spurn these gallant attentions in front of her guests, reluctantly gave Charles Eden her arm. It was better, she thought, to pretend to have no hard feelings than to create a scene.

Arm-in-arm with Mary, Charles Eden felt a sudden heaviness of spirit. Why had he let this lovely creature slip away from him? The answer to his question lay in the conspiracy to capture the silver. It had not been so painful for Eden to lose Mary at first, but as time went by and Blackbeard began to claim her as his own, the thought of losing her had become more and more heartbreaking to Eden. He questioned why Blackbeard should have this woman.

Gazing into Mary's eyes, Charles Eden was not aware of the source of his feelings. The fact of the matter was, although he thought he was in love with Mary, he was not. If truth be told, he envied Blackbeard. He wanted to be the pirate. And he wanted everything the pirate had. If that included Mary, then he wanted her, also. Men like Charles Eden know little of love—and what emotions they do feel can be easily misinterpreted.

Eden watched a slender white ankle appear from the girl's dress as she thrust her leg forward. In a sudden flush of passion, Charles Eden spoke, "You're looking quite attractive tonight, Mary," he commented.

Mary felt her face flush. She had behaved herself quite well this evening, said nothing concerning Eden's previous slights to her, remained calm in the face of adversity, but with this comment her anger burst forth. "I have heard tell that you find Anne Hassell quite attractive."

"Perhaps," Eden said in his usual cool, high-handed way.

Mary was reminded that she never liked Charles Eden's way of answering questions. He was always evasive, willing to be misinterpreted; in a word—political—and now it made her more angry than ever. She, on the other hand, was not about to be misunderstood. She looked at him directly. "Correct me please, if I am wrong, but I have also heard tell you escorted Anne Hassell to this party."

"You are correct."

Mary took a small fan from a pocket in her dress and began to fan herself hurriedly. It was hot this evening, but the anger she felt at the governor was what was making her blood boil. "I find that highly unusual, Governor."

Eden raised an eyebrow.

Mary took her arm from him. "Governor Eden, you know as well as I, you have never in your life been seen in the company of an ugly woman." She turned to look into the man's eyes. She had been hoping to find something there, but there was not a glimmer of an expression. Instead, Eden only replied. "Well, then, Mary, perhaps she has other attributes."

Mary snapped back. "Perhaps not. I suspect some ulterior motive."

Governor Eden gave a sidelong glance. Then he shook his head.

Mary began to divine something. Continuing to fan herself, she remarked, "I suspect another motive, nonetheless."

As Charles Eden contemplated this lovely creature, he thought, why are we arguing in this garden, with the birds singing softly in the evening breeze? Suddenly, he took her by the shoulders and whirled her around to face him. The fan fell to the ground. Giving full vent to his feelings, he kissed her on the lips.

Mary struggled furiously to release herself from the governor's grasp and then gave him a slap in retaliation for this ungentlemanly behavior.

Surprised, Charles Eden put his hand to his face, rubbed it and glared at Mary. "Why you little wench," he said furiously. "You'd spurn the advances of a governor and yet you'd proceed with a pirate."

Mary was furious at his insinuation that she had let Blackbeard have his way with her. "Proceed with him! Why, I've done nothing of the sort. But I'll tell you, Governor, my so-called pirate is more a gentleman than you'll ever be." And with that, she took her leave of the governor, preferring to be unescorted rather than be alone with him.

Charles Eden shrugged. His ideas of courting Mary dissolved. Let her go, he thought to himself. He didn't want to complicate his plans for the conspiracy anyway. He stayed in the garden for awhile before joining the others, hoping to walk off his anger.

When Mrs. Ormond talked about Mary that evening she kept one eye on the liquor table to be sure glasses were always filled, and one eye on the garden path, from whence her daughter was scheduled to come at any moment. When Mary finally did make her appearance, she looked quite flustered and out of breath and a curl had fallen over her face. "Mary, darling," her mother greeted her. "You needn't have hurried yourself so."

Mary did not answer her mother, nor tell her the cause of her disheveled appearance. Instead, she kissed her mother lightly on the cheek and went to find Captain Teach. When she found him telling one of his sailing stories to a fascinated group of listeners, she took him away from the group for a moment to be introduced to her mother. He bowed stiffly, a feat he had perfected now, and kissed Mrs. Ormond's hand. Quite impressed with the man, for he did cut a fine figure, Mrs. Ormond offered him a drink. "Do you take punch, Captain Teach?" she asked.

"Ah, by gum, I do," Blackbeard said, holding out a silver tumbler to be filled. "Yes, I take to punch like a fish takes to water."

Mrs. Ormond thought the captain a little quaint really, and his expressions, although somewhat on the barbaric side, at times, quite delightful. She continued to chat with him and her daughter until the three were joined by Captain Richard Fenwinkle, who owned a trading vessel recently bound from Barbados. Fenwinkle had established quite a profitable trade in sugar between Barbados and North America, that is, when pirates didn't see fit to plunder his vessels. A short, pudgy man with a shock of white hair and a coarse little beard, he was known to stand rigidly at attention and salute whenever he made someone's acquaintance. He did so now.

"Why Captain Fenwinckle," Mrs. Ormond said, suddenly recognizing the man and addressing him, "I don't believe you've had the pleasure of meeting my daughter or Captain Edward Teach."

Fenwinkle gave Mary a smile, but for Blackbeard he reserved a frown and the remark, "Alias Blackbeard the pirate, no doubt." When it came to pirates, Fenwinkle was quick to dispense with socialities.

Blackbeard stood with his feet planted firmly on the ground, preferring not to answer this obviously distasteful affront.

But sooner than say nothing at all, Mary was quick to defend her new beau, breaking into the conversation with the words, "Captain Teach is no longer pirating."

"On the contrary," Fenwinkle replied, "I've heard tell his men are taking small trading vessels off our coast."

Mary opened her mouth in surprise.

But before Mary could say anything, Fenwinkle continued, "And I find it highly undignified that a lady of your breeding should fraternize with common pirates."

At this remark, Mary turned quite red.

Mary's mother, obviously embarrassed, thought perhaps she should have heeded her own instincts and not included the pirate on her guest list. Unaccustomed to confrontations, she could only lamely reply, "I'm sure Captain Fenwinkle has made a mistake." However, the phrase was said with much uncertainty because Mrs. Ormond had only recently made the acquaintance of Captain Teach. Quick to change the subject of the conversation, she offered Fenwinkle another cup of punch.

Fenwinkle flatly refused.

So the four stood in virtual silence for a full minute until Mrs. Ormond caught sight of Governor Charles Eden. With a sudden flourish of violin music, he approached their little gathering. "Oh, how nice to see you again, Governor Eden," Mrs. Ormond said much too gaily, for she was relieved someone had come to rescue the conversation.

Eden addressed Mrs. Ormond in his usual charming manner and Mary too, but she said nothing in return.

Mrs. Ormond, thinking her daughter quite rude this evening, nudged her and said, "Governor Eden spoke to you, Mary."

Mary glared at the governor, curtsied, and said, "Good evening, Governor Eden." She turned on her heels and left abruptly.

Speechless at Mary's rudeness, Mrs. Ormond reminded herself to talk to her daughter later.

After gathering her former composure, Mrs. Ormond continued, now addressing Eden. "The men were just speaking of sailing," she said.

Obviously, sailing was the only thing Mrs. Ormond felt Captain Teach and Captain Fenwinkle had in common, for standing opposite each other with grim faces and set lips, they looked as if they might come to blows at any moment.

With contempt in his voice, Fenwinkle remarked, "I have heard tell this colony is harboring a pirate." He made no pretense as to whom he was referring, for he stared directly at Blackbeard.

Eden was quick to defend his colony. "On the contrary, I must inform you that Captain Teach has retired from piracy."

"Of course he has," added Mary's mother, who was hoping Mr. Fenwinkle would not spoil her party by slandering her or her daughter's good name.

But Fenwinkle stood his ground. "There's many a vessel in Bath that's been robbed by the Jolly Roger lately, madam. I've a good mind to inform the governor of the colony concerning it."

Eden remarked, "Sir, I am the governor of this colony. And I think you've had your say concerning Captain Teach."

To say Mr. Fenwinkle was shocked by Eden's remark would be an understatement. His small beady eyes opened with surprise. And then without so much as a "Nice to have met you," or "Good evening," Captain Fenwinkle took one last look at the governor, and then sticking his nose in the air, stalked off in fury.

Embarrassed, Mrs. Ormond quickly excused herself with the words, "I believe the punch bowl needs refilling." But she did turn around as she left to give Captain Teach a most curious look.

Governor Eden, on the other hand, did not walk off. Instead, he took the pirate aside and said, "I warned you when first we met to stop your pirating of the traders of Bath. People will get suspicious."

Blackbeard was startled at Eden's words. "I haven't set a foot on my vessel when she was plundering a ship, Governor, I swear to you."

"Then why has this man seen your ship pirating?"

Blackbeard sighed. "The long and the short of it is, it's my men, Governor. None of 'em's fit for a landlubber's life. I'll stake my life on it, the men's been using the *Adventure* to plunder."

Governor Eden looked fiercely at Blackbeard. "We can't have that, do you understand?" Then unconsciously, he took the man by the collar. He paused, then turned around to find several people in the crowd staring at him. Eden, realizing he had made a scene, let Blackbeard shake himself free of his grasp. The governor stood silent for a moment, drinking and smiling until the guests resumed talking once more. Then he turned to face Blackbeard again.

Meeting the governor's eyes, Blackbeard spoke. "There's no way to control my men, Governor," he said. "Not unless you tell 'em of the conspiracy. That'll keep 'em quiet, no doubt—aye, if they knew there'd be plunder soon enough."

"Tell them of the plate," Eden continued, "and the conspiracy's off."

"Off?"

"Yes," Eden said. "And you'll end up with a knife in your back." Staring straight at Blackbeard, mouth firmly set, the governor didn't look like he was bluffing.

"Well, then when will we be telling them?" Blackbeard asked.

Eden finished off his drink. "The last moment we can possibly manage. I've seen too many men sun drying at Execution Dock because the word was out too soon. No, they'll know when the time comes and not a moment before."

"Well, now." Blackbeard was clearly upset. "You're a tight one. High and dry, you are."

"That is why I'll never be strung up." Eden gave Blackbeard one of those twisted smiles the pirate had often seen the governor make when he thought himself superior to others around him.

The smile made Blackbeard feel uncomfortable and he soon separated from the governor to seek Mary once again. He found her by a table set with drinks. When Mary saw Blackbeard, she made some excuses and went to join him.

The two didn't say much, but when Blackbeard asked Mary to come with him down one of the garden paths to a bluff overlooking the river, she readily agreed. The guests were tiring her, and the previous conversation with Captain Fenwinkle had made her uneasy.

When the two came to the end of the pathway, Blackbeard took Mary by the waist and pointed out a house in the distance. It overlooked the harbor, much the same as Mary's home, but it was located at Plum Point. It was a two-story structure, larger than Mary had ever seen in Bath Town. It was newly built.

"That's my house," Blackbeard said proudly.

Mary uttered, "It's lovely." Somewhat in mild surprise, she looked at Blackbeard, for a man living alone in a house like that could be terribly lonely.

As if reading Mary's thoughts, Blackbeard replied, "It would be for my family, Mary," he said. He was now on a first name basis with her.

"Your family?" she asked. Blackbeard had never told her he had a family. When the thought crossed her mind that he might be married, perhaps even have a wife in another port, she paled. She would not be made a fool of twice in one summer, that was certain. She was about to say something when Blackbeard spoke up.

"Well, I ain't got a family now, lass."

This statement offered Mary sufficient consolation and her lips parted slightly from the firm set they had achieved only moments before.

"But, given time, why, in time, I'll have a wife and little ones."

"Oh!" Mary pressed her lips firmly together again. So he was about to be married. It was as she suspected. She was indeed being made a fool of. "And who is your betrothed?" she asked of Blackbeard, backing away from his hold around her waist.

"Why, Mary, don't you know?" Captain Teach asked.

Mary shook her head.

"Why, you, of course," Blackbeard said.

And as the sun set slowly in the horizon, the shadows steadily becoming longer over Plum Point, the pirate took the lady firmly in his arms and kissed her, deeply, longingly and hard.

Prisoners In The Inquisition

Arms crossed behind his back, worry lines furrowing his brow, the captain-general of the *San Rosario* paced the stone floor of the Inquisition building in Cartegena. All day yesterday and now today (it was six o'clock in the afternoon) he had paced in just this manner, back and forth, back and forth, his relentless routine of steps broken only by the intermittent screams of tortured prisoners. The fierce, proud face of the captain-general was lost in thought. By God in heaven, it certainly took these friars long enough. They made everything so complicated—all those routine questions and answers in their interrogations, all those intricate methods of torture—the water cure, iron maiden, the rack and the pendulum. It was his opinion all these complications were a waste of time. If asked, he would have said that torture was really quite simple. Thinking now of his own expertise with a whip, he felt he could have dragged whatever information he needed from a prisoner in half the time it took these befuddled friars.

Just as the captain-general was in the process of berating the clergy, one of those befuddled friars opened the door of the torture chamber, quietly walked out and closed the door gently behind him. The captain-general had just enough time before the door was closed to catch sight of a woman, stark naked, being taken from the rack. But the door was closed all too quickly and the sight lost from his view. His lascivious desires left unsatisfied, the captain-general returned his thoughts to the matter at hand. He waited impatiently, tapping his finger on a small table beside him, while the Franciscan bowed his bald head in prayer and crossed himself. The captain-general would have spoken sooner, but he did not wish to appear irreverent, so he waited for sufficient time to lapse.

"Have they rendered up any information concerning the silver?" he asked firmly.

The friar thought the man was unduly anxious. "No, *señor*. Not one of those men has said anything concerning the silver. Please be assured if they knew anything, we would break their minds." The friar fiddled impatiently with his rosary beads. He wished to get to his daily devotions in the church, and the captain-general, by his repeated questions, was keeping him from them. So far, the captain-general had asked the same questions four times in the last two hours—enough to stretch the patience of any man.

Just as the friar was mulling over in his mind how best to dispose of the captain-general, from the torture chamber came an earsplitting shriek. That scream must have been emitted from the young man dragged in earlier today, for it was an octave lower then the woman's.

Taking no more than a passing interest in the screams, unusual because the captain-general habitually took sadistic pleasure in torture, the captain-general continued his conversation with the friar. "You are aware, of course, how important this shipment of silver is to King Philip."

"*Si, señor*," the friar said, "and at your request we are torturing all foreigners brought here. You must understand though, Captain-General, that the only foreigners arrested in the last forty-eight hours have been some smugglers."

"Smugglers?"

The friar nodded. "These smugglers were captured not far from Porto Bello. They were trading with some Spanish merchants dressed as peasants and carrying jars of what looked like grain, but underneath were silver pesos. The *Guarda La Costa* brought them in."

"Smugglers," said the captain-general, half to himself, half to the friar. He paused to give himself time to collect his thoughts.

The friar wished to ease the captain-general's needless anxiety, and he continued, "But, Captain-General, not one smuggler has rendered up even the remotest reference to a secret treasure ship. I think your anxiety is unfounded."

The captain-general did not like to be told he was in the wrong. He, the commander of a Spanish armada, he, who had never lost a ship at sea, he, the eldest son of a nobleman from Cadiz, who had, thank the Lord, not a taint of foreign blood in him, *he*, was in the habit of telling others their mistakes. But he did not want to make the friar angry, so he did not comment on the remark.

One had to be quite careful with members of the Spanish Inquisition—quite careful, indeed. The Inquisition had the power to arrest, detain, imprison, torture and murder almost anyone, short of the king himself, on flimsy, trumped-up charges.

The captain-general, returning to his earlier thoughts of the silver, commented, "I must take all precautions." Never before in the history of the Spanish Empire had so much treasure been placed on one ship. Never before had one man, he, Don Pedro, had so much trust put in him by the king. It was unnerving to have this much responsibility.

The friar, his patience wearing thin, fiddled with his beads. He sighed. "Perhaps, *señor*, your time would be better spent in tending your ship instead of waiting here. I'm sure the Inquisitor will inform you of any breakthroughs with the prisoners."

"No," said the captain-general in a very determined manner. "I'll wait." He put his arms behind his back in the same posture as the friar had seen earlier.

The friar looked directly at the captain-general and then shrugged as if to say, "Suit yourself." He hurried off to his duties, leaving the captain-general, his brow knit in thought, a stony look in his eyes, pacing back and forth.

Inside the chamber, a truly hideous room filled with innumerable devices for the torture of the body, and—as the friars believed—the soul as well, the friars made ready for their next victim. Besides the torture devices, other small things about the room told of much suffering; specks of dried blood where someone had been wounded, and on the wall, marks made by scratching fingers and holes where iron instruments of torment had been placed.

As the friars hurried about, from a small inner doorway stepped a stout man swarthed in the traditional garb of black reserved for members of his order. Underneath his somber robe he sometimes wore clothes of the French style—shirts with gold buttons, red velvet coats, fringes of white lace at the wrists.

Indeed, the man's corpulence bespoke his own self-indulgence. He had sired innumerable bastard children from his mistresses and from some of the female prisoners who had been taken advantage of during their stay in the Inquisition. He stared wantonly at the naked woman who was being taken out of the room and he made a note to himself later to find out from one of the friars what cell she was in. She would be quite accessible, for he had a master key to all the cells.

Well over three hundred pounds in weight, it required the services of three men to seat him, but once he was seated he became composed and grandiose, nodding with ponderous dignity at the other men. He noted with pleasure that all was ready, the other two chairs occupied by the friars, the notary waiting to take the minutes. From deep within his overstuffed belly came a rumble and then he belched—loudly.

One of the friars looked up. The holiest of holies, the grand master of them all—the Inquisitor, had burped. After months of habitual interrogations, the friars had learned the burp was a signal to the others that the Inquisitor's dinner was digested and they could bring on the next prisoner. There was a good deal of arguing about who would go and get the culprit, and then finally, one friar followed by two guards, left the room.

Face drawn, the next victim opened his eyes. For several days he had been provided with only bread and water and consequently, passed out from utter exhaustion and hunger. Now, looking around, he could see nothing but darkness and a thin sliver of light from the cell window in the door. After a moment, he remembered where he was. He was in the *carcelas secretas*, the secret prison of the Spanish Inquisition in Cartegena. He tried to move his arms and legs but they were attached to the wall. His head was also immovable. Something iron was holding it in place. Realizing he was in chains and his chin fastened to his neck by a device called the *pie de amigo*, an iron fork to keep the head rigidly fixed, he moaned. The agony of this device was becoming more and more unbearable. Unbearable, too, was the cold. Earlier they had stripped him naked.

It was yesterday that he was arrested—or was it yesterday? He suddenly realized that here in this prison, he had no sense of time. It could have been minutes, hours, or days since he had passed out. The sailor noticed that the tiny sliver of light from the cell door was dimming. The beadle must be making his rounds, he thought. As time went by the light grew dimmer, but strangely enough, he began to make out several shapes in the room, perhaps because his eyes were growing more accustomed to the darkness. On one side of the room was a small window. Even if his body was loosened from the chains binding it, he doubted he could ever escape. The slit of a window on the upper wall of the cell was barely large enough for an arm to get through. Gradually, he began to concentrate on small things—a rat scurrying across the floor with a bit of straw in its mouth, a hairy tarantula making its way toward the door. The cell was damp. Having nothing else to do, he counted the drops of water dripping from the ceiling. But even counting drops of water could not dispel his thoughts of torture in the Inquisition.

Once he had met a Negro who had escaped from Spanish-occupied Hispaniola. The Negro had told the smuggler of the *estancias* where after hours of torture, Negroes had been buried to the neck in the ground with their mates and left to die.

The smuggler suddenly heard footsteps approaching his cell. As the bell of the Angelus pealed the *Ave Maria*, voices spoke garbled Spanish. Then there was a turn of keys in the lock, a creak of the door, and in a ray of light, a friar in a long, black robe entered the cell. The friar looked at the smuggler for a moment with a glance of extreme disgust. He had been nibbling on some sort of sweetmeat, but he dropped it on the jail floor as he entered. Immediately, he took out a piece of cloth from his robe and put it to his nose to disguise the smells. The smuggler had been unaware of the odors, but in the light he could see in the far corner of the room the remnants of some human excrement. The friar approached the smuggler and undid the iron utensil around his neck.

Two jailers unfastened the chains that held him to the wall and immediately tied his hands behind his back. He was pulled to an upright stance, but his legs buckled under him. Sitting for so long in one position had made it extremely difficult for him to stand. The two men picked him up again and dragged him through the doorway and down a long flight of stairs until they came to an inner chamber.

Just outside the chamber, the smuggler was aware of footsteps and he turned for a moment to catch sight of a man, clothed in a white frilled shirt and heavy boots, pacing back and forth. His face was set firmly, but the smuggler noticed he had a cruel smile. As the smuggler passed, the man's face suddenly lit up, his malevolent eyes glittering.

The smuggler gritted his teeth as the door to the chamber swung open, but he could not take the shock. Appalled at the severity of the torture instruments and the condition of the human beings inside, he began to struggle frantically. His heart pounded as never before. The crack of a whip against his back silenced his screams. How strange, he thought. He hadn't realized he was screaming until a silence fell in the room. He was mute as he followed a man toward a table where he noticed sitting between two friars, the fattest man he had seen in his life.

The fat man listened to the pacing of feet outside the chamber. "Is the captain-general still outside?" he asked the friar next to him.

The friar nodded solemnly.

The fat man set his teeth firmly as if trying to remain patient, and then continued. "Did you tell him all was being done that was possible?"

The friar nodded again. "Yes, my lord. But he prefers to wait."

The fat man heaved his shoulders. "We should have made this chamber more soundproof, for the convenience of those inside as well as out."

Then the Inquisitor turned his attention to the matter at hand. He sniffed disparagingly at the prisoner, glanced at the culprit's records which had been placed before him, and then, looking up to the heavens, crossed himself as if to gain inspiration from the Lord in such matters as now concerned him.

"I am the Inquisitor," he finally said, obviously in deep satisfaction with himself. He paused in his monologue for his title to have the reverence it deserved and then continued, "God was the first Inquisitor. When Adam sinned, God asked '*Adam ubi es*'—Adam where art thou? Adam presented himself and God began his interrogation. You were in Nombre de Dios. I could inquire what business you had there."

Although his name had not been mentioned, the prisoner took the question to be meant for him because the Inquisitor had now deigned to stare in his direction. "Trading," he said. "I was trading."

"Smuggling," the Inquisitor corrected. "Smuggling is heresy. It is a sin against God's laws. What have you to say in your defense?"

The smuggler could, in fact, think of nothing to say. But knowing something was expected of him, he answered with the words, "There are worse things."

The smuggler did not know the Inquisitor would be shocked—indeed indignant—at this remark. Provoked now by the prisoner, he opened his mouth in mild surprise and said, "That is heretical blasphemy."

The prisoner, now shaking with fright, tried to think of anything to appease the Inquisitor. So when he spoke again it was to say, "But, sir, this smuggling—it was against my will. I was forced to do it. Forced by my own countrymen. Stolen from my mother's arms when just a boy, I was." The majesty of his lie overwhelmed him. Here he was, captured by the Spanish Inquisition, and all because of a freak accident that happened as a child. In a sudden reaction to danger, exhaustion and horror, he burst into tears.

The Inquisitor made a remark in Spanish and then turned his attention again to the prisoner. "Do you wish to confess?" he asked. "God will forgive you if you confess."

God might forgive him, thought the smuggler, but not these men. He had heard about the Inquisition. Once you broke down and told them your true business, they tortured you all the worse. No, he would not confess. Tears now abated, he said. "An't please your honor, I do not wish to bear false witness against myself."

Perturbed by the prisoner's evasions, anger curling his fat lips, the Inquisitor shouted in Spanish and then pointing to the rack, said in English, "Begin the torture."

Immediately, the smuggler was grabbed by the two guards and taken to the rack. Laid flat on his back, the prisoner had ropes tied to his arms and legs.

"Do you wish to confess now?" the Inquisitor asked, smiling deviously.

The prisoner shook his head. Consequently, the ropes began to stiffen around his hands and legs. Straining every muscle and bone in his body, the ropes gradually grew so tight the smuggler could stand no more. Soon he said, "I confess—I'm a free-trader."

The smuggler thought the ropes would ease up then. But, on the contrary, there was another strong wrench in his arms and he felt as if his muscles would separate from their bones. He believed it was the policy of the church to cease torture once the sinner had confessed. The thinking of the church's lawmakers was, however, that the heretic must also pay for his crimes and in this case, they also wished to discover if the heretic had an inkling of an idea about a Spanish treasure ship.

"Answer the Inquisitor, sir, and confess," said a friar who had walked over to question the prisoner from directly across the room. He was a skinny little man with a large emerald-studded cross draped around his neck, which he constantly admired throughout the interrogation. A present from a bishop, the cross had only recently been given to him. The friar passed a glance to the Inquisitor, who nodded. Both wanted to have a confession if one existed—a confession concerning King Philip's silver.

"I humbly beseech thee, tell me what to say," the smuggler said. He was frantic with fear that he would not survive this incident, and if he did, that he would be disfigured for life. "Loosen the cords," he pleaded.

The friar merely glanced at the cross again and answered, "Confess," in the same determined manner.

It was almost as much torture to wonder what these men wanted from him as to be placed on the rack. But the smuggler changed his mind as he heard his bones crack when the cords were tightened.

"My arms!" the smuggler screamed. "My arms!" But there was no one to answer his cry for help.

"Tell me all you know," the friar coaxed.

Sweat poured from the prisoner's brow. Suddenly, he urinated on himself in an unconscious reaction to fear. "Pray, tell me what you want to hear," he begged. "Tell me what to say. Release me and I'll tell all."

The smuggler saw the Inquisitor whispering to two friars seated beside him. The two got up and helped the Inquisitor to his feet. At once, the fat man waddled over to the friar who was questioning the smuggler. The two Franciscans whispered together.

The smuggler happened to glance at the notary. The notary had, in fact, never even looked at the prisoner during the entire interrogation. Now he was preoccupied with some doodling in the top left-hand margin of the page.

The whispers from the Inquisitor and the friars were almost inaudible.

In time, the two men stopped their conversation to peer at the prisoner. Eight rungs were all this culprit's arms could take. They knew if they tightened the rack again, his arms would break. They whispered to each other to determine whether to continue. Suddenly, the two came over to the prisoner to loosen the cords.

"It is the law that torture can not be repeated," the friar said. He moved his emerald cross slightly so it caught the light of the candles.

The smuggler closed his eyes in relief. "Then it is over," he mumbled.

"On the contrary," the Inquisitor said in a condescending manner. "It can be continued. We will continue on the morrow." Trained expertly in logic, the Inquisitor knew how to get around about everything.

The smuggler immediately opened his eyes. "But I confessed all," he said, extremely puzzled. Oh, merciful God, he thought. What did these men want from him?

"On the morrow," the Inquisitor said, deigning to look at the ragged, sweaty man on the rack, now wet with his own urine.

The Inquisitor turned his back on the prisoner and left the room.

The captain-general looked up inquisitively when he saw the Inquisitor in the hallway.

The Inquisitor responded by shaking his head to inform the captain-general no new information had been discovered concerning the silver. But as he passed, the captain-general pulled him over to talk. "I have just heard, *señor*, that a smuggling ship escaped from the *Guarda La Costa.*"

"No one ever escapes from the *Guarda La Costa*," the Inquisitor said flatly. Never in all his years in Cartegena had he heard of a ship getting away from the *Guarda La Costa*. To prove his point, he added, "The prisoner inside was on a smuggling ship—the *Providence*."

There are always exceptions and the captain-general had one. "On the contrary," he said. "This ship did."

"What was the name of the ship?" the Inquisitor asked.

"The *Bachelor's Delight*," the captain-general replied.

The Inquisitor looked surprised, but he shrugged it off. "Captain-General, it is highly improbable that anyone knows of the silver. As you see I have tortured all these men at your own request and not one smuggler has rendered up even the remotest reference to a secret treasure ship. I think your anxiety is unfounded."

"Unfounded?"

"*Si*," the Inquisitor said. "Can't you understand Spanish? Unfounded. And I see no need to make any alterations in your plans. Proceed with the present plans for shipment of the silver."

"Very well," the captain-general said.

The captain-general watched as the Inquisitor walked away. When the figure disappeared, he began pacing once again.

In an hour's time, when another friar opened the door of the torture chamber from the inside, he regarded the captain-general with some disturbance. He noticed his stern brow wrinkled in thought. As he closed the door, the friar made a note to himself to talk to the Inquisitor later about the captain-general's lack of composure. Although the captain-general was King Philip's most experienced sailor, if he was this worried about such a small event as the escape of a smuggler, then perhaps he shouldn't be entrusted with such a large responsibility as the shipment of the silver. Indeed, the captain-general was overreacting to such a minor incident, wasn't he?

An Account Of The Plate

Blackbeard sat down to a lunch of pigeon pie washed down with rum. The ship's cook had been preparing the pastry all morning, and Blackbeard, sitting in the *Adventure*'s cabin staring at the delicacy, felt his mouth water in anticipation. Scarcely had he raised the first steaming biteful to his mouth when there was a knock on the door. Regretfully, he lowered the spoon to the table, and his mouth screwed up in apparent disgust. Blast whoever it was who kept him from his lunch.

The man he had blasted was none other than Charles Eden, who, when he entered the cabin, disturbed not only Blackbeard, but his parrot as well. The parrot, perched in a bronzed cage in one corner, let forth quite a loud curse, then commenced to scale the wires of the cage with a prodigious agility.

Presumably, the governor was here on a matter of no small importance, for all courtesies had been dispensed with.

Without his usual charming greeting, the governor sat down in the chair opposite Blackbeard and spoke, "He's here."

Blackbeard surmised correctly that the governor had inside knowledge of Taylor's safe arrival in Bath Town's harbor for when he answered the governor with the word, "Taylor," Eden nodded.

In all truth, Charles Eden had word from a passing merchantman owned by the syndicate that the *Bachelor's Delight* had been sighted ten leagues from Ocracoke and was scheduled to dock any time. In fact, the captain of the merchantman had stopped to talk with the captain of the *Bachelor's Delight*. The captain of the merchantman, obeying his orders, reported back to Eden that Taylor was safe and sound and also handed the governor a sealed packet given to him by Taylor. This packet, Eden presently had in his waistcoat pocket.

It was plain to see Blackbeard was excited by the news of Taylor's arrival, for he pushed the pigeon pie aside with no apparent regret and it was left all but forgotten on a corner of the table, steaming and bubbling to itself.

"You've seen him with your own eyes, have you?" Blackbeard asked, a gleam in his eyes, his fingers trembling with anticipation.

"No, but one of the men in the syndicate has," Eden explained. From his pocket he withdrew a pipe, lit it, and then offered some tobacco to Blackbeard, but the pirate, shaking his head, declined. Blackbeard's state of mind was all too anxious to think of enjoying a smoke. His face was animated now with a marked excitement that came from an overwhelming desire to know what Eden had discovered.

On the other hand, Eden had had enough time previously to dwell on Taylor's arrival and the obvious consequences. He exhaled a puff of smoke slowly and evenly so that the two, sitting opposite, presented a picture of decided contrasts—the cool, calculating governor and the hot-headed, blustering pirate. But even though they were so unalike, Blackbeard and Eden had established a kind of intimacy that can develop only through shared danger.

"The wind blew Taylor in yesterday afternoon," the governor said.

"A tall, lanky man?" Blackbeard asked.

Eden nodded, exhaling another puff.

"With a twitch in his left eye?" Blackbeard continued, just to be certain the governor was not mistaken.

"Yes," Eden agreed.

Blackbeard, who had been anxiously leaning forward in his chair to face the governor, sat back, still a bit stunned by the news. "Ah, that's Taylor." Blackbeard paused to collect his thoughts.

Eden simply sat and waited.

After a moment's consideration, Blackbeard's eyes once again lit up, and he bounded to his feet, pushing back his chair. Then he immediately put his pistol in his sling and grabbed his hat. "Well, where is he?"

Eden opened his mouth to answer the pirate, but Blackbeard continued talking at such an incredible rate the governor could hardly get a word in edgewise.

"I'll just go to that Taylor swab," he mumbled to himself as he straightened his hat. "Yes, I'll go right now, and he'll tell me what I need to know. Where is he?" he repeated.

Clearly the governor was irritated at Blackbeard's excitedness. He raised his hand to calm the pirate. "If you'd stop being so confoundedly hot-headed so I might get a word in, I'll tell you."

The pirate took off his hat again, placed it on the table, and after sitting down and rapping his knuckles on the table, stared impatiently at Eden.

What ensued was a discussion concerning the packet Eden had in his waistcoat pocket. Eden withdrew it—a sealed envelope, spotted with droplets of sea spray, but still in good condition. Blackbeard gazed curiously at it and then he met Eden's eyes once again.

"If you're agreeable, I'll open this," Eden said. "There's a map inside it. Taylor's given us the passage."

Blackbeard nodded. Quickly, he closed all portholes so the men outside could not hear their conversation. Then he lit a candle in a lantern. He watched as Eden unsealed the wax binding the envelope in several places. Eden broke the seals with great care and then withdrew a map of the Caribbean. The course had been drawn between Crooked Island, Mayaguana, Caicos, Turks Island, Mouchoir and—last of all—the Ambrosian, north of the Ambrosian Banks. These were five passages. Crooked Island Passage marked in red had been underlined as the one to be steered. Eden felt bound to acknowledge his ignorance.

"For the life of me, I can't make head nor tail of it," confided Eden in utter confusion as he gazed at the map. Then he leveled his eyes at Blackbeard.

Obviously in deep thought, Blackbeard stared at the map. "Well, it's clear enough to me," he said. He reached for a candle that had been placed on a desk behind him, lit the wick and then held it over the map. A drop of wax fell on the parchment. "See here," he said, his voice rumbling deeply as he traced the lines for Eden's sake. "These lines here, they're the five passages the Spanish armada took in years past. Must be one hundred and fifty years agone since they used these passages. Off Crooked Island, see," Blackbeard said, pointing to some lettering.

Eden squinted in the candlelight and nodded.

"Crooked Island," Blackbeard continued, in a steadily deepening voice. "That's the passage they'll take this year. Our ship will have to be stationed here at this small island where they will water. There we'll take the *San Rosario*." He reflected for a moment. "God help the poor souls that went those passages in years past—coral long ago—for these is the roughest passages ever to steer—reefs that'll break a ship's hull in two." He paused for a moment in deep contemplation, then returned the map to the packet. Then meeting Eden's face head on, Blackbeard asked, "Now what's the time she'll be weighing anchor? We'll need to be stationed at that island thereabouts."

Eden paused for a moment to exhale tobacco smoke into the air. When he was ready to answer, he leaned forward, tipped out the tobacco ashes from his pipe, and said, "Taylor will tell you all that soon enough. First he wants his pieces of eight."

During the course of this conversation, the parrot had finally tired itself out on the bars of the cage, but the words "pieces of eight" brought it rigidly to attention. Quite familiar with these words, it began to repeat them in harsh shrieks so loudly, that both Eden and Blackbeard paused to glance at the bird.

"Now that bird is maybe one hundred and eighty years old, Governor—they lives forever mostly, and if anybody's seen more devilry, it must be Beelzebub himself. She sailed with Tew, the wickedest of them all, the great Tew. She's been at Madagascar and at Providence and Porto Bello. She was at the fishing up of the Spanish treasure wrecks off Florida's coral shoals. It's there she learned pieces of eight and no wonder; hundreds of thousands of 'em, Governor. She was at Hornigold's surrender, she was, and to look at her you'd think she was in her prime. But you heard the cannons roar and the guns thunder—ain't you Cap'n?" Teach said, addressing the bird.

"Stand by to fire," the parrot screamed. And then it began to swear.

Blackbeard, in a customary gesture used to quiet the bird, reached for a cracker that was contained in a little box on his table and gave it to the "Cap'n." The bird took the cracker in its right claw and then raising the claw to its beak, began to crunch on the cracker, sending most of the biscuit into the air instead of down its gullet.

"Here's this poor blameless bird o' mine swearing blue streaks and she's none the wiser, make no mistake," Blackbeard continued. "She would swear the same before the pulpit, in a manner of speaking. But she's a poor innocent soul at heart. Like your old captain you are, ain't you?"

"Like your old captain," the bird repeated. It finished the cracker and watched Blackbeard with unblinking coolness.

"We're three of a kind, ain't we Cap'n?" Teach said, still seemingly talking to the parrot. "You and me and the Governor, here. We all look to be what we're not." At that point, Blackbeard threw the governor a quick, but all too obvious glance.

The governor knowingly returned the glance. "Taylor's waiting," he said.

Blackbeard shook his head sadly, determined to have his say. "It were New Providence that put me here," he said. "Hornigold and New Providence."

If Eden had any compassion for the pirate, he certainly did not show it. But then, insensitivity was a part of Eden's strength. He simply did not care that much for other human beings, and this let him take actions necessary to reach his goals that others would have balked at. Foremost in Eden's mind was the silver. "I'm having Taylor watched," Eden said.

Blackbeard was obviously surprised by this statement for he raised his eyebrows. "Watched?"

"Yes. By one of the merchants in the syndicate." Eden passed a description of the man to Blackbeard.

Blackbeard nodded at the description, but he wanted to know why Taylor was being watched.

In the candlelight, shadows flickered and died across Eden's face. He neared Blackbeard, closer than before. What he had to say to Blackbeard had an evil ring of truth to it. As he whispered his words in the semi-darkness, Blackbeard shivered. "You and I and Taylor are the only ones that know of this treasure ship," Eden said, lighting his pipe again with the wick of the candle. "And there's one thing I'm afraid of."

"What would that be?" Blackbeard was almost afraid to ask.

"Blabbing," Eden answered, putting down the candle on the table once again. "Someone who can not hold his tongue." He exhaled a puff of smoke into the air, and Blackbeard watched it rise.

Blackbeard cleared his throat. "Well, now," he said, "you know I'm as silent as the tomb."

"We both are." Eden watched Blackbeard keenly as the pirate's hand went for the glass of rum poured earlier for lunch. The pirate lifted the glass to his mouth, then downed half of it in one gulp.

"Listen," Eden said, leaning even more closely to Blackbeard until the pirate could almost feel the governor's hot breath on his neck. "You and I have money to gain by silence. But Taylor can only gain by telling. Taylor's a smuggler. Smugglers are bold, desperate blades. And I believe Taylor's bound and determined to get more money. I believe he'll tell."

Blackbeard felt a chill run though his massive frame. "And if he does?"

Eden slid a finger across his neck.

Blackbeard shivered. The governor's uncaring nature had put a strain on their relationship from the start. Behavior that might seem heartless seemed perfectly natural to Charles Eden.

The pirate backed away. What was it that made the governor so cold, so uncaring? The governor had within him absolutely no conscience. With all inner uncertainties resolved he had, more than any other man, complete free will—free will to act exactly as he wanted, free will, if he pleased, to damn himself to hell. Never in Blackbeard's life had he met a man with so much ruthless strength, so much power. It was frightening.

Blackbeard eyed the governor, and then reaching for a handkerchief from his waistcoat pocket, he pulled the piece of cloth over the cage, while talking to the parrot. "The governor looks a gentleman, he do. They say he's been in Parliament. And rides in a carriage, he does. But underneath his heart's blacker than the devil's own, Cap'n."

The parrot cursed and then replied. "Pieces of eight, pieces of eight."

The governor straightened his wig and his waistcoat and coughed uncomfortably. "Listen, it's been one year since I first heard tell of the *San Rosario*. In that one year I've been waiting and scheming, scheming and waiting, for the treasure in her hold. And by God, I'd care little for someone who talked."

"But even to the point o' murder, Governor?"

The governor nodded his head calmly.

"You'd do anything for the *San Rosario*," Blackbeard said, shaking his head in a puzzled manner at the governor, who seemed to be a driven man. "Aye, you're a true criminal, Governor. Only a true criminal would do anything for that ship."

"Yes, anything," Eden said firmly. "Even give up the woman I love."

Apart from his talk of the silver, this last sentence was said with more unbridled emotion and more remorse than any other statement Blackbeard had ever heard the governor make. Blackbeard was understandably puzzled by it, because he had no idea that the governor had ever cared for Mary. The pirate and the lady had never discussed their past loves, instead preferring to devote all their attentions to each other, so that now Blackbeard could only dismiss Eden's statement as something said lightly in passing.

Blackbeard downed the last of his drink and then in a gruff, rumbling voice whispered, "Well I'll help you get your ship, Governor. I told you that before. I'll help you sail her up to Execution Dock, if that's what it takes, by thunder, I will at that."

And with those last words, an uncanny silence fell on the room.

Sometime thereafter the two parted, Eden making his way to the plantation home and Blackbeard striking out to the wharves to meet Taylor. Blackbeard found the smuggler not far from the *Bachelor's Delight*. He was enjoying a smoke beside a slaver recently bound from Africa. The slaver smelled of vinegar from a recent washing and fumigation, but unfortunately, the overpowering odors of urine and perspiration were already beginning to permeate the air.

Before the pirate approached Taylor, he stood watching the smuggler light his pipe again and smoke it. It was not to stall for time that Blackbeard did this, but merely to see if he could spot the man whose job it was to watch Taylor. Presently, he caught sight of him no less than ten yards away. He was a tall, broad-shouldered fellow with a black cap on his head and he leaned ever so slightly against a post. From Eden's previous description given in Blackbeard's cabin, the fellow was not hard to miss.

As Blackbeard approached Taylor, he stopped to look at the slaver. He had always been rather amazed at the cargo. The natives were separated—the males on one side of the ship, the females on the other—but both sexes chained together at the legs to prevent any attempted escape. This particular captain of the ship was almost ready for the citizens of Bath to board for inspection, for he was letting down the gang plank.

As was presently the case, there was always a mad rush to gain entranceway to the ship, for slaves were still fairly rare and hard to come by in the colonies. If the natives were frightened by this mad rush to examine them, some would usually try to escape by jumping overboard, so that the captain always kept an eye out for just such an episode.

When one of the slaves would catch a spectator's eye, a process of inspection would begin which, Blackbeard thought, was unequaled to any cattle market in England for its minuteness. The potential buyer, having been assured that there was no defect in the faculties of hearing or speech and that the slave was free from any debilitating disease, would next proceed to examine the native fully, not excepting the breasts of the young girls, many of whom were handled most indecently. But more interesting to watch were the small English boys who grinned as if somewhat pleased by the degrading and indecent examination.

Blackbeard noticed there was a curious smirk on Taylor's face as if he guessed what Blackbeard was up to. Almost at once, the smuggler revealed his state of mind. "She's the *capitana* of the plate fleet, ain't she matey," Taylor said, his eyes firing with an inner emotion. "You can't deny it. I've seen the silver with these very eyes, I have," he declared, pointing to his pupils which were dilated with excitement. "Ah, yes, King Philip's sailing his ships, once again, eh? And it's the plate fleet you're after, ain't it, mate?"

Taylor was right. Blackbeard would have been foolish to deny what Taylor had seen. So he made no attempt to hide this knowledge from the man. His eyes twinkling, a smile playing about his lips, Blackbeard nodded. "Aye, she's the *capitana* of the plate fleet at that," he said. "Pesos, bars, ingots, all King Philip's silver. More money than you can ever imagine, just a'waiting for my men to lay their hands on it. Blast me, t'will make me a gentleman o' leisure, a gentleman o' leisure, to be sure."

Taylor eyed Blackbeard curiously, because for the life of him, although he had been mulling over the ship in his every spare waking moment, and sometimes even in his dreaming ones, he could not figure out how Blackbeard could capture an entire plate fleet. "There's many that's tried for the plate fleet and failed," Taylor said, who did indeed look baffled, for wrinkles appeared on his forehead when he frowned. "None's had success but one, and he was a Dutchman. And that was long before the fleet was guarded. Now it's near impossible to take the Spanish plate, matey, and you as well as I knows that. So how are you proposing to take an entire fleet is what I'd like to know?"

Blackbeard gave Taylor an all too forbidding look. "You'd like to know, would you, matey?"

Taylor nodded enthusiastically.

"Well, by thunder, I ain't a'telling you, you may lay to that." Blackbeard glanced at Taylor's perplexed look. To gain a moment of respite, he turned to glance at the spy who had now walked away from the post, but was still watching them with a fixed and unmoving eye.

No doubt, thought Blackbeard, Taylor deserved a warning of his intended fate should he betray the plan for the capture of the silver. In a gruff, terrifying voice he faced the smuggler and looked him straight in the eye. "Now then, me hearty," he said, "there's lubbers that would like to get wind of the plan; lubbers as couldn't keep what they got but would want to nail what is another's. So you'll be telling no one, you understand?"

"Aye," Taylor said, eyeing Blackbeard uncertainly.

"And you've told no one, have you?" Blackbeard asked. The unsure way Taylor had answered his question made him doubt the man.

"No. I swear it." Small beads of perspiration formed on Taylor's forehead.

"You're sweating, you mealy-mouthed rascal," Blackbeard said angrily. "Sweating overmuch it seems to me."

"I swear to you," Taylor said, trembling. "Wild horses couldn't draw it from me."

Blackbeard gave the smuggler a sidelong glance. Then using a scare tactic he had learned once under Hornigold's command, he retrieved a bottle of rum and a pouch of gunpowder from his waistcoat pocket. Almost at once, he mixed the gunpowder into a dram of rum he was holding. A match was subsequently lit to the mixture and when the concoction was on fire, Blackbeard proceeded to guzzle the entire dram. Taylor gasped in response. Blackbeard, satisfied now that he had Taylor's undivided attention, continued the conversation.

"Now," Blackbeard said, "if someone ax's you what'd you'd be doing with Blackbeard the pirate you say you'd just be with him for pleasure. With him for pleasure—them's the words, you understand?"

Taylor nodded fearfully.

"And if they ax's you more you say you like a drink now and then, says you, and you say you like a fine lady sometimes, that's what you'll say. And then you'll give him a nip like I do now, see?" He pinched Taylor.

"Aye." Taylor winced with pain and fear.

"There's no one that turns traitor on Blackbeard the pirate," Blackbeard said, suddenly grabbing Taylor by the collar. "Or he'll do what must be done, you gets my drift?"

"Aye, aye, sir." Poor Taylor was shaking from head to toe.

Blackbeard released his grip on the man so that the smuggler stumbled backwards. "I have a way with me, I have," he growled. "When a man slips his cable—one as knows me—it won't be the same with Blackbeard. 'Lamb' ain't the word for me."

It was no modest fear that Taylor felt now as he glanced away from Blackbeard, but an all-consuming, deadening panic and horror that made him sick to his stomach. For the smuggler was about to betray Blackbeard, was, in fact, already betraying him as of this moment. But even looking away from the pirate did not help matters for his gaze came to alight on the slaver.

At the moment the captain was disposing of the more sickly slaves by having them thrown overboard. This little ritual was called the work of death and was being performed remarkably fast. The captain held the opinion of most educated men of his time who assumed the natives were heathen, if not "set a'dunking in the holy waters of the baptism." Anyway, when it came down to the hard, cold facts—money—he certainly could not pay for their upkeep. However, he was always quick to disappear below deck before the ritual began. The natives, who suddenly realized their fate, were letting out pitiful moans and whimpers. Taylor smelled death all around him. It was, to say the least, unnerving.

Blackbeard watched Taylor, trying to detect if he had frightened the man sufficiently. Satisfied that he had, he reached into his pocket.

Indeed, Taylor was trembling from head to toe. All qualms now passed, the pirate withdrew a small bag from his waistcoat pocket.

Taylor's attention immediately returned to the pirate as the money bag was withdrawn. When it was opened to reveal pieces of eight, Taylor's hand greedily went for the bag.

"By gum," Blackbeard said, watching Taylor's reaction with interest. "You're a plucky one when it comes to money." He snatched the bag away from the smuggler's grasp. "But not so fast," he continued.

Despondently, Taylor took his hand away. "Never trust a pirate to keep his word."

"You'll get your money, mate," Blackbeard said. "But in time."

Taylor's face seemed to brighten a bit at this last statement and he listened intently as Blackbeard had his say.

"Now," Blackbeard said, "first things first. First you tell me whence she sets sail, now matey."

"October 22," Taylor said.

"Hm," Blackbeard said, putting his finger to his head and scratching it. He paused. Obviously, he was deep in thought. Then thinking out loud, he said, "Hurricane weather. Seems the Spanish is more afraid o' pirates than a northeaster, to be sure. Taking their chances with this shipment o' plate."

Taylor glanced anxiously at Blackbeard, his face now imploring the pirate. Clearly, he wanted his money. The pirate wasted no more time in responding to the smuggler. He handed the bag to Taylor.

Taylor quickly grasped the bag of money and held it closely.

Blackbeard studied the tall, lanky man. "You're plucky enough when it comes to cob." But then he glared at the man. "Taylor," he added.

"Aye," Taylor said, his eyes now gleaming as he ran his hands through the gold.

"I'm warning you, if you lied to me, things will go bad for you."

"I have not lied," Taylor said, but he hung his head so that Blackbeard could not see his left eyelid twitching.

"Very bad," Blackbeard repeated, and as he looked away from Taylor, he chanced to see the man with the black cap not more than ten feet from them.

Taylor did not happen to catch sight of the man with the cap until he had taken his leave of Blackbeard and was almost at his next destination,

The Lion And The Unicorn, where he had another very important appointment. The man, he noticed, was walking at an even pace not far behind him, and Taylor surmised he had been doing so for quite some time. He loosened his collar when he did spot the man, because he felt it was choking him.

In actuality, it was not the collar that was choking Taylor but his own guilt and fear. Fear—that was something Taylor had lived with day in and day out, year after year as a smuggler. But he wouldn't have to live with it anymore, he told himself, once the next part of his escapade was over. Soon, he would be set up for life, and the fears, the terror of being caught, would be over. Ah yes, his pot of silver was close at hand.

But Taylor was not quite in the clear as yet. He realized that when he rounded a building and found the man with the cap still following him. The man was so close, Taylor could see the features of his face. It was a face that made him shudder because it had a large purple scar running all the way from its jawbone to its forehead.

Even when Taylor shouldered his way into the tavern and took a seat beside a sailor with rusty hair and a tan complexion, the man with the scar was never far from Taylor. Unlike the smuggler, he did go to the bar and order a drink. But his eye, even from a distance, didn't leave Taylor.

"You look a fright," the sailor said, addressing Taylor. The sailor simply sat and lit a long, clay pipe.

"Well, they're out for me, they are," Taylor said, leaning closer to the sailor. He pointed to the man with the scar.

The sailor looked, but said nothing.

"See, he's got his weather eye on me, he does," Taylor said. "In a moment I'll put out another reef, matey. Yes, I'll buck him. I'm not afraid. Almost gave him the slip before."

"So, you have the map," the sailor said, hardly concerned with Taylor's position.

"Aye, I does at that." Taylor took a packet from his pocket similar to the one he had previously given Eden.

"And you gave Blackbeard the wrong one," the sailor said.

"Aye." Taylor glanced once more over his shoulder at the man with the scar. There was a bulge in the man's waistcoat that clearly revealed a weapon underneath.

Taylor felt himself sweating again. "'Listen," he said to the sailor. "If there was ever a seaman that needed rum, it was me." He held out his hand. "Look how my fingers shakes and I can't stop 'em, not I. Not one drink I've had this blessed day. Just you get me one drink and I'll show you this map."

The man threw Taylor a disgusted glance. Clearly, he felt put out. But nevertheless, he rose from his chair. "I'll get you one drink, and no more."

Taylor nodded anxiously. His clothes were wet with perspiration.

The man made his way to the bar to get a drink, turning his back on Taylor as he did. " A dram o' rum," the sailor shouted to the barman. He turned around to look at Taylor. He thought the man was overly nervous. He turned his back on Taylor once again and took a drink from the barman. Then he made his way to the table. It was so crowded in the room, he lost sight of Taylor for a moment. When he sighted the man again, he was not more than five feet from him. Blood was gushing from a wound on his neck. The sailor rushed to the table and pulled Taylor to an upright position.

Taylor's hand caught his attention almost immediately, because it was twisted in a contorted gesture around a crumpled packet. But inspecting the packet closer, the sailor found it was empty. Whatever had been inside was now gone.

And Taylor? He had fallen lifeless in a moment, the victim of a premeditated, cold-blooded murder. He lay quite dead in the tavern, his throat slit by his own knife.

A Duel Fought Over a Lady

After Charles Eden's initial meeting with Miss Anne Hassell he began to meet the woman for social events about the town of Bath. The first encounter, so Anne's family thought, was apparently accidental, but later by a sort of mutual understanding these meetings occurred with increased regularity.

Anne Hassell's life began to take shape around these meetings with Eden. She spent all her morning hours preparing for them, and all her evening hours discussing them. Her friends complained that she spoke incessantly of the governor, and her father complained of his daughter's insatiable demand for fashionable garments.

The unattractive woman apparently never thought it odd that Charles Eden would select her from a throng of considerably more desirable ladies from Bath Town society. She was completely captivated by his attentions. Indeed, she thought Eden most serious. However, Eden was later to describe his conversations with her as light and trivial.

One of these conversations occurred on a fall afternoon when they met at Anne's home for tea. The couple was walking together through a maze of hedges in the garden. The maze had been contrived by Anne's father as an amusement for their guests. Exploring it had become a favorite pastime for Anne, and she was thoroughly familiar with its tricky pathways. As they strolled, Eden made the flattering remark, "You're very intelligent, Anne." He knew full well that this was exactly what Anne wanted to hear.

Clearly, Anne wanted to believe Eden, but her face suddenly screwed up in a wry expression. "I don't see how I could be," she replied. "Everyone says I'm a silly, dull-witted girl. Mother and father both say so." The poor girl's lips trembled, and her eyes became moist with tears.

Making a show of tenderness, Eden took the woman into his arms. "There, there," he said, "they just don't know the real Anne as I do."

Anne choked back some sobs and then, breaking away from Eden, searched for the handkerchief she carried. "You think so?"

"I know so. You have a wonderful intelligence, a wonderful mind. I knew that when I first met you. I've often thought what interesting opinions you have."

Thus reassured, Anne stood beside a row of shrubbery, dried her tears and smiled. "Well, I do have a fair amount of opinions," she answered, sniffing softly. "But people, you see, don't listen to me...no one, that is, but you." She looked longingly into Eden's eyes.

Charles Eden made a pretense at a smile and then laid his hand lightly on Anne's arm. "Your opinions are what make you so attractive."

"Well, I do have a lot of opinions. I mean, I think beggars can't be choosers. Do you think so?"

"Oh yes," Eden said as they continued walking down a pathway. "Oh yes, I think so."

"I think beggars can't be choosers," Anne airily repeated.

"What else do you think? I'm interested in knowing everything you think."

Anne's face was suffused with color, her pupils dilated. "Well, my opinion is life is not a bowl of cherries."

"I agree." Eden secretly laughed at the woman. "What do you think about men?"

"Men?" Anne asked, completely taken by surprise.

"Yes, men," Eden replied, gently leading the woman into a conversation concerning a certain councilman. "For instance, Edward Moseley."

Anne took this remark exactly as Eden expected her to take it, as a note of jealousy on the governor's part. But, in actuality, Eden was interested in finding out what type of skullduggery his adversary was up to. He knew that if anyone knew, it was Anne. For wasn't she Moseley's intended?

"Oh, you're jealous." Anne tapped his cheek lightly with her fan as they continued through the maze.

"Perhaps," Eden said, committing himself to nothing.

Anne was thoroughly delighted, for never in her life had two men vied for her love.

"I don't see why I shouldn't be jealous. After all, you're a very attractive woman, Anne." He grabbed her playfully around the waist.

Anne giggled. "You silly goose," she said, pushing him away. "You needn't be envious. He's away now."

"Away?" Eden had no idea Moseley was not in Bath.

"Yes, silly." Anne coyly offered her hand to the governor as she led him on. "In Virginia."

Eden took her hand and listened intently as the woman continued chattering aimlessly.

Charles Eden was about to question Anne further regarding Moseley's trip when the two were suddenly interrupted by Mrs. Hassell coming down the pathway to meet the two. "Tea time," she said. "Come along."

Charles Eden could say nothing else for the time being. He took Anne's arm in his, "Shall we?"

Anne nodded, although she thought that she detected a note of annoyance in Eden's voice.

The two were accompanied by Mrs. Hassell to the rear lawn of the home where tea was being served in delicate china cups by a servant clothed in white.

While Mrs. Hassell poured tea and constantly chatted, Mr. Hassell commented on a workman nearby who was patiently installing a gazebo. Not far from the gazebo, a gardener was planting some ivy to trail up the structure. This was quite a quaint piece of architecture, fashionable at the time, and everyone who could afford a gazebo installed one.

"When will it be completed?" Eden asked.

"In about a week hence," Mrs. Hassell said, "if the workman continues at his present speed. It will be quite lovely, don't you think?"

"Most impressive," Eden smiled charmingly at Anne, who was sitting beside him. His fingers, long and white, slipped off some silken gloves and laid them on the tea table.

"Of course," Mrs. Hassell continued, staring at the gazebo, "we will have to wait for the ivy to grow before it has the proper appearance."

At the moment, Anne stood to take a sweetmeat from a tray, and Charles Eden's eyes alighted on her with apparent delight. Mr. and Mrs. Hassell both noted Eden's reaction and their eyes met in acknowledgment.

"Anne," Eden said, "you always take me quite by surprise."

"Is that to my advantage?" Anne asked, glancing at Eden as she took her place once again at the tea table.

"Wholly to your advantage," Eden concluded in his usual charming manner as he waved an ungloved hand in the air.

His gallant attentions had the effect of shocking the Hassell family, for Anne seldom received compliments of any sort.

Anne colored at this remark that was said so openly before her parents, and began to fan herself quickly. Mr. Hassell cleared his throat. Mrs. Hassell picked up the tea tray and offered some small cakes.

"Will you try one of these, Governor?" Mrs. Hassell asked.

"With gratitude, madam," Eden said, accepting a cake.

For a moment the conversation stopped of its own accord.

"I trust you are telling no more tales of your travels abroad," Mrs. Hassell said, addressing Eden.

"I am telling no more tales, madam," Eden replied. "But if I may confess, I find the countries abroad much more civilized than our own."

"Mrs. Hassell was just remarking on that." Mr. Hassell, who had drained his cup, handed it to Mrs. Hassell to refill. "There is more savagery on this continent than anyone in Europe can possibly imagine."

"Mr. Hassell is referring to the heathen, of course," Mrs. Hassell said, stretching out her hand to refill Mr. Hassell's cup.

"Ah, yes," Eden remarked.

"I have hopes," Mrs. Hassell said, "that with the coming of civilization to the American lands, these Indians will soon vanish."

"Let us hope so, madam," Eden replied.

"These savages are quite beyond me," Mrs. Hassell continued. "Worshipping pagan gods, living in those filthy, makeshift huts, and performing the most wicked and atrocious acts. Our poor Mr. Lawson."

"Poor Mr. Lawson" was one of Bath's most honored citizens who had been killed before Eden had arrived in the colony. He was tortured to death when the Tuscarora drove lighted splinters into his legs.

Mrs. Hassell was obviously upset by the memory of Mr. Lawson for she took out a handkerchief and sniffed into it. "You can't imagine, Governor, what the recent war was like. You weren't in the colony."

"Ah," Eden said. "I have been previously informed from Chief Justice Gale that it was indeed atrocious. Mr. Gale informed me that pregnant women had their unborn children ripped out and hung upon trees. Women were laid on house floors and great stakes driven up their bodies."

Mrs. Hassell gasped in her usual, ladylike manner. "Well, one needn't be so graphic."

"There, there, dear," Mr. Hassell said.

As readily as her mother gasped, however, Anne smiled with abandon. She found the governor's tales most stimulating. Stuck in a house all day, little exposed to life and its dangers, she never came in contact with foreign lands or peoples, and Eden's stories never failed to interest her. She had already remarked to her family that she found Eden quite charming in a "rough sort of way." Indeed, with his charm and wit and his ability to tell stories, he was the type of man who by his mere presence had the power of captivating most people.

The governor knew this, of course. And that is why he continued to tell his tales. The tales and the flattery were aimed at one objective—impressing Anne.

But he made amends to Mrs. Hassell by apologizing for his strong language.

Mr. Hassell was about to change the topic of conversation when Edward Moseley did it for him. He appeared quite suddenly, clothed in a waistcoat of a remarkably light color. At the moment, he was heading down the garden path towards the little gathering of tea takers.

Presumably, thought Eden, the man must have only just returned from his trip to Virginia.

When Moseley arrived, he bowed graciously and smiled at the family. When his eyes came to alight on Charles Eden, however, he scowled.

Mrs. Hassell, totally unprepared for this unexpected visitor, nevertheless tried to make the councilman feel at ease. She motioned for him to sit down.

"How nice to see you again, Mr. Moseley," she said. "A totally unexpected pleasure." She glanced anxiously at her husband for she did not feel entirely comfortable having two suitors taking tea with Anne at once.

Anne, however, did not mind in the least. Indeed, her color was high, her lips bright. Eyelashes batting, giggling profusely between sips of tea, she was perfectly pleased.

Moseley bowed most charmingly to Mr. and Mrs. Hassell and kissed Anne's hand graciously, but for Governor Eden he reserved a cold shoulder and the patronizing words, "I see you have another guest."

"Ah, yes," Mrs. Hassell said, seeing things weren't going as she had planned for her daughter. "Governor Eden arrived only shortly before you. Won't you have a cup of tea?" she asked, trying to keep the conversation light.

"Most willingly," Moseley said, taking a teacup and a seat with the others and smiling politely at Anne. He had managed to overlook her obvious disadvantages in favor of her large dowry which would exceedingly enhance his present estate. This estate he was extremely proud of, and he never failed upon making someone's acquaintance to list all his property.

Eden studied his enemy intently as he sipped his tea. With eyes that looked away, Moseley's secrets could not be fathomed. He also was a sagacious and enterprising politician who had by sheer pluck and endurance attained a wealth of political power in the colony. He would employ any means to attain his end. He was a formidable enemy.

Now that Eden's party had gained power, Moseley's party was virtually as harmless as a sleeping dog. But Eden knew Moseley was only waiting for the right moment to awaken and take action, and the governor was not about to let sleeping dogs lie. He knew Moseley's one weakness. He knew him to be a boastful man. And that was where Anne came in. Looking at Moseley, he rightfully guessed the man was after her for her money.

Anne's girlish laughter rang through the air. In the garden, birds sang, bees hummed. A leaf lightly dropped to the ground. From time to time, Anne nodded to her two suitors. She was indeed in high spirits. Charles Eden winked at her as her mother passed the tray.

All the while these little glances were being exchanged between Eden and Anne, Moseley became more and more enraged. What right had Charles Eden to try to win his intended? Moseley suddenly directed his conversation to Eden. "I see that you have been telling the ladies tales of piracy on the high seas. Your tales are quite remarkable, Governor."

"Quite," Mrs. Hassell said, remembering how angry she had become at Eden's earlier coarse remarks.

"Now dear," Mr. Hassell began, looking at his wife.

Governor Eden made no attempt to respond. Instead, he simply winked at Anne. He displayed an air of confident superiority.

Anne giggled and moistened her lips.

Moseley felt sorely aggrieved by this show of affection on Anne's part. The two were trying his patience beyond all ordinary limits. With considerable anger on his pink face, he declared, "Yes, Mrs. Hassell tells me you've had quite a few encounters with pirates."

Moseley's words hit home this time and Eden put down his teacup and fired Moseley a questioning look. No doubt Moseley knew something concerning his dealings with Blackbeard. He stared the councilman straight in the eyes. "I merely spoke of an engagement with one, Henry Avery," Eden replied. He was referring to his previous conversation with the Hassells, although he knew Moseley's insinuation was concerning Blackbeard.

The Hassells—mother, daughter and father—naively looked on as the two eyed each other.

"Governor Eden's tales are quite quaint," Anne broke in, unable to think of anything else to say.

"I'd say they were uncommonly rude," Moseley said, in a deriding tone.

Anne broke in. "Oh, not at all."

"The lady's only being polite," Moseley said, his mustache bristling.

Trying to quell what she saw was an ensuing argument, Mrs. Hassell airily waved a hand at the sky and remarked, "Isn't it lovely weather we're having."

Neither Eden nor Moseley answered her.

Instead, Eden very steadily returned Moseley's gaze and declared, "I'll have you know, Edward Moseley, the lady's enjoying my company."

Moseley flatly denounced Eden. "I trust not."

Temper flaring now, Charles Eden's hand went for his pistol. Why not end the man now and have done with it? "Are you challenging me to a duel, Edward Moseley?" Eden asked. A duel was the perfect way to get rid of Moseley. He knew Moseley was a bad shot, even from a short distance, while Eden had a reputation as an excellent marksman. By custom, if he shot Moseley in a duel, he would be immune to arrest. And Moseley could no longer threaten his plans for the capture of the Spanish treasure ship.

Mrs. Hassell, seeing that this affair was getting quite out of her hands, quickly offered another cake. Mr. Hassell made a remark about the gazebo. And Anne, who had never in her life had two gentlemen fight over her, clapped her hands to her face in complete adoration.

Moseley was utterly amazed. Although much was written concerning duels, seldom were they carried out in the colonies. "What the devil?" Moseley asked, looking at the governor as if he had gone mad.

"A duel it is then," Eden said dramatically. "I have drawn blood more than once where a woman is concerned." He drew his pistol from his waistcoat pocket.

Moseley rose to his feet. To back down now would have made him look like a coward. That, he could not stomach. His honor, as well as his life, was on the line. He reached for his pistol.

Anne would have been disappointed to know that Eden's challenge was not made for her, but for twelve million pesos worth of silver. Suddenly put in a position of being what she thought was a woman fought over, she did the first thing that came to her mind. Standing up, she announced, "I think I shall swoon." Her face grew quite pale. She fell backwards against Moseley, almost knocking him off his feet.

All, however, quickly recovered from this minor accident and the two duelers once more challenged each other.

"Ten paces," Eden shouted, raising his pistol to the air, and the two men faced each other for one last moment before they turned back to back.

Mrs. Hassell, who feared for her tea things as well as her life, quickly ordered the servants to clear away the cups and trays while she and her family ran for cover behind a stone wall.

At ten paces the two duelers stopped and then turned. Through the still air of an autumn afternoon, the Hassells heard the click of pistols being cocked.

And then, all at once, the most amazing thing happened. Anne Hassell let forth the most earsplitting shriek Charles Eden thought he had ever heard.

Off went the guns in an explosion of gunshot! There was the acrid smell of spent powder. Slowly, the smoke cleared. The Hassells, who had expected to see one dead man, perhaps even two, instead saw two men very much alive, facing each other with a look of shock on their faces. Anne's scream had caused them both to miss.

However, the shock of coming this close to death's doorstep so frightened Moseley that he fell to the ground, crying, "By God, the shot has struck my bowels."

The governor looked incredulously at the man squirming on the ground and then his lips turned into the scornful smile that was so characteristic of Charles Eden.

Anne, thinking her former lover cut a cowardly posture, sniffed disparagingly at Moseley.

Anne's father ran to comfort the councilman. He appeared quite worried as he tried to make the man understand he was still very much alive. Looking up at Anne, he remarked, "Come help your suitor."

Anne, however, stood back and waited until Moseley rose to his feet, trembling and white. In a voice loud enough for everyone to hear, she remarked to her father, "He is my suitor only if I continue to see him."

This sudden haughtiness, a characteristic of more beautiful women, tended to make Anne look absurd.

Little did she suspect that she was on the verge of turning down her one and only offer of marriage. Her father muttered under his breath, "Damn the spinster."

Anne tossed her head to one side. Dreamily gazing on Eden, she waited while he remarked to Moseley, "I trust you will not mistake my opposition to you so lightly in the future."

Thinking the opposition Eden was speaking of involved her, not Blackbeard, the lovestruck Anne gave her hand to Eden, and the two headed back up the garden path towards the house.

The poor girl had no idea she was being taken for a fool.

Great Talk Of Separation

The wharves of Bath were no place for a gentleman, especially after nightfall on a misty autumn evening. Deserted by all but vagrants, misfits and sailors, clouded in a wet grey shroud of fog that conveniently hid all misdoings—they were the perfect setup for a crime. Seldom would a man of means venture the twisted streets in this area without fearing for his life.

Yet on this dark and dismal evening, a clean-shaven man in fashionable attire braved the fog-filled, cramped and narrow streets. Remarkably, the vagrants and sailors watching this gentleman made no attempt to attack him. No doubt, they observed the bulge beneath his waistcoat that might conceal a weapon. It is also conceivable that the very boldness of this foolhardy act intimidated those criminals who might be tempted to waylay him or abduct him onto a ship.

The gentleman chanced to stop below a streetlamp. There he stood, a solitary and lonely figure, for upwards of twenty minutes or more. To dispel the chill of the evening, he lit a pipe. Only moments later, as if by predetermined arrangements, those watching caught sight of another gentleman, bearded, massively framed, who appeared just as suddenly out of the fog. The two, oddly enough, began a conversation in these dangerous and forbidding surroundings.

"Taylor double-crossed us," the clean-shaven man said. When he stepped into the lamplight, his face was recognizable. The cool, unemotional eyes, the slightly upturned leer of the mouth, were characteristic of Governor Charles Eden. He exhaled tobacco smoke.

Blackbeard fired him a questioning look and the governor responded almost immediately. "He gave us the wrong passage."

Blackbeard shook his head. He should have guessed as much from a smuggler. "So the scurvy wretch turned traitor on us, did he?"

Eden nodded.

Blackbeard studied the governor. By no means did he seem disheartened. He drew in on his pipe calmly. From his assured countenance, Blackbeard assumed the governor had located the correct map.

In confirmation of the pirate's thoughts, the governor took out a packet from his waistcoat pocket and broke the seals. "I have the correct passage." The governor handed the map to Blackbeard.

Curiously, Blackbeard eyed the faded sheet of parchment—a precisely drawn paper with arrows marked in red to show a passage. In the foreground was a representation of a small ship leaving Havana.

The pirate's fingers moved slowly over the map as he traced the lines from the south of Florida all the way to the European continent. "From the looks of this she'll leave Havana October 1 and steer her course amidst the Straits of Florida, further north to Carolina." He thrust the paper into the lamplight so Eden could examine it more carefully. "See, here's a strong current runs from the south of Florida and then easterly. She'll follow that and then she'll steer northeast to the Canaries, and then the Azores. Yes, this looks a more likely map at that," he continued in a steadily deepening voice.

Eden nodded. Anxious to learn more of the passage, he pressed Blackbeard to continue. "Go on."

The pirate, in a voice that from time to time rose and fell with the lapping of the sea water against the ship's hulls, spoke. "Now there's three large hills just across this island near the Outer Banks. She'll water there." He pointed out the island. "Now see these three large hills marked in green. I'll just keep my lookout on this hill to the southward here—that's the big one—they usually calls it Spy Glass, by reason the lookouts keep watch here when its time for anchorage clearing."

Eden nodded.

"Nobody puts in here, but gentlemen o' fortune nohow," Blackbeard continued. "And if the weather's fair and the wind's free, why on October 15 or thereabouts, this galleon, she'll round Spy Glass Hill, and no mistake. There we'll take her." With a smile on his lips he whispered in Eden's ear. "Aye, Blackbeard, here knows the Outer Banks better than his own palm, he does. I'll take her easy, you can count on that."

Eden smiled as the pirate returned the parchment to him.

Blackbeard broached the topic of Taylor with some circumspection. "And Taylor?" he asked.

"What about him?" Eden replied in his usual, arrogant manner as he pocketed the map.

"What's become of him?" Blackbeard demanded, more directly than before. No doubt, the man had come to no good end. Eden was not the type of man to let a betrayal go unrevenged.

A smile played about Eden's lips. "What do you think?" Eden asked.

Blackbeard studied his companion, trying to guess his innermost thoughts. "You could have put him ashore like a maroon. That would have been Hornigold's way. Or you could have cut him down like butcher's meat. That would have been Tew's."

"Tew was a man for that," Eden responded, eyeing Blackbeard.

Blackbeard sighed. "So he's come to port, then."

Eden, his eyes staring fixedly into the darkness, only replied, "Dead men don't bite."

Blackbeard shook his head. "Oh," he said, his voice breaking dryly. He had not bargained for killing. As he studied the governor, he came to the conclusion that a vital ingredient was missing in his nature. There was the charm, social ease, and wit about Eden, but the pirate was left with the cold impression of an intensely self-reliant man, one who repels sympathy by his own conceit.

The governor, in turn, bent his attention to the pirate. Blackbeard was dressed in the height of fashion this evening. He watched the pirate primp in his waistcoat. Underneath the waistcoat was a shirt of the French fashion, a tiffany whisk and a gold fringed handkerchief folded in his left pocket. Eden blew another smoke ring into the air, and then after looking off into the distance, returned his gaze to the pirate. "I hear you're to be married this evening," he said. He spoke easily, fluently, without the least hint of emotion in his voice. The emotion was hidden.

"Aye," Blackbeard said, his attention diverted to more immediate matters. "The Captain's about to be wed and to a grand lady at that— Mary Ormond." Proudly he twirled the gold cane he was bearing about his fingers, and then tipped back his hat with the top of it. Clearly, he was exultant at the thought of his approaching marriage. He whirled around on his heels to display the rest of his apparel to Eden. "Like it?" he asked.

Eden nodded in approval.

"I may speak coarsely enough, Governor," Blackbeard said. "But I warrant I have the appearance of a refined man of means."

"You do at that," Eden replied. But the next remark Eden made came somewhat unexpectedly. Indeed, it shocked the pirate. Eden took a puff from his pipe and then calmly looking the pirate straight in the eye, asked in a somewhat defiant manner, "Is it the lady you wish to wed or the respect?"

Blackbeard's mouth opened in surprise. He held the woman he was to marry quite close to his heart. But he could see where a man such as the governor would ask such a question. Mary had great wealth, intelligence, and influence—all very valuable attributes for a man who was considered an adventurer by the people of Bath. Blackbeard braced himself and made a reply to the governor that was quite assured in its tone. "It's the woman I love, Governor," he said. He sounded certain.

"Well, sir," Eden said, pausing to tip out the tobacco from his pipe. "Your intended is no common woman."

"Aye, she has a remarkable way with her, Governor."

Blackbeard watched the governor, wreathed in a fringe of smoke, benevolently smiling, complacently leaning against the lamppost. Nothing could less reveal the nature of this formidable man who was now struggling with violent emotions. As he nodded a goodbye to the pirate and watched him turn on his heels and leave, his chest smoldered with passion and jealousy. For Eden lived in a world of private egomania and he could not bear either a partner or rival. Lashed to his ambitions, he had let Mary slip through his fingers.

But now that Blackbeard had Mary, Eden wanted the woman more than ever. He was determined to have whatever the pirate had and that included Mary. Ah, yes, he would have her. As he walked blindly home through the twisted and narrow streets of Bath, he heard the laughter of prostitutes drifting through the air. When one tempted him by opening her blouse in a doorway, he thought of Mary and his lust was aroused. That he expected Mary to still love him after he had cast her aside showed a certain blindness in Eden's character brought on by arrogance. Usually, he had a clear eye in matters around him, for he was the type of man who accepted the world as it was and worked within it, doing the best for himself. It was just that he was often vain and boastful, and that, indeed, was his fatal flaw.

Blackbeard, unaware that the governor intended to take his beloved, put on a pair of silk gloves, placed his cane over his left arm and walked lightly through the fog-filled streets, whistling a little tune to himself. From time to time drunken sailors passed him in twos and threes, so closely he could smell the liquor on their breath, but he barely noticed them, for all his thoughts were on Mary Ormond. Far off, a ship's bell tolled the hour and then all was still save for the sound of the pirate's footsteps muffled in the damp and greying fog.

He was just about to turn down Carteret Street when he was somewhat taken by surprise. In the distance, some sailors had begun singing a round of familiar songs. Before he knew it, he was humming along with them. The song was one composed for Captain Kidd at his hanging:

> *My name was Captain Kidd, when I sail'd, when I sail'd,*
> *And so wickedly I did, God's laws I did forbid,*
> *When I sail'd, when I sail'd.*
> *I roamed from sound to sound, and many a ship I found,*
> *And them I sunk or burned, when I sail'd.*

Urged on by the singing, remembering the old swashbuckling days on the high seas, he approached the sounds. His feet thumped heavily on the wharves, until he came upon the source of these songs. Only yards away, he discovered a small group of sailors huddled together around a bonfire on the beach. About them was strewn rubbish of every kind. They were busy roasting some meat over the fire and guzzling mug after mug of small beer. To his surprise, the sailors were his crew members. Not wishing to make his presence known, he made himself small behind a piling and listened to them. They were dressed in old rags, with limbs that stuck out from their shirts in an odd fashion. They looked as if they'd steal the clothes from a corpse if given half a chance. The few ships that they had managed to plunder had not provided them with sufficient supplies.

Straining to hear their voices, Blackbeard bent down lower, his ear to their direction. He caught the last of a sentence drifting through the night air. "A toast to the pirate's life. Aye, a toast to the pirate's life. And damnation seize the landlubber."

Another, who seemed to have some impediment that made his speech almost unintelligible, remarked, "Whe...Whe...Where's our captain?"

"He's not about."

Still another, whom Blackbeard recognized at once as Israel Hands, his first mate and dearest friend, spoke in sudden indignation. "He's been keeping himself gone overmuch it seems to me."

A scrawny little fellow who went by the name of Richard Stiles broke in. "He's always with his wench, Mary Ormond."

"His wife, lads, no more his wench," Hands said. "Leastways in no mor'n an hour, she'll be his wife. Why, he's to be married this evening, all proper and such-like. But he couldn't invite no scurvy tars. Too respectable he is now. Why, you should have seen him decked out tonight lads, a gold watch and all."

Blackbeard turned away from the group, for their words stung his ears. What they said was true. He had been ashamed of his shipmates—embarrassed at their vulgarities, lack of manners and social graces, so he had not invited them to his wedding. Indeed, how could he invite this rough, raucous group of felons, thieves, perhaps even murderers to an event that would be attended by the social elite of Bath? It would have been a mockery.

"Our captain's a landlubber," Richard Stiles said, denouncing his captain's ungenerosity in the wedding invitations. Although none of the men actually said it, they were clearly all hurt by the fact their captain was ashamed of them.

Blackbeard, quite aware now that he had had a falling out with his crew members, listened more intently.

"A regular gentleman," Hands said, nodding in agreement and downing a drink. "Respectable-like."

"Respectability," Stiles replied, acidly. "Damn it."

"Lads," Hands said, proceeding to demolish his captain's reputation, "there never was a respectable man that was worth a sailor's damn."

These last words hurt Blackbeard more than all that was said before, not because they were so harsh, but because they came from the lips of his best friend.

"Well, a toast to the secret trade," said the first who had spoken. He gulped down some more liquor. "A toast to tropic isles. To go ashore among'st the negro ladies."

And the others joined in another round of drinks. Once finished, they smacked their lips, wiped them on their sleeves and then struck up the second stanza of the song composed for Captain Kidd.

I murdered William Moore, and laid him in his gore,
Not many leagues from shore,
When I sail'd, when I sail'd.
Farewell to young and old, all jolly seamen bold,
You're welcome to my gold, for I must die, I must die."

Richard Stiles, however, interrupted him before he could proceed any further. "Oh shut your mouth, you fool. And stow it. Damn, I'm fully tired o' singing."

The first mumbled a retort that was scarcely heard by the others. They huddled closer to the fire now as the smells of roasting meat wafted through the air.

Hands spoke up defiantly. "I've had just about all I can stand o' Blackbeard. I'd be wanting a share-out, to go on the account, to pirate again. What do you say, lads?"

Blackbeard recognized the anxiety in Hand's voice. The long, slow, uneventful days in Bath were taking their toll on the pirates, making them restless.

"Aye, he's hazed me enough, by thunder," another said.

"Now look here, men," Richard Stiles broke in. "You know as well as I, we can't be a'pirating—Blackbeard won't allow it."

Hands, however, was quick to argue this point. "Ain't we all pirates?" he asked, taking a swig of beer. "Ain't we all seamen here?"

"Aye," mumbled the others.

"Then I suggest we go athwart him," Hands said.

Silence followed this remark. Never before had any of these pirates considered going against Blackbeard's command. Indeed, it was a dreadful moment when Hands spoke these words.

Taken aback, Blackbeard recognized at once why Hands said what he did. The man had a terrible fear of starving. Ever since Blackbeard had picked Hands up in the streets of London, famished and undernourished, at death's doorstep, the fear had never left him for an instant. He had joined with Blackbeard because the pirate promised he would never be in want again. But now there were no prizes and no money. The promise was being broken. Hand's actions now were not the sly, ruthless maneuverings of a cunning man, but instead the steps of a frightened individual in the throes of desperation.

As the pirates continued to talk, Blackbeard moved not a muscle, said not a word, despite the defiant tones in the voices of the crew.

"Aye," Israel Hands said. "We'll go athwart him then. There's a couple o' Frenchmen coming from Antiqua, I've heard tell. They'll be coming to port soon enough. I say we capture one, and if Blackbeard gets in the way I give my vote—death!"

The words were razor sharp in the night.

"Aye," Stiles said. "There'll be no more of this blessed hanging in stays and a teaspoonful o' flip a day."

"Here, here," all the men shouted in agreement. They seemed pleased enough with this solution, for they finished off another round of flip in high spirits.

Blackbeard's rise to such a commanding position among his men had come because he had seemed to his crew the most murderous and fierce pirate of the lot. Now that he had settled down, he seemed only mild compared to Hands, who was next in command. Blackbeard was not the man he once was. A respectable gentleman could not command such a murderous group of cutthroats as these pirates.

The pirates would have never tackled a quarry that was too big for them. But now that Blackbeard had lost his power they quite naturally turned to other leadership, to the most murderous and reckless man in the lot—Israel Hands.

Tears welled up in Blackbeard's eyes as he came to the realization of his predicament. He had been dealt quite a blow by his men that night. Henceforth, he would have to tread softly among them.

Abandoned by his men now, Blackbeard listened to the sailors sing the third stanza of their song:

> *Farewell to Lunnon Town, the pretty girls all 'round,*
> *No pardon can be found, and I must die, I must die.*
> *Farewell for I must die. Then to eternity in hideous misery,*
> *I must lie, I must lie.*

The men's coarse laughter echoed over the sea.

There was a worried expression on Blackbeard's face as he left the wharves that night. But as the time passed, he straightened the ruffles on his waistcoat and jiggled the chain on his watch. His thoughts turned to Mary Ormond. He smiled and lit a pipe. Almost at once, he succumbed to a private world. His vision of respectability was close at hand. No more would he be a pirate, no more would the society of Bath look down on him—for he was about to marry Mary Ormond.

As he exhaled tobacco smoke into the night air, he began to hum the wedding march. But the tune of the pirate's songs overpowered his humming. His marriage procession, blending in with the strains of Captain Kidd's hanging, seemed strangely incongruous in the night air. It was a portentous night.

An Unexpected Turn
of Events

The marriage of Captain Edward Teach to Mary Ormond was the most magnificent affair ever held in Bath. For miles around guests came in carriage and on foot, on horseback and even by ship from as far away as Philadelphia. No bride more radiant had been seen in Bath nor groom prouder than Blackbeard as he carried his bride across the threshold.

After the two took up residence at their new home in Plum Point, a whirlwind of parties and social affairs continued. Happy voices echoed through the hallways of Blackbeard's estate. Wine flowed freely. Rounds of guests came and went in a never-ending stream. Never a day passed when Blackbeard did not hear his wife's laughter in the courtyards or in the gardens or in the bedrooms where the two fulfilled their amorous desires—the young bride delighted in the thrills of her first love; the groom ever amazed at the new pleasures he could bestow upon her. Oh, that a love like this should never end.

Blackbeard delighted in gazing warmly at his young wife as she went about her daily chores of directing the cooking, gardening or cleaning. Mary, seeing her husband return from the shipyards on a new business, welcomed him home joyously.

Blackbeard loved his wife as he had loved no other woman in the world. Near her, he was in ecstasy. Her mere presence thrilled him. However, he was still such a good-looking man that when he was alone, other women pursued him. They asked him into their houses, seized him in garden paths, and one in a deserted alley by the shipyards even went so far as to pull down his trousers, but thus unencumbered, the only love he had was for Mary. From the moment he had seen her on the wharves of Bath, he had a singular attraction that he had never felt before and would never feel again.

Thus, the time passed. The two were deliriously happy, blissfully content. Days passed into weeks and weeks into months until one day when the wind blew cold across the sea and a chill set in that was never to end for the happy couple. On that day two marshals came to the door of the mansion at Plum Point and after knocking, marched inside uninvited. They interrupted the two in the middle of a meal, and the captain, with mouth open in amazement and still full of pigeon pie, was handcuffed and taken away to Bath Town.

As the jail doors clanged shut and the sound of a key rattled in the lock, Blackbeard was left alone to contemplate his fate and to wonder why he had been arrested at the height of a respectable life in Bath. It was even more of a paradox that Governor Eden would let him be jailed before the *San Rosario* would round Spy Glass Hill. This thought and others went through Blackbeard's head as he lay on a bed of malodorous straw, his body tired, hungry, shaking with cold and yearning for the warmth of his young wife beside him. At night while sleeping, he felt such love for his wife he leaned over in his dreams to call her name. The sound of his voice woke him, but once awake, he found she was not there.

Instead, she was at Plum Point, sobbing herself to sleep. Finally, in sheer desperation, she put on her bonnet and shawl and went to pay a visit to Governor Eden. Certainly he would be able to tell her why Blackbeard was in jail. Mary also thought that Eden might release her husband. After all, a governor could pardon anyone—even a pirate.

She found him sitting in an elegant room set off in Queen Anne furniture. A bar had been laid out and he was sipping quietly on a drink. But when he saw her, he immediately set the drink down and bounded to his feet. "Mary!" He extended his hand to her. "How good to see you again."

She was saying something, some casual greeting as she removed her bonnet and shawl and was seated on the sofa, but Charles Eden did not hear her. All he could do was gaze with awe on those lovely white arms and red, red, lips that were no longer his, but Blackbeard's. His entire being smoldered with jealousy. He must have her—he would have her—he thought, gazing into cornflower blue eyes that danced in the flickering candlelight.

"But I shan't waste time in idle conversation," she was saying, pausing just long enough for him to acknowledge the remark.

"Of course." He pulled up a chair near her and made himself comfortable.

One might think that Governor Eden had planned this entire scene and had indeed purposefully seen to it that the pirate was arrested. But this was not the case at all. Although this was the perfect set-up for a psychologically forced rape—the vulnerable woman now begging a favor—the man consumed by passion and desire—Eden had not planned it this way. This was one time when in this strange, unpredictable world, things naturally fell exactly into place.

"Will you have a glass of sherry?" Eden asked.

Flustered and frightened, she accepted the offer and, in all, drank two full glasses before speaking again. Pleased, Eden offered her another, but she refused. "I have a matter of utmost importance to discuss with you," she said. Her lips moved again. "It's about my husband." She bowed her head in humility.

Mary Ormond was a proud woman. Beautiful, rich, a lady—people naturally gave her whatever she wanted, usually before she even asked for it, as if it were the accepted thing to do. A woman such as Mary would always get by in life, no matter what the circumstances. Never having been put in a supplicating position, it was particularly hard for her to plead with Eden now. She handled it badly. She perspired, she wrung her hands, her voice faltered. "He's been arrested," she continued, her voice breaking dryly.

"So they say," Eden replied. The pitiful wavering of her voice touched him, although he was touched even more so by those long, white arms of hers.

"But how could you let this occur?" she asked, now distraught with emotion.

"I had no part in his arrest. The townspeople found a Martiniqueman had been pirated, and all evidence pointed to Blackbeard and his men as the culprits."

Mary was quite beside herself. She stood up from the sofa and walked to the window.

When she had calmed down, she took a seat again. She looked him straight in the eyes. "Blackbeard could not have taken that ship," she said firmly.

"And why, pray tell, is that?" Eden asked.

"Why, he has been with me every night," Mary said, quite naturally.

The picture painted in Eden's mind by this comment only served to arouse him even more. He saw the pirate take her in the dim light of the moon, saw him shudder at the height of passion, and after the cravings of the flesh had quelled, subside into sleep. He threw back his head and laughed. "You must be keeping your pirate quite satisfied, Mary," he said.

Mary Ormond reddened.

Eden smiled in his usual smug manner. "Only commenting," he answered, and he helped himself to another drink.

Mary Ormond was a lady. In any other circumstances she would not have stood for this language. The liberties he was taking with her now were well beyond what any man had taken before. But in this situation she had no choice but to sit and endure this humiliation. So she sat, eyes slightly lowered, biting her lips.

"Governor, I know my husband. And my husband would not do such a thing."

"All women think they know their husbands," Eden commented, casually.

"All this is beside the point," Mary stated. She took a deep breath and then came to the point. "Governor, I wish you to pardon my husband."

Eden could not help but laugh. "Pardon him! Why we'd both be strung up for piracy, the townspeople would be so suspicious."

"But you must," Mary pleaded, her hands now clasped beneath her throat. "You must," she repeated, her eyes begging, a desperation in her voice.

The moment Charles Eden had been waiting for had arrived. Cooly, calmly, he rose from his chair and ventured toward the sofa. He took his place beside her with calm efficiency. Then taking her hand in his, he gazed into her eyes. A smile was on his lips. "Then you must do something for me in return, Mary."

It was suddenly all too clear what Eden wanted. She recoiled in terror at the thought of relinquishing herself to the governor. But it was no good. It was useless to struggle for he already had her in his arms, holding her tightly.

He suddenly forced her down and lifted her skirts. Legs between her thighs, his blood pounding, Governor Eden would have surely reached that pinnacle of passion that unites the male and female into one had not the pounding of fists been heard at the door to the parlor. Charles Eden scarcely had time to jump to his feet and straighten his clothes before the doorknob turned and a servant entered, announcing that several council members were at Eden's home to discuss Blackbeard's arrest.

Peering through the door that was slightly ajar, Eden saw several members of the syndicate. He gazed once more at Mary. The promise of sexual union stirred him again so that before she left, he gave his word he would help Blackbeard. She could only hold her head in shame as he said those words because she knew in her heart, she would not send her husband to his death.

Governor Eden kept his word to Mary by visiting Blackbeard the very next day. Blackbeard's cell was, as jail cells go, not too bad since it had been cleaned out that morning, but it was dark and damp, and there was a dankness in the air.

Within, sitting on his bed, his head hanging low, was the pirate. When he saw the governor enter his cell, he bounded to his feet. As the marshal uncuffed his hands, he let forth a torrent of curses. "Hands off me, ye lily-livered scalawags!" Blackbeard shouted. "Or I'll break yer arms. I'm afraid o' none, not I, not the great Blackbeard!" He dusted off his waistcoat and then watched the marshal as he closed the cell door behind Eden.

It was clear to Eden that the pirate handled his role of prisoner as badly as Mary had handled her supplicating role with Eden. It was not an easy thing for Blackbeard to ask for his freedom. The tables were turned. He was no more the intimidating pirate, but the one in need.

His eyes had a puzzled look as he stared at Eden. It was clear Blackbeard did not understand what had happened to him. One moment he had been in the peak of happiness. He had been adored and happy and full of animal spirits. Now, he stood in a dark cell—deprived of his prowess, his home, his wife, of everything that had meant anything to him. So, he walked angrily up to Eden and his beard bristled as in the days of old and his voice rumbled and growled in a threatening manner. In his high-handed, quick-tempered way, he held onto his former image stubbornly. "T'was a good lay o' theirs, coming to my house by surprise. I won't deny I was shook. But it was only from drinking too much rum, it was. So the town o' Bath better come to terms. My crew'll take me back soon enough. And what's more they'll blow this whole town clean out o' the water into blazes first." Blackbeard glared at the governor. "I thought you was square. You promised me nothing would happen to me in Bath. But the devil take me for a fool you was a scoundrel, you was.

Ah, it was a sad day when I fell in with the likes o' you. I've sailed with the bloodthirstiest hounds that put to sea, ships so overloaded with gold they was fit to sink, and so run amuck with red blood there wasn't a clean spot to stand on, but on my account, yer the worst of the lot. You think I'm a sheet in the wind's eye, don't you? But you'll see soon enough. Cross Blackbeard the pirate and you'll breathe your dying breath, you will."

The governor broke in. "No one's crossing you," he said calmly. All was confidence on his side and suspiciousness and fear on the other.

"Well, damn me to hell!" Blackbeard shouted, his eyes afire, his muscles hardened. "What would you call coming to my house in the dead o' night and taking me hostage? Would you call it a party, Governor? No, by the powers I'll teach your town better. Cross me and you'll go where many a seaman's gone before, some to the yardarm, some by the board, and all to the fishes in the deep, blue sea." If he could have performed any of his old tricks to scare the governor, he would have performed them now, assuming the image of the devil himself, by putting lighted matches to his hair or putting his hand in a lighted flame. Since his matches had been taken from him by the marshal, he could only stand now and flex his muscles and bang on the wall of the cell. The tendons in his neck protruded hideously.

Eden shook his head to let the pirate know he intended no harm and then reached inside his coat pocket and withdrew a bottle of rum. He handed it to the pirate who grabbed the bottle, uncorked it, sniffed the contents and then took a gulp, all the while keeping one eye suspiciously on the governor. Then, rather despondently, he put the bottle aside and sat down on his straw bed, his back against the wall, knees propped up. A hint of fatigue was on his face. The governor took out a pipe, lit it and then offered a smoke to the pirate, who refused.

"I had no part of this," Eden said. "It was all the marshal's doing. I knew you'd be out of sorts." He blew tobacco smoke gently into the air.

Blackbeard eyed the governor indignantly. "Out of sorts!" he shouted. "Without I gives you a hint, them's precious little words for what I feels, Governor. But I'd like to know why they went and did this damned fool thing."

The governor pursed his lips. It was hard to keep control when Blackbeard was having one of his rages, but he made an effort to reach some sort of understanding with the pirate. "Your men captured a French Martiniqueman," the governor said, leaning against the wall of the cell.

Blackbeard put his head between his hands. "Ah, the ship bound from Antiqua," he commented.

Eden nodded.

Blackbeard reached inside his shirt pocket for some chewing tobacco that the jailer had missed in his search through Blackbeard's belongings. "Got a knife, Governor?" Blackbeard asked. "I'll cut me a quid."

Eden instinctively removed a knife from his pocket, but hesitated before giving it to the pirate.

"Blast you, I ain't a'going to escape with that knife, Governor," Blackbeard said, reading his thoughts.

Eden nodded and then gave the knife to Blackbeard. The pirate cut himself some tobacco, chewed it, then returned the weapon to its owner.

"Of course there'll be a trial," Eden said.

"And if they find me guilty, Governor, I'll be strung up for sure." He raised his eyes to meet the governor's. His face assumed a distinctive plea for assistance. It was clear Blackbeard wanted the governor to help him out of the situation. But if he had known that his wife would have to give into Eden's desires in order for him to escape, he wouldn't have been so anxious.

The governor glared at Blackbeard. "We made a bargain in the beginning. You weren't to take any ships. But you did it anyway. Took a ship even when I warned you of the hazards."

"Well, now, Governor." Blackbeard spat out his tobacco. "My men had a powerful urge to go a'pirating, a powerful urge. Them's the kind that can't lay to and whistle for wind, on my account. If we had told them of the conspiracy..."

"No," the governor said in a hushed voice. He paused, seemingly in deep thought. Then, he spoke. "You could have stopped them."

"Stopped them, Governor? Nohow could I have stopped them. If I had spoken, swords would have been going in two shakes; there would have been a tiff soon enough and a new captain aboard the *Adventure*."

The governor shook his head.

Blackbeard lowered his eyes.

The jailer came back and slipped a tin plate and mug through the door. On the plate were a few dried beans. The cup held some water. Blackbeard took one look at the plate and then pushed it aside. Clearly, he had no stomach for prison food. He took another gulp from his liquor bottle. At length, he raised his eyes to meet the governor's again.

"Believe me, Governor," Blackbeard said, "it would have been far pleasanter for the old captain here to have come to blows with them ruthless dogs. I was rough and ready, I was. But there would have been no help to it. And duty is duty. I know'd we needed the hands for the *San Rosario*. No, I'm an easy man. I know when to lay low and wait."

The governor paced the floor of the cell. Clearly, he saw the problem they were up against, for his brow was wrinkled in thought, his body tense. Blackbeard's worries were indeed well-founded.

"Yes," Blackbeard continued, "it's a mess. Me arrested afore the *San Rosario*'s to pass this way. With me in jail there's no one to sail the *Adventure* nor capture the treasure. If you don't figure out something, you'll be making a hash o' this treasure ship—you're a bold man to say no to that. You'd bungle this whole thing, would you? Aye, my heart's sore thinking on the loss o' that treasure."

"But what would you have me do?" Eden suddenly whirled around on his heels and glared fiercely at the pirate. "I'm the governor of North Carolina. I have to obey the law. I just can't set you free."

"I ain't denying that, mate."

The governor stared at Blackbeard. There was a worried expression on his face. "The people expect certain things of a governor. I have an image to uphold. If I were to let you off free there would be questions asked...suspicions raised...and sooner or later maritime attorneys coming to my home like the devil at prayers. I cannot help what I am."

"Nor I what I am, Governor," Blackbeard added. "We all haves our images. But if you had the pluck of a weasel, you'd save me."

Eden shook his head. This was a mess.

"If you don't get me out, it's the noose for me, Governor," Blackbeard said, pressing the point. "And a fortune in silver lost for you. Yes, from the looks of it you're in a bad way as far as I can tell. Treasure lost and this whole *San Rosario* business gone to wreck. Aye, in no time the *San Rosario* will round Spy Glass Hill. And where will Blackbeard the pirate be? Why in jail, that's where. And the ship, why she'll sail on by the Outer Banks to King Philip and his money lenders."

Eden paced the jail cell. He turned to the pirate. "But I just can't pardon a pirate outright. It would put me in...ah...a very bad position."

Blackbeard took up the bottle again. "Then, Governor, I'll thank you for a last sip o' rum." He poured half the bottle down his throat. "Aye, now that's good rum," he said, licking his lips in satisfaction. "I've lived on rum, I have now, Governor. Been in places hot as flames and mates dropping round with the black vomit...but I've always had me bottle. It's saved me from the fever and more, Governor. Helped me bide my time easy when times was rough." Gradually his voice took on a different tone—pleading in its expression. Perhaps the governor would have a change of heart. "Bear it in mind, it ain't my life only, Governor, now it's the treasure in the bargain as well. When a man's steering this near the wind as me, you wouldn't think it too much to give him one good word, would you? You'll speak me fair now and give me a bit o' hope to go on, eh, Governor?"

Eden lowered his head, unable to face Blackbeard's gaze. The expression was not much consolation to the pirate. At length, Eden turned to leave. But before he did, Blackbeard retorted with a statement that shook the governor up considerably. "That treasure," Blackbeard said, "t'would have made a man o' you, Governor."

The governor whirled around on his heels to regard the pirate. Blackbeard grinned. He had obviously hit a sore spot.

The pirate threw back his head, laughed, and then raising the bottle to his lips, downed the last of the rum.

As the governor called to the jailer to unlock the door, he had to admit to himself that Blackbeard was right. For Eden, there was too much at stake here to let the pirate hang—much more than even Blackbeard fully understood.

Villainy in a Vice-Admiralty Court

A courtroom was no place for a man who had no conscience at all. And yet here was Charles Eden, the governor of North Carolina, filing into this courtroom—a large, bare room plastered on the interior with white lime. He followed the other citizens of Bath—the men in homespun jackets and pants, the bonneted women in drab greys and browns. In orderly procedure, he was seated.

It could be assumed that upon entering this courtroom with its severely plain walls, bare, straight-backed benches and hardwood floors, that one should realize some clear distinction between right and wrong, good and evil, just as that thick law book placed on the judge's bench suggested. However, Eden held the opinion that there was no such distinction, and perhaps that is why he felt uncomfortable.

He did indeed look out of place here. This could in part be explained by the expression on his face, which was not serious and somber, as were the faces of the other citizens who shuffled in, but rather mocking and scornful, evidenced by the faint, half-quizzical smile that played about his lips.

Was it also true, that this smile was due in part to some scheme he had planned to free Blackbeard? One would almost think so, for his eyes alighted on Blackbeard's wife and stared straight through her. And Mary, what of her? What were her innermost thoughts as she felt Eden's eyes upon her and quickly bent her head?

Those guesses, however, were not the concerns of the common men who were attending today due to the notoriety of the case. They were packed elbow to elbow. The benches were filled to overflowing. Garrulously, excitedly, they spoke of the character of the culprit. Their voices created a continual buzz. The courtroom, to them, was the very fiber of their being, the lifeblood of their moral existence. It was the common bond that held their society together. Charles Eden sat apart.

Gold cane in hand, gloved and powdered, handsomely featured, Eden cut a striking figure. But even if he had been as splendid as a Greek god, it is doubtful anyone would have paid him any mind. For suddenly the culprit entered the room—a muscular man with a swarthy complexion and a mass of black hair. All heads turned and breaths were caught in mid-air. The din of voices ceased. Blackbeard the pirate was brought up the aisle by the sheriff of Bath.

The citizens regarded him with marked curiosity. Every detail was noted—the cut of his clothes, the way his eyes met those of Mary's. Some even remarked afterwards that as he walked past the governor, a knowing glance passed between the two, a glance barely noticeable to any but the most astute observer.

They watched the culprit take his place at the bar, watched his hands being unbound, and watched the sheriff go to the door to prevent any attempted escape.

Momentarily, Tobias Knight, chief justice of the colony, joined the courtroom. Knight's powdered wig and black robe gave him a look of dignity. As the bailiff cried, "All rise!" the citizens stood until the judge was seated. As he sat down, Knight's eye caught the eye of Charles Eden.

Before speaking, Knight coughed, which caused his powdered wig to fall over one eye knocking his spectacles to the floor; whereupon it was necessary for all procedure to stop immediately, and the clerk of court to hunt for the spectacles. When the spectacles were retrieved and placed once more on the nose of Tobias Knight, the trial began, to be interrupted occasionally by Knight's sniffing and coughs. Obviously, he was still suffering from his cold.

Once Knight gained control of his voice, he spoke. "Captain Teach, before the trial is there anything you wish to say in your defense?" He turned to face the pirate.

Blackbeard had the face of a downhearted man pleading for mercy. When he addressed the jury, it was with an air of humility, for he was fully aware his life was in their hands. But his voice still had some of that force and vigor that characterized his days as a pirate. Now that his hands were free, he took off his hat and placed it in his lap. "Gentlemen," he began, bending his head, "I know there's many among you here today what has old scores to settle with me." He looked several of the jury straight in the eye and they dropped their glances as if in confirmation of his feelings. "Ah yes," he said, his voice deepening steadily, "many of you, I knows, wants me dead now and under hatches." He broke off suddenly, overcome with emotion. It was several minutes before he was able to gain control of his feelings. "Now you can kill me if you please or you can spare me. Let the worse come to worse, if need be. But it'll be my life on your shoulders, gentlemen, yes, my life on your shoulders." He cast his eyes to the floor.

In a few moments, he regained his composure and continued, this time more demanding than before. "See here now, all the captain's asking for is a fair trial—fair and square. This trial here's to judge me on whether I took that Martiniqueman, not on any piracies before that." He clenched his fist. "And I say to you, gentlemen, I in no way unlawfully took that Frenchman. No, I nor any o' my men." He paused. "Once I were a pirate, gentlemen, I won't deny that," he remarked, staring the jury straight in the eye. "But that's not the course I lay now, no sir." He shook his head. "Wasn't it me who struck my colors and come before Governor Eden to surrender?" he asked, more fervent than before. "Do I look the part of a pirate a' standing afore you now?" He spoke his final words. "No, I'm an honest man now and no more a pirate. I say let bygones be bygones. Look here, I was once a gentleman o' fortune, I was once the fiercest pirate ever to sail the seven seas, but I have a wife now. I'm no more a pirate. Well, that's all I have to say in my defense," he finished, lowering his head.

The emotionality of this appeal tended to have a decided effect on the audience. There was a good deal of talking, so much in fact, that Tobias Knight had to rap his gavel on the bench for silence. It was said later by several members of the jury that Mary took out a handkerchief to hide the wellsprings of emotion that were so clearly evident in her eyes.

When all was quiet, the clerk who had been scratching on some papers with a quill, rose and faced the jury. He spoke in an articulate, well-modulated voice. "You gentlemen of the jury that are sworn, look upon the prisoner and harken to his charge. The jurors of our sovereign lord the king do upon their oath present Captain Edward Teach, alias Blackbeard, late of Bristol, England, mariner, the twenty-sixth day of August in the fifth year of the reign of our Sovereign Lord George, by the grace of Great Britain, France and Ireland, king, defender of the faith, by force upon the high seas in the latitude of thirty-two degrees or thereabouts and within the jurisdiction of the Court of the Vice-Admiralty

of North Carolina did fall in with a French merchant ship and did piratically and feloniously set upon, break and did board and enter this Frenchman bound from Martinique and within the jurisdiction aforesaid, piratically and feloniously did steal, take and carry away the said merchantman and also several diverse hogsheads of sugar and cocoa and within
the jurisdiction aforesaid, against the peace of our now sovereign lord
the king, his crown and dignity, upon this indictment he has been ar-
raigned. Upon this arraignment he has pleaded not guilty and for this
trial he has put himself upon God and his country which country you
are. Your charge is to inquire whether he is guilty of the felony and
piracy of which he stands indicted or not guilty. If you find him guilty
you shall inquire what goods or chattels, lands or tenements he had at
the time of the felony or piracy, committed, or at any time since. And
hear your evidence." The clerk took his seat promptly.

The attorney general rose, approached the bench and then, turned to
face the jury. The attorney general was a short, sharp-chinned man who
had a mass of salt and pepper hair. What he lacked in height he made up
for in his reputation in the colony, for seldom had he lost a case. Although at first glance he appeared laughable, he was quite a formidable
figure.

The attorney general strode rapidly toward Blackbeard until his short
figure was within a hairsbreadth of the defendant. He stared at Blackbeard
with malignant, beady eyes.

However, Teach maintained a great amount of self-assurance at this
affront. Failing to get a rise out of him, the attorney general left off
Blackbeard and then walked in an aggressive manner to the jury box.
Folding his hands behind his back, he began to pace back and forth.
Then, with acrimonious words, he stated his case. "The piratical captain
at the bar is now to be tried. He says he has taken the pardon and is no
longer a'pirating, but the ship and effects mentioned earlier only show
that indeed he continues in his unlawful ways as a beast of prey upon all
mankind, his own species and fellow creatures. And by law, if he continues preying after taking the Acts of Grace, he should be hanged by the
neck until dead." The attorney general paused to make a sour face at
Blackbeard. "And now, gentlemen of the jury, I must remind you of your
duty on this occasion. You are bound by your oaths and are obliged to
act according to the dictates of your consciences, to go according to the
evidence that shall be produced against the prisoner without favor or
affection or pity. And you are not allowed a latitude according to will
and humor. Gentlemen, Captain Teach and his crew members did board,

break, and enter the aforementioned French vessel. We shall call the evidence and prove the fact fully and clearly upon him. And so, we doubt not but you'll find him guilty."

Soon after the attorney general had finished his speech there was a good deal of shuffling of papers by Tobias Knight. Understandably, Blackbeard was a little on edge after the attorney general's vicious attack and he glanced in Charles Eden's direction, wondering if the governor had the same feelings. But Eden only stared straight ahead, in his usual assured and confident manner. Indeed, there was no evidence from his posture that he was in any way in collusion with the pirate.

The attorney general proceeded to call his first witness against the pirate—John Jeffers—a man of ordinary stature, well-set and fresh-colored.

The calling of this witness took Blackbeard completely by surprise. The fact that one of his shipmates would testify against him was almost more than he could bear. His jaw fell open in surprise as Jeffers walked down the aisle.

Blast Jeffers, thought Blackbeard, as he watched the mariner, sworn in now, take the witness stand. Never trust a pirate.

Jeffers was engaged in listening to the attorney general's questions with rapt attention, and when the attorney general made a reference to Blackbeard, Jeffers sat straight up.

"You've clapped eyes on this Black...Captain Teach before, haven't you?" the attorney general asked.

Jeffers glanced at Blackbeard and his lips trembled slightly in apprehension as he spoke. "Yes sir," he whispered. Obviously, he was very much afraid of the pirate for he put his hand over his mouth as if to stifle himself.

The attorney general frowned. The man's voice was barely audible in the courtroom. "Speak forthrightly, Mr. Jeffers," the attorney general stated.

"Yes sir," Jeffers said, a little louder. Hesitantly, he continued. "I know...him...very...well."

The attorney general turned his back on the witness and then strode to the jury's box. Facing the jury, he remarked, "You seem timid, Mr. Jeffers. Or are you just stupid?" He whirled around on his heels to face Jeffers.

Obviously, Jeffers did not like being thought of as ignorant. "I ain't stupid, sir," he said. "It's Blackbeard, I swear to God. For it's anyone that would know that beard—black as the lord of hell's riding boots."

Tobias Knight, sitting placidly at the bench, suddenly cringed. "Strike out that last from the record," he shouted at the clerk. And then addressing Jeffers, he said. "Mr. Jeffers, kindly refrain from using profanity in this courtroom."

"Yes sir, Your Worship, sir," Jeffers responded.

"Now then," the attorney general said, continuing his line of questioning, "you know of Blackbeard and his behavior, don't you?"

"Yes sir." Jeffers sat calmly in his chair. The only evidence of his uneasiness was a slight trembling of the lips from time to time at the pause of each sentence. "If I do rightly recall, Your Lordship, it was just after Governor Eden issued some clearance papers for a trip to the island of Saint Thomas that Captain Teach headed north for a little trip to Philadelphia. But Governor William Keith of Pennsylvania issued a warrant for Teach's arrest. Teach, soon learning of this come aloft our ship, of which I was myself a crew member. He talked o' going a'pirating once more, he did." Jeffers paused.

The evidence had a decided effect on Blackbeard. The whites of his eyes became filled with blood. His beard bristled; he cursed under his breath.

Jeffers saw all this out of the corner of his eye, for he was too afraid to look directly at the pirate. Blackbeard's reaction had a decided effect on the crewman. Indeed, he could hardly sit still. The attorney general felt as if the man might just jump up momentarily and bolt for the door.

For this reason, the attorney general walked to the witness box and stood directly in front of Jeffers. "And what else was Blackbeard jawing of on his voyage?" he demanded. "Pipe up now fellow, what was it?"

Jeffer's attention was immediately diverted from Blackbeard. "Well, Your Worship, he talked of using the cat on some that disagreed with him."

"The cat, eh?" The attorney general turned around instantaneously to face Blackbeard and pointed a finger at him. "And a mighty suitable thing for him, the cat." He faced Jeffers once more. "Anything else?" he fired.

"Well," Jeffers said, his jaw more firm than before. "He was saying he wished to be a free man and loathed the landlubber's life."

In the box, Blackbeard's massive frame trembled in anger. Damn the mongrel of a sea dog, Jeffers, he thought. Oh, if he ever got hold of the man he'd feed his body to the maws of sharks!

"And what else did he talk of?" the attorney general asked.

"I don't rightly know, sir," Jeffers said, who in all truth had taxed his brain beyond ordinary limits for a man of his intelligence.

"Don't rightly know!" the attorney general shouted. "Do you call that a head on your shoulders or a crow's nest? Perhaps you don't rightly know if you're a pirate yourself."

"Oh, no Your Worship, I ain't no pirate," Jeffers said, quickly interrupting. "I had no designs to go on the account. I told Captain Teach that myself, told him he could not force me to it and that it was against my will." Jeffers had no intention of confessing to piracy, simply for the reason that he might be tried for it at a later date.

"Well, it's good you weren't mixed up with the likes of that," the attorney general said, turning his head in Blackbeard's direction. Then he turned to Jeffers once more. "So you refused to go on the account."

"Aye, Your Lordship. But he was a rascal, he was." Jeffers nodded his head at the pirate. "Took my possessions and goods and set me ashore on an isle without water or victuals."

"And what did you do?"

"Well, Your Worship, marooned three weeks I was, and lived on nuts and berries and oysters. But thence I resolved to escape and hailed a passing ship."

"A merciless scoundrel," the attorney general said, now facing the jury. This disquieting news created several outraged whispers from the jury.

"Did Teach's ship bear arms on it?" the attorney general asked.

"Aye," Jeffers said. "For it's naught I know of the contrary. All the crew members were in arms, Your Lordship."

"That will be all." The attorney general seemed satisfied with the information. Jeffers' evidence would carry a good deal of weight with the jury, for who could sympathize with a merciless scoundrel who would maroon his own men?

Jeffers stepped down from the chair, looking at the forbidding figure of Blackbeard over his shoulder, and scurried to the back of the courtroom. Blackbeard's frame heaved with hatred and his lips pursed as he looked at Jeffers.

The attorney general regarded Blackbeard's state of anxiety as a good sign. He had learned throughout the years that he was able to get more out of a witness when he was emotional. He could use these emotions to his advantage.

On the other hand, Charles Eden remained cool, calm and collected. Mindful of the impression he was making, he even went so far as to light a pipe he had placed earlier in his breast pocket. The tobacco smoke drifted lazily through the air. Indeed, as far as the eye could detect, Charles Eden had no more than a passing interest in this case.

In fact, no one in the audience caught the slight nod of the head Eden gave Blackbeard as the clerk spoke up—no one except Mary who, by chance, happened to glance at Charles Eden in disgust.

"Have you anything to say to the king's evidence, Captain Teach?" the clerk remarked.

Captain Teach regarded the person of Jeffers with marked hatred. Then all his reserve burst forth. "You're a nice one, ain't you Jeffers? Broken my trust, you have. Once I thought there was few seamen far better than you. Never a month passed but I gave you a rightful share-out for yourself. But now that I'm pretty low you've gone and deserted me." He shook his head in apparent retrospection. "Oh, it's a dark conscience that makes you afeer'd o' me, Jeffers. Ah, there's many a man what's swung for want of an honest word. Aye, my blood'll be on those that find me guilty."

"May it please Your Honor, we will call another witness," the attorney general interrupted. He clearly wished to proceed with the case.

Tobias Knight began to nod from lack of interest and the clerk found it necessary to prod him to keep him from falling asleep.

"Call Samuel Baley, ordinary keeper," the clerk shouted.

Blackbeard recognized the figure of Samuel Baley—a freckle-faced man, plump of figure and small in features, who often had waited on his men at a tavern in Bath.

After being sworn in, Baley settled into his seat.

"Now, Mr. Baley do you know the prisoner at the bar?" the attorney general asked.

"I certainly do," Baley said, regarding Blackbeard. "He oft frequents the tavern."

"Well, how about telling us of Blackbeard's dealings with you," the attorney general continued.

Not so easily intimidated as the other witness, Mr. Baley spoke. "He comes into my tavern as oft he does, him and his boys, between nine and ten of the clock. Them's once been pirates, you see, sir, so mosts of the gents in the tavern lets 'em be no matter what. I've no mind neither to get into trouble, so I lets 'em be, too."

"Please continue, Mr. Baley," the attorney general remarked.

"Yes sir," Mr. Baley declared. "Well then, later I works my courage up, and I asks where they'd received the cocoa. They says it's from a

French Martiniqueman taken in August of late of which they had all received their shares, and if'n I would care to see the vessel, I could. So's being that I'm the curious type, I goes to Ocracoke Inlet and there in plain sight at the south tip of the island is the French Martiniqueman sitting there as pretty as you please. And it's anchored in full view still."

At this moment Knight yawned. "Have you any questions to ask the king's evidence?" he asked, looking at Blackbeard.

"No sir. There's always those that puts their trust in scoundrels, sir, them that lives in lies and sin." Blackbeard glared at Baley.

The attorney general smiled in calm satisfaction with himself. He had certainly proven that Blackbeard was in possession of the Martiniqueman. With the remarks of his next witness, he would have the case sewn up. It was certain Edward Turner would tell the jury exactly how the ship was taken.

However, with the calling of the third witness, no figure bounded to the bench as beforehand to be sworn in, not a soul stepped up to take the stand. How odd, thought the attorney general.

But it did not seem odd at all to Charles Eden, who calmly puffed on his pipe. Indeed, he did not even lift a brow at this unusual occurrence. Instead, he merely waited as had been planned until a tall man stood up in the crowd.

"Edward Turner was found dead this morn," the man said.

A murmur of surprise rippled throughout the courtroom.

"Drowned," the man continued. "We fear he overdrank himself and fell into the sea. A frightful shame it is, a frightful shame. God rest his soul." He took out a handkerchief and blew his nose before taking his seat.

Tobias Knight rapped his gavel on the bench to quiet the crowd which had grown quite lively. When silence once again prevailed in the small white room, the judge nodded for the case to resume.

Of course, the attorney general was mortified at this turn of events. His lower jaw fell open; his face grew livid; the veins on his neck grew to bursting. His main witness had just been disposed of. All his previous evidence would not hold water without him. He could lose the case.

Quick on his feet, he thought to call Governor Eden. Previously, Eden had assured him he would testify against the pirate.

Governor Eden, dressed impeccably in his tiffany whisk and silver-buckled shoes, stood up and walked erectly across the room. He looked the part of a forthright, honest governor. Indeed, no one in the jury suspected less as he took the stand. They failed to recognize the sly and ruthless maneuverings of a cunning man.

The attorney general began his questioning. "Governor, do you have any idea how Teach got the Martiniqueman?"

Governor Eden cleared his throat. Just the slightest trace of a smile was seen around his lips. He glanced at Blackbeard who immediately returned the acknowledgment by a slight nod of the head.

Eden shifted his weight in the chair. "This is what Teach told me. The crew spotted the Martiniqueman watering in the Caribbean. But when he hailed her, there was no reply. So he boarded her and found she was empty, a regular ghost ship. She was a derelict at sea."

"Derelict at sea!" the attorney general shrieked in a high-pitched voice. This was not the testimony he had expected at all.

The crowd turned boisterous at this moment, and Knight immediately glanced at the onlookers and shouted, "Silence!" between his coughs.

Hardly had Knight finished speaking when Eden continued, "Yes, that was the way it was. On September 24, 1718 Teach reported to me that he had found a French ship at sea without a soul on board her. He and four members of the crew testified to this."

At this instant, the attorney general was rendered fully speechless. He was outraged. He gritted his teeth. Governor Eden had played him for a fool. He had been shamed before the entire Bath community. He could not bring himself to continue with this case. Morose and stifled, he retired, stating, "No more questions, Your Honor."

Tobias Knight turned his attention to Eden. Eden nodded, and as if this was a signal to proceed, Knight began to speak. Several citizens remarked after the trial how calmly Knight proceeded in the light of all this startling information and how quickly he formulated his judgment. Indeed, for a man who habitually mulled over facts for hours before reaching a decision, it was extremely remarkable how speedily his opinion was rendered. "Gentlemen of the jury," he said immediately, "the prisoner at the bar stands indicted for piracy committed on the high seas. In the light of this new evidence the case involves the doctrine of salvage." He paused to cough. "Since there is no claimant for the Martiniqueman or its effects the court rules herewith that the aforementioned property has been brought back into circulation when it otherwise might have been lost. The true owner belongs to the Crown. The court therefore awards Captain Teach a compensation as a reward for bringing in the ship and gives to the Crown the hogsheads of sugar—twenty of which will be kept by Tobias Knight and sixty by Governor Eden until sale at public auction."

The effect of these proceedings were marked. Immediately, the crowd rose from their seats and began to talk garrulously among themselves. Mary, in a state of ecstasy, leapt from her seat and rushed to her husband, hugging him joyfully. However, at the sight of Eden approaching Blackbeard, Mary's face turned livid, and she whispered in her husband's ear, "I'll go and tell the servants to get the carriage." She rushed from the courtroom, in such a tizzy that there were those who wondered if she were indeed so ecstatic to see her husband freed. However, they need not have wondered. For it was not Blackbeard who Mary had on her mind at the moment. It was Governor Eden. She knew full well that sooner or later he would come to claim her. And what would she do when he did? If she did not give in to his desires, would he imprison her husband again?

Governor Eden watched the woman leaving and his eyes smiled deviously. He knew exactly what she was thinking. He thought of the ripe, full lips that would soon be his.

It was not long before the room was emptied of all save for Blackbeard and Eden. There was the echo of boots against the floor as Captain Teach boldly approached Governor Eden.

"T'were remarkable good luck that Edward Turner did not testify," Captain Teach said. "Very remarkable good luck." He fired a questioning look at Eden.

"Yes," Eden said. "T'was the hand of fate that pushed him, poor dog."

"Or thy own," Blackbeard said, eyeing the governor shrewdly.

Eden didn't trouble to answer.

Blackbeard studied the governor. "And you, Governor. Your testimony saved me from the gallows. Now if I didn't misjudge you, Governor. And me thinking your heart was as black as pitch. But see there— you risked your life for an old tar like Blackbeard. Aye, it makes my heart warm just thinking on it."

The governor ignored this remark. The pirate didn't know the half of it. "Whence does the treasure ship round Spy Glass Hill?" Eden asked, changing the subject.

"Two weeks hence," Blackbeard said. "Two weeks," he repeated, before he knocked the ashes out of his pipe and put it back in his waistcoat pocket.

A Contrivance
for the Lords Proprietors

harles Eden took a drink. Then he took another. God only knew what more trouble that Martiniqueman would give him, he thought, as he stared out the crack of his parlor door at the gentlemen standing in the hallway. First the trial and now this! He did not need "this"—a little man barely over five feet with a tiffany whisk and brocaded waistcoat, threatening to cause more trouble, and perhaps ruin everything.

The "this" Charles Eden was referring to was one of the lords proprietor's secretaries, Lord Carteret's to be exact, who had just announced to one of Eden's servants that he would like to see the governor. In the secretary's words, which had been delivered to Eden on perfumed note paper by one of the governor's servants, the secretary was there to "investigate the Martiniqueman more fully, having been given a testimony by a seaman aboard the Martiniqueman at the time of its capture by the piratical Captain Teach." The visit by Lord Carteret's secretary would be followed by the seaman's visit to primarily identify the ship.

It was altogether not a good time for the secretary's visit, not good at all, thought Eden—just a week before the *San Rosario* was to round Spy Glass Hill.

"This" was now tapping his foot impatiently in the hallway, and Eden, realizing he would have to see the secretary sooner or later, braced himself and downing the last of his drink, decided on sooner.

Eden ushered the secretary into the parlor and before the governor had a chance to offer a seat, the secretary took one. Eden noticed the secretary was wearing gloves with silk tops which he immediately took off, so that every now and then he could dip some tobacco from a little gold snuff box which he carried in his waistcoat pocket.

"Make no mistake, sir, this business of piracy in the colonies is most scandalous, most scandalous," the secretary said between dips.

Charles Eden shifted his weight uncomfortably in the chair. "Well, it's most distressing to all concerned." In actuality, Eden was more distressed by the secretary's business in the colonies than any pirates.

The secretary raised an eyebrow at Charles Eden's remark. "I should hope, Governor Eden, that you take an intense dislike to pirates. However, I have heard comments to the contrary."

The secretary made the governor feel uncomfortable. His comment gave the governor the intuitive feeling the secretary was about to spring something on him at any moment. But Charles Eden was able to keep up his calm countenance, even in the face of such a rascally little man.

The secretary paused to taste the tobacco now in the intercises of his teeth. "I'll have you know that the king, Lord George, by the grace of Great Britain, France and Ireland, defender of the faith, hardly knows what more to do. He has been most generous in giving the pardon, most generous."

"Most," Eden commented.

"As I remarked—most generous," the secretary said, eyeing Eden rather strongly for cutting off his thoughts. He was not in the habit of being interrupted by anyone—anyone save the lord proprietors of the king. He frowned at Eden. "But what is His Most Gracious Majesty to do with this laissez-faire attitude in the colonies?"

Obviously this question was rhetorical, for Eden had barely opened his mouth when the secretary continued, waving a glove in the air. "Ah yes," he said. "Pirate crews circulating freely along the wharves and in the stores of Boston, Providence, Newport, New York and Philadelphia; young men from respectable families hastening to join in their maraudings, claiming that in the Red Sea money is as plenty as stones and sands. Shameful!"

Eden opened his mouth to comment and then, on second thought, closed it.

He watched as the secretary helped himself to a drink and wondered all the while how the dickens such a small man could be so intimidating.

When he had settled himself into his chair once again, the secretary gave a sharp glance at Eden. "What do you suppose," the secretary said, emphasizing the word *what*, "could be the cause of this piracy?"

Charles Eden had supposed that the secretary would continue in his monologue, but the man paused and looked straight at him. After giving the question some thought, Eden responded. "It seems the people want the money. They complain about the taxes."

"Fiddlesticks," the little man snapped.

Charles Eden had the distinct impression that he might as well have said nothing in response. He did not trouble to comment further, but instead merely waited for the secretary to continue.

The secretary did so after helping himself to another drink. "I fail to see taxes as a reason. I dare say, taxes are forever a problem. Nevertheless, it's no excuse for hobnobbing with these infidels."

"I understand." Eden would have offered more of a response had the secretary given him time to get a word in edgewise. However, he did not.

"I would hope you would understand," the secretary said. "But as I said, there has been much talk of your taking a liking to these villains, Governor. Your testimony in court..."

Charles Eden could no longer stand this constant prodding of the secretary. He interrupted the secretary this time. "Forgive me, sir, but the Martiniqueman was a derelict."

The secretary pressed his lips together. "Was it, Governor?" he asked shrewdly. Then he edged in a bit closer to Eden, causing the governor to back away.

To calm himself, Eden poured another drink. Then after taking a sip, he continued. "I assure you, sir. I have an extreme dislike for piracy." The comment was said in Eden's usual charming voice with enough firmness to sound convincing.

However, the secretary proved by his next statement that he was not convinced at all. "Then you should have no objections to me seeing the ship."

"Seeing it?" The comment hit Eden like a bolt out of the blue. What in the devil did the secretary want to see the ship for? But if he had asked the question aloud, Charles Eden couldn't have received a quicker answer.

"Yes." The secretary smiled deviously as he took a final dip of snuff from his little gold box. "Since this seaman has informed me of a few details regarding the vessel and since you have such a distaste for these pirates, Governor, I'm sure you won't mind in the least, if I take a look at it."

Eden was so stunned, he said nothing.

"Well, Governor?" the secretary asked, smiling.

Eden coughed uncomfortably. "Well, of course, sir, I'll make arrangements immediately."

"Fine." The secretary rose to go. He put on his silk-tipped gloves and then bade his farewells. He gave Eden a little sidelong glance as he left which seemed to say, "Now I've got you where I want you," retrieved his hat and coat from the servants, and then was on his way.

That the secretary had put Charles Eden in a most awkward position did not trouble the secretary in the least. He often put people in awkward positions. At dinner parties he would make snide remarks to the hostesses, or break the china or spill drinks on women's dresses. But the hostesses of these parties were always careful to overlook these "little" faults of his. He would be asked back again and yet again to remake snide remarks or rebreak china or respill drinks, merely because he was the secretary of Lord Carteret. His title gave him just enough power to make others cringe in his presence and cower in his footsteps.

The secretary expected people to cringe and cower. He wouldn't have it any other way. At ceremonies, red carpets were laid before his feet; he received six-gun salutes; he spent much of his time waving from carriages. Everywhere he went doors were thrown open to him. Heaven forbid that Lord Carteret's secretary should ever come to part with his title!

So as he walked up the gangplank of the Martiniqueman that very afternoon, careful not to muddy his silk-tipped slippers, he expected the trumpet salutes and stands of attention that he received from Blackbeard and his men who were now manning the ship. And when Blackbeard welcomed him politely aboard and Charles Eden addressed him in his usual charming manner, he never suspected for a moment that either one of the men had a thing up their sleeve. He merely took it for granted that the two were treating him with the usual pomp and ceremony so common to the rest of his admirers. As he walked, a black lackey, carrying a green parasol just above the little man's head, followed behind like a well-trained puppy dog. The lackey did not, on any occasion, let the sun shine on the secretary's face, for that, indeed, would have ruined the secretary's complexion—and the secretary was a very vain man. He often wore on his face the fashionable little black patches of the time.

After he had given the Martiniqueman an overall glance, he proceeded to examine the ship more closely by walking fore and aft and hemming and hawing at each French *culverin* or *fleur de lis* he sighted. Charles Eden walked beside him and the little lackey followed a few feet behind. All the while the secretary continued this examining process—stopping beside the binnacle, pausing beside a mast—Charles Eden's anxiety increased until finally, his curiosity got the best of him.

"I am quite anxious to hear the seaman's account of the vessel," Eden said.

This remark by Eden seemed to satisfy some unanswered question in the secretary's mind concerning Eden's character, because he turned to face Eden with a shrewd expression on his face and replied, "Are you?" Then he smiled knowingly and continued looking directly at Eden. "Yes, I should think you would be anxious."

Charles Eden frowned in response to the secretary's statements. Had "this" (for that was all he could think to call the puffed-up little dandy with powdered wig and perfumed handkerchief), yes, had "this" stopped beside the *culverins* and *fleur de lis*, paused beside the binnacle and mast, only to increase the governor's anxiety to the point where he would incriminate himself? Lamely, Eden commented, "Yes, I'm quite anxious. For if you are correct I will hang these sailors immediately. Pirates—vile villains."

The secretary smiled, studied Eden for a moment longer, and then muttered to himself, "We shall see, we shall see."

Then he asked to be taken below deck and ordered the lackey to stay above. The two descended deck after deck—the secretary still hemming and hawing to himself until they reached the very hold of the vessel. Then all at once, the secretary sniffed.

It was not the strange, little sniff the secretary always gave when he opened his snuff box and fine particles of tobacco dust wafted through the air to the secretary's nostrils. No, this was quite different—something like the kind the secretary gave when he was coming down with a cold. "Quite dampified down here, if I do say so," the secretary said. He came to a standstill.

There was not the least hint in Eden's voice that he had previously known of the ship's condition. He looked completely surprised when the secretary now sniffed the air with the nose of a bloodhound. "No!" Eden remarked with a contrived look of disbelief.

"Yes!" the secretary said.

It seemed to Eden as the secretary stood between decks, now taking out a handkerchief to blow his nose, that he was seriously debating whether to continue his examination of the Martiniqueman. Actually, Eden was not far from wrong. The secretary was not fond of dampness and often made it a point to stay inside on cold, rainy days in London. The thought crossed his mind that perhaps he had seen enough of the Frenchman to report directly to the lord proprietors. However, duty was duty to the secretary (and title and position were everything) and so he decided after much thought, that he would continue.

However, they had not gone much further when there was a sudden gasp from the secretary, his powdered wig fell askew, and he rushed right back up the ladder, almost bumping into Eden in his mad scramble to get above deck. "Bless my buttons!" he yelled, face to face with Eden. "This ship's taking in water. She's bursting her seams!"

"You don't say!" Eden's countenance would later be described by the secretary as one of extreme horror and disbelief. It is a shame that the little man, in his mad dash to climb above deck, did not see a slight curl on the governor's lips—a twisted smile that would seem to indicate that the governor was laughing at him. Yes, in the secretary's rush he created untold problems.

One was that he did not even bother to wait for the lackey to shelter his face from the sun. It is quite possible that at this very moment, the secretary obtained just the slightest blemish on his complexion, an ugly little brown thing on his cheek—in short, a freckle, which he afterwards discovered. But that was for the secretary to notice later in one of his calm moments as he stared in a mirror late at night in his lodging place. Presently, blemishes were the last thing on his mind, and he approached Blackbeard at the forecastle with utter and fervent intensity. "Your ship is rotting, Captain Teach," he said between sniffs.

No one would have doubted for a moment that Blackbeard was genuine in his feelings as he looked at this puffed-up little dandy before him and remarked in disbelief. "Well, shiver me timbers. And how do you like that—me thinking she was all shipshape. A sorry ship this is, and no mistake," he remarked, turning quickly so as not to break into guffaws at the little man's perplexed look. When he had composed himself, he turned a concerned face to the secretary. "You don't suppose she'd be sinking, then, matey?"

The secretary paused for a moment to consider the pirate's question. "Sinking? Well, it's quite possible." He took out his handkerchief and sneezed into it. He did not seem to be thinking any further on the possibilities connected with the ship's sinking so that it was necessary for Blackbeard to resume the conversation by prodding him further.

The pirate took on a contemplative air, putting his hands behind his back, bowing his head to the ground and then looking into the secretary's face with marked concern. "This is bad, very bad," he said. "For England, that is."

"Bad?" the secretary asked, blowing his nose.

"It's just..." Blackbeard continued, breaking off his thoughts.

"Well what?" the secretary asked, impatiently.

Blackbeard continued. "Why, she might just sink and so stop up the mouth of the inlet."

"Stop up the mouth of the inlet?" the secretary repeated in surprise.

"Blast me!" Blackbeard shook his head. "Why no ship would be able to get in or out of the harbor."

Slowly but surely, the secretary was beginning to divine what both Blackbeard and Eden had in mind. A shadow crossed his face. It was with acute anxiety that he now looked at Blackbeard who had just been joined by Governor Eden and the lackey. "If this ship sinks, no one will be able to get in or out of the harbor," the secretary repeated, half to himself, half to Blackbeard.

"No one whatsoever," Eden said. "No trade at all to England. No taxes. Nothing."

Now it was Lord Carteret's assistant's turn to be discomforted. He no longer had the upper hand. He stared at the governor in horror. His mouth opened wide. "No trade?" he gasped. He paled.

"No timber, no tar, no rosin, no tobacco," Eden said, shaking his head. "No taxes," he repeated.

The secretary looked worried. "That would make the lords proprietors extremely angry, I'll stake my wig on that. They expect their goods from North Carolina."

"Be that as it may," Eden said, mindful of the impression he was making on the secretary. "We can do nothing about it. Unfortunately, we must wait for the seaman to come to North Carolina and identify the ship."

The little man threw up his hands. Worry lines crossed his brow. This would not do, not do at all. "If this ship sinks, the lords proprietors will never let me hear the end of it." They might even take his title away, he thought, although he did not say it. "Oh dear," he uttered in perplexity. He called to his lackey and immediately began to pace back and forth across the deck of the ship, the lackey scurrying after him.

Eden followed after him. "I insist, sir, that we keep this ship here to be identified by the seaman. I won't allow it to be destroyed. Not when I think it might be a pirate ship." How utterly pious Eden sounded as he paced with the secretary, how utterly upright in his wish to fight for law and order.

"It must be destroyed," Lord Carteret's secretary said.

"Never," the governor said. "If we destroy this ship, we'll never discover whether she's a pirate vessel or no."

"That will have to be," the secretary snapped.

"But," Eden broke in.

"Damn it, Governor," the secretary said, fiercely stomping his foot. "I realize your hatred for pirates. We all do. And I will surely report to the lords proprietors that they have misjudged you. But a trifle more of this arguing, and I shall explode. Now I'm ordering you to destroy this ship."

"There's nothing I can do to change your mind?"

The secretary shook his head.

The tables had definitely been turned on the secretary. He left the Martiniqueman that day in a state of acute discomfort. Tablets, long periods of rest, hot baths failed to completely cure him. Indeed, his stay in the colonies was to be marked by cases of nerves and morose spells of depression. Even after his return to England, he suffered a noticeable change. Peculiarly enough, for several months at parties, he was unable to break the china, spill drinks on women's dresses or make snide remarks. In short, he seemed to have lost some of his old ability to put people in awkward positions.

Some thought this change for the better could be attributed to his vacation in the colony and suggested he should get away more often. But all this soon passed. In time, the secretary returned to his former self. It was just that when the Martiniqueman was mentioned, the old symptoms of anxiety returned—the unsteady hands, the ashen face, the trembling lips. For this reason alone, the lords proprietors thought it best not to mention the incident and after awhile it was all but forgotten.

As for Eden and Blackbeard, the two enjoyed a smoke together, laughing all the while at the look on the little man's face as he left the Martiniqueman that afternoon. Soon, they turned their thoughts to other matters. Blackbeard's voice took on a more serious tone. "You saved my skin at the trial, Governor," he said. "So I saved yours this afternoon. Tit for tat, eh?" He nudged Eden in a friendly manner.

The governor did not take Blackbeard's remark as the pirate would have hoped. Instead, in a voice as cold as ice, he remarked, "That's the trouble with you. You're too soft-hearted. I turned the trial to get the treasure, not to save your life. And if I had a choice between you or the treasure, you'd know what I'd choose."

Blackbeard cast his eyes to the deck. Eden's voice sounded strangely harsh in the warm afternoon sun and Blackbeard was reminded again of how insensitive the man could be. That insensitivity would keep them apart forever.

As if reading Blackbeard's thoughts, Eden commented. "Remember what I said. Remember why I'm the only man who can get this treasure—because I won't be swayed by some damn fool notion in my heart." Eden stood up then and walked the length of the ship—turning his back on Blackbeard. Obviously, he did not want to hear any more of this.

Blackbeard said nothing. He only shook his head sadly, for he suddenly understood the governor's heart could never be touched. But putting aside all these thoughts for the moment, he turned his mind to other matters. Presently, he cleared his throat. "Well, we might as well get down to business, Governor."

Eden turned around. He was ready to listen now. He returned until he was in front of Blackbeard again.

"Well, then, Governor," Blackbeard said, staring the man in the face. "Now how's the ship to be destroyed?"

Eden looked at the sparks from Blackbeard's pipe, the fiery cinders alive and glowing in the hollow bowl of wood. "Burn her," he said.

And that night the Martiniqueman went up in flames.

Going on the Account

The scene was all too typical, thought Blackbeard as he raised the spyglass to his eyes and descried his wife standing at Plum Point. He had seen it, oh, so many times during his life. The woman stands at the edge of the water; the wind blows her hair; her hands shade her eyes from the sun. She strains to catch a glimpse of her departing lover as his ship sails off into the horizon. When she can see no more, she turns her back on the sea and walks home again to await his return.

Oftentimes he had seen that scene, played it out, in fact, with others—the parting words of sorrow, the half-choked sobs, the questioning looks. Would he return, they would ask? Yes, of course, he had said, as he had sailed out of their lives forever. For the sea had been his only true love—always the sea calling him to different horizons. He thought of his men—locked to their duties, to services, to their ambitions—locked like him, now, to this one last voyage.

He had answered her as he had answered all the other women in his life. Oh, yes, he had said, as he dried her tears on his shoulder. I'll come back. Only with her, he had meant it. Quite naturally, he thought of her suppleness, her wiles. He would have given up all this—the sea, the pirating—would have laid down his life at her feet, if only he could. He knew, of course, that this was little consolation to her now as she stood on the shore, wondering why he was going at all. Oh, yes, he said to himself, as he watched her praying to God for his safe return, oh, yes, I'll come back.

The emotions must have been too great for her to watch any longer, for she turned away from the ship before it was underway, wrapped her cloak tightly around her and returned to their home. He was glad she had turned away. Her figure, staring after him, had become almost unbearable to watch, the sorrow of parting was so great. He paused for a moment to gather control of himself. Tears passed, he put his spyglass aside.

He turned his attention to his men and his ship. He struck his finger out to test the wind. It was rising slightly. Still, the ship was not at all straining on the heavy cable that held her at anchor, but instead, floated calmly on the waves, her towering masts seeming to stretch into the wisps of grey clouds that had settled across the sky. Earlier he had given orders not to sail until the wind picked up.

Yes, earlier he had blamed his inability to get underway on the wind, but he knew in his heart he had delayed because of Mary. An old salt such as himself would have had the ship underway even in the earlier calm. He guessed his men knew that. But now that the wind was rising, he knew his men would not stand for his hesitation much longer. They'd be calling down at any moment from the topsails, for they were anxious to make the voyage, although they, like Mary, did not know what it was about. He could not hold them off much longer.

As if in confirmation of his thoughts, the sailing master cried, "The land breeze flutters aloft, sir. If our light sails would draw we might be able to cast away."

Blackbeard heaved his shoulders. "Hail the tops," he said to the master. He already knew what the men's answers in the topsails were going to be.

"Is there wind aloft?" the sailing master shouted to the men above. Obviously, he was quite excited for his face was ruddy, his eyes, bright.

"Aye, a light cat's paw," one shouted. "But our topsail winks not."

"Shall we sail then, Captain?"

Blackbeard felt the eyes of all his men upon him. He knew what they were feeling then—the excitement of the chase, the thoughts of booty in their minds and what they would do with that booty. He could not hold them off now if he tried.

"Trip the anchor then, you dogs, and we'll be heading out to sea," he cried.

At the sound of his command there were hurrahs and huzzas as in the days of old, and shouts of "aye, aye, sir" as the men hustled and bustled about the deck.

He gave his orders. As the men's measured tread was heard, the capstan was set in motion. The anchor was tripped and heaved up. The sails were loosened from the spars, and yard after yard of billowing white cloth unfolded. As the sails hung from the yards, the master cried, "Ready the foreyards." Another called, "All ready aft."

"Let fall your foresail," Blackbeard shouted. "Now your mainsail. On with your bonnets and drabblers." As the sails filled with wind and the ship drew ahead, Blackbeard steered her easily toward the dreaded bars of the Pamlico Sound.

The *Adventure* ran off free, her bowlines hanging loose and all her canvas rapt full. She sailed through the water, one league, two leagues, three, until Blackbeard could no longer sight the land. In time, he put aside his spyglass to stare at an occasional gull wheeling free through the air or a flying fish skimming along the water. Sea spray stung his face; sea salt, his eyes. It was like the days of old, he thought, like his pirating days.

But not quite. His men were too restless. Even now as they went about their duties, there were occasional scowls on their faces or wrinkles on their brows. They were discontent. He knew why. He had paid them a barbarous insult—he had given them up for his wife, and even worse, he had given up the pirate's life for his life of respect. Ah, yes, feeling was running high against him. He could hear it in their voices, low and grumbling at night; see it in their eyes that gave him evil sidelong glances; feel it in the way they took his commands with frowns and scowls. Even now, a group of them had gathered around his second-in-command, Israel Hands, and were muttering to each other. Surely, they were wondering what he was up to—if he had indeed chosen the pirate's life once again. As these thoughts crossed his mind, Israel Hands' eyes met his, and Blackbeard's eyes turned away with a stabbing look of pain. He was heartsick. His choice of Mary had strained their friendship to the breaking point.

The thoughts of this hurt him so that he suddenly whirled around on his heels and shouted contemptuously to Hands. "Hands, you're getting to be leading man here. You'll be captain next, and little surprise it would be."

The small group of pirates stopped their grumbling and turned to face him. A look of rage swept across Hand's face. He gave full vent to his anger. His voice was taut and harsh. "Captain, this ship's been in stays much too long, it has. This ship weren't christened to be in stays."

Hands glared at Blackbeard. The second-in-command was as heartsick as his captain. For the man whom Hands had thought to be the greatest pirate of them all had broken his faith. He had given up the pirate's life, and for what? Solely for a woman. It was contemptible, thought Hands. He could not look Blackbeard in the eye but feel a smoldering rage. Blackbeard had betrayed him.

Furiously, Hands raised his fist to the high heavens and cried, "These men are gentlemen of fortune. They've kept company with the best of them, with Tew, at Madagascar, and Calico Jack at New Providence. They've smelt powder, these men have. They ain't respectable such as you—they're pirates!" That was quite an emotional speech, so emotional that Hands had to turn away from his captain for fear the emotions welling up inside would burst forth in a flood of tears. When Hands turned around again, his face was rigid.

Blackbeard paused for a moment. When he spoke his voice was firm. "I'm still captain here, Hands."

Excitement ran wild through the crowd of men. It was a moment when sudden violence could burst forth, when anything could happen— but nothing short of bloodshed and sudden death. The time had come to test Blackbeard's strength.

Hands did not back down. "Well, when are we to capture a ship?" he shouted. "How long are we going to stand off and on? We want a prize, we do." It was clear he would not be satisfied until he knew what their position was and this position would have to be that of pirates on a pirating ship, not sailors on a respectable vessel.

Blackbeard, studying the men, judged they would not back down at this point either. If Hands gave the word, they would certainly mutiny. They were ready—fingers itching to pull the triggers of their pistols, hands ready to draw their cutlasses. What he said in the next few moments could determine his fate. He decided to tell them of the treasure ship.

Carefully, Blackbeard chose his words. "When, by the powers, are we to capture a ship, you ask? Well, now, if you want to know I'll tell you when. Today. For there's a prize to be had."

The men stirred at the words. Whispers of a "a prize" ran through their numbers. The excitement was wild.

However, Hands eyed the captain suspiciously. He was not one to be swayed by words. He spat on the deck of the ship. "Are you certain? For I want some goods, by thunder. I want some sugar and wines and such not."

The color rose in Blackbeard's cheeks. He gritted his teeth. Hands had always taken him at his word. Now, he seemed determined not to trust him. This was a barbarous prejudice, an unjustifiable insult. He hurled his words in fury at Hands. "Damn me!" he shouted. "I seen a thing or two at sea, I have. If you'd only lay your course and point dead ahead, you would ride in carriages, you would. But not you." He shook his head at the crew. "No, not you. You'll have a gulp o' rum and go hang. Bless my soul, I've a sick heart to sail with the likes o' you."

Immediately, a roar went through the crew. There was much tongue clucking and wagging of heads. Several of the crew went for their pistols.

Teach acted quickly. He withdrew his cutlass. It flashed brilliantly in the sunlight as he pointed it toward the heavens. "I say we sail today," he shouted, beard bristling, eyes fiery. "Aye, if we have favorable winds and a quick passage, there'll be money to roll in, money that'll keep us in carriages for ever after."

Teach had said the magic word. "Money?" Hands asked aloud, and immediately his eyes lit up with eager anticipation. No more starving in the streets.

"Aye, money." Blackbeard should have known what effect the word would have, for immediately his second-in-command lowered his cutlass. "No more begging in the streets nor sponging for bread," Blackbeard added.

Several of the crewmen thrust their pistols back in their belts. Clearly, they wanted to know more about this money before they took any action.

"How much money?" Hands was as curious as the rest. "What's the ship? Whence does she weigh anchor?"

"You ask a sight o' questions, Hands," Blackbeard remarked.

Hands fumed. Self-willed, impatient, the second-in-command replied, "Maybe that's because you're a man what's not to be trusted." Being a pirate he looked for duplicity behind every apparent altruism.

Blackbeard straightened to a ramrod posture. Hands had dealt him a mighty blow. He hurled one back, equally as vicious. "Well, your brains tarn't much and never was, Hands. But I'm supposing you can hear, leastways your ears is large enough." Hands had no time to reply to this insolent remark for Blackbeard continued immediately, "Now we're not after no measly sloop o' wines and sugars. No, I say, we're after King Philip's own plate, I tell you."

The words "King Philip" and "plate" hit the group of crewmen like a bolt of thunder.

However, Hands was not so easily convinced as the others. His jaw remained firm, his eyes set. He took a step forward and struck the sharp edge of his cutlass on the deck of the ship. The cutlass remained in the wood of the deck. "How are we, a handful o' men, to capture an entire plate fleet?" he shouted defiantly. "We'd all starve for King Philip's silver."

The men grumbled in agreement. Clearly, Hands had a point. A handful of men could not capture an entire plate fleet, that was certain. There were smirks and sly remarks now as they looked at Blackbeard again. All was wariness and suspicious curiosity on their side, confidence on the other.

"The plate's aboard a secret ship," Blackbeard shouted. "One ship and one ship only will cross the ocean with that treasure. And by God, we'll capture her."

Hands was surprised. He had heard about these secret ships but he had never believed the stories. Suddenly, the men broke into riotous clamor. Blackbeard knew he had won them over. It would only take one further push to have them back on his side again.

Blackbeard stepped forward to meet Hands' challenge. "But, perhaps you can't understand English, Hands," he roared. "Maybe you thought you was captain here. But I'm captain by election. I'm captain because I'm the best man to ever sail the seas. And you'll obey me, you may lay to that, as long as I have the tip-top post here. Now do you men want the plate or no?"

There were excited cries from most of the crewmen. "Aye, aye."

"Well, now you men choose your captain," Blackbeard said. "You take another ship and you'll have me as captain no more. Who's the better man I'd like to know? Israel Hands or Blackbeard the pirate? Elect who you please to be captain now. I'm done with the post o' captain."

"Blackbeard! Blackbeard, forever!" the pirates yelled in unison.

"So you've changed your tune, have you?" he shouted. Then directing his words solely to Hands, he said, "Well, Hands, I reckon you'll have to wait until another time to be captain. And lucky for you I'm not in a revengeful mood. For I'd splatter your guts on the deck o' this ship, I would." With those last words he walked up to Hands, grabbed his cutlass from the deck of the ship and thrust it into his second-in command's hands once again. Hands could no longer meet Blackbeard's stare. He took the cutlass in silence. There was little more to say.

Blackbeard sighed in relief as he turned away from Hands and went about giving orders. For the time being, the Spanish silver had quelled a mutiny. But suppose, by chance, they didn't get the silver. Would they attempt another mutiny? The answer was all too clear. He only questioned how they would kill him—in his sleep with a knife in his back or in broad daylight by pistol fire. He shivered at his thoughts. With all this in mind, he raised the spyglass to his eye and peered out into the vast immensity of sky and ocean. Somewhere out there was the *San Rosario*.

If Blackbeard could have seen farther into the distance, indeed, much, much farther southward, he would have caught sight of a Spanish galleon in the early mist of morning, her complicated tracery of ropes taunt, the proud display of spars and booms uplifted, the broad folds of canvas filled. Peering closer, he would have seen the captain-general, a well-favored man, pacing the deck, arms crossed behind him.

Upon first glance, it might appear that the captain-general was lost deep in thought. But this was not the case. Indeed, the captain-general was not thinking but praying. He prayed to God and Saint Elmo, the patron saint of sailors, whose light from a little candle in a lantern dangled from the stays. The sailors called it *corpos santo*.

The captain-general was like most Spaniards, very religious. However, he was also very superstitious. To a Spaniard in the 1700s, religion and superstition went hand in hand. One was hardly distinguishable from the other.

The fact of the matter was that luck had not been with the captain-general on this voyage. Only a short while after the *San Rosario* had embarked from Cape San Antonio in Havana, the ship had been rammed straight through by a swordfish and major repairs had to be done to her hull. Later, when they had been navigating through the barrier reefs, her hull had scraped bottom. It was only a minor scrape, but enough to scare the men, making them fear for their very lives.

This was the captain-general's third such trip carrying cargo of treasure for King Philip, but never had he made the trip alone without an armada and never had he beheld such bad omens. They could only be premonitions of future disaster, thought the captain-general.

His brooding thoughts turned to the silver. Too much responsibility for only one man, especially when God was not with him. Below, in the hold of his vessel, were four thousand five hundred and eighty wooden chests, weighing one hundred and sixty pounds each. In each of these chests were silver bars weighing seventy pounds apiece, wedges, weighing twenty pounds, and some pesos mined from no base metal but from the highest grade ore. The ship rolled slightly. The weight of the silver made her tender.

All day the captain-general pondered upon these oracles and even as the day was dying, he continued to brood. His men noticed he was not himself, and they commented on it. Not once did the captain-general use the cat on his men, not once did he send one to be keelhauled. He seemed distracted, distant. The stony look had left his face to be replaced by one of puzzlement.

Death by drowning, thought the captain-general. What would it be like? Once he had seen a young boy in Cadiz washed up on the beaches—hair matted, eyes glossy, skin white as ash. He shuddered. Would Don Pedro look like that if he drowned?

His thoughts returned to the oracles. The only relation between the two signs was the damage to the hull of the vessel. He prayed to Saint Elmo to give him another sign into the mystery of the oracles but the saint did not answer him. He slept little that night.

As he fitfully turned and tossed in his sleep, the ship sailed on. At 8.3 knots she made her way easily past the Spanish fortresses of Florida and then gradually passed into English waters. Once during this time, the captain-general drifted off to sleep. But he dreamed bad dreams. He felt he was being stabbed from below and when he awoke, he found a pebble in his mattress just below the small of his back. He threw the pebble out of his bed, but still he did not sleep well.

Come morning, the captain-general awoke to find the ship sailing at 29 degrees northern latitude, past Cape Fear and Topsail Inlet. He spent the rest of the morning taking readings. He wrote in his log—"passed Cape Lookout two leagues to the east and at latitude 35.8, Ocracoke Inlet."

The captain-general went about his normal duties until the ship began to slow down. When the topsails on the main and mizzen masts would draw no wind, he put aside his log and went to investigate the trouble. He ordered the sailors to scurry up the ratlines to set the topgallants, but still the ship would not sail ahead. They had lost the wind.

The captain-general impatiently walked to the bulwarks and peered over the edge. He hated delays, but one had to expect them in a voyage such as this.

Suddenly, without any warning, the ship began to roll. The captain-general's body tensed. There was a heavy ground swell. Although there was no wind, the dashing of long sweeps of water against the ship's hull was plainly felt.

There was a deathlike silence from the men. They all knew what these ground swells meant—a gale.

The captain-general had thought they might run into a gale. Hurricanes came frequently along the American coast in the fall and they were to be expected. But the captain-general was not afraid, for he had the instinctive feeling his ship and the men were not destined to perish in this storm. Death from a storm would have been portended by signs from above the water and not below—not those deadly slashings to the hull. What could they mean? He stared at Saint Elmo's lantern, but still the saint did not answer him.

The captain-general had learned how to read signs from an old aunt in Madrid. He had gone to visit her every summer as a boy, and she had taught him all the saints and what they stood for.

He repeated them on his lips now as he walked among his men. At first he had not believed the old woman when she had told him the saints gave you signs, had laughed in her face, in fact, but one day his aunt had seen a meteor in the sky and said there would be a tremendous fire in the town the next day. When the fire did indeed occur as she predicted, the young Don Pedro no longer doubted his aunt. From that moment on he had become a deeply religious man. He spent all that summer, and succeeding summers, learning the signs. Now he walked among his men, fingering the cross at his neck.

The vessel began to roll heavily, causing an occasional expansion on the sails which made the more experienced sailors doubt which way the currents of air were passing. Suddenly, the ship yawed off course and became unmanageable, falling broadside to the sea. The men feared she would broach to. But the captain-general feared not. His men marveled how when the wind rose to a high pitched whine, he shouted calmly through his speaking trumpet, thundering orders for the sails to be shortened and the ordnance lashed sure.

The faces of his sailors turned instinctively toward the yards. They knotted the reef points and passed the gaskets until the unruly canvas was confined and exchanged for staysails and trysails. Gloomy apprehensions mounted as they waited anxiously for the fury of the gale. But Don Pedro told them not to worry. They would survive the storm. The sailors wondered how he could be so sure. The captain-general told them to trust in God. God, he said, had not meant them to die in this storm. Since God was all they could trust in now, the sailors crossed themselves and were glad they had a captain who was so religious. It instilled confidence.

The wind that had whistled through the shrouds began to howl. The foam glittered in white curls and an endless succession of whiter surges rose above the heavy billows. In time, the whole ocean became white with foam and the waves, instead of rolling about in steady surges, now ripped about in mad gambols.

The captain-general ordered the anchor cable payed out. As the storm increased, the sea seemed to threaten destruction. But still Don Pedro was not afraid. He ordered his men to the bilges to pump water and bale with buckets. He commanded coopers to fill the gaps with caulking where the ship had burst her seams.

Suddenly there was a strain on the rigging and it broke. This was followed by a rending of wood and spars crashing to the deck. Booms knocked two sailors down and they were washed overboard. Surely, thought the men, God had meant for the crew to die in this storm. They waited fearfully for the ship to founder. Some frantically began to confess their sins. But the captain-general walked fearlessly among them telling them death would not come from this storm. No, death would not come from above, the captain-general said. He failed, however, to mention the other signs of death from below—the swordfish, the barrier reefs, the pebble in his bed. Why, thought the captain-general, would God send them this storm when they were to die from other means?

Meanwhile, not more than ten leagues away, the *Adventure* scudded before the gale, her sails bellying out. The sudden storm had forced the men to reef the fabric displayed earlier and to substitute in its place, storm canvas. She had a close-reefed mainsail and foresail and the bonnet off her jib.

Some of the men were extremely fearful the ship would not weather the shore and that she might be broken on the sand bars. The sea churned now, creating tides and eddies around the bars that could dash the vessel to bits. Spray filled the air and stung the men's faces. If the ship weathered the shore, it was certain she would be able to find safe anchorage. But the drift was becoming awful. Blackbeard kept his eye fixed on a point, a certain dune of sand and watched the drift from it. The wind was pulling the vessel to leeward with portentous speed. The men watched as the ship rode the waves toward their doom.

But suddenly the ship felt an undertow of current and was breasted to windward. It had caught the ebb tide. Captain Teach was careful to keep close to the south breakers over the bar where it had two fathoms and a half. The crew made a cast of lead. With the certainty that there was enough water to keep him clear of the bottom at low tide and that his anchors would hold, Captain Teach made a flying moor and payed out the anchor. In the sound side of the inlet, the vessel was safe. The wind could do nothing to them now but whistle in the cordage and spars aloft.

But it was not the wind Blackbeard was worried about, nor his own vessel. He had calculated the *San Rosario* was also in the gale. And if her captain had no knowledge of the Outer Banks, she would be dashed to bits on the treacherous bars, and her treasure lost forever in the depths of the ocean.

Death from below—it was the sand bars of the Outer Banks that God had meant for the captain-general's destruction.

Captain Teach Takes a Prize

When the storm passed that evening at eight o'clock, Blackbeard called down the curses of the heavens upon gales. Gales were the causes of all man's woes from the beginning of time. Deaths at sea, shipwrecks, even pestilences were attributed to gales, although heaven only knew how the last ever could be logically connected to thunder, rain and rising seas. Little did that matter, though, to the pirate who continued to call down God's wrath between prodigious quantities of rum brought to his cabin every half hour by a cabin boy clothed in blue. These curses continued, in fact, until one of the sailors on board the *Adventure* hailed a small dory approaching the pirate vessel.

The figure in the dory was a mysterious one, cloaked surreptitiously in black, his face unrecognizable—due, in part, to the clouds scudding across the wind-swept sky which hid any light from the moon. The figure carried a small lantern by which he had guided himself and a speaking trumpet from which he had hailed the *Adventure*. Curiously, Blackbeard eyed him from the porthole of his vessel, wondering in his unsobered condition who would have the nerve to approach a pirate vessel unaccompanied, and so it seemed, unarmed. He could think of only one man with such unmitigated gall.

His thoughts were confirmed as the man stood up in the flimsy, rocking boat, (wet through by the pounding surf) tossed his oars aside, and then climbed up a rope ladder with the aid of several crewmen. As he stood on deck and tossed his head up into the light of the ship's lantern, Blackbeard could see the granite face of Charles Eden flecked with sea salt and foam.

It was only a moment before the governor disappeared down the hatch and stood dripping water onto the already wet planks just outside

Blackbeard's cabin. He was announced by the cabin boy who set down another round of rum on the table. Eden took off his cloak in the dim cabin, lit only by a flickering candle. The sailor lad said a final word and departed, the parrot in the bronze cage ruffled its feathers, and the two regarded each other with a taciturn solemnity brought on by the seriousness of the hour.

Finally, Blackbeard spoke with a weary voice. "My men are none too happy with the course of events, you may lay to that. Most likely they're scheming for the captainship right now. There's none that's standing by me but one lad as I've took a liking to."

It seemed Eden could only nod in agreement as he reached for a glass of rum. A drop of water fell from the boards as Blackbeard took his pipe and helped himself to some tobacco in a tin on the table. "Damn, dampified planks," the pirate muttered as he struck a match, lit a pipe and then stood up to throw the remains of the matchstick out the porthole.

"Ah yes, me mates would have it out with me sooner or later, they would," Blackbeard continued as he eyed the governor, who was in the midst of pouring himself another drink. "Since you're pouring yourself a glass o' rum, Governor, I'll be so free as to do likewise." Eden poured a glass and Blackbeard swallowed the whole in one gulp.

Neither of them spoke of the *San Rosario*. It seems that often the mention of some catastrophic event in a person's life can create a trauma surpassed by just its thought. Both of these men were not the type to break down in front of another human being, so neither of them broached the topic of the gale, although each knew it was on the other's mind. They could see it in each other's eyes—the look of dogged, defeated resignation.

They drank together for a good part of the evening, conversing on other matters not so relevant. When the two had drained the liquor bottle, Blackbeard called for the cabin boy once again.

The boy, in his haste to be at his captain's beck and call, stumbled and almost spilled the contents of the liquor bottle onto the floor, as he breathlessly opened the door and announced, "I'm come, sir!"

Blackbeard caught the bottle just in time, however, and the next round of drinks were saved. It seems, even in a drunken state, Blackbeard was slow to lose his faculties. The cabin boy waited as the pirate uncorked the bottle and poured two glasses, one for himself and one for Eden.

"Chill enough for you, lad?" Blackbeard asked, in idle conversation as he placed the bottle on the table.

"Aye, sir," the boy said. "A stiff wind blows outside. The sentinel complains."

Blackbeard took up a spyglass and walked to the porthole. Then he raised the spyglass to his eyes and looked out to the land. For as far as they could see stretched the great sand dunes of the Outer Banks—mighty sculptures of wind and time, towering monuments of nature's artifice. Blackbeard had sailed the entire eastern seaboard but he had never seen taller dunes than these. Sometimes, it took a man forty-five minutes to make a trek to their peak. On the highest of the dunes, Blackbeard sighted his sentinel staring out to sea. In the winter when the cold winds began to blow in November, the sentinels would oftentimes find it too cold to keep watch and would consequently come down to the ship.

"Tell him to keep a lookout still," Blackbeard said, his brow knit in thought as he put his spyglass down again. "There may be some wreckage from the Spanish ship."

Governor Eden started at the words "Spanish" and "ship" but he said nothing.

"What's the time, lad?" Blackbeard asked, raising his glass to his mouth.

"Second bell on the middle watch, sir," the boy said. Noticing that his captain was in a talkative mood, he requested from Blackbeard a pirating tale, for he was especially fond of tales of romance and adventure on the high seas. Captain Teach's tales were the most remarkable he had ever heard, and he yearned one day to emulate his captain.

Blackbeard responded by taking the boy aside and remarking that he would be glad to tell him a tale, adding humorously, if it would not "hurt the governor's ears."

Eden shook his head good-naturedly, and the tale began amidst dramatic flourishes of Blackbeard's arms and great gulps of rum. "T'was in Queen Anne's War, when I was barely mor'n a lad such as yourself here," the pirate said, his voice rumbling and deep as he remembered his earlier days on the sea. "I was in Hornigold's crew then. I was quartermaster. We fell in with a Spanish ship. Bound from *Tierra Firme*, she was."

"The bloody Spaniards," the boy remarked, balling his fists into a knot, for he hated the Spanish as much as the next English seaman, and he was proud to say so. He listened enthusiastically as Blackbeard continued.

"Aye," the pirate said, taking a swig from the glass. "And we battled fore and aft a spell and finally we won her."

"Hooray for that," the boy shouted, imagining himself in Blackbeard's position. No doubt, the two could have won a ship here and now, so ready was the boy to do battle with the bloody Spanish.

"Aye," Blackbeard continued. "Now upon this ship, wedded with the captain, was a Spanish lady."

The boy nodded and watched now as the pirate reached for his bottle and poured a drink for the youngster. "Now," continued the pirate, handing a drink to the lad, "I asks the captain, I did, if the lady had any booty."

Then the governor and the pirate watched with marked amusement as the boy, wishing to appear manly, drank down the liquor given to him. It was much too strong for him and he choked once. Nevertheless, he finished off the entire dram. When he had finished, Blackbeard continued his story.

"Now this captain, he said there was no booty to be had aboard his ship. So's we cut off his little finger; a fat little pinky he had too, for we know'd he was lying. He finally come to tell us the lady had a diamond as big as my knuckle." Blackbeard chuckled secretly. "So's upon my account the men searched the lady, but found it nowheres upon her. Now the men growing frightfully angry was about to set upon and kill the captain when his wife speaks up to me, 'I'll show you the whereabouts of the diamond. But the quartermaster must take me to my cabin.' Now then, the lady took Blackbeard here to her abode, and she told him the diamond was in a most private place which she most willingly asked me to remove. And so I did," Blackbeard said, finishing off his tale with a hearty laugh and a great belch.

The boy seemed to enjoy the tale too, for the chuckled in response, no doubt imagining himself in the pirate's shoes.

Eden smiled, but as he did a feeling of fierce envy stirred within him, a feeling that was all too evident. Blackbeard caught the remnants of it in the shadows of the candlelight that flickered and died across Eden's face. In response, the pirate sent the lad off with the empty bottles, mentioning that the sails wanted mending.

When the boy was out of earshot, the pirate stood up, walked to the porthole and threw the tobacco ash from his pipe into the ocean. He made no attempt to hide his feelings as he turned to speak to Eden. "So the governor still wishes to be a pirate."

Governor Eden stared at Blackbeard. Suddenly, things he had hitherto left unsaid were said. "Damn you," Eden said, slamming his fists down on the table. "You don't know how it made the rest of us feel when you first came to Bath Town. It was just you, mind you, a man in black boots and hat and people came from miles around just to talk with you, just to see you."

Blackbeard nodded in understanding. He had never seen the governor quite so emotional. "Aye," he answered. "Women flocked to keep company with me. People were so prodigiously afraid of me, why, just to hear my name they'd shiver in their bootstraps. My match has never been seen before—and never will be seen again."

In frustration, Eden sent his glass flying through the air. It shattered against the ship's deck. He gritted his teeth. "Just once, I wanted to be like you...to be a pirate...to be the greatest."

"Aye, the great Blackbeard," Captain Teach shouted and his strange sardonic laughter filled the night air. "Everyone wants to be him...even that sailor lad."

Eden must have indeed wondered then why a pirate such as Blackbeard, the greatest of them all, should mock himself so. But the pirate did not explain his actions—dared not, in fact, tell Eden why his dreams were all idle fantasies, his hopes groundless. For all that would be gained by telling would be disbelief or, if believed, the gallows, so instead he let the governor think what he wished.

The governor was puzzled at the pirate's laughter. But his attention was caught now by laughter from other quarters—specifically from above deck. It was so boisterous that both Eden and Blackbeard left off their drinking to find out what was going on. They found the crewmen making fun of an old fisherman they had persuaded to come aboard ship. He had become the sport of these murderous cutthroats. After he had gulped down several drinks, one of the pirates had taken the opportunity to grab the poor man's watch and chortling that it made a pretty good football was now kicking it about the deck of the ship.

The fisherman, whimpering that the watch was his only valuable and to "pray please have a care," only caused to excite the other pirates even more, and now they, in turn, joined in passing the watch to each other as they scuffled about the deck. The poor man tried to retrieve the piece of metal, but only succeeded in getting his ass kicked in the process. When the watch was finally retrieved and the man remarked that it would take a great deal to mend it, a bucket of sea water was poured on it to see if that would help mend the works. The pirates could not help but burst into boisterous laughter at this episode.

In the midst of all this commotion a voice was heard, shrill and clear across the expanse of land and sea. "Sail, ho!" It was the sentinel on the highest dune telling of a passing ship.

Immediately, the crew froze in their tracks. The fisherman was forgotten. All eyes were turned toward Blackbeard as the pirate became rigid with attention.

With a wild look of excitement in his eyes, Blackbeard spun round to face the sentinel and cupped his hands about his mouth. "How stands she?"

"To windward," came the voice almost immediately back across the wind-swept sky.

"Her burden?" Blackbeard asked.

"From the beacon on her mast she seems fifteen hundred tons," was the response. "She might be a Spanish galleon."

To Eden, the words were miraculous. He had concluded earlier, along with the others present, that the galleon had been lost in the storm. This was nothing short of a godsend. He whirled around to face the pirate. Immediately, their eyes met and Blackbeard, in response, clapped the governor warmly on the shoulder.

A roar went up from the crowd of pirates, so loud that Blackbeard had to threaten death to quiet them.

The crew was ready to fight the ship and board her, and they said so in voices loud and mingled in the night air. But Blackbeard held them back. They were outnumbered by the very size of the galleon. To do battle with the *San Rosario* now would mean the *Adventure* would be blasted to smithereens.

"Hold your fire," Blackbeard shouted to the men at the guns. Understandably, the men were upset by Blackbeard's unwillingness to do battle and they grumbled and growled as they took turns looking through the spyglass at the ship on the horizon. Twelve million pesos worth of Spanish silver was floating idly past them on the horizon.

They were even more upset when the sentinel cried, "She plies to windward." It was now or never if they were to take the silver.

Blackbeard knew all this, of course, and his face was the very picture of gloom as he paced up and down the quarter-deck, his brow knit in thought, his hands behind his back. He gazed out at the galleon slowly passing them in the night.

It was then that Eden took it upon himself to step forward. He lunged at the fisherman who had been all but forgotten in the sudden appearance of the ship.

"Oh, do not clout me," the fisherman shouted. "Have mercy, sir, for I'm but a poor, miserable fisherman with little to call my own." He trembled, not unduly, after the beating given him earlier by the pirates, and he hid his head in his hands.

The other pirates including Blackbeard looked at Eden with a certain degree of irritation.

Not only was Eden worrying the fisherman now, but the governor was demanding his horse—a poor, mangy nag not worth a guinea since she was lame. This was quite clear to the pirates who could now see her limping up and down the beach slowly as she waited for her master. However, the fact that the horse was lame seemed to excite Eden even more, so that most of the pirates formulated the obvious opinion that Eden had gone quite mad. For what did he expect to do—ride out to the ship on a horse?

Eden was now asking Blackbeard for a lantern from the ship.

Blackbeard was about to agree with the crewmen on the subject of the governor's madness when he recalled an old pirate's trick he had learned from Hornigold years ago. How Eden knew about it, he didn't know, but when he turned to face the governor, his face did not hold the puzzled look of his crewmen, but a look of enlightenment and hope.

Quickly, he ordered his men not to stand there like nitwits but to "bear a hand" and "fetch a lantern" and "to bring forth matches from the magazine."

The pirates looked at Blackbeard with a dazed expression on their faces. But at Blackbeard's insistence they followed orders, returning with matches and a lantern for the governor. Before they knew it, the governor had taken his dory and was steering toward the land.

Eden wasted no time in shoring the boat. Rushing toward the horse, he mounted her. He kicked her heartlessly and she started up, trying to get air in her lungs—an old bag with the airs of Aeolus bellowing through her. She wheezed and snorted and breathed heavily until she finally got her second wind and then she took off as in her more youthful days, toward the nearest sand dune that rose two hundred feet into the starless sky.

After much prodding, she reached the dune. Here she slowed down, her hooves sinking into the soft sand as she began to climb the towering mass of slowly shifting earth. Eden urged her up the steep mound.

At the peak Eden dismounted her, keeping her at his side as he struck a match to the edge of his boot. Sparks fired. Swiftly, he touched the flame to the lantern, watching it take on the look of a beacon in the night. That done, it was only a short while before he had the lantern tied to the mare's saddle with a lanyard. Holding the mare's reins in one hand, he walked her across the dunes, the uneven gait of the horse making the lantern bob up and down.

On board the *Adventure,* the crew suddenly surmised Eden's plan, and from the deck of the ship Blackbeard was heard to whisper to himself, "Blast me, he just might have the makings of a pirate." For the horse, walking on the dune, looked to the crewmen like a ship's lantern floating up and down on the waves.

To the lookout on board the *San Rosario*, that light bobbing up and down was unmistakably a lantern which was always placed at the top of a ship's mast. He called to the captain-general to check, and the both of them, taking turns at the spyglass, came to the conclusion that it was owned by a ship of approximately fifteen hundred tons, for it had at least a two hundred foot mast.

The captain-general was most relieved that there was another ship in view. It confirmed his idea that he was in deep waters for a ship with a two hundred foot mast would have an extremely deep draft. Earlier he had taken soundings and was satisfied the waters were deep enough, but one could never be too sure of anything at sea. He would have liked to be even more certain of his location, and for that reason he had earlier tried to take the latitude. But no reading could be attained since the north star was still obstructed by clouds.

Unknown to the captain-general, the gale had blown his ship quite close to shore. He was correct in assuming he was in deep waters, but approximately two leagues dead ahead lay the shoals of the Outer Banks.

The captain-general was also relieved to see this ship for another reason. The *San Rosario* was badly in need of repairs and could not make an ocean voyage. If this merchantman was friendly, he could trade off some of the silver for supplies, and if she wasn't, he certainly couldn't be any the worse.

Indeed, the *San Rosario* was little short of being a wreck. In the storm, the mainmast had broken. Falling over the side, the mainmast had brought down the mizzen-mast and all its hamper. To add to this misfortune, the foremast had snapped. All that remained was the mutilated foremast, the foreyard and sail and the fallen head gear. All the rest was strewn about the deck. Crosstrees and trestletrees rose on the summits of the swells. The eyes of the men that had survived the gale were desolate. The tracery of ropes and rigging was now a mutilated heap of rubble settling on the troughs of the ocean.

It was a matter of luck that the ship had not been completely wrecked, and Captain Don Pedro gave his thanks to God and Saint Elmo for this, although the storm had taken half his crew. He looked at the survivors, worn out, hungry and already sick. But he still wondered why God had sent the storm and what the oracles had meant. He crossed himself as he turned over the signs in his head—the swordfish, the pebble, the reefs. Then crossing himself again and praying for luck, he set his course to the southwest. The *San Rosario* proceeded toward the light.

The *San Rosario* proceeded boldly through the billowing waves, her bow pointed toward the deadly sand bar. She advanced on the towering dunes that rose as the masts of a ship.

Suddenly one of the men caught sight of a curl of white water directly ahead. Then the appalling sound of breakers was heard. The captain-general paled. Instinct or experience he knew not, but his throat went bone dry. The oracle...death from below. Within a moment, the captain-general knew they were about to hit bottom.

Quickly, he ordered the helm to be kept fast. The foreyards were swung heavily against the wind and the vessel was soon whirling around on her heel. However, sudden movement did little good. The sea was now covered with foam. The captain-general heard the dashing of breakers against the shore. They were already in the jaws of destruction.

Aware now that it was too late to do anything but watch in horror, the captain-general waited as his ship shattered her timbers on the sandbar across an inlet.

The crew on Blackbeard's ship shouted for joy.

It was only awhile before the *Adventure* had set sail and was headed straight for the Spanish vessel. The pirates wasted no time in hurling their boarding axes across the ship that had now settled and was no longer taking on water.

Not knowing what to expect, they were elated to find the Spaniards in such poor condition that they surrendered without so much as one cutlass being drawn.

The pirates were quick to dispose of their enemies—stabbing most of them and throwing them overboard. Their screams could be heard over the churning foam of the breakers. But the pirates took little notice of the screams or of the blood that was slickening the deck of the galleon. Instead, they turned their attention to the treasure.

From the shattered hulk of the wrecked vessel tangled in broken cordage and mutilated spars, the first chest was brought up from the hold. For a moment the pirates stood transfixed by the thought of its contents, and then all at once there were the sounds of hurrahs and huzzas as they leapt at the booty. With groans, they thrust it at the feet of their leader. And then Captain Teach stepped forward. Wielding his cutlass high in the air, the pirate hurled the weapon against the wooden chest. The wood rended and pesos flew under the pressure of the heavy metal. Glittering in the darkness, they spilled onto the deck of the ship.

The men grabbed handfuls of the plunder, and after gleefully examining it, they began stuffing their pockets with the swag, cramming it into their clothes until they were brimming. Amidst the sounds of the sea pounding against the shore was the noise of their unmitigated mirth. In another moment, the pirates had gone into the hold again and had brought up more booty—this time wedges and ingots of the precious metal. They were unbelieving at first and then amazed at the vast wealth that was now theirs. They ignored the dead bodies of the Spaniards around them. The wealth of the Indies was at their feet.

Blackbeard lowered a dory into the water to head to the land. He must see to it that the treasure was put on board some vessels that Eden had hired earlier. It could then be stored away as soon as possible so that no one could detect the deed the pirates had just committed.

When Blackbeard had shored his boat, he saw a figure appear on horseback and make its way toward him. The horse stopped. The deep, yet steady voice of Governor Eden was heard to say only two words, "The plunder."

Blackbeard smiled and pulled a small bottle of rum from his pocket when he saw the man admiring the rewards of his work. "To a fellow pirate," he said, throwing the bottle in Eden's direction.

Eden caught the bottle, took a swallow, wiped his mouth across his sleeve, and returned the bottle to Blackbeard. Some crewmen who had come to shore stood about him and let forth a round of cheers in gratitude. Several hoisted the governor on their shoulders and carried him about the beach.

When they let him down he was laughing, and Blackbeard noticed it was the first time he had ever seen the governor laugh. As the pirates danced and shouted among themselves, throwing coins of silver into the air, Blackbeard approached Eden. He took the governor aside.

They stood together on the beach out of hearing distance of the crewmen. Their faces were lost in the shadows, the only light coming from the reflection of silver in the pupils of their eyes.

"Now, then, governor," Blackbeard said softly. "When's the time my men will be getting their shareouts?" The light created a devilish look in his eyes.

It was all too evident from the crewmen's actions here tonight that they expected to take the silver immediately. Already they were talking of what they would buy with the booty.

"They'll get it in time," Eden said, his eyes turning away from Blackbeard and watching the pirates making merry on the beach.

Blackbeard knew he couldn't keep his men waiting long. When he spoke again, it was with an intensity which his character was accustomed to only in the most emotional times. "Now, Governor," he said loudly, "Between man and man, this ain't good enough. I done your bidding, you can't deny that. But if me and my men don't get our fair share of this treasure soon..."

Eden shook his head at this point.

The pirate braced himself. He was getting nowhere with this line of reasoning. With all the cunning he had gained in his years of piracy, he began to argue in a more subtle and yet powerful way. "Avast, me hearty," he said, his eyes now glittering wickedly. "Now what do you think would happen if I was to let that fisherman on the ship go? Why, he'd go straight to the sheriff, no doubt, and the sheriff, why, he might just investigate the goings-on. T'wouldn't do you good to be found with a buccaneer such as myself, and you may lay to that. Aye, you'd be found consort to a pirate. Upon my affydavy, t'would fair ruin your reputation as governor, and them's my views."

For the first time, Governor Eden trembled in Blackbeard's presence. Then he winced. "So you're crossing me."

"Aye," Blackbeard said, his eyes twinkling as he reaffirmed the governor's thoughts.

The governor turned away from the pirate now and stood in deep thought for a moment. Then his eyes looked straight at the pirate. What would happen, he thought, if he called the man's bluff? So in a voice clear and calm, he said, "Go ahead and let him go. I could just as soon say I'd found you hereabouts with this treasure."

"Found me?"

"Yes, found you," Eden repeated craftily. "And was arresting you for plundering a ship from the king of Spain."

Blackbeard stared at Eden. Suddenly, the smile vanished from his face.

"Go ahead," Eden said, glaring at Blackbeard now.

Blackbeard was silent, pondering thoughts in his head.

Eden grabbed the pirate by the waistcoat. "Go on," he whispered in his ear. "You forget who I am—representative of His Majesty, the king of England—the arm of the law—the governor of North Carolina. Go ahead, and I'll have you arrested, and you'll lose your precious life."

"Now then, Governor, no need to be handling the materials roughly," Blackbeard whispered, shoving away Eden's hand. He took a step backward from the man and frowned. "There ain't a particle o' service in that, and no mistake." He paused to gain control of his emotions. "Now I never meant you no harm, Governor. I'm on your side, you can count on that." He dusted off his waistcoat. "You see, freebooters usually puts little trust among themselves and right they are to do so. Now, then, matey, you mightn't know where we might be getting some brandy would you? Yes? Well, many a night I've been dreaming of fine brandy—Portuguese mostly—and woke up again and found nothing."

"We're in this together, then?" Eden nodded and gave Blackbeard a piercing glance.

Blackbeard was quick to avert his eyes. "Aye," he said. "You and me must stick close like, back to back, that's clear."

Blackbeard trembled again. He should never have pulled that trick on the governor. All he wanted was the money for his men. But he knew Eden wasn't bluffing. The man would do anything for this treasure. That thought scared Blackbeard more than all else.

Blackbeard put his hands in his waistcoat pocket. He didn't want the governor to see they were still trembling.

When Blackbeard stepped forth from the shadows to the shoreline, he gave his men a reproachful look and suddenly he drew forth his cutlass, hurling it dramatically in mid-air. "Unhand that, you scalawag," he shouted to one of his men who had pocketed some of the silver. With the tip of his weapon, he ripped the man's pocket to shreds. The silver spilled out onto the beach.

Quite naturally, the pirates were upset. They thought the treasure rightfully theirs and they turned to face their captain with scowls and curses. Didn't they capture the treasure? Wasn't it theirs to do with as they wished?

Blackbeard began a subtle yet sanctimonious browbeating. "Now as I'm speaking to you there, I'm speaking to you all," he said, still pointing his cutlass at the sea dog who had his pocket ripped. "Now, then, you'd bungle this whole thing would you?"

The sea dog grumbled in response. He made a circular pattern in the sand with his feet as Blackbeard continued. "Don't you know there's them that would question the whereabouts of our sudden wealth?"

A crewman objected at this point. "We'll go some place else and spend it."

"And what honest English official would take this silver without question?" Blackbeard argued.

The crewmen grumbled. Another spoke up. "There's plenty of dishonest officials."

"None that won't demand a share and leave you penniless," their captain retorted. Still receiving objections, Blackbeard threw up his hands in a gesture of weariness and defeat. "Go ahead and take it then. But mark me, you'll rue the day the *San Rosario* sank off this here coast."

Some of the crew members picked up a few coins then, but they hesitated before putting them in their pockets.

"Aye," Blackbeard said, realizing his words were having the intended effect. "You'll rue this day, you will. Take it and by gum, we're that near the scaffold that my neck's stiff with thinking on hanging. You've seen 'em maybe in chains—sea gulls about 'em, peck, pecking their eyeballs, seamen pointing 'em out to passers-by. Well, them's will be us, by the powers. They'll say, 'I knowed him well. There's Blackbeard the pirate, fiercest of them all.'"

Several of the men, crestfallen now, looked at the silver in their hand and placed it back in the chests. "Aye," the pirate said. "Wait is what I say until a few months pass and this *San Rosario* ship is forgotten and no longer missed by Spain."

Thus it was that after some argumentation and quite a few frowns, it was decided the treasure would be stored in Tobias Knight's barn. Here there would be little interference from governmental officials. Already the contents of the French sloop from Antigua lay there.

The discussion was ended only moments before a streak of lightning swept across the sky and a crack of thunder was heard. The storm wasn't over yet, thought Blackbeard, as he ordered his men to begin the loading of silver on Eden's ships.

Blackbeard's Quartermaster Clapped in Jail

For the past several weeks Alexander Spotswood's preoccupation with capturing Blackbeard the pirate had gradually increased to the point where he thought of little else.

It was Spotswood's unquestioned assumption that only the capture of the pirate could restore unity, peace, and harmony to his world, now threatened by rebels, anarchists and other destructive forces. In the past, the cause of all his grief had been pirates, and one pirate in particular had come to represent them all. In the governor's mind, Blackbeard had come to symbolize evil, a black spot on an otherwise pure and harmonious world—a spot that must be removed at all costs if England and his government were to survive.

Each exterior threat only served to deepen his conviction. Now that threat was William Byrd of Westover, Virginia who had been sent to England by several of his council members who objected to Spotswood's rule. Spotswood was convinced Byrd was influencing the king to remove him from office. Byrd was a wealthy and well-known figure, both at home and abroad, and Spotswood feared the worst from him. If he were to become an influential figure among that small but powerful group of Londoners who frequented the Virginia Coffeehouse (a social coffeehouse that had become political because of the influential politicians that frequented it) the effects could be disastrous. In fact, at this very moment Spotswood was writing a letter to Colonel Blakiston, agent of the colony of Virginia, telling him just that. "I think it is doing little honor to the government of Virginia to have its council appointed by the Virginia Coffeehouse," he wrote.

Katherine Russell had noticed her uncle's paranoia and his unnatural preoccupation with Blackbeard. This preoccupation did not affect his daily activities, however. He took his tea promptly at four o'clock. He still walked Rover every afternoon at precisely five o'clock. He went to church every Sunday, and he still picked quarrels with those who sought to drag the flag of England in the dust. It was his nighttime activities that Katherine was worried about. For the rampant rumors of Spotswood's relations with his niece were not unfounded—indeed, the two were participating in an incestuous relationship. But in the past month Spotswood had had trouble keeping up his end of the relationship with Katherine.

Impotency in the eighteenth century was regarded with a great deal of anxiety and vexation. Little was actually known about the act of sex itself, much less the lack of it. Causes of impotency were attributed to venereal disease or improper diet. Cures included anything and everything, and often included black magic. A gentleman suffering from this malady was obliged to eat much ginseng and oysters. For the past month Spotswood had lunched upon generous helpings of oysters and dined upon boiled ginseng roots. Since Spotswood detested oysters and was not fond of roots either, the servants naturally suspected the problem, and there was much suppressed laughter with the service of each meal— an embarrassment both to Katherine and Spotswood.

Katherine could remember distinctly the first time Spotswood's deleterious condition had occurred. She had greeted him from her bedroom one evening with nothing on but a hat. When she had asked him if he liked what he saw, he had answered by saying he thought the hat suited her but it should have another feather in it. Then he sat down on the four-poster bed where it was their custom to make passionate love. When she asked him what he was thinking about, he had merely said, "pirates."

"Pirates!" she said, surprised.

"Yes," he remarked, striking up a conversation. "These people in the colonies have the supinest notions. They feel that either their poverty will discourage or the wilderness frustrate any invasion. But let them beware. The Spanish are below, the French to the north and the pirates in North Carolina."

She nodded in agreement.

"We must add to our defenses," he said.

Katherine couldn't imagine why they would need any more defense in the colony. A true military man, Spotswood had already increased

Virginia's defenses to the point of stationing a squadron of the Royal Navy to patrol the coast, building a magazine, and leading an expedition across the Appalachians to discover the situation of the French. But she did not state any objection. When he left her room that evening, he gave her a kiss on her cheek and asked if she shouldn't have something more on. "You don't want to catch a cold, my dear," he said. From that time on, Katherine had found their nightly sexual escapades had been replaced by talk of pirates.

A case in point was only two days later when she had found it necessary to become a bit more bold when he entered her room.

"The pirates, so I hear, are planning to build another Madagascar at Ocracoke Inlet," he said, sitting on the bed.

"Oh?" She sat down beside him on the bed and began to unbutton his shirt. She mentioned she had heard something to the effect of a buildup at Ocracoke. Madagascar was the pirate haven in the Indian Ocean. She doubted that a small island such as Ocracoke could ever be a hang-out for an entire hoard of pirates, but she assumed Spotswood could use this as an argument to increase defense in the colonies. She laid his shirt on the bed and then took off his powdered wig. He seemed not to notice what she was doing, but he did cough as some of the dust from the wig circulated in the air.

"Perhaps you also heard mention," Spotswood continued, "that Vane sailed into Ocracoke and exchanged mutual civilities with Teach."

She had heard the name "Vane" before. "Isn't that the selfsame sea dog from Providence?" She massaged his back a bit, and then began to undo his belt.

She thought he was nodding in response to her massaging, but the nod was actually in response to her question.

"Calico Jack joined them," he said. "William Rhett of South Carolina was sent to capture the rascal, but he mistook Major Stede Bonnet· for Vane and captured him instead."

"Bonnet." Katherine pondered the name. "Isn't that the fop that sailed with Blackbeard?"

"The very one."

"The gentleman pirate, they call him."

"Yes," Spotswood said. "Rhett received great honors for capturing Bonnet and a great deal of money—pirate gold, of course."

"Of course," Katherine repeated. It was an unquestioned assumption, founded on rumor, suspicion and hearsay, that pirates had hoards of gold and silver. In actuality, those pirates that had treasure were few and far between and were often robbed of it by legal or illegal means.

Katherine began to reach down at the buttons of Spotswood's pants, but he did not seem to notice.

"Blackbeard still plagues Virginia's capes," Spotswood said with a slight hesitation in his voice that seemed to indicate some frustration. He also began to display some discomfiture evidenced by a nervous tapping of his feet and a slight whistling under his breath.

Katherine nodded and then reached down. He was limp as a wet noodle.

Katherine had no idea why Spotswood was substituting pirates for sex in his nightly rounds to her room. Little did she know that Spotswood was feeling a failure in his political life, and therefore, could not function well sexually. But she did not entertain the thought of a relationship between sex and one's daily life. So, naturally, Katherine assumed the worst. She thought the fault lay in herself.

She did everything she could possibly think of to put some romance into their life. On one occasion, she fainted on the dining room table. Smelling salts would not revive her. It was only when her dress was entirely unbuttoned that she finally came to. She tried going to his room in various stages of undress. But all her sexual underthings seemed to remind him of was pirates, be it garters or corsets. He seemed to have forgotten that the act of intercourse even existed. Finally, she wrote love letters to him in invisible ink. But Spotswood's elixir failed to work and he never read the letters. In exasperation, she began to threaten and cajole. But all this was to no avail. He still remained steadfast.

Given Spotswood's reluctance to participate in the act of copulation, it is a wonder that Katherine Russell even bothered to continue her escapades. Nevertheless, she did, and her concern mounted as his interest decreased. After a few more incidents of disappointment, she made one last effort a fortnight later. She went to considerable expense to have transported into her boudoir a number of mirrors, because she knew looking glasses held a unique fascination for Spotswood.

When Spotswood entered her room that evening, he found the air softly scented with the fragrance of jasmine. But Katherine, instead of combing her hair, was undressing before a row of mirrors. Spotswood thought the mirrors gave the room an air of decadence as she casually undressed, placing her clothes on a walnut chair with silver snuff covers.

He sat down on the bed and watched her, his eyes glowing with excitement. The mirrors had aroused him. But he was even more aroused by what he had to tell her, and he took great pride as he reconnoitered the day's events. He, Spotswood, had been in luck. Two of his marshals had just arrested William Howard, one time quartermaster of Blackbeard. Strolling the streets of Williamsburg, the wizened little man, rascally of eye and with a shock of unkempt hair, had just come from a seaport town where he had attempted to induce sailors to join him in forming a company which would then seize a vessel suited to his purpose and set out to sea for plunder. On the charge of vagrancy, he had been detained in the Williamsburg prison. Although he had put up a good fight, hiring the lawyer Holloway (who was represented as supporting pirates and who had Howard's arrestors jailed under charges of unlawful detainment) Howard was still imprisoned. Indeed, Spotswood had visited him that very morning.

While speaking with Howard, Spotswood had made a bargain. He would restore Howard's freedom if the pirate would cooperate by giving him some valuable information.

Dressed only in her corset and stockings now, Katherine listened patiently as she doused the lights from the flickering candles in the room.

Spotswood's eyes followed her as he talked of Howard. "I've found his lurking hole," Spotswood said. "He weighs anchor near the south tip of Ocracoke Island."

"How many vessels are under his command?" she asked casually.

"Only one, the *Adventure*." He walked the length of the room to stand over her as she undid her stockings. He put his hand lightly on her shoulders and she kissed it ever so softly. He smiled. It would be an easy victory for Spotswood if he caught Blackbeard off guard. "He no longer has a fleet," Spotswood continued. "The *Queen Anne's Revenge*, the French Guineaman of forty guns, ran aground on a sand bar. And Major Bonnet took the *Revenge* of twelve guns."

"How many guns does the *Adventure* have?" she asked.

"Eight."

"Only eight!" she responded in surprise.

"And only forty hands," he replied.

"You're very lucky," Katherine said. "You'll defeat him easily."

"I should think so," Spotswood said, smiling at the thought.

"Of course, you won't free Howard before you capture the pirate. He just might get word to Blackbeard," she added.

"Free him!" Spotswood said. "I have no intention of freeing the man. He'll be strung up like any other ill-looked sea dog."

"But you said..." Katherine began, looking puzzled.

"What I said and what I do, my dear, are two entirely different things. Do you think I'd actually restore a pirate's freedom who had my marshals arrested? Certainly not!"

"Oh." Katherine knew very little of political matters. Furthermore, she was more concerned with Spotswood's hand on her shoulder than a pirate's life at this moment.

So she stood up and caressed him softly, leading him to the bed. In the corner of the room was his silver hilted sword and her eyes swept across the erect tip.

When they were in bed, she moved her body over his, her mouth touching his neck, her hands caressing his shoulders.

For a moment his eyes glowed; but then they went blank again.

She lay back in bed. Here, Katherine, for all her persistence, seemed to falter.

"I can not, my dear," he said, unable to bring himself to look at her. "It seems I please no one now. Not the king, not the people. Powerless, I..." His voice broke off with emotion.

In that one instant, Katherine must have finally began to divine the underlying cause of Spotswood's inability to maintain an erection, for in that one instant she gave no indication of going ahead with her seduction. Instead, she answered him by saying, "Soon you will capture Blackbeard."

Lying back in the bed, staring at the ceiling, for her sake, she hoped it would be soon.

A Visitation
to the Silversmith's Shop

The sight of Charles Eden entering James Geddy's silver shop one fine fall day was not uncommon, for the governor took quite a liking to silver and often shopped here. He also came here for other things, since the silversmith was also a gunsmith, founder, cutler, blacksmith, jeweler, engraver, watch finisher, milliner and import merchant of Bath.

What the silversmith found uncommon was Charles Eden's behavior. It was apparent from the first that he was reluctant to enter the shop, evidenced by his hesitation at the door—a full minute in duration. Once inside, his hesitation was even more apparent. Instead of greeting the silversmith in his usual manner, his eyes made a clean sweep of the room, inspecting every corner; he glanced suspiciously over his shoulder; he watched the passers-by outside the shop's windows with an extreme intensity. Only when the silversmith, a short black-haired man, put aside the watch he was cleaning and stood up behind the counter did the governor speak—and then most strangely.

"Evening governor," Geddy said.

"Good evening," Eden answered. This answer was the governor's only response for a half-minute or so. Such an unwillingness on the governor's part to make his request known prompted Geddy to continue the conversation.

"How may I be serving you, sir?" Geddy was quite anxious to please the governor for he considered himself only an average man in the daily affairs of the world. But when the governor became one of his clients he felt a certain headiness because he was serving such an outstanding gentleman. Geddy seemed to gain an air of distinction when associated with those of breeding. Even now his speech became markedly improved, his bearing more refined.

Eden knew all this, of course. He had been a client of Geddy's for years. Indeed, for a moment he gazed on Geddy with an air of marked amusement. But his humor quickly changed. He showed a trace of concern as he looked about the shop. "Are we alone?" he asked.

The silversmith raised an eyebrow. What was the governor up to, he wondered? He leaned closer to Eden at this instant, and remarked in a voice softer than before. "Yes sir," he said, not a hairsbreadth from the governor. "We're alone, sir, or my name isn't James Geddy." His curiosity aroused, Geddy waited in anticipation for the governor to speak.

The governor raised his shoulders and braced himself before he responded. Finally, he took a deep breath and said, "I'm looking to have some casting done."

"Casting, sir?" asked the obviously inquisitive Geddy.

"Yes," Eden responded.

"I do all you see, sir," Geddy said, waving his hand about the room.

Eden directed his attention toward these few small articles and then shrugged. Seemingly, he was dissatisfied. "Perhaps I have been told wrongly."

"Told wrongly?" the silversmith asked, puzzled. "What is it you were told, sir?"

Without even waiting for the silversmith's explanation, Charles Eden backed away toward the door. Clearly, his hesitation seemed confirmed. "I need some things made into rather large casts," he said. "Perhaps, you don't have the facilities." His hand on the doorknob, he was about to leave when the silversmith responded.

"Well, what manner of casts did you have in mind, governor?" Business was slow this year and he didn't want to lose a customer if he could help it, especially such an important customer as Eden. Geddy often boasted in private of the governor's frequent visits to his shop, and when he bought an article, Geddy was sure to pass on word to his customers, for Eden was a trend-setter in the community.

Governor Eden paused for an instant, his hand leaving the doorknob. He turned back around to face Geddy and then in a voice firm, yet quiet, he said, "I need some anchors cast."

The silversmith looked puzzled. "Anchors?" he asked. Anchors were usually forged and he did not have the facilities for forging. "Don't you want them forged, sir?"

"No. I wish them cast."

"Well, it's possible," Geddy said. "But they won't have the strength needed."

Eden nodded, then continued speaking. "But this must be a goodly number."

"A goodly number?" The silversmith wondered what number Eden had in mind. He was not equipped to handle large orders.

"Actually," Eden said, looking around the room to reassure himself that they were truly alone, "I'll need twelve."

"Twelve!" The silversmith was surprised. "That's a quantity."

Eden began to edge toward the door again, remarking, "If you don't think you can handle it..."

Looking back on the incident the silversmith acknowledged that he would have referred Eden to another shop at that moment had not Eden phrased his remark in such a way that it was a direct challenge to Geddy. He felt a necessity as of that moment to uphold his shop's reputation, and so, he remarked, "Wait now. I can handle it. All I said was I reckoned twelve a quantity."

"Good," Eden said. Thus reassured, he made a final decision to stay in the shop for the time being. He took a pipe from his breast pocket and lit it.

In an attempt to reassure the governor still further, Geddy brought himself to the front of the counter and crossed the room. In an instant he had locked the door and closed the blind to the small silver shop, so that those passers-by outside quite naturally assumed the shop was closed for the day. Then placing the key to the shop in his pants pocket, he returned to his former position.

This time Geddy leaned closer to the governor in a conspiratorial fashion. "Now, then, governor, if this is something you'd rather not have known you can count on me, sir. I won't breathe a word." Geddy awaited Eden's answer with breathless anticipation, for he would have liked nothing better than to be "in on" something with such an outstanding personage as the governor.

However, Eden did not make his intentions known so soon to Geddy. Instead, he exhaled his smoke, watching the curiosity on Geddy's face mount with each passing minute. Actually, he found all this circumspection tedious, but it was necessary to convince Geddy of the genuineness of his transaction. So he adopted a pose of extreme nervousness, drumming his fingers anxiously on the counter. It was evident from his posture that he did not trust Geddy quite yet.

Fearing that he might lose all his headway in this agreement, Geddy coughed abruptly and then continued the conversation. "Well, sir, will you be wanting the anchors cast in iron?"

"It's not iron," Eden said, displaying some discomfiture at the thought of revealing more information.

"Bronze, is it then?"

"No." Eden bit his lip. To all appearances, he seemed put in a spot.

"Then what?" Geddy asked impatiently.

The time had come, thought Eden, to reveal to Geddy what he had come here for. So, with the necessary dramatic flourishes brought on by the governor leaning closer to Geddy and speaking in a voice much softer than before, he said, "Silver."

"Twelve silver anchors!" The silversmith's eyes opened wide in astonishment. Never in his life had he been asked to do a job quite so absurd and quite so costly.

Eden put his finger to his lips when Geddy shouted, and Geddy looked nervously around the room as Eden had done before him. Then he blinked. He stared up at the ceiling then and plucked his lower lip.

Eden could almost see Geddy's mind working, thinking over the meaning for a request for twelve silver anchors. It implied something criminal. If Geddy were to take the information to the right sources, he could make quite a bit of money if he knew the details.

"Why, sir," Geddy said, "I hardly know where I could get that much silver. Nowhere in the colonies, anyhow. Not in Boston, surely, no not there. New York, now maybe. Bless me, it'll have to be shipped, and there's shipping expenses to be added to the cost, now, let's see that's two shillings per pound export taxes and..."

"Quiet!" Eden could stand no more of the man's constant chatter. "I'll be bringing the silver around. All you have to do is the casting."

"You will, sir!" Geddy said, amazed at the thought of anyone having that much silver in North Carolina. Then pausing to collect his thoughts, he stared suspiciously at the governor. "Now where'd you be getting all that silver?" he asked.

The governor had been counting on Geddy's question. In fact, he knew the success of his entire mission this day depended on how Geddy would take his response to it. He made a depreciating gesture with his hands. "It's for the king, you see."

"The king!" Geddy said, puzzled. Surely the king wouldn't be involved in anything illegal. His thoughts along that line ended as abruptly as they had started.

"It's most secret," Eden said, taking Geddy fully into his confidence. Now that his information was out, he seemed more nervous than before. "That's right," he said, glancing this way and that. "It's for the king."

"Oh, I take your meaning." Geddy really understood quite little of this conversation, although he had figured by now that he was involved in quite an important undertaking. All suspicions of Eden's involvement in something illegal vanished from his thoughts. He, James Geddy, was to be part of a mission for the king. His life suddenly had meaning, purpose, a destiny. He fairly beamed with excitement. He was intoxicated with the thought of being associated with royalty. Perhaps he would be famous after this, his works displayed by the most important personages in London.

"How long will it take?" Eden asked.

"Take?" Geddy's concern now was less with the anchors than with the fame that would soon be his. "Oh, it shouldn't take more than a month, sir. I'll have to make the casts, you see, and then there's the..."

Eden shook his head. "That won't do. I need them in two weeks."

"Oh, it can't be done, sir," the silversmith said. "I couldn't possibly..."

"Two weeks," Eden repeated firmly.

The silversmith shuffled about on his feet nervously and plucked his lips again.

"Three, sir. How about three?"

"Three," Eden said. "Whence is that?"

"Thursday, there, sir." The silversmith pointed at his calendar on his shelf behind the counter.

"Thursday, then. What time, Thursday?"

"Thursday, noon," the silversmith said.

"Good." The governor stared directly at the silversmith again and then took from his pocket some gold. "You'll get the rest when they're finished," he said, placing the gold on the counter.

"Yes sir," Geddy said, gathering up the money.

"And James," the governor said.

"Yes sir," Geddy answered.

"This must be kept quiet. The king would be most upset."

"I understand perfectly, sir. My lips are sealed. For the king, hisself," he said in awe and amazement that he, James Geddy, had been chosen to do work for the king. "I'll not say a word—you can count on that, Governor."

"Good." Eden smiled. The silversmith had reacted just as he had planned. That part about the king had worked just perfectly. He placed his hand on the silversmith's shoulder, to give his plan the final touch. "You have my fullest confidence."

The silversmith glowed with excitement. Pumping the governor's hand, he hustled to the door and opened it obligingly for Eden.

Geddy watched the governor leave. The silversmith's eyes sparkled with excitement. Standing in the door he felt ten years younger than his thirty-seven years. Immediately he went to work on the design of the molds.

But as the time drew closer for Eden's arrival with the silver and his elation wore off, Geddy couldn't help thinking to himself that casting twelve silver anchors was the oddest request he had ever had, even if they were for the king of England.

He would be even more perplexed to know that Governor Eden had visited smiths all up and down the coast and given identical orders to them—totaling four hundred tons of silver.

Soon, Geddy's original question came back to him. What would anyone be doing with all that silver?

An Urgent Message
Dispatched

Over the course of the last several weeks, Charles Eden had be came quite persistent in his courting of Anne Hassell, so persis tent, in fact, that it drew the attention of Bath society. At social events about the town, Charles Eden's wooing of Anne became an inevitable topic of conversation. Rumors ran rampant as to the reasons why a charming, eligible bachelor would woo such an ugly old maid. People conjured up wild and fanciful accounts of the man's style of living, but none, indeed, seemed to be adequate. Finally, Bath society remained as mystified and puzzled as it was when the topic was at first brought to its attention.

As for Anne, for the moment she was enjoying her popularity to the fullest. Once the brunt of much derision and scorn, she was now an object of awe and admiration. Stunning young beauties felt a nip of jealousy when she made her appearance. Young men who had never even glanced at her began entertaining thoughts of calling at her home. Edward Moseley, frantic at the thought of losing her dowry, pursued her with a vehemence hitherto undreamed of.

It could only be expected, then, that as others' opinions of Miss Hassell underwent a transformation, so, too, would Anne's opinion of herself. Indeed her ego became highly inflated. She spent long hours gazing at herself in front of a mirror. Her friends complained how she talked constantly about herself, a habit Eden was encouraging wholeheartedly. Anne's personality began to acquire qualities of a haughty, stunning beauty—qualities tolerable in a woman of that nature, but quite intolerable for a woman such as Anne. Unintelligent, ugly, and now conceited, the woman became, in short—insufferable.

Indeed, Anne continued to think quite highly of herself until one day when she attended a party with Governor Charles Eden. Here, she suffered somewhat of a blow.

The two were taking drinks in a private corner of a large ballroom furnished with appointments of taste and quality. Eden was bored silly by the girl's endless chatter, but he was putting up a good front. By chance, so it seemed, he began a conversation.

He turned in his chair to face Anne who was directly across from him. "I see, my dear, that my main rival for your hand is not about." He smiled his usual charming smile.

Anne looked about the room to confirm Eden's thoughts. "So he's not," she said, tittering happily as she sipped her drink.

"It's all the better for me," Eden said. "I shall have you wholly to myself this evening."

Anne tittered again and replied that he was a bold rogue to flatter her so openly. "One might even suspect an ulterior motive," she said, laughing.

"Heavens no!" To further reassure her, Eden placed his hand lightly and briefly over hers.

For an instant the two paused to admire the fashionable splendor, bright lights and gaiety of the occasion. A waiter refilled their drinks and offered miniature cakes. Eden refused, but Anne took one. In a moment, Anne resumed the conversation concerning Moseley. "I had heard that Edward only recently left for another trip to Virginia. Perhaps he has not returned."

Eden raised his brow at this point, but no other gesture seemed to indicate he was overly interested in Moseley's trip. "I have been informed," he remarked, most casually, "that Virginia is quite the place to be this time of year. Does Mr. Moseley find it so?"

"Believe me, I have no idea," Anne said, taking another cake.

Eden raised his brow again. "No idea?" he said. "I should think that he would enjoy discussing his adventures with you. I certainly do." He squeezed her hand quite gently at this instant, and Anne laughed gaily. Eden's admiration, the drink, and festivity of the occasion had made her quite giddy.

She turned to face him and batted her eyelashes. "Charles, I should be delighted to regale you upon Mr. Moseley's trips, but he keeps them exceedingly secret."

Anne went on chatting about something else then, but Eden did not hear her. These trips of Moseley had caught his attention.

"I don't suppose you are aware of why Mr. Moseley makes his journeys?" he interrupted, returning to the former topic of conversation.

"Why no," Anne said, the smile on her face suddenly replaced by a look of puzzlement. "Should I be?"

Thinking over her conversation with Eden at a much later date, Anne would remember that Eden paused here for a much longer time than was necessary. The pause aroused her curiosity. Why, indeed, was Moseley taking these trips?

Eden knew that Moseley was up to some skullduggery. Obviously, these trips meant trouble. But what kind of trouble?

"I have noticed," Anne said, looking about the room at the other guests, "that he is a different man each time he leaves for his trip. He is distant and preoccupied."

Eden's brow wrinkled. He sat his empty glass down on a table beside them. "Distant and preoccupied?"

"Why, yes. So much so that I fear he has something so deep on his mind that only excessive drink could cure."

"I pray you exaggerate, madam."

"Well, he does act strangely and no mistake."

Eden's attention was diverted here for a moment by an especially attractive female spinning and whirling past them in dance. All too well, Anne noticed then that her escort's gaze was not fixed on her, but on the elegant young woman. She turned away in anger.

Eden caught Anne's feelings almost immediately. The elegant young lady, staring unabashedly at him as she danced, suddenly gave him an idea. Make her jealous, he thought. Of course.

"Well, I think Mr. Moseley should act strangely," Eden said.

Anne stopped munching on her cake to stare at Charles Eden. She had a look of bewilderment on her face. "And why is that?"

"Why Anne, don't you know?" Eden asked, showing a trace of concern.

"Know? Know what, Charles?" she asked in exasperation. She suddenly did not feel hungry and she put her cake down on the table beside her.

"My dear Anne," Eden said, aloofly watching the dancers again, his eyes no longer fixed on Anne. "A woman in your position should not take these things so lightly."

"My position?" The poor girl's face went white.

"Well, it seems most obvious to me," Eden said.

"Obvious?"

Eden turned to regard Anne sternly. "Anne, has Mr. Moseley ever asked you to accompany him on his trips?"

Anne's face wrinkled up in thought. "Well, no."

"Well, then, you see," Eden said, quite naturally. "It's most obvious."

"Not to me." Anne looked as if she might burst into tears at any moment. The gay surroundings did not give her pleasure any longer.

"My dear," Eden said, gazing deeply into her eyes as he took her hand, "I naturally thought you would suspect." His voice broke off for a moment. "But if you don't know, I think it hardly proper for me to be the one to inform you."

But by now the harm was done. Anne was curious to the point of destruction. "Do tell me, Charles, what you are talking about!"

Eden shook his head in marked astonishment. "Well, I confess it takes me quite by surprise that you have not guessed. But very well, I shall tell you for I feel it is my moral duty to do so." He hitched his shoulders at that point and sighed.

"Do go on," Anne said, vexed. Impatiently, she waved away a waiter who had returned with more drinks.

"Edward Moseley is courting you, is he not?"

"Of course he is. You know that, Charles. And he is most serious too—in fact, he only recently asked me to marry him. But my mind is unmade as of yet." She fluttered her eyelashes and smiled at Eden. Clearly she was considering him as a husband.

Eden gave the woman no cause to doubt him. He straightened one of his gloves, and replied, "Well, my dear, I trust Mr. Moseley is not as serious as it would seem."

"And why is that?" Anne retorted.

"Because, my dear Anne," Eden said, suddenly bringing himself to look at her, "it is perfectly clear that if he keeps his trips so secret from you then it could only mean one thing—another woman."

Anne colored at this remark "Another woman!" she said, startled. Her outburst was so loud it caused several guests to turn their heads in her direction.

Actually, on an earlier occasion before Eden had courted Anne, she might have taken this information with more humor. She might have even chosen to overlook this slight upon her character. But as it was, she had grown too proud and haughty for this indiscretion to go unnoticed.

"My dear Anne," Eden said, making a show of surprise, "I had hoped you would not take this so strongly."

Anne could do nothing but repeat the words, "Another woman." Her hands trembled and her voice shook. She did not even seem to see Eden. She rose from her chair in mild fury.

Eden rose with her and then turned her around to face him. "My dear," he said in the most gentlemanly manner possible. "I fear I have distressed you." To all appearances, he seemed dreadfully sorry.

Anne's lips were immediately firmly set. "Not at all," she said.

"Then shall we dance?" Eden asked, taking her by the arm. And before the poor girl even had time to answer she found herself swept off her feet and onto the dance floor by the governor—who now seemed to have entirely forgotten the conversation concerning Edward Moseley. In the aftermath, Eden would congratulate himself on the ease in which he conducted this entire episode.

But Anne would be quite distressed—so much so, in fact, that she would dismiss the advances of Edward Moseley for the next week with a zeal unusual in even the most spurned lover. Within a few days, Edward Moseley found the flowers he brought to Anne thrown out the window, the door to her home slammed in his face, and his love letters to her returned unread. That he had become the object of her contempt was only too apparent.

Unable to fathom the cause of all this rejection, Moseley waited until she came forth from her home one afternoon and then approached her. However, this too was to no avail. Callously, she shunned him. She stepped into her coach without a moment's glance in his direction. Dejected and downcast, all Edward Moseley could do was to throw his hat furiously on the ground and stomp on it in exasperation. Whatever had gotten into the woman?

Thinking of her small fortune, he swallowed all pride and went to her. Only after much pleading, and then a bribe to the servants, did he gain admittance to the Hassell household. Evidently, the servants had gotten wind of Anne's contention for they fairly snatched his hat and coat from him as he entered. Then they did not bother to put the garments away, instead flinging them on a chair. Obviously, they felt his stay would not be that lengthy.

He was received in a parlor most coldly. Anne sat stiffly in her chair, wearing a high lace collar, nose in the air, a look of wounded egoism on her face. Though the room itself was prepossessing, furnished in rich drapes and fine Persian carpets, Anne, herself, had indeed an unfortunate aspect.

"I suppose you have come to apologize," she said, haughtily.

"Apologize?" he asked, looking puzzled. "For what, I ask, should I apologize?"

Anne's overweight figure rose from her chair and waddled across the room. Then she looked him straight in the eye. "Do you think me an utter fool?" she shouted.

The thought had often crossed Moseley's mind that the girl could indeed very well be a simpleton, but being a fairly well-cultured gentleman, he had never said so, especially to her face. So, he simply sat and said nothing when the inquiry was posed to him.

That Moseley did not bother to answer her did not deter Anne in the least. "Yes," she said, turning away from him and recrossing the room, "I suspect you do take me for a fool, Edward Moseley. Well, I shall disabuse you of that notion."

Moseley shook his head in utter bewilderment. "You must forgive me, Anne, but..."

"Never," she interrupted, breaking off his words in mid-sentence. "Do you think I could ever show my face in Bath society again?"

"I don't see why you shouldn't, Anne." He wished to add that if she had done so up until now, he saw no reason not to continue. Her face was shocking enough at first glance, but somehow one grew accustomed to it.

"You have come here to apologize," she went on. "You suspect you can gain my forgiveness."

"—Anne, please—"

—"but on the contrary, I shall never forgive." Her eyes flashed as she fairly flew into a rage.

He sat up stiffly in his chair and then spoke his thoughts. "Anne, whatever you imagine I might have done..."

"Imagine? You call another woman imagination?"

He opened his mouth in shocked surprise. "Another woman! Why, whatever gave you such an idea?"

She sat down on a Turkish chair once again, staring him in the face. "Don't try to hide the facts from me, Edward Moseley. Those secret trips to Virginia in the dark of night..."

Edward Moseley threw back his head. So that was why she was in such a state. She imagined he was seeing another woman. He finally broke into laughter, the thought was so absurd. "So, that's what is on your mind—that I have another woman in Virginia."

"And what else?" Anne demanded, her beady eyes staring wickedly at him.

"Oh, dear Anne," he said, rising from his chair and crossing the room to take her hand. "You are a silly goose."

"You are not seeing another woman?" she stammered in perplexity.

"Of course, I'm not."

She sighed. "Then why do you make such journeys?"

"Dear Anne," he said, heaving his shoulders as if he carried the weight of the world on them, "I am not at liberty to tell."

For an instant she seemingly returned to her former state of mind. "There, you see, it is another woman!"

Moseley shook his head in utter frustration. "Anne, you must come to your senses. There is no other woman than you in my life."

"I don't believe it. Nor shall I be satisfied until you give me a proper explanation." She pressed her lips together firmly. "Now, good day, sir," she said, rising to leave.

"Anne, wait," Moseley said. By the sheer pressure of his hand on her shoulder, he forced her to stay. "Very well, you give me no choice. I shall tell you. But it is most secret," he added.

"I shall not breathe a word of it," she answered.

"Well then, Anne it's this. Each time I travel to Virginia, I take some arms—weapons, guns, ammunition. If you wish you can inspect my coach."

"Arms?" Anne asked, curiously. Her face wrinkled up.

"Now you see, dear, would a lover take weapons on his trips?" he asked, staring her straight in the face.

"I suppose not," she reasoned. "But I am still dissatisfied. Why do you carry arms to Virginia?"

Moseley's jaw became rigidly set. "I do not wish to tell you anything further," he answered, releasing her.

"My dear Edward, I assure you that is not a sufficient explanation. If that is as good as you can do, then you may as well go and never show your face in my home again."

"Anne," he begged, "you press me beyond all reason."

She turned to go, giving him one last look over her shoulder.

Vexed and frustrated, Moseley finally gave in. Her sharp rebukes were more than he could bear. "Well, if you promise not to press me further I shall tell you something more."

"I promise," she said, smiling in satisfaction with herself.

"The truth is that Virginia and North Carolina are planning a secret invasion, and I and no one else am to be in charge of North Carolina's entire part of it."

"You are!" she said. Anne's mouth opened in surprise. "In charge of the entire troops!" She now regarded him with dizzy admiration. Evidently, his stature had risen in her eyes, for he was to be commander of the colony's entire armed forces, a position of great respect.

"Yes," he said proudly.

"Tell me more. What country? And where?"

"You promised to ask no more questions," he said, holding her hand. "But within a week I promise you'll know it all. Until then, I ask you to wait for me, Anne. And pray for the satisfactory conclusion of this invasion."

"Of course, Edward dear," she answered, still in awe. Perhaps he would never again return to her! Her voice broke off in dismay. "Believe me, had I known..." she began.

"There, there, dear," he said, patting her briefly on her shoulder and holding her closely. "It's perfectly forgivable."

But as Edward Moseley left the Hassell household that evening, he could not help but recall, with some delight, the topic of Anne's concern. "Another woman," he said to himself, as he hailed a passing coach. The thought struck him that that was not such a bad idea, at least for a brief encounter, and especially after looking at Anne's face for an entire evening.

It was only a short while after Moseley's coach pulled away from the Hassell household that another coach drove up. This one was occupied by an equally elegantly attired gentleman caller of Anne's—Charles Eden. The governor had, in fact, in a rather sleazy, underhanded manner seen Moseley entering the house and had merely waited around the corner until he had left. Suspecting from the relieved expression on Moseley's face that the two had cleared the air, he now descended from the coach and approached the house, assumingly to pay his respects to the young lady.

He was greeted warmly. "Why Charles!" Anne said. "Do sit down and tell me about your day. I've had a most interesting one." Before Eden had a chance to open his mouth, she began to recount her activities, from the foods she dined on to the chores she had done. Charles Eden sat and listened politely to her mindless chatter, although he found her conversation tired him. Finally, after a half hour of trivia, the conversation turned to other things.

"I must apologize for any duress I caused you the other evening," he said.

She rose from her chair and turned her back to him. "Charles," she said sternly, "I am inexperienced in the means men will use to win a woman, but I am rather shocked that you would stoop so low as to try to win me by unfair advantage. If you think you can succeed in marrying me by causing undue suspicions in my mind concerning Edward Moseley, you are wrong."

Eden raised an eyebrow. Obviously, the woman had learned something more concerning Moseley's trips to Virginia. Perhaps, he thought, if he played along with the woman he would find out more. "Indeed," he said, hanging his head, "I am most ashamed. I beg your pardon." He turned his head away and added. "My dear, you know I want you so."

"I know," Anne said, now twittering and fluttering her eyelashes. "And for that reason, I forgive you." She turned to face Eden with a look of dazzled admiration in her eyes. "If only for love," she said, placing her hand over her heart. She was enjoying immensely the thought of having two lovers fight over her. She crossed the room to sit beside him. "Nevertheless, you were a scoundrel to pretend you didn't know why Moseley was going to Virginia."

"I'm dreadfully sorry," Eden said again.

"Yes." Anne took Eden's hand in hers. "Pretending you knew nothing of his taking arms to Virginia, pretending you knew nothing of the invasion." Anne, of course, was assuming naturally that the governor would know of his state's foreign policies—an erroneous assumption on her part.

"Invasion?" Eden asked.

"Now don't play the fool with me, Charles Eden," she said, laughing. "You know perfectly well there's to be an invasion. Moseley told me all about it. He's to be head of North Carolina's troops. Now you will tell me what invasion you're planning, won't you, Charles? Or is it secret?"

Eden hid his surprise of the invasion extremely well. "It would be unwise for me to give out such information, Anne. Politics," he whispered.

"Ah, yes," Anne said.

"In fact, I only recently learned of this invasion, myself." That was true. But Eden had heard of the invasion much more recently than Anne had thought.

"Well, I shall know within the week," she said. "But my! Isn't it a lovely evening?" She rose from her chair to throw open the doors to the veranda.

"Lovely," Eden agreed, rising to meet her. "Exquisitely lovely. But no more lovely than you, my dear."

"Oh, Charles." Anne gazed into his eyes. "I am so happy with you."

"And I with you," Eden said, leading the woman onto the veranda. For he now had the information he needed from her.

As he returned home that night, he was absorbed in his thoughts of the invasion. He was certain Moseley and Moore planned to invade North Carolina. And if so, the invasion was to capture Blackbeard. Surely that was their reason for the taking of arms and provisions to Virginia because, for any other invasion into a foreign territory, Spotswood would have notified Eden, and not Moseley and Moore.

He wondered what Spotswood planned to gain from all this. Did he plan to take over the government by proving Eden corrupt? Would Moseley and Moore head North Carolina then? He did not know.

But he did know the poor colony of North Carolina could never defend itself against the combined forces of Virginia troops and rebel forces. Eden didn't even have an army. But he could keep Blackbeard from being captured and he could keep evidence of a corrupt government from Spotswood. That was his only hope. Without the capture of Blackbeard or any proof of the pirate's dealings with the North Carolina government, the invasion would be worthless.

On November 16, Eden spoke with Tobias Knight concerning the matter and on November 17, Knight drafted the following letter to be taken directly to Captain Teach.

November 17, 1718

My friend,

If this finds you yet in harbor I would have you make the best of your way up as soon as possible your affairs will let you. I have something more to say to you than at present I can write...

I expect the governor this night or tomorrow, who I believe would be likewise glad to see you, before you go, I have no time to add save my hearty respects to you, and am your real friend.

And Servant
T. Knight

After the letter was written there was nothing else Eden could do but simply sit and wait.

The Particulars
of the Land Invasion

Governor Charles Eden crossed the room to the fireplace, threw another log on the fire and returned to his former position at the upstairs window. He had been staring out the window for well over an hour now as he had done every evening about this time for the past six days. Those accustomed to the governor's habit of socializing at this hour might well wonder what had caught his attention to such a degree that he would spend his time in such an unusually solitary and lonely manner.

Actually, the governor was staring out to the harbor of Bath Town and searching for a ship—the *Adventure*. For a week the ship had not been in harbor, and the meeting the governor had planned with Blackbeard had never occurred for this reason. The governor had marked the number off his calendar with the dreadful fear that Blackbeard's days were numbered also.

It was November 23 now, and still Eden caught no sight of the pirate's flag. He stood poised at the window until late afternoon when the beacons from the ships in the harbor began to be lit with increasing regularity. Just as he was about to turn away from the window, an unusual sight met his eyes—a figure running directly to his home. As the figure drew nearer he could make out the shape of a woman, her hair flying about her in a wild fashion, her cloak billowing in the wind. It took him by surprise, for seldom did a woman venture out alone in Bath, especially at this hour of the evening. She was already at the gates leading onto his lawn before he recognized her. It was Mary Teach.

His momentary reaction was one of arousal for he was reminded that she had not yet returned his favor for helping Blackbeard. But this reaction was replaced by one of curiosity and then an awful, sickening dread. Something was wrong. It was not the habit of a young lady to come tearing towards his home on foot, but to be ushered gracefully by servants from her carriage to his door.

He half expected what he was about to hear as he was called to meet her in the parlor.

"Please be seated, Mary," he said, taking her shawl. He noticed her shoes were muddy and the edges of her dress covered with briars. When he offered her a drink, she refused, stating frankly, "I have but little time, Governor." She did not bother to remove her gloves, but instead, wrung her hands together in anxiety.

From Mary's appearance, the governor felt he needed a drink himself, and he poured one. He sat down to prepare himself for the news.

Mary had a wild, startled look in her eyes. "Governor," she said, "I fear my husband is to be arrested—and if arrested, he shall surely hang."

"Arrested?"

Her voice was strident now. "I believe you know of what I'm speaking. You directed Tobias Knight to write a letter to him on November 17."

Governor Eden's eyes dropped.

"Yes," she said. "I am well aware of that letter. But that is beside the point. You see, he is always in the hands of death. And warnings to him are as worthless as the paper they're written on. He tossed it aside."

Charles Eden took a deep breath. "I see." He took another sip of his whisky. Hunted men always took life more casually than others because they lived on the edge of death. Damn, he had been a fool not to have counted on that. Suddenly, another thought crossed his mind. "Mary," he asked, "how do you know your husband's in immediate danger?"

Her voice trembled as she spoke. "Captain Ellis Brand of Virginia came to my home tonight searching for him."

Mary knew she must have shocked the governor, for he braced himself before rising. He put his glass down, stood up and began pacing the floor. The invasion from Virginia had already begun, he thought. It was only a matter of time now before Brand would be at his home demanding Blackbeard and whatever else Virginia's governor was after. A worried expression crossed his face as Mary told him how her home had been surrounded by armed forces, how she had come here through a secret, underground passageway Blackbeard had built of ballast stones that led down to the sea, how she had risked her very life and limb to hire a boatman to row her across the creek to the governor's home, and how she had run more than a mile to his plantation. When she had finished she broke down, weeping into a handkerchief she had earlier tucked in her bag.

Eden walked over to comfort the woman, but she would have nothing to do with him. In a fit of fury she suddenly forced back her tears and rose from her chair. Her eyes flashed now as she clenched her fists in a fit of stifled rage. "I blame you for all this, Governor. You put him up to this. He wouldn't have pirated if it wasn't for you."

The governor showed a trace of discomfiture at Mary's remark. He had, over the past several months, gone to considerable expense to keep his collaboration with the pirate secret, and now here was this woman sniffling into her handkerchief and angrily telling him she knew about the affair. This would not do at all. She could, if the mood struck her, make things extremely difficult for him—furthermore, she could stand to gain quite a bit by telling. It was necessary to find out just how much she knew. Had the pirate at some weak point told her of the conspiracy to steal the treasure? In a calm and determined manner, he asked, "What did he tell you?" he asked.

"Enough," she said, glaring up at him through wet lashes. "Enough to know he's been pirating and you put him up to it."

"And anything more?"

"No," she snapped.

Mary thought she heard Eden breathe an audible sigh of relief at this point and in the aftermath, she would wonder what more there was to know. But now she was concerned with more pressing matters. After putting her handkerchief back in her bag, she turned her face upwards. "Governor, do you know where he's keeping himself at this moment?"

Eden frowned. He walked to the window and stared out to the horizon once again. He could still make out the shapes of the ships, but not one resembled the *Adventure*. He had been concerned about Blackbeard's whereabouts all week, but as yet he had only one notion of a hiding place. "I have been thinking about a place," Eden said. "One place on the south tip of Ocracoke. No one puts in there but pirates."

The thought that Eden might actually know of Blackbeard's whereabouts caused Mary to become extremely excited. She was frantic again now. Her eyes showed it—startled eyes, wild eyes.

"Then perhaps you could do something," she pleaded. "Perhaps you could save him."

"There's a chance I could dispatch a ship," he said, putting quite a good countenance on his selfishness, for it was not for Mary's sake or Blackbeard's that he wished the pirate's freedom, but to save his own skin.

Mary, however, sighed in desperation at Eden's suggestion. "By the time you give orders to sail, two sloops out of Kecoughtan, Virginia will be holding all ships. Brand told me the Virginians plan to block Ocracoke Inlet."

Eden started. "I could get someone to ride around the sound," he said. "Then a ship could be dispatched."

Mary shook her head. "The town's under martial law," she said. "No one goes in or out. Brand's orders."

"I see." Eden heaved his shoulders in utter hopelessness. "So there's no warning him."

"I suppose not." The thought of their failure to arrive at a solution caused Mary to burst into tears again.

But in a moment the air of impending gloom that had settled over the parlor was immediately interrupted by an outburst from Mary. "You put him up to this, Governor," she shouted. "And if some remedy is not found, I'll tell the whole town you were pirating."

Eden was alarmed. The last thing he needed right now was a witness to his collaboration with the pirate. Frantically, he clutched her shoulder in desperation. "Mary," he said, his jaw rigidly set, "you mustn't tell, you understand."

Mary gave him a serious look.

My God, but she was stubborn, he thought. "Listen, you'll only harm your husband, if you tell. You wouldn't want that, would you?" he asked.

"No," she said, shaking her head sadly. Her mood changed, she suddenly grasped him by the hand. "But you will do something, won't you?"

"I'll do what I can, Mary," he said, pressing her hand in return.

For the moment, bowing her head, she seemed satisfied. It was a relief to him that she had cooperated, for he still thought she was beautiful with her chestnut hair falling softly over her face. It would have been a shame to have silenced her in other, more harmful ways. For an instant he was reminded that in rather different circumstances, he would have pressed a kiss on her warm, full lips.

But as it was, he had neither the time nor inclination even to approach her, for already the two were interrupted by the sounds of horses' hooves on the front lawn. In alarm, she whirled around to face the governor. "It's Brand," she said, and the two gazed at each other in shocked silence.

"He's come," Mary said, wringing her hands. "If he finds me here he shall surely take me as well as my husband." She began to sob hysterically.

Frantic to calm the woman, he took her by the shoulders and shook her. The jolt was the only thing that seemed to shock her into a state of silent submission. Wasting no time then, he pulled her toward the door and called one of the servants. Breathless with excitement, the servant arrived in only a moment. Giving her over to him, he said, "Take the back way out. John, here, will saddle a horse for you."

As soon as Mary was hurried outside, a footman was at the door of Eden's home, requesting and then demanding to see Eden. When he could no longer be put off politely, the governor met Brand at the door. Eden apologized for his tardiness, making an excuse that caused Brand to feel guilty about the fifty horsemen that were now on Eden's lawn, tearing up his flower beds. Brand apologized then, explaining that his only reason for being here was a search for Blackbeard. He would leave quietly enough when the pirate was found. He hoped he hadn't disturbed the governor.

With the calm assurance of a guiltless party, more deserving of public support than condemnation, Eden shook his head. Would Brand come in, he asked? As Brand followed the governor into the foyer and down the hallway, Eden openly acknowledged his distaste for piracy in the colonies. The thought crossed Brand's mind that perhaps Governor Spotswood's ideas about Eden were wrong.

Comporting himself with extraordinary dignity, Eden threw open his doors to an impressive study furnished with gilt leather books and fine Persian carpets. As Brand looked about the room his thoughts were confirmed. Surely, he thought, Spotswood had made some error for here was Eden not only offering him a seat but also his support in locating the pirate. He apologized again as he took a letter from his waistcoat pocket and handed it to Eden.

The governor grasped the letter and scanned its contents.

Williamsburg, November 1718

Dear Sir:

Give me leave to enumerate to you perils which if not avoided with prudence and circumspection, your enemies may take the advantage thereof to your great detriment.... Therefore I write this to take notice of some proceedings in your government, which I fear may in the end badly affect you if continued longer in the same course.

The reception that Teach and his piratical crew have hitherto had in your province begins mightily to be canvassed here and will assuredly make a great noise after the evidence given in yesterday upon the trial of his quartermaster William Howard, who now lies here under the sentence of death, for being clearly convicted of manifest piracies since the fifth of January last.

I know not whether you and your people be well apprised of the extent of the governor of Virginia's power and authority with relations to pirates; whereof I have chosen to recite the same the more particularly in an instrument which Captain Brand carries with him...

I hope you will put a favorable construction upon the friendly advice he brings you, and whatever just reason you may have had for suffering Teach and his accomplices to live in your province hitherto unmolested you will now exert your endeavor and heartily join with us to bring these villains and their accomplices to punishment.

It's very possible that I may have been misinformed as to several extraordinary passages that I hear with respect to the pirates in your province, and it may give less offense to open such matters to you by a prudent friend and an intimate acquaintance of yours, than to offer any imputations of that kind in writing, wherefore I shall herein add nothing farther on that head but refer you for particulars to Captain Brand and to conclude with assurances of my heartily aiming at your welfare as being with great truth and esteem.

> your most obedient
> and most humble servant
> A. *Spotswood.*

When Eden returned the letter to Brand, the captain handed the governor another document citing a crown colony's authority to legally enter a proprietary government in search of pirates. When Eden had done with that also, he gave the document back, stood up and walked to the liquor cabinet to pour himself a drink. "Will you take one?" he asked.

"Never touch liquor myself," Brand said.

Eden studied the man thoroughly. He was a short, stocky man who was easily impressed by elegant surroundings. That was certain from the way he shifted uncomfortably in his chair as he gazed about the room. Probably from the lower class, Eden thought.

Eden's thoughts were correct. Brand had worked himself up to a very high position in the army. Now he associated with people such as Eden, wealthy people of high social breeding. He had been careful as he made his way up the ranks to study aristocratic manners and dress, and he imitated them copiously. But he could never quite overcome his feelings of inferiority in an aristocrat's presence.

In part, these feelings were due to the fact that he knew deep down inside that he was as much unlike them as ever. Aristocrats had made their livings through inheritance of vast family wealth. Brand made his living by killing and robbing (he had spurred his men on even now with promises of Blackbeard's treasure). He knew he was no better than a pirate or ruffian at heart. These men like Eden, thought Brand, what did they know of the dirty side of life? They had not seen the horrible, brutal things Brand had in wars. They did not have to see them—living safely in their refined homes. When he took from them in time of war, he felt justified. He deserved it. He even felt triumphant.

But in the presence of a man such as Eden, a man of such superior social breeding, Brand was too easily impressed. Eden sensed this.

Eden took a seat directly across from Brand. "I was under the impression that Blackbeard had given up piracy."

Brand shifted uncomfortably in his seat again. Then he coughed. "Well, sir, it has come to Governor Spotswood's attention that the pirate has been molesting small trading vessels off your coast."

Eden paused for a moment to collect his thoughts and then glanced at Brand. "I see." He took a sip of whisky.

Brand could not bring himself to look at the governor for a moment. When he did speak his voice was oversmall and squeaky. "And the governor is also under the impression that there may be a possible misunderstanding concerning the Martiniqueman."

Governor Eden shifted his gaze. "But why has he sent you to me? Surely you don't think Blackbeard's here."

Brand braced himself before continuing. "Governor Spotswood has sent me here for the express purpose of confiscating the goods from the Martiniqueman. These goods will be used as evidence at a trial."

Governor Eden said nothing, but he did take another sip of whisky.

Brand drummed his fingers on the edge of the chair. "I trust sir, that with all due interest in your colony, you will be more than willing to help rid your coast of these pirates."

"Nothing would give me more pleasure," Eden said. However, at the instant he made this statement, he choked on his whisky.

Brand was obliged to offer a handkerchief when the governor coughed. However, Eden waved the handkerchief away. The captain returned the bit of linen to his waistcoat.

This cough did little to give the governor away. Already won over by the man's good manners and genteel breeding, Brand now took the governor completely into his confidence. "Governor, you don't know how happy it makes me that you are willing to help. For we have a problem."

"A problem?" Eden couldn't imagine Brand having a problem— what with fifty horsemen and half the North Carolina citizens backing him as well as the governor of Virginia. It was he, Charles Eden, who had the problem.

"Yes, we have a problem." Brand fidgeted in his seat. "For we have evidence that some of Blackbeard's effects are in Tobias Knight's storehouse."

"I see," Eden remarked, placing his finger to his lip. Then he downed the rest of his whisky.

"If I'm not mistaken, Knight is one of your councilmen."

This time Eden shifted uncomfortably in his chair. "Yes," he answered.

This remark seemingly put Brand at ease. He smiled slightly and then spoke with a bit of enthusiasm in his voice. "Then would you be so kind, Governor, to visit Tobias Knight's barn with us? The commissioner has stubbornly refused to let us enter. A governor of the king such as yourself, sir, not wishing to be maliciously and falsely accused of accompaniment in piracy, would, I'm sure, be able to convince Knight to open up his storehouse."

Brand had put Eden in rather an awkward position. "Yes, well..." he said, brokenly. He stood up and walked the length of the room, his hands behind his back. For a moment he stopped beside the window to peer at the horsemen in his front yard. He knew a refusal to help Brand would only incriminate him. And he felt a need now to uphold the reputation of North Carolina. "I am amazed Captain Teach told me wrongly concerning the Martiniqueman." He turned to face Brand.

"Yes, well, it seems he did," Brand said, waiting anxiously for the governor's response.

Eden braced himself. "If you'll just excuse me, I'll just get my coat and go with you, sir."

"Of course," Brand answered, but as Eden walked out of the study, the captain noticed that a most peculiar look came over the governor's face.

Having been in bed, Tobias Knight was startled from his sleep as he heard the approaching sounds of horses' hooves beating the grass outside his plantation home. Coughing from the illness he had not yet been able to shake, he grabbed a pewter candlestick beside his bed and after lighting the wick, tossed the bedclothes aside and stepped into his slippers, starting down the long staircase to the bottom floor. His nightclothes flapped wildly about his thin figure and his nightcap fell lopsided on his head as he rushed to open the door, just barely enough to see outside.

Brand didn't waste any time in idle conversation. "We have the governor with us this time," he said, "with an order for you to open up your storehouse."

Knight peered nervously at Eden from the half-cracked door. His eyes clearly pleaded for support, but the governor did not respond in the slightest. Instead, he stood next to Brand, arms crossed in front of him, with all the appearance of siding with the captain. This shocked Knight to no end. Had the governor lost his mind, he wondered? Did he know he was setting himself up as well as Knight to be hanged, drawn and quartered? He regarded the governor with fear and trepidation. But what made him even more fearful was the fact that Captain Brand was continuing to voice his demands, "Well, will you show us the goods or no?"

Knight was about to close the door in Brand's face and take his chances on a quick escape from the entire scene when Eden spoke up. "Mr. Knight," he said, giving his councilman a severe look, "I hope you'll be so good as to show Captain Brand the effects."

"And if not?" Knight asked fearfully.

Brand lost his temper at this arrogance. Quickly he withdrew a pistol from his waistcoat pocket and aimed it between Knight's beady, little black eyes. "If you don't step to it, Mr. Knight," he said, "I've a good mind to put lead in your carcass."

Knight jumped. Clearly, the man meant what he said for he cocked the pistol at this moment. Knight shivered like a leaf. "These goods, *wheeze*, sir," he said, "they are all honestly come by."

Brand tried to remain calm even though his patience was wearing precariously thin. "T'would not seem so," he said.

Knight continued, however, with his excuses. "Merely, sugar loaded at the request of Captain Teach, *wheeze*," he remarked offhandedly, "only 'til a more convenient store could be procured by the governor."

Brand measured the man up and down. The man was putting him off, he thought. "Sir, let us see the particulars," he said calmly. "And no more beating about the bush."

Resignedly, Knight opened the door the rest of the way. Candle in hand, nightclothes flapping about him, he led the captain, Eden and the entire troop of fifty horsemen to a storehouse behind his home. There he stood, eyeing the little house as if it were the arm of death.

Knight gave every effort to avoid opening the door to his storehouse. Looking warily at the men, he made a remark now that caused Brand to throw up his hands in disgust. "T'is much of a bother," he said. "The latch's broke."

"I'll wait," Brand said.

After fiddling with the lock, a matter which took a full five minutes, the latch to the storehouse finally was unlocked.

"Pluck up the latch," Brand ordered in a clear, strong voice.

Knight jumped and the door swung open, revealing a pile of hay and fodder inside four walls. The barn smelled of oats and urine.

Brand entered, followed by Eden and several of the horsemen, who measured the barn up and down, peering this way and that to discover its contents.

"Now then, Mr. Knight," Brand said, turning to face the sickly, little man again. "Show us the goods. And you'd best do it quickly."

"Yes," Knight mumbled, moving back through the storehouse. "You shall have them all, of course," he continued, pushing aside some of the fodder. Underneath were two large, burlap bags of cocoa, perhaps four feet in diameter. Knight opened the bags to reveal their contents to Brand. "Very fine cocoa," he said. "Very dear in Virginia, I warrant. A man hither wants to buy this cocoa from me, and you know what he offers me, *wheeze*? Two pounds, he offers me for one bag."

"I understand," Brand said impatiently, "but, I..."

"This," Knight continued, "this is the finest cocoa in the colonies, I warrant. Very dear, *wheeze*, very dear. And all yours for the taking, sir, all yours. *Wheeze*, yes, very costly cocoa. T'will bring a pretty price in Virginia."

Brand looked at the cocoa. It was good cocoa, no doubt, but hardly what he or his men were looking for. No, what they were after was not worth a pretty penny, but a fortune in pirate's booty. The fact of the matter was he had heard rumors of the Spanish silver. Cocoa be damned. He and his men wanted pirate's treasure. However, the sight of Knight making such a to-do about the cocoa made him laugh.

"Yes, well, t'is a bit of a joke," Knight said, moving around the enclosure. "But not when you get to this here. Not here, there's no joke." Knight called for the men to give him a hand in lifting an armload of hay. Underneath were several large bags similar to the others in shape, but heavier. "Sugar, sir," Knight said, pointing to the bags. "Brought hither from Barbados. I trust you'll find it well worth your trip."

Brand shook his head, firmly.

"But it's very fine sugar, very fine. It will do you proud." He glanced fearfully at the governor then, but Eden gave him no sign of encouragement.

"I want all the goods," Brand said.

"That's all there is, sir, I swear it," Knight said, trembling and throwing up his arms.

The captain crossed his arms over his chest and tapped his feet.

After a very long silence, Knight said, "Well, then there are a few other things. Nothing special. This way, *wheeze*, sir," he said, leading the men to an enclosure on the side of the storehouse. Eagerly the men began tossing aside the hay and fodder. Gradually, pieces of some heavy substance was seen.

"What is it, then?" Brand asked, peering closer with curiosity.

Knight merely stared at Brand.

"Come, come, man," the captain said. "Speak up."

"It's anchors, sir," Knight said, trembling again.

"Anchors?" Brand asked in surprise.

"Anchors," Knight repeated. "Painted, sir."

"I can see that." Brand examined the hardware. "Black, aren't they?"

"Yes, sir," Knight said.

"How many?"

"Two hundred."

"Two hundred anchors!" Brand said, disappointed beyond belief. "Now what in the world would a pirate be doing with two hundred anchors?"

Knight shrugged.

Brand bent down and examined one of the anchors. "It weighs too heavy to lift and carry," he said. "We'll have to take them back aboard ship."

"You weren't thinking of taking these, sir?" Eden broke in. It was the first remark he had made since coming to the barn. "They're from the Martiniqueman."

Brand nodded. "King's orders. We have orders to take everything—all Blackbeard's effects," Brand said, turning to face the governor. "But we thank you for your help, Governor. I'll be sure to report to His Excellency, Governor Spotswood, how you were most helpful. I am thoroughly convinced Governor Spotswood was mistaken concerning your character."

Brand thrust out his hand for the governor to shake, but he noticed that as the two shook hands, Eden's face turned quite pale. Afterwards, he would wonder whether the trip to Knight's house so late at night had disturbed the governor's constitution.

But right now he was more concerned with his men. Their shoulders drooped, their mouths made a downward grimace. That they had not found a hoard of pirate treasure had hurt their morale. Brand encouraged them by demanding that they search out the barn completely, but in an hour's time after the barn had been completely ransacked and still nothing more had been found but two hundred anchors, all black and all weighing a total of four hundred tons, Brand ordered that his men begin loading what little remained of the Martiniqueman into the wagons.

As the men loaded up, Brand noticed how Knight cast wild glances in the men's directions and how even Eden seemed slightly disturbed. What concern could either Eden or Knight have with sugar, cocoa and several hundred anchors? He gave it little thought.

Quite the contrary, Eden and Knight gave the matter more consideration. In fact, it was all they could think of as they stood outside the storehouse. They watched in dismay as the cocoa, sugar and finally the anchors—a fortune in melted down silver coins and bars—were loaded into the wagons to be taken back to Virginia.

In The Lurking Hole
of Captain Teach

T
he day was dying. With the fading light, the visibility of objects along the horizon was next to impossible to the naked eye. The sailor keeping watch in the crow's nest of the *Adventure* squinted. He could hardly make out the shape of Ocracoke Island that stood two points starboard of the ship. Momentarily, he applied his spyglass to his eye. Eventually, this, too, was of no further use to him, and he laid it aside. For several moments, he sat, arm under chin, staring into nothingness. At length, what caught his attention was a great deal of commotion going on down below. Looking down from his position one hundred feet above the quarterdeck, he stared at the other crew members aboard the *Adventure*.

A party was in progress down below, that was plain to see. Earlier in the evening Blackbeard had arrived on board ship with a great many half-hogsheads of beer and bottles of claret and French brandy. The crew was already commencing to knock the heads out of the hogsheads and nick the necks off the bottles. By morning all the liquor would be gone, he was sure of that, and there would not be one sip left for him. At the thought of the French brandy his mouth watered.

He tried not to think about the brandy. Instead, he took the spyglass and reapplied it to his eye. Still nothing, not even a beacon flashed by from a passing ship. He sighed. If there had been more light, he certainly would have seen two sloops steadily advancing upon the seaward side of Ocracoke, and most assuredly, he would have notified his captain to prepare to do battle. But, as it was, his view was limited by very large and very close sand dunes.

He thrust aside his spyglass. Eyeing the carousing crew members, he decided that no one would notice if he stealthily stole down the rat lines for just one drink. He was correct in his assumption, for no one paid him the slightest attention as he glanced anxiously over his shoulder and then headed down to the quarterdeck. Quickly snitching three bottles of the finest brandy he could find in the lot, he went off to drink himself to sleep in the magazine of the ship.

Most assuredly if Blackbeard had been his old self, he would have taken note of the sailor's actions and sent him scurrying up the ratlines. As it was, he was lost deep in thought. He had been this way for days— no longer joining in on the crew member's boisterous games and activities, no longer even taking drinks with the men. Of late, he kept to himself. Something was on his mind. Some guessed it was his wife, Mary; others assumed it was the new life he had taken up in Bath. It was generally acknowledged aboard ship that Blackbeard had lost all interest in a pirate's life. He was distracted, distant, preoccupied.

Blackbeard sat on an old hogshead propped up beside the bulwarks and stared out to sea. The *Adventure* strained slightly on the cables that held her at anchor. Pipe in hand, Blackbeard watched the ringlets of tobacco smoke he exhaled drift casually upwards. He paid little attention to his men. Even the cockfight the men had started near the mizzen mast failed to rouse him. In his old days there was nothing he would have enjoyed better than to join his crew, who were urging the roosters on with shouts of, "Go get 'em boy!" and hear the betting, "A pittance on Simon Whifflepin. A quarter cask of Madeira wine on Timothy Tugmutton!"

Something must have struck Blackbeard as he sat on his hogshead staring out to sea—perhaps the urge for more tobacco (the remains of which were sitting in a box in his cabin), perhaps the wish for a drink of some Barbados rum (in his cabin also, packed away in a chest stolen from a West Indiaman), because he rose now from the hogshead, tipped out his ashes and walked in the direction of his cabin. But hardly had he gone ten paces when he caught sight of a group of his crew, Israel Hands among them, huddled together in conversation. Sitting on some crates that held the French brandy, they passed a flint among themselves to fire their pipes. The flint lit up in such a way that every now and then their faces had a ghostly appearance. Their voices were harsh and hard in the night air.

Evidently, the men had not heard Blackbeard approach nor did they see him now, for the darkness hid his presence extremely well.

Blackbeard, too, would have taken little notice of the men had not his name been mentioned in passing. For this reason, he paused for a moment before stepping down the hatch. What he overheard shocked him so, that in the aftermath, he forgot the purpose of his visit to his cabin and instead, gave his thoughts to other things.

"Now, look here, men," Johnathan Davis said, spitting on the deck of the ship. "You know as well as I, Blackbeard ain't the man he once was." He passed the dying flint on to Israel Hands. Blackbeard could see the whites of Hand's eyes glisten in the night, his proximity to the men was so close.

Only feet away from Blackbeard, Hands paused to exhale some tobacco smoke. "Well, I for one, have had just about all I can stand o' Blackbeard," Israel Hands said harshly. "He's hazed me enough, by thunder! I'm no respectable gentleman as he thinks he is. Aye, he forgets who he is, I can see that. And who made him captain."

"We did," Davis returned, taking a bottle from one of the crates, uncorking it, and then guzzling down the liquor.

"Aye," Hands said defiantly. A trace of bitterness was in his voice. "You remember how we took to sea, gentlemen o' fortune we was, happy to fly the Jolly Roger, you make no doubt o' that. We was his mates. It was proud we were to sail with him."

"Aye, aye," the others said in unison.

"Aye," Hands remarked. "We stood through thick and thin together. Our match was never seen upon the high seas." Suddenly, his voice grew vengeful in tone. "But now I spit on his name, I do. Nothing he is, but a lily-livered coward. No more the great Blackbeard."

High-handed and quick-tempered, Davis felt for a knife in his pocket, took it out, thrust it into an apple barrel beside him and impaled an apple on the blade. After taking a bite, he remarked, "Ain't we all pirates? Ain't we all seamen here?"

At this instant there was a good deal of grumbling and agreements of, "Aye, aye."

When the conversation of the men stopped of its own accord, Davis suddenly lowered his voice and whispered, "I suggest we go athwart him." For a moment no one spoke, for this was no small thing Davis had suggested.

Then Israel Hands took a swig from the brandy bottle he had propped between his knees, and after wiping his mouth on his shirtsleeves, he agreed with Davis. "He deserves it. For he's an ungrateful scamp. Soon he won't be able to go back to his own for we won't have him, and as for him being a gentleman, well, he ain't one of them and never will be. Sooner or later, he'll be all lonely by himself."

Provoked now, indeed indignant from the conversation, several of the men could hardly sit still and their hands went for their knives and cutlasses. "Let's mutiny now," one said.

But Hands held them back. "Not now, but later tonight," he said. "When I give the word, we'll give him the knife. Until then, mum's the word."

"Aye, aye," the men said, their eyes gleaming wickedly in the light of their pipes.

"Now, then," Hands commented, "look lively, men. Forget the mutiny now and go about your work proper so's not to raise any suspicion. And when the time's ripe, I'll give you the word."

Blackbeard turned away from this scene with a heaviness of spirit unusual to a man who took hardships so casually. As he quietly walked to his cabin, he remembered how he had found Hands, starving and sick, in the doorstep of a filthy garret, how he had taken him through street after stinking street in London Town to get him aboard ship. He remembered how they had handed and reefed and steered together, how they had drunk together. The thought that his friend would repay him with a knife in his back made him heartsick and desolate.

After he entered his cabin, his feelings suddenly burst forth and he hurled a piece of furniture across the room, sending it crashing against the bulkhead. Then, emotionally drained, he sat down in his chair, head in his hands.

Thus he sat, not speaking, except for an almost unidentifiable moan every now and then. But by the time fifteen minutes had passed, he rose from his chair. Heaving his shoulders in sorrow, he was only too aware of what he must do as the captain of a pirate vessel. He could not permit himself any more time mulling over his past friendship with Hands. He knew that. It was either act now or perish at the hands of his crew.

Across his shoulder he slung two pistols hanging in holsters. He strapped a broad belt around his waist containing an assortment of daggers and an oversized cutlass. For a finishing touch, he tucked under the brim of his hat, fuses made of hemp cord that had been dipped in a solution of saltpeter and lime water. Striking a match to the fuses, he became wrapped in wisps of smoke. Indeed, if his purpose was to look frightful, he had accomplished it extremely well, for when he looked at his own reflection in the cabin's mirror, he gave a start.

When Blackbeard sauntered onto the deck of the ship, the oaths and curses circulating among the pirates suddenly stopped. A deathly silence fell upon the deck.

He strode the length of the deck, clothed in an aura that sent fear through the very bones of his men. Here was the mystery and power of the most dreadful pirate to ever sail the seven seas. They trembled in dread.

Suddenly turning to them, he shouted, "Avast you boozy lot of sea dogs."

The men shivered in their bootstraps. One poor fellow who had had too much to drink earlier in the evening and had fallen asleep suddenly awoke from the roaring sound of Blackbeard's voice. Turning over on a crate of liquor bottles, he opened his eyes to come face to face with this picture of terror. The sight of his captain, unrecognizable to his enfeebled mind, sent him into a state close to hysteria. "Egad, t'is Beelzebub!" he cried at the top of his lungs.

Then he raised his hands to the heavens and in a praying posture began to whimper, "Oh, Lord, do not send me to hell. Have mercy on me, poor miserable wretch that I am." Then he looked at his mates and pointed an accusing finger at them. "T'was those scurvy knaves that forced me to go a'pirating. T'was no fault of my own, Lord. Oh do not send my soul to fry in hell!"

"Z'wounds, stop your blubbering, ye scurvy wretch," Blackbeard bellowed, sauntering up to the man. "Or I'll tan your hide and set it a'drying in the sun."

The poor fellow, dizzy already, immediately passed out on the deck.

"A toast to the skull and crossbones," Teach said, taking a bottle from his coat and drinking from it. Then he spoke in a wheedling voice. "Well, now, my lads, having a bit o' fun, are you? Just oblige me with a match, will you, Hands? This pipe won't draw."

Hands brought forth a match, struck it, and ran up to his captain to light his pipe for him.

"There, that's better now," Teach said, eyeing Hands and drawing in on his pipe.

The other pirates passed looks from one to another, wondering what their captain was up to.

"Now then, it's a drink I've been wanting of late, but I've no company to help me take it. Why, I've got me some o' the finest Barbados rum in my cabin." He surveyed his men and smiled. "Come now, no one's a'pressing you. It's just some company I wants to spend the time with."

Most of the crew members gave him a black look and one scowled.

Hands, realizing his captain might suspect something, suddenly spoke up. "Aye, sir," he said, cheerfully. "T'would be nothing in the world I'd rather do than drink with my captain." He poked Richard Greensail, the crew member standing next to him. "Ain't that right, Greensail?"

"Aye," Greensail said.

With a broad smile, Captain Teach clapped the two on the shoulder warmly, making a show of friendship. Indeed, he gave no indication at all of the falling out he had had with Hands or the other crew members. Arms on their shoulders, walking between the two, he laughed and joked lightheartedly as he led them into his cabin. But he was extremely careful when the three sat down at his table to station himself near the door.

Captain Teach soon put the men at ease with his laughter, tales, and good drink, and after several rounds, the men found time going pleasant enough in their captain's company. They gulped their liquor down, licked their lips and chatted gaily as in the old days—forgetting for a moment the recent strain that had been put on their friendship. For an instant, time stood still. What more could a pirate want but lively conversation, good company and a bottle of rum?

But, at length, for Hands, the old fears came welling up inside him once again—pictures of his captain deserting him, pictures of himself starving in London. The moment of intimacy for himself and his captain passed.

Regarding his captain with shifty eyes, Hands downed his rum, then turned the topic of conversation to other things. "Now Captain," he said, leaning forward in his chair. "It's known well enough you have a reputation for having a great deal of money."

A pause lasted for several moments as Captain Teach slowly smiled at the slightly overweight fellow with glinting eyes. Then he gave a great belch, thrust his rum down on the table and bellowed, "Damn my guts," he said, guessing Hand's thoughts. "That I do. Yes, I don't spends my money that freely—I puts it away, some here, some there, and none too much anywhere for the reason there's them that'll cut my throat for it." He gave Hands a direct glance.

The first mate could not bring himself to look in his captain's eyes. Instead, he refilled his glass, turning it nervously around in his palms and staring at it. "Now let's suppose something were to happen," he said.

"Happen?" Teach asked, throwing his first mate a questioning look. He leaned in closer to stare at him.

"In a battle, let's suppose," Hands said, still staring at his glass.

"Aye." Blackbeard leaned forward with even more enthusiasm.

"Well, sir..."

Blackbeard pounded his fist on the table so hard that it almost put out the light from the candle on the table. "Speak your mind, Hands," he said, "and be done with it."

"Well," Hands blurted, "would Mrs. Teach know where you had buried the money?" He took a swig of rum now and stared at his captain.

Captain Teach leaned back in his chair and roared with laughter. "Blood and thunder, ye sway bellied oaf," he shouted. "Nobody but myself and the devil knows where it is and the longest liver shall take all!" Then the two watched in amazement as he opened another bottle of rum and gulped down the entire bottle at one time.

It was Captain Teach's tolerance of liquor as well as other things that created his marked reputation as the greatest pirate that ever lived. Now he lived up to his name, taking out another bottle and refilling the men's glasses as well as his own. As the rounds increased, the steadiness of his hands remained the same, while his mates reeled in their chairs and sang drunkenly. By the time the second bell tolled on the watch, Hands was almost ready to pass out from excess. Amusedly, Blackbeard watched his two mates throughout the evening until the wick from the candle had burned halfway down. Then, unknown to his mates, who were too drunk to notice anything, a shadow crossed his face. Slowly, but surely, his hand reached down to feel the cold, hard metal of his pistol. Not permitting himself to feel the least compunction, he drew it from his holster and cocked it.

Greensail was the only one of the two crewmen who heard the clicking of the firearm. Even in his drunken state the awareness hit him that something was awry. Suddenly, he bounded to the door, muttering, "Something's afoot!"

Hands seemingly did not notice him. Lost to the world, he continued to toast himself drunk until Blackbeard softly blew out the candle. The room was suddenly pitch black.

"Now who's gone and doused the light, eh mates?" he asked, suddenly stopping midway in his song to stare about the room.

No one answered him, for Greensail had left quietly and Blackbeard was not speaking.

Instantly, the sound of gunfire shattered the air.

Hands felt a jolt of pain in his knee. It ran through his entire body.

Letting out a long, bloodcurdling scream he fell backwards to the floor. Madly, he dragged himself to the door of the cabin and opened it.

What the crewmen saw when Hands crawled to the quarterdeck of the *Adventure* was a sight worse than death itself. A face contorted in pain met their eyes. They drew back from the scene in fear and loathing, shocked into silence, as the fellow slid along the deck of the ship, pulled only by the strength of his hands. The clothes at his right knee were shredded and torn, and a steady stream of blood trailed behind him. Panting heavily, he struggled to the bulwarks of the vessel and laid against them, the blood now forming a pool around him. Although the gunshot wound would cripple Hands for life, Blackbeard had not been able to bring himself to kill his first mate.

It was only a short while before Teach appeared in the opening. One of his boots trod in Hands' blood as he walked across the deck, pistols in both hands, the slowly burning matches in his hair still smoking.

Horrified, the men shrank back in fear. They watched in breathless silence as he walked the deck of his ship, his huge cutlass swinging back and forth at his waist. Finally, one whispered, "Damn him, he's a villain." Another muttered, "Now wherefore did he do that?"

Quickly, whirling around on the heels of his boots, Blackbeard answered the man in a snarling voice, the tone increasing in depth. "You speckle-shirted dogs. You sons of whores. If I do not now and then kill one of you, by thunder, you'll forget who I am."

Then as quickly as he had appeared on deck, he put his pistols in their holsters and recrossed the ship to disappear below. He left his men trembling in fear. For the moment, all the crew's thoughts of a mutiny had been quelled.

But the possibility of mutiny were still on Blackbeard's mind as he walked below deck. And as he relit the candle on the table in his cabin, he muttered to himself, "Well then, they got what they wanted, an infernal lubber and a villain, at that."

As he sat down at his table, a tear fell on the candle flame, causing it to flicker for a moment. Blackbeard couldn't remember a time when he had seen himself so disheartened. "But I ain't such an infernal lubber," he muttered.

Then he reached down in his liquor chest, took out another bottle of rum and uncorked the bottle. "Aye, I can't do it and no tears, Hornigold," he said with a sob. Another tear fell on the table. He forced back more sobs. "Now look a here, is this a proper way for a pirate to behave, a pirate as was taught years and years ago by Hornigold? Ah, he was a man to have a headpiece, was Hornigold."

He took a swig of rum. "But, what if I told you, Hornigold, I ain't strong enough and I don't like the job o' being a pirate?" He sighed. "Ah, well, I can see it makes no difference nohow what I want. They were dead against me. Israel Hands would have been captain next, I shouldn't wonder. And I would have been dead with a knife in my back."

Between sobs, he blew out the candle.

The Battle by Sea

The morning of November 22 broke grey and cloudy on Ocracoke Inlet. On the *Adventure*, the men were still asleep, most of them hung over from the night before.

Had the pirates been keeping a proper lookout, they would have seen two sloops from the Royal Navy anchored at the entrance to the inlet. The king's sloops, the *Jane* and the *Ranger*, has been leased by Spotswood at his own expense, because the drafts of His Majesty's ships, the *Pearl* and the *Lyme,* were too deep to enter the shallow waters of Ocracoke. They had weighed anchor out of Kecoughtan, Virginia at three o'clock in the afternoon of November 17, under the overall command of Lieutenant Robert Maynard. Twenty-five seamen from the *Lyme* were manning the *Ranger*; thirty-five out of the *Pearl* were manning the *Jane*. Although neither vessel was mounted with large cannon, their men were ready to do battle. They had arrived the evening before, but because the king's men were unfamiliar with the deadly channels and shoals, they had waited for early dawn on the morning of November 22 to make their attack.

Presently, the men on sloops were hoisting and bending sails to the yards and in a moment they were underway, the Union Jack blowing in the breeze as the two ships proceeded around the south tip of Ocracoke Inlet. As the sloops crept through the treacherous sand bars, the men were preparing for battle by mounting swivel guns and piling cutlasses, muskets and boarding axes in strategic points.

Blackbeard had slept lightly the entire night. After preparing some coffee and taking a pipe from his pocket, he made his way topside, pipe in one hand, coffee mug in the other. It was not a pleasant morning—cold and misty with waves that chopped roughly against the side of the ship. He looked at his men sleeping side by side, made a comment about them "a'kenneling like hounds," and put his coffee mug on the bulwarks of the vessel. In its place, he substituted a spyglass. He surveyed the island.

What he saw startled him. He drew his breath in between his teeth in surprise. Was that the king's flag? He thrust aside his pipe and readjusted the spyglass. He placed it to his eye. Sure enough, there was the Union Jack, flying above two ships headed directly for the *Adventure*.

Damn, he thought! Why hadn't the lookout sounded the alarm? Glancing up at the empty crow's nest on the mainmast, he knew the reason—the party the night before. His men had grown soft, not expecting a battle after taking the pardon.

Immediately, Blackbeard rang the alarm. "A sail!" he cried. "On your feet, you lazy dogs. Make ready for a close fight, fore and aft. Every man to his charge, by thunder!"

It was all too clear from the dazed, hung over faces of the twenty-one men who staggered to their feet, that they were in no condition to fight a battle. Nevertheless, a battle they must fight. Their captain kicked them to their feet and threw buckets of water over their faces. In no time, they were stacking powder, scrap shot and cannon balls near the guns; soaking blankets to smother any fires that might break out; and piling cutlasses and pistols near the battle stations.

Blackbeard surveyed the scene once again and formulated plans for battle. He could see the two sloops clearly on the horizon, and from the way they were stationed on the inlet, there would be no escape for the *Adventure* to the open sea.

He had hoped that as the ships drew nearer, they might wreck on the shallow bar across the inlet, but the tide was high now. The shallow draft vessels floated easily over the bar and then into six fathoms of water. They were steering north directly toward the ship. He guessed correctly that the ships had been to seaward of Ocracoke Inlet all night, waiting for high tide.

Damn his lookout! But there was no time for other curses for a rowboat was already proceeding directly ahead of the first vessel, taking soundings. Every minute brought them closer to a battle. The excitement on the deck was wild. Blackbeard reached over to grab a tall negro racing by.

"Caesar!" he cried.

"Aye, sir," Caesar said, halting in mid-stride.

"Caesar, I'll be posting you in the powder room." Blackbeard reached into his pocket and withdrew a match. "Light this if the ship's taken. It will blow the ship to smithereens."

"But, sir," the Negro began, not understanding why the ship should be blown up.

"Do as I say," Blackbeard ordered.

"Aye, aye, sir." Blackbeard had freed Caesar as well as several other Negroes on this ship. For that, Caesar was extremely grateful. He never disobeyed an order.

Blackbeard watched the man climbing down the companion ladder. To Caesar, he had entrusted perhaps the most important part of this entire battle plan, for if the king's men took the ship, no doubt, they would come upon some very important papers on board, papers that could be extremely harmful to those in the North Carolina government. He feared for those governmental officials as well as his men, but even more so for his wife, Mary. The image of her cornflower blue eyes and chestnut hair came painfully to mind. He paused for a moment to get his bearings, and then heaving his shoulders regretfully, he walked to the bow of the *Adventure* and gave his first command. "Lads, hail them with a chase piece!"

White smoke suddenly burst forth with a roar from a muzzle of one of the eight cannons followed by a whizzing sheet of fire that sent the men in the small rowboat rocking to and fro so wildly that the pirates felt they had overturned it. Terrified, the men in the rowboat quickly scurried back to the larger vessel, unwilling to continue taking soundings.

Blackbeard laughed at their lack of bravery. His men were equally jubilant, shouting hurrahs. For the moment, they had the upper hand.

From what Blackbeard could discern though his spyglass, it appeared that neither of the sloops mounted heavy cannon. If that was so, they would have to give chase and try to get close enough to the *Adventure* to engage in battle.

From the king's ships, sounds of drum rolls rattled clear across the water. In a moment, the battle would begin.

In response to the drums, the pirates sent up a wild cacophonous clatter of their own, beating on anything in sight including pots and pans and shouting obscenities at the top of their lungs. Clearly, they were ready to do battle with the enemy, no matter how formidable.

Blackbeard had to smile at the bravado of his men, but then his expression became more serious. He could have evaded his attacker, perhaps, and steered northward through channels thoroughly familiar to him. But, he was not the type to back down from a fight. Plus, they would probably seek him out again, at a later date. Better to have it out now on his own territory than in some Godforsaken place he did not know.

"Stand by to send the swan shot!" Blackbeard bellowed. "Aim for the quarterdeck, ye tars. Fire!"

Blackbeard watched as the first shots fell short. "Let them have another round," he yelled. "Blast them, if they like the sport, we'll play a game of long bowls with them!"

The men heeded to his words. They continued to fire. The sloops moved closer, returning the fire with swivel guns, their shots falling just short of the *Adventure*. The pirate's hearts raced; their eyes glittered with excitement. As the struggle became closer, a great mass of smoke rose over both the sloops.

But the struggle was useless. Neither the sloops nor the pirate vessel was damaged to any degree, because they were still too far from each other. Blackbeard was the first to recognize their predicament. Shoving his helmsman aside, he took the wheel and began easing the *Adventure* toward the beach at Ocracoke Inlet.

The gunners stopped lighting touchholes and looked at each other in puzzlement. They were amazed at the course of action, which if continued, would lead them directly onto the shore.

Thomas Miller, the quartermaster, ran towards Blackbeard. "She'll run aground," he said, grabbing the pirate by the shoulder and pointing to the approaching land. "Have you gone stark raving mad?"

But Blackbeard did not listen to Miller. He shoved him aside, knocking Miller to his knees. Abruptly, Blackbeard changed the course of the *Adventure*.

Quickly, the other crew members divined Blackbeard's plan. They were entering a narrow channel that would separate the *Adventure* from their attackers by an unseen sandbar.

"Fetch the sounding line!" Blackbeard cried.

A line was drawn from the ocean's depths. "By the mark five," shouted the leadsman at the bow, looking at the piece of white bunting. "By the mark, three," he shouted as he saw the three strips of black leather. And finally, "By the mark two," as they sailed into twelve feet of water.

The *Adventure* sailed in with a fair wind. "She bears in with the land," Blackbeard shouted. "Hold off. Hold it fast with nippers."

After the *Adventure* had glided over the deepest part of the bar, Blackbeard moved to the stern to watch the two sloops. He guessed their drafts to be six feet at the most. If they continued on their present course, they would plow right into the sandbar. The larger of the two continued her course, tacking towards the unseen sandbar. The other vessel maneuvered a little to the left, following close behind.

From the stern of his vessel, Blackbeard grabbed the speaking trumpet and yelled, "Damn you for villains! Who are you and from whence come you?"

"You can see by our colors we are no pirates!" came a voice back across the water.

"Hoist out your boat and come aboard, so I might see who you are," Blackbeard shouted.

From across the waters, the voice yelled back. "I intend to come aboard you. And I'll send you to kingdom come, by God, or my name isn't Robert Maynard."

Lieutenant Robert Maynard! His old nemesis. Blackbeard had been in battles with him before. Once, Blackbeard had been so close to the man, he had seen the color of his eyes—grey and cold, the color of a sea in a storm. Under Governor Spotswood's command, Maynard had been tireless in his pursuit, searching up and down the coast for pirates. Most men would have given up the hunt for Blackbeard by now, but not Maynard. Those ruthless grey eyes had gazed on the pirate so determinedly that Blackbeard knew Maynard would follow him to the grave.

Blackbeard had escaped Maynard in other skirmishes. He prayed it would be the same today.

Blackbeard did well to pray. Maynard was a very cool and very practical lieutenant of incredible confidence. The men under his command felt him quietly and precisely imposing his will. He had a reputation in the colonies for capturing more pirates than any other man alive and he captured them, not to enjoy success, but to prepare himself for the next and greater capture. There was no man he wanted more than Blackbeard, for he was the greatest challenge of them all.

Furious, Blackbeard placed the speaking trumpet to his lips. In his other hand, he held up a bowl of liquor from last night's celebrations and shouted back, "I drink to you, sir with these words. Damnation seize my soul if I give you any quarter or take any from you." Then, he drank the entire bowl, his men cheering him on. Here was the old Blackbeard they knew so well—ferocious, indomitable and unshakable.

In reply, Maynard yelled, "I expect no quarter from you, not shall I give you any." Obviously, he was about to issue additional orders for his men to fire on the *Adventure*, because Blackbeard's men saw guns being aimed at them. The *Ranger* followed the *Jane*, both sailing full speed toward the *Adventure*. But, before they could reach the *Adventure*, Blackbeard's crew heard the sounds of one light crunch and then another, as the *Jane* and then the *Ranger*, plowed into the sandbar.

"They've run aground," Blackbeard shouted joyfully. His men burst into boisterous laughter. No doubt their enemies heard the laughter, but Blackbeard heard no words from Maynard floating across the inlet.

While Maynard's men were in confusion, Blackbeard prepared his attack with tremendous cunning. If he was lucky, he might end this battle here and now. "The larger sloop has but a small waist!" he shouted at his men. "Give her a broadside, you dogs!"

The *Adventure*'s cannon were aimed at the attackers. At a signal from Blackbeard, the thunder from the cannon echoed across the dunes. A cloud rose above the vessels so thick it completely concealed the ships' dark hulls. But when the smoke cleared, the sight was devastating. Streams of blood ran through the scuppers of both the *Jane* and the *Ranger*. The sound of moans and wails was so pitiful, it was as if the very bowels of hell had been opened.

Blackbeard's men yelled shouts of victory and began jumping up and down for joy. But Blackbeard was not so jubilant. The mighty recoil of the cannon had also shoved the *Adventure* onto the shoreline and she was stuck. He, too, would have to wait for the rising tide before his ship could be set afloat.

Blackbeard placed his spyglass to his eye and studied first, the larger sloop and then, the smaller. He saw no sign of life anywhere—not a man even rose to show a flag of truce. Neither did he hear a single moan or groan from a man. Indeed, his shots had been fired to maim and kill. They were not the large heavy cannonballs, but smaller swanshot and glass and metal wrapped in burlap. Still, had they really done that much damage?

Joining their captain at the *Adventure*'s stern, the pirates peered out across the waters. Well, thought Blackbeard, they would have their answer soon enough. The larger sloop with Maynard on board was breaking free from the bar, heading straight in their direction. Blackbeard's men grabbed axes and irons and prepared to board the ship as soon as the *Jane* came alongside.

As the *Jane* drifted closer, Blackbeard held his men back.

"Better to be safe," he shouted. "Lead with the grenades! There may be some still alive!"

The men grabbed case bottles filled with powder and small shot, slugs and pieces of iron. Lighting the fuses, they threw them on the deck of the *Jane*. The grenades exploded, sending up a foul smelling, suffocating smoke that would have finished off anyone caught on the deck.

Blackbeard shouted to his men. "They was all knocked on the head but three or four! Blast you, board her and cut them to pieces."

The men's pulses beat quickly; their faces lit up with renewed vigor. As the stern of Maynard's sloop brushed the bow of the *Adventure*, grappling irons were hurled across the bulwarks of the enemy vessel. Carrying a rope, Teach locked and made fast the two sloops. He was the first aboard.

Blackbeard glanced about the deck of the ship and then turned away from the scene in loathing and horror. The blood ran so thick it had slickened the deck and several of the pirates, in a mad rush to board the ship, had slipped and fallen in it. He paused for a moment to collect his thoughts and was about to give another commend, when suddenly he heard a voice he recognized immediately. Maynard!

"Boarders on the starboard quarter!" the lieutenant shouted.

As Blackbeard and his men opened their mouths in amazement, half of Maynard's men burst from the hold of the vessel.

"It's a trick!" Blackbeard shouted. "Half are still alive!"

Cutlasses were drawn, pistols pulled, and knives flashed out as the pirates were thrown into the midst of hand-to-hand combat.

Rallying his men on, Blackbeard called in a daring bloodthirsty voice, "Away there! Leave not a man to sup his flip again!"

Bearing up gallantly, he sprung into the fighting with an air of confidence that concealed his real fears and dreads. Blackbeard had previously avoided hand-to-hand combat by scaring his enemy into submission through treachery and cunning. Maynard's men often engaged in combat with pirates. They had Blackbeard at his weak point.

Nevertheless, Blackbeard and his men strove valiantly against his enemies. The shouts and tauntings of the combatants, the clashing of cutlasses, and the deadly fire of pistols clanked and clattered and clashed in the air. The pirates fought in the midst of the remains of twenty torn and mangled Englishmen lying about the ship. As they skidded on the deck and sought to regain their balance, they heard the groans of dying men beneath them. The sea was red with blood.

Blackbeard wildly swung his cutlass round and round his head, dealing anyone in his pathway a fatal blow.

He made his way toward Maynard. Some of the lieutenant's crewmen fired their pistols at the hulk of the man, but the shots had no effect. He kept on coming.

Finally, Blackbeard stood no more than two feet away from his old adversary. The steel grey eyes looked at him, menacing and terrifying.

Blackbeard tried one last time to frighten Maynard into submission. "You lily-livered rascal," he cried. "How dare you come athwart the great Blackbeard!"

Undaunted, Maynard didn't even flinch. He stood his ground. Blackbeard's old tricks could not aid him now. He had met his match.

The two men each cocked their pistols and fired. Rushed suddenly from all sides by Maynard's crewmen, Blackbeard missed his target. But Maynard's shot plowed through Blackbeard's body. Even this failed to halt the pirate.

As Maynard reached for his sword, a powerful blow from Blackbeard's cutlass snapped it off near its hilt, sending the blade flying into mid-air. Such a blow ordinarily would have knocked a man down, but Maynard still held onto the hilt with a frenzied grasp, even thought the blow had grazed his knuckles.

Maynard drew another pistol. Blackbeard raised his cutlass for a finishing blow. But the moment he swung his cutlass aloft, a sailor, barely more than twenty, gave Blackbeard a terrific blow to the neck with his sword.

Blood gushed from the wound. Blackbeard staggered, grinned at the boy and yelled, "Well done, Lad!"

The young boy raised his sword again. "If it not be well done, I'll do it better!" he shouted, giving Blackbeard another blow to the neck.

The pirate fell to his knees. Other seamen now fell in on him, shouting defiance. Ducking in behind him, they pricked him with their swords. He cocked his pistol, but it fell from his hands. His eyes rolled in terrible wildness; he writhed for a moment in passing agony and then, he fell to the deck, the blood pouring from his gored neck.

As Blackbeard gave his final moan, his crew stopped their fighting and froze in silent horror at the sight of their slaughtered leader. Then they fled; some jumping overboard, others, calling out for quarter.

Hearing these shouts Caesar, who was in the powder room, well understood the goings-on outside. He moaned for a moment, then spoke, "A good seaman he was, not your fresh water, wishy, washy, fair weather fellow. Many a gale of wind we weathered together. Here's to him with all my heart." He lighted the match and was just about to set the magazine on fire when Maynard's men burst into the hold and stopped him.

As the action ended, the _Ranger_ drifted into the _Adventure_. Her seamen jumped on board and attacked the last of Blackbeard's crew.

When the bodies of the slain were removed and the prisoners taken into custody, the Union Jack was raised aboard the _Adventure_ amidst a chorus of exhultation. When the final flush of victory subsided, the king's men made a thorough inspection of the _Adventure_. Aboard the ship, they found some gold dust, plate and other small articles of value. These, they brought back to Lieutenant Maynard to examine along with some papers they had discovered. Some was correspondence between Blackbeard and some prominent New York traders. A more interesting document was a letter from Tobias Knight dated November 17, 1718. The gold and plate, Maynard distributed among his men. The papers were kept by Maynard for further inspection.

Wounded and desolate, the rest of the pirate crew consisting of nine men including Caesar were brought onto the deck of the _Jane_ as prisoners. They stood huddled around the body of their captain.

Maynard walked into their midst and gloated over the pirate. He had killed the most infamous pirate of them all—the great Blackbeard. He, Robert Maynard, was no ordinary man. His name would go down in history.

At length, Lieutenant Maynard proceeded to examine the huge body of Blackbeard. Conducting an informal autopsy, he passed his hand over the bloodstained clothes and pushing them aside, found that his victim had died with five pistol balls in him and no less than twenty severe cuts from swords. "I must say he was courageous," Maynard commented. "Not an ordinary man at that. He might have passed for a hero had he been employed in a good cause."

It was said later that Caesar, who had been standing with the other prisoners beside the bulwarks, made the comment, "I think he would have liked hearing someone say that. He always wanted to be employed in a good cause. T'is a shame he never was."

But no more was said concerning the major adversary of Lieutenant Maynard's career, and after these final comments on Blackbeard's character, the lieutenant lay aside all feelings of compassion. Raising Blackbeard's own cutlass over his head, Maynard slung it down on the pirate's throat, severing his head from his body. The body, he threw into the sea. The head, he hung from the bowsprit of the _Jane_, to be taken back to Williamsburg and Alexander Spotswood.

XXVIII

A Eulogy for a Pirate

It was said later by the servant who delivered the message to Charles Eden, that the governor took the news of Blackbeard's death very lightly. Indeed, he seemed to show only the slightest concern over the incident, asking for a brief account of the particulars leading to the tragic occurrence which would be reported in the minutes of the North Carolina Colonial Records. It was only natural, then, that most would reach the inevitable conclusion that the two had only the most casual of acquaintances.

But those that knew him better would report that the governor rarely showed emotions, even on the most mournful occasions, and that his reaction to the news could not be taken as evidence of a lack of collaboration on Eden's part.

The servant reported that the governor sat listening to the news in silence, casually sipping wine by a fire lit in the library of his home. Once, while the servant was speaking, he rose to stir the coals in the fireplace, and then seated himself once again. Only a slight tremble of the glass at the initial report gave any indication of shock or bereavement. The servant, after reporting the news, closed the door gently behind him and left.

As far as could be determined by those servants who passed outside, the governor crossed the room several times to either refill his wine glass or turn the coals. All else was heard by one older servant who had the habit of listening through keyholes. She heard at one time—the most unusual rattling of papers coming from the area of the room occupied by the governor's desk. The governor rattled the papers for a full half-hour, then crossed the room to the area of the fireplace. The servant heard a few loud crackling sounds such as burning paper makes and then all was silent. It could be assumed that those crackling sounds were made by burning correspondence between Eden and Blackbeard. However, this is not certain. All was quiet then in the library, save for the hourly chiming of the grandfather clock...

Quiet, until there was a heavy knocking on the front door that was opened to reveal a most startling guest—a young woman, hair flying wild about her face and wet from a recent thundershower. In her haste, she had lost her bonnet and her shawl was loosely arranged about her shoulders. She did not wait for the servants to take her wrap nor for them to announce her arrival, but instead, burst into the library, unbidden and unheralded.

Governor Eden whirled around on his heels as the door opened to admit Mary Teach, tears in her eyes, voice shaking as she spoke. "Tell me it's not true," she said. Her face was drawn; her eyes red.

He raised the glass in his hand, half-filled with wine. "To Blackbeard," he said. "A man who was a match for the devil himself." He sent the glass through the air and it shattered against the fireplace. Flames from the liquor shot up for a moment, threatening to engulf the wall, and then subsided. It was the only outburst of emotions he had shown all evening, and whether these feelings were on behalf of the pirate or his own loss has yet to be determined.

Eden's reference to Blackbeard in the past tense confirmed what Mary had heard. She sunk down into a chair. "Then it's true," she said. "I had prayed it wasn't."

He laid a hand on her shoulder in a gesture of comfort, but it did little good. The emotions welling inside her burst forth in a torrent of tears. A handkerchief offered to her was refused for one of her own.

She wept long and bitterly and then suddenly she turned the face of an anguished woman on him. "You sent him to his death, you scoundrel."

He looked at her face, her lashes wet, her cheeks streaked with tears, and then turned away. He spoke exhaustedly. "He went to sea of his own free will."

She sniffed. "I don't believe that."

"How could I have made him go on the account?" he asked, praying she didn't know of the two's collaboration.

Mary shook her head. "Don't ask me, for I don't know, Governor," she answered. "But I know you for what you are, a scoundrel of the most common sort. You had a kind of evil power on him, I know."

Eden began to pace the length of the room. "He was a pirate."

She spoke softly now, her voice hushed yet firm. "He was not a pirate. Not at heart."

Eden walked to the liquor cabinet and poured himself a drink. He offered one to Mary also but she refused, her lips pressed together tightly.

For an instant, he studied the woman. She was speaking out of love, he thought, and not with any real logic. He could perhaps agree with her—that Blackbeard had wanted to settle down, to start a family—but at heart, he was a pirate. The sea was in his blood, his brain, his heart. Ah! Sentimentality, thy name is woman, he thought, sipping his wine.

As he gazed on the woman, her cheeks flushed, her eyes dewy and soft, the old feelings of jealousy and lust stirred within him, and he wanted to crush out that love of hers for the pirate and replace it with a love for himself. Standing over her, he smirked. "You're being ridiculous. He was just a common pirate. He would have had the inclination to go on the account again—if not now then later. It was only a matter of time."

"No," she said, her lips curling in anger.

Eden put his glass down on the table. God, but the woman was stubborn! "Listen," he said, suddenly flying at her. "I'll tell you the truth about your wonderful, beloved husband."

She watched him in puzzlement as he rushed over to his desk, opened the drawers and gathered a pile of papers from a bottom drawer on the right hand side. He brought them to her and she looked at them curiously. They were from all over the world—England, the Barbados, even Africa. In all there were thirteen of them.

"He gave them to me for safekeeping," Eden said.

"What are they?" she asked curiously, before reading.

"Marriage documents," he said. "He had thirteen wives other than you."

She put her hand over her eyes. "Lies," she said.

"Lies? In black and white? Mary, he had fourteen wives—one in every port. And all those marriages including your own are as worthless as the paper they were written on."

Her eyes flashed furiously as she gave the papers back to him, unread. "You're even more a scoundrel than I thought—for telling me that," she said. "You should have left me with my memories."

Eden sighed. He stood up and returned the documents to their drawer. Then he spoke in a softer tone. "Why live in memories, Mary?" He crossed the room and sat down beside her once again. "Mary," he said. "I still want you more than ever. Come and live with me in this house."

She looked at him, appalled.

"Marry me," he said.

His eyes were in shadows.

"Mary," he said, "I have everything he ever hoped to have and more. Riches, power, respect in the community. They're all mine. And they can be yours."

She withdrew from him and rose from her seat, trembling from head to toe. "How dare you compare yourself to him!" she said, her face coloring. "You are more a villain than I thought. You thought to blackmail me earlier, to force me to submit to your desires. Now my husband is dead, and you can no longer force me to do as you want."

He rose from his seat and drew her to him.

She thrust herself away. "Don't come near me," she shouted. "He was a gentleman, a true gentleman. You shall never equal him, Governor. You shall always remain an abominable, blackhearted scoundrel. Compare to him? Hah, never in your life!"

Eden was aghast. For the life of him, he could not understand this woman. He could offer her so much more than Blackbeard. And she was turning it down.

"But I don't understand," he uttered.

"And I'm certain you never will, Governor," Mary said, rising. She seemed to have gained her composure again, and in a very ladylike manner she put on her gloves and turned to face him. "I'll find my own way out," she said heavily.

Mary Teach was never quite the same after Blackbeard's death. She stayed in mourning for well over six months and even after she stopped wearing black, her eyes appeared sunken and her cheeks hollow. She received only a few guests in her home at Plum Point, and eventually those stopped their visits, so melancholy and sullen were the encounters. Invitations to parties, she refused; suggestions of overseas trips were shrugged aside. She never married again.

She was seen by the citizens of Bath only by chance and only from a distance—mostly on the widow's walk of her home overlooking Bath harbor. Passers-by frequently reported they saw her staring from an upstairs window of her home in that same direction, like a mariner's wife who waits for her husband to return from the sea.

Eden, on the other hand, apparently suffered no long-lasting effects from Mary's abrupt departure. There were those that said he drank himself into oblivion that night, for he ordered two bottles of Barbados rum from the cellar, and then he did not leave the room all evening. Come morning, when the servants knocked gingerly on the door, they found him dressed in the same attire of the preceding day. He needed a shave and his breath smelled badly of alcohol, but by mid-morning he was up and about, conducting business as usual.

But one servant while cleaning up about his desk did take note of two peculiarities that would seem to indicate the governor had not drunk himself into oblivion that night at all, but, on the contrary, had been far from idle. The peculiarities were a candle, burned down to the bottom of a wick (a brand new candle, at that) and wads of paper thrown into a waste basket—wads the servant was sure were not there before since the wastepaper baskets in the house were emptied daily. One of these wads when unrolled revealed that the governor had addressed a letter to the lords proprietors of North Carolina.

Actually, the governor had been quite busy that night for he had some most pressing matters to look into that took priority over love, namely, those items carried off by Captain Brand and his men the night of his entry into North Carolina. His letter, sent off as soon as possible the next day, vehemently implored the lords proprietors to force the governor of Virginia to return these items (sugar, cocoa and, notwithstanding, anchors to the number of two hundred) at once, for, complained the governor, the entry had been illegal and uncalled for.

The letter, when opened in England by the lords proprietors, was received at first with some consternation and, at a later date, with growing anger. The fact that a crown colony had invaded a proprietary government under a separate jurisdiction was regarded as an unjustifiable act. In response, a series of letters ensued that created a flurry of excitement throughout the English government.

The lords proprietors wrote to the king stating they would soon declare war on Virginia if the goods weren't returned to North Carolina where they could be sold and the proceeds handed over immediately to them. The House of Burgesses informed William Byrd that Spotswood's reputation was none the better for the illegal entry, for he did it "understanding that there was a great deal of money and a great many Negroes in the case," and Byrd, wishing to oust Spotswood from office, immediately drafted a note to the king giving him all the details concerning the invasion. Spotswood in turn sent a letter to Lord Carteret stating that he would certainly be the gainer from the confiscation of the loot transported to Virginia, "where there are many more purchasers for such commodities than in North Carolina and I may say...much better payment." However, he did think the lords proprietors should reimburse him for the efforts to take Blackbeard, and this would take all the money from the sale of the goods.

At length, Spotswood wrote to Governor Eden stating the reason he hadn't informed him of the design was, he said, merely a "friendly concern for your safety, for if the pirates found out you knew you would certainly be exposed to the pirates' revenge." A letter was then posted by Spotswood to the lords proprietors, hoping they would give little credit to clandestine testimonials by Eden when the lords proprietors would soon be hearing, "how dark a part some of their officers have acted, particularly the chief justice who concealed a robbery he committed and received and concealed a considerable part of the cargo of this French ship which he knew Teach had no right to give or he to receive, admitting the same had been wrecked goods as pretended."

Eventually, the king, totally confused at the course of events and all these letters, requested and then demanded to know why Spotswood had made an illegal entry into North Carolina when Blackbeard had the king's pardon and there was no proof of him having pirated after settling down in Bath. The implications of the king's correspondence with Virginia's governor were only too apparent—Spotswood had better be justified in invading North Carolina's lands or, in other words, he had better have some evidence of a corrupt North Carolina government. If not, things would get very unpleasant for Spotswood.

An Interlude
With an Old Acquaintance

Not long after Blackbeard was killed, Charles Eden was seen walking along Beaufort Street. Gold cane in hand, powdered wig atop his head, he was dressed so smartly that several young ladies stopped dead in their tracks, quite struck by the character that he cut. He stopped to bow to these ladies, who were, no doubt, flattered by his attentions for they giggled profusely, and then he walked on. For an instant, he tipped his hat to several other gentlemen. Then he continued at a leisurely pace, apparently just out for an afternoon stroll. He appeared carefree and untroubled, untroubled that is, until he stopped to watch some reflections in the glass windows of an establishment at the corner of Beaufort and Carteret Streets.

He was not particularly pleased with what he saw, but he was totally unprepared for what happened next.

He caught a quick glimpse in the window of a most ugly face wrapped in a hoodwink. Then he heard a familiar voice cry, "Charles, dear Charles."

Groaning inwardly, Charles Eden turned to face Anne Hassell waving at him from across the street.

He would have perhaps taken off running, given the opportunity, but already it was too late; for in no time she was standing no more than two feet from him. Knowing he had no choice, he braced himself, took her hand and kissed it graciously. "What a pleasant surprise!" he said.

Anne stared at him from under a sea-green cloak called a cardinal that was partially open in front to reveal a tabby dress underneath. For a moment she smiled at Eden, a smile of intense excitement and pleasure. It was quite obvious she was glad to see her old beau. She was in high spirits. "Yes, I..." she began, and then stopped in mid-sentence. A sudden thought seemed to have crossed her mind, not very pleasant, and now in another frame of mind she quickly snatched her hand away from Eden's grasp. Then just as quickly, she spoke. "Why whatever has become of you, Charles? I have not seen you in a month's time." She seemed quite angry.

Eden coughed, looked at his feet and then waited a moment before speaking. He gave himself just time enough to think of an excuse. Then quick on his feet as always, he looked her in the eyes. "I must apologize. I was called away on business."

"Oh?" Anne asked.

"Yes," Eden said, coughing again. His face assumed a contrived look of pain brought on perhaps by unrequited love. "And when you did not respond to my letter," he continued, his voice breaking in mid-sentence.

"Letter?" Anne asked. Her eyes went blank. "What letter?" Her former look was replaced by one of hurt confusion.

Eden appeared quite emotional, tapping his head with the palm of his hand. "Hell," he said, and then immediately apologized for using such strong language in the company of a lady.

Anne accepted the apology.

For a moment they stopped their conversation to greet some neighbors on a shopping spree. Before they resumed, Eden noticed a puzzled expression on Anne's face.

Eden responded to Anne's look. "But did you not receive my letter?"

"Why no!" Anne said, all the while wondering what Eden was getting at.

"Had I only known!" Eden dramatically assumed all the looks of bewilderment, anguish, and utter hopelessness, in that order. "But I did not suspect," he continued. "And when you did not reply, naturally I thought you angry at me."

"Angry?" Anne asked, her state of mind now one of total confusion. "But I assure you, Charles..." she began.

"Yes," he said interrupting her. "So you see when I returned it was most difficult for me to visit you."

"But when did you return?" she asked.

"About two weeks ago," Eden said, rubbing shoulders with a gentleman who passed them.

Anne paused to collect her thoughts until the man was well out of hearing distance. She looked Eden shrewdly in the eye and remarked slowly and evenly. "That is odd! My father told me he saw you at Madam Worsley's ball. I did not attend for I was a bit under the weather."

For an instant, Eden looked taken aback. His excuse, which had been going along so well up until now, seemed about to be undone. However, quickly he regained his former composure and said, "I assure you, Anne, I do not wish to contradict your father, but I've been back only two weeks." Cleverly, he changed the subject. "And how is your father?"

"My father?" Anne said, totally exasperated with Eden. "My father is quite well, thank you." She returned to the former topic of conversation very adroitly, considering her reputation for stupidity. "My father had some unflattering things to say concerning your person."

Eden hemmed and hawed for a moment, but all he said was, "Did he?"

"He called you a womanizer," Anne continued. "And worse."

"Well, that is understandable, given the unusual circumstances," he said, concentrating his attention on a carriage across the way.

"But," Anne said, with sudden determination, "since you've returned, I hope we'll be seeing you at the house again." Evidently, she was ready to forgive him—even though his behavior had been despicable.

Eden looked extremely uncomfortable. The girl was not easily put off. Finally, he took a deep breath. "Anne, when you did not answer my letter I felt you were displeased with me and well, as the days passed.... My dear Anne," he stammered, "I hardly known how to say this." For a moment his voice was drowned out by a group of laughing children racing down the street. When they had left, Eden suddenly straightened up. "Anne," he said, "I deeply regret to inform you that I am to be married."

"Married!" Anne exclaimed. Her face turned positively livid.

"Yes, I am afraid it is so," Eden said, shaking his head sadly.

Anne stared at Eden. Then her mouth fell open. "But to whom?" she asked.

"To a lady from Barbados," Eden replied. To the eye he appeared quite upset—a pained expression crossing his face. He continued to shake his head in regret. "Yes, I fear it is true, all true. I have given my word," he said lamely. "You see I was dreadfully upset when I did not hear from you." He paused.

Anne's mouth made a downward grimace and her lips trembled.

Eden raised her chin with his finger. "Ah, but how unhappy you look, dear Anne," he said. "I thought you would be happy for me."

Anne jerked her chin away in dismay. "Happy, Charles!" she said, now on the verge of tears. "I was in love with you."

Eden appeared totally surprised. He placed his hand over his heart as if it had skipped a beat. "Why Anne!" he exclaimed. "I had no idea. I never thought so…ah, but it is too late now," he continued in a sad, drawn voice. "I was in desperation when I did not hear from you. I thought you no longer cared. I never suspected. Ah, I hope you do understand," he finished, so sadly one would think tears were welling up inside him.

Anne's reaction was one of positive amazement. "Indeed I do understand, sir," she snapped. Quite briskly, she turned on her heels and stalked off in fury.

Eden remained standing on the side of the street, trying to look as forlorn as possible until she had stepped into her carriage and had driven off. Then he continued down Beaufort Street whistling softly under his breath. Nothing in his manner indicated the least remorse. Indeed, on his face was that expression he often had when he had made a fool of someone—that strange, marring and twisted smirk of a smile.

Eden continued down Carteret Street until he came to the wharves. Crossing the street, he disappeared into a tangled maze of alleyways along the waterfront. He passed a lodging house where drunken seamen slept the night for a penny, so squalid and malodorous were the accommodations. Through half-glazed windows, he saw sailors packed elbow to elbow at eating places. He hurried on, trying not to notice the dilapidated buildings whose doors were falling off their hinges.

However, when Eden came to one building in particular he stopped, gazed at the sign of a fish's head above its door, and then pulled a scrap of paper from his waistcoat pocket. The note had been delivered to him that morning. All it said was, "Meet me at the *Fish's Head* at two o'clock. Barnes." Curiosity had gotten the best of him and Eden had decided to do as the note said, but he had no idea who Barnes was or why the note had been written.

He entered the building. The first floor, a fish shop, was closed. He pushed his way past a throng of dirty, ragged children and climbed some creaking stairs to the second floor and then knocked on a door. A woman, stoop-shouldered, her hair matted and filthy, answered it, and through a half-cracked door he could see a dozen men crowded into one room,

drinking and talking. At a side table, several of them were playing cards.
The woman stared at him for a moment. No doubt, she had not seen a
gentleman in a long time. Then, she brought a man in rolled-up
shirtsleeves to the door.

"Are you Barnes?" Eden asked.

The man nodded and the two, Eden and Barnes, descended the stairs
together, into a cramped room barely large enough for the table and two
chairs it held. The man glanced cautiously over his shoulder and then
closed the door. Eden handed him a gold guinea which he bit between
his four front teeth, for that was all the teeth he had, and then he put the
guinea in his pocket and flashed a smile.

"Bit late," Barnes said.

"I ran into an old acquaintance. Nothing of any importance."

"I see," Barnes said. He pulled out a whisky bottle from his shirt
pocket, offered Eden some and when the governor refused, took a swig
for himself. Then he wiped his mouth on his shirtsleeves and set the
bottle on the table.

"Now then, what's this all about?" Eden asked, pulling forth the
note.

Barnes looked at the note, turned it upside down and squinted. "Don't
read myself, Governor," he said, giving it back to Eden. "But if you're
wanting to know why I asked you here, I'll tell you...my seamen friends
seems to thinks I have something you'd want."

"What's that?" Eden eyed the man quizzically.

"Well, sir," Barnes said, leaning closer to Eden and breathing more
softly, "I just come to work this morning, you see, sir, over to Lovick's
house."

"John Lovick, secretary of the colony?"

When Barnes nodded in response, Eden immediately tensed up. He
drew his breath in, causing the candle on the table to flicker.

Barnes continued. "I come to work at seven o'clock, seven, as I
always do, and there's the house all locked up and bolted and some
gentlemen standing about watching. And that's how I found out, sir."

"Found out what?" Eden asked, looking rather irritated.

"Well, sir, it's Moseley and Moore."

At this instant Eden leaned closer to Barnes. "Tell me about Moseley
and Moore."

Barnes smiled. "Well, they've gone and taken the records of the
province, they have, the journal, everything, and they've locked themselves up in Lovick's house."

"Well, what of it?" Eden failed to see the gist of the man's message.

"They're saying, sir, that Governor Spotswood has new evidence."

Eden started. "What evidence?" Barnes was beginning to make more sense.

"That I don't know, sir, save it's of your being an accomplice and an abettor in piracy."

"Damn!" Eden thrust his fist down on the table so hard that the candle would have fallen over had not Barnes steadied it.

"They're saying, sir, that the people will rebel when they hear the news. And there's more, sir."

"More?" Eden certainly didn't need any more bad news.

"Aye. Those troops of Spotswood's. The ones in the Pamlico Sound. The ones that took Blackbeard."

"Yes."

"They're saying those troops will come direct down to take over once the rebellion's underway."

"My God!" Eden said in dismay.

"They say there's no way to stop it. Not if Spotswood's got the evidence, sir."

"I wonder what this evidence is..." Eden said, thinking aloud.

"I wouldn't know, sir."

"Well," Eden said, standing up, "you did have something I'd want, Barnes." On the way out he gave the man another gold guinea and then left Barnes biting the second coin between his teeth.

Eden retraced his steps to Beaufort Street, leaving the filth and grime of the waterfront. At one point he cuffed a small boy who tried to pluck a coin from his pocket. He came out of a narrow alleyway, turned onto Beaufort Street and joined the well-to-do in front of a high-class establishment, blending in extremely well in his gold cane and periwig, and finally disappearing into the crowd.

A Stratagem
to Uncover the Syndicate

S hortly after his meeting with Barnes, Charles Eden met with Tobias
Knight at the governor's home.

At first glance, the meeting with Knight appeared to be social in
nature, for the two talked quietly together, sipping wine across from a
lighted fire in the governor's library. But the more careful observer would
note that the governor glanced at his watch every now and then as the
two conversed, and that Tobias Knight on every quarter hour rose from
his chair, crossed the length of the room, and drew back a curtain from a
corner window to stare outside. Indications were the two expected someone.

The expected visitor was, by no means, of any small importance.
This was more apparent by the way the two glanced anxiously at each
other when a door was heard to open and slam shut outside the library.
Sounds of voices, pounding of feet across the floor, and finally, a sudden
loud knock brought the governor and Knight quickly to their feet.

The door was opened to reveal a sailor in the hold of an armed
guard. The sailor looked appalling. He was emaciated from scarce meals,
tired from lack of sleep, and dressed in tattered clothes, now many sizes
too big and hanging curiously from the shoulders. Upon being thrust
inside the room, the men noticed the sailor had a limp in his left leg. On
closer inspection the man was revealed to be none other than Blackbeard's
first mate, Israel Hands.

"You may set him down," the governor said, nodding to the guard.
In response, the guard grabbed Hands roughly by the shoulder and

dragged him across the room to a wainscot chair. Hands sat down, glaring with small malevolent eyes.

When he had settled down, the prisoner spoke his thoughts in rough seaman's language. He directed his attention to the governor. "So, your shirking lubbers found me for a marked man, did they?"

The guard moved in at this moment, ready to hold the prisoner back should he try anything, but Hands, weary and tired, could only give the guard a sour look. "Tell them to let me be," he said, nodding at the guard, but speaking again to Eden.

The governor did not comply with Hands' request too hastily, despite the look of anxiety in the prisoner's eye. He crossed the room, took a pipe from a table, lit it and exhaled. "So they roughed you up a bit, Mr. Hands."

Hands fumed in indignation.

Eden stared steadfastly at the prisoner, but he was quick to add, "No one is going to hurt you, Mr. Hands...as long as you see fit to cooperate." Smoke rose in long, easy curls throughout the room. Then with great composure, Eden walked across the room until he was directly in front of Hands. Feet planted firmly apart, staring down at the man, he made his next statement with the calm assurance of a man used to having his own way. "Of course, if you don't cooperate my guard will begin by cutting out your tongue—we should have done that long ago. It would have spared us this meeting, and you, untold anguish."

The consequence of this last remark was an emotional outburst from Hands. He glanced first at Tobias Knight, still sitting by the fire, then at Eden standing above him, and then began to bewail his own misfortunes in a shrill, pitiful voice. "I know'd if ever I was to get off clean, if Spotswood set me free, I mean, you'd have the black spot on me. Here I was about to swing from Gallows Road when the king issued another pardon. And what becomes o' me? Why, I'm done for again by you. By the powers, this tops the stiffest yard it do." His face wrinkled up; he put his head in his hands and broke down sobbing.

Eden withdrew from Hands at this instant, crossed the room, and turned the coals in the fire. When Hands had sufficiently recovered from bemoaning his own fate, Eden turned to him once again. "Mr. Hands," he said, looking the man directly in they eye, "you are correct in assuming our syndicate was on the lookout for you."

Hands gritted his teeth in a sudden fit of stifled rage. "Well, you've run me down, and here I am. What's it you want?"

Eden, who had finished his smoke, turned his back on Hands, poured himself a full glass of liquor and drank half. When he sat his glass down on the table, he turned back around to face Hands. His face had a most severe look. "I believe you know exactly what we're after, Mr. Hands." He motioned to the guard who suddenly grabbed Hands, jerked him to his feet, and twisted the prisoner's arm behind his back.

Hands let forth a piercing shriek of pain. When the guard eased up, he sunk back into his chair, his senses exhausted. "You gave me your word you'd let me be," he moaned.

Eden's jaw was rigidly set. "Only if you'd cooperate." He retrieved his glass, drank another sip, and then exchanged glances with Tobias Knight. "Now," Eden said, pausing for a moment to collect his thoughts, "I heard tell you turned king's evidence on us at a trial held by Spotswood. That wasn't a very noble thing to do, Mr. Hands."

Hands was quite upset by Eden's knowledge of the trial. His hands trembled. "Well, he roughed me up, Spotswood did," he said, making an excuse. "Just as you."

Eden finished off his drink, set it down and walked toward Hands again. When he was only a few feet from him he stopped and looked directly at the prisoner. "Tell us what you told him," he said, in a steadily deepening voice.

Hands sat motionless in his chair, saying nothing.

Tobias Knight, still suffering from his cold, let forth a sneeze so loud at this instant that it caused both men to start.

After a moment's hesitation, Eden spoke. The man was trying his patience. "I promise you, Mr. Hands, upon my honor, you're as good as dead by tomorrow if you don't speak up."

Presumably, Hands must have decided that doing what Eden wanted would be better for him in the long run, for what ensued was a conversation concerning the trial in Williamsburg. "The silver, sir," he said. "That was kept secret."

Eden pressed his lips firmly together. "You blabbed."

Hands' lips quivered. "I never told of that, sir, so help me God, I didn't. Not to a soul." Momentarily, his eyes brightened. "Spotswood, he was saddened by the merchandise, he was. The anchors. Never suspected, sir, not him, even though rumors of the Spanish galleon were passed on by the fisherman. Spotswood still doesn't suspect. The anchors are locked in a barn with the other merchandise to be sold at public auction."

"I see." Eden went to his tobacco box again, refilled his pipe and began another smoke. Then he began to pace the floor, turning over thoughts in his head. He decided to find out about the trial from Hands first. Then he would find out about the silver. "Well, perhaps, Mr. Hands, you'd better tell us what you do know. Now you were captured. There was a trial in Virginia. And you turned on us, became king's evidence."

When Hands did not react to this remark, Eden stood up and went to the fireplace, probing among the logs for a fresh light. Then he faced Hands again. "Come now, Mr. Hands, you can tell an old shipmate, surely." Eden motioned to the guard again. The guard responded to Eden's signal immediately by reinstating his former torture.

Hands let out an earsplitting shriek and then flew into a rage. In a headlong torrent he spoke. "I can see for myself I ain't got no choice. You governors are all the same, you are. Dogs and murderers, the both of you. You're within sight of the gallows and what's a long sight worse, of torture, with a governor. But I'll tell you what I told him." Hands finally settled down and rubbed his arm to relieve the pain. "I told him of the French ship."

"Told him you captured the Martiniqueman?" Eden asked, instantly removing his pipe from his mouth in surprise.

"Yes," Hands continued, his eyes flashing in anger. "Told him how we spied the two merchant ships and made ready for battle, and how one crewman come on deck with his head all done up with smoking matches, looking a fright just like Teach and how he gave a signal to raise the Jolly Roger."

"Damn you!" Eden said, all his spiritual reserve bursting forth. He went to the liquor table and drew some cognac into a glass. Then he took a swallow of the liquor, shaking his head like a man looking forward to the worst.

"But that ain't the half of the evidence he's got on you," Hands said.

Eden whirled around on his heels. "Well, you'd better tell me the rest at the risk of losing another limb." Eden's face was livid with anger.

Hands regarded his wounded leg and then trembled with sudden horror. "The evidence is William Bell's periauger that Teach captured the night after he took the goods from the Frenchman to Knight's house."

Eden's brow wrinkled in thought. "But Bell told me he didn't see the man that rifled his boat."

"No, he didn't, sir. T'was four Negro slaves what seen it. They went with Teach. They saw and they turned king's evidence, too. Now Spotswood knows Teach was a'pirating and he can prove it."

Eden raised an eyebrow. "I see," he said. He looked worried.

"And putting two and two together, they now suspect Knight. Knight told Bell he didn't know of anyone on the river, and yet Knight had just received the goods from the Martiniqueman. It looks mighty suspicious, sir. They know'd Knight lied. And they knows you are in with Knight for the reason o' the letter Knight writ to Blackbeard, November 17."

Tobias Knight, who had been relatively silent up until this point, looked extremely discomfited now. All color drained from his face. He began to wheeze so heavily that Eden insisted upon refilling the man's glass and then demanded he drink at once.

Hands, noticing the man's anxiety, commented, "Aye, if you don't smother things up, it looks as if you two will be swinging from the gallows." He laughed and instantly spat on the floor. Then he wiped his mouth on his shirtsleeve. Out of one eye, he saw the guard approaching him again, but Eden shook his head.

"Let him be," the governor said, "and take him away. I want him out of my sight...forever."

Instantly, Hands fell to the floor in supplication and began to weep piteously. His eyes pleaded with the governor. "Now, listen, sir. I've told you all so give me a bit o' hope, eh, for the sake o' mercy. You'll not forget I told you. See here, I could have kept silent. Spare me, governor."

Eden gritted his teeth. "I'll give you a piece of advice, sir. Don't turn traitor on anyone again. As you wish, I'll give you a concession. I'll spare your life, Mr. Hands. As long as I never see your face again in North Carolina. Now get him out of my sight," he said, shouting to the guard once again.

Hands, now on his knees, thanked the governor profusely. "For my life, I'll be telling you something else. Be prepared for Moseley. He'll be here soon enough."

"Moseley?" Eden looked puzzled.

"Aye," Hands said. "He'll be here with a deposition for your arrest."

That was the last Charles Eden ever saw of a member of Blackbeard's crew—a supplicating, lame man whose name was Israel Hands and who was once first mate of the great Blackbeard. From a corner window, Eden watched the man. He limped piteously across the courtyard, an old tattered hat in his hand, his pirate boots worn out and of no further use. The governor never heard of him again. When the man was out of sight, he drew the curtain and began to prepare for the arrival of his old foe and adversary, Edward Moseley.

Hands had been true to his word. Moseley arrived at Eden's home in approximately three hours time, pushing his way past the servants. Unheralded and unbidden, he entered the library to find his old foe in very much the same position Hands had found him three hours earlier, talking casually with Tobias Knight before a roaring fire in the hearth. Only this time it was Moseley who had the upper hand, or so it seemed, and Charles Eden and Knight who were the prisoners. For outside, a small band of armed guards waited impatiently for a signal from Edward Moseley to declare Charles Eden's home under military rule and Eden and Knight its hostages.

Throwing open the doors, Edward Moseley walked inside the library, a broad smile on his face. He paused for an instant to curl his mustache. Then he faced Eden and Knight, his military accouterments flashing in the light of the fire.

Charles Eden felt bound to acknowledge his rival's presence. "Good evening, Mr. Moseley," he said, about to rise. "And what brings you on such an unexpected visit?"

"Please don't get up, Governor," Moseley said, crossing the room to take a seat not far from the two. "I believe you'll need your seat soon enough." He propped his feet up on one of Eden's imported English tables and took a box of tobacco from his pocket.

Eden raised an eyebrow. Although he had remained quite calm until this point, the sight of Moseley using his table for a foot rest infuriated him. "I find this quite presumptuous of you, Mr. Moseley," Eden said, "coming to my quarters unannounced. Mr. Knight and I were in private conversation. I must ask you to leave."

Moseley, however, refused to budge, preferring for a moment to look for the whereabouts of a light to fire the pipe he now had withdrawn from his waistcoat pocket.

Eden pressed his lips together firmly. "I'll have to call my servants," he said, suddenly standing.

Instantly, Moseley took his feet down from the table and Eden caught sight of a pistol in his left hand. "Not so fast." Moseley aimed the pistol at Eden and motioned for Eden to take his seat once again. "I would warn you not to call your servants, governor," Moseley said. "Or things could get very nasty. Now *sit down.*"

Eden took his seat promptly. He exchanged glances with Knight. "And what, Mr. Moseley, do we attribute this unexpected visit to?" Eden asked.

A trace of a smile played around Moseley's lips. In the next instant, he stood up, walked across the room and took a lighted candle from a desk. He lit his pipe, all the while keeping one eye on Eden and his pistol aimed at the governor's heart. When he had taken a puff from his pipe, he reached into this breast pocket and retrieved a piece of paper. He handed it to Eden and then waited until both Eden and Knight had time to examine the contents.

A most peculiar look came over the chief justice's face.

"Well, Mr. Knight," Moseley said, grinning, "what have you to say in regards to that paper."

Knight wheezed and coughed and carried on to kill time. Finally he spoke up, but it was not at all what Moseley had expected him to say. "Well, I'm a sick man, Mr. Moseley, very sick," he said. "It would do little to question a man what's sick."

Moseley looked him straight in the eye. "That deposition accused you of being in league with Blackbeard the pirate. Don't you have anything to say in your defense?"

Knight put his hand over his heart. "I knew a man once was taken ill with fever," Knight said. "He expired on the same day. He, *wheeze*, had the same as I have, that's why I mention it."

Moseley pressed his lips together. "Well, you'll answer soon enough in court," he said.

Eden interrupted. "I dare say, Mr. Moseley, you wish to have Knight and me arrested."

Moseley threw back his head and laughed. "How observant you are, Governor."

"I'm not as ignorant as you believe, sir," Eden said. His voice had taken on quite a serious tone. "If you'll just take a look out that window," he said, nodding at a corner window.

Moseley permitted his eyes to stray in the direction Eden had indicated.

"Yes, that's the window, Mr. Moseley," Eden said. "You'll find your guards have already been overpowered by my men. We heard from sources unknown to you that you might be paying us a visit."

The smile on Moseley's face suddenly was replaced by a look of shocked surprise. Very slowly and deliberately he eased his way to the window, careful to keep his pistol still pointed at the governor. He drew back the curtain. His face paled. There in the courtyard, were not his soldiers at all but Eden's men, their pistols aimed in his direction. Angrily, he turned around to face Eden. He had been tricked.

He walked straight toward Eden now, pulling back the hammer of his gun, ready to fire at any instant. "I still have you as hostage," he said, glaring at Eden.

Eyes flashing, head thrust back, Charles Eden smiled. "I'm not much of a hostage, Mr. Moseley. Shoot me and you'll have my blood on your shoulders. It's not likely a murderer will get the governorship of North Carolina. And you'll hang soon enough. Now I suggest you put that gun away. It's quite useless." Eden, who had been drinking steadily all the while, now laughed, toasted the man and then downed his entire drink. It was Moseley's turn to be discomfited. But Moseley was not so easily dissuaded and he was not about to put his gun away. He kept it riveted on the governor. "That deposition will show what a scoundrel you are, Governor," he said, frowning. "The people will not mind me murdering a ringleader of a band of pirates."

Moseley's remark did not seem to trouble Eden in the least. In fact, he poured himself another glass of wine and settled back to relax in his chair. He sipped his drink. "You are smart, Mr. Moseley, but not smart enough. And let me tell you why. First point, as for the evidence of Mr. Hands, it seems he was coerced into telling it. He'll testify to that and swear all the evidence he gave was a lie. Second point, all the evidence given by these men is hearsay. Pray consider the evidence of Mr. Hands. From this deposition, Mr. Hands seems to swear positively that Teach went from his boat with a present for Mr. Knight and yet this is out of reach of his knowledge since he was all the time at the inlet thirty leagues from Knight's house. Third point, William Bell did not know positively who the white man was who robbed him. Fourth point, this letter of November 17 doesn't imply any illegal consorting with Captain Teach. And fifth point...and really Mr. Moseley, this is one you should know. In fact I'm surprised at you—a smart lawyer, like yourself not having enough sense to know the law."

"Know the law?" Moseley asked, puzzled.

Eden turned his face in Moseley's direction. "I believe, Mr. Moseley, the four Negroes were the only ones to actually see Captain Teach on board Bell's periauger. Is that not true?"

"Well, yes," Moseley said, looking askance at the governor. "But they'll testify to his guilt under oath."

"I hardly think that evidence will stand up in court."

"And why not?"

"I believe it is expressly stated by law and custom that Negroes ought not to be examined as evidence. That Governor Spotswood used them as evidence is surprising to me. But let me assure you, North Carolina has never and will never let a Negro testify against a white in court. I have the king's word on that."

Moseley looked startled. He had been taken for a fool. His hand began to tremble so that he could not hold his gun and it fell to the floor. He would have said something, but he had been rendered fully speechless.

"So, you see, Mr. Moseley," Eden said. "Your deposition is not worth the paper it was written on." Eden proceeded to shred the paper into scraps and then threw the scraps into the fireplace. They immediately turned to ashes.

Then all at once Eden crossed the length of the room and threw open the door. "Guards!" he shouted.

Moseley spun around to face five armed guards now bounding through the library door.

Both Eden and Knight watched in silence as Eden's council member was cuffed and then taken away.

When he and Knight were alone again, Eden sighed in relief. He had done it. He had pulled off the largest robbery of the century.

Now all he needed to know was the whereabouts of the anchors.

The Whereabouts
of the Plate

Alexander Spotswood was busy putting a leash on Rover to take him for his afternoon walk when there was a knock on the door to his study. This perturbed him a little for Rover bounded from Spotswood's grasp before the leash could be securely tightened. The dog began to yelp excitedly. Spotswood, leash in hand, rose from a kneeling position on the floor as the door opened to reveal a squarish man with whiskers and a clean-shaven lackey. The lackey left Spotswood alone with the man who was carrying a strongbox.

Spotswood recognized the man immediately as the auctioneer he had hired to dispose of the piratical goods from the invasion of North Carolina. Rover continued to bark excitedly, growling and snarling to show his viciousness, but, in fact, the dog had lost his teeth from a recent gum disease. He continued to snarl and pull back its lips menacingly, which made the auctioneer laugh.

"He is a bit of a joke," Spotswood said, calling his dog. "Lost his teeth a fortnight past, but still thinks he's as vicious as ever. Here, Rover," he said, calling the dog to his heels.

The dog bounded back to Spotswood while the auctioneer, taking off his hat, took a seat directly across from the governor. Rover settled down below Spotswood's chair, one eye closed and one eye directly on the auctioneer.

"Well, sir, I sold the lot." The auctioneer smiled in satisfaction with himself. He fished a key out of his pocket, opened the strongbox and then turned it around for Spotswood to examine. "All totaled it come to two thousand, two hundred and thirty-eight pounds, sir. All is before you here."

Spotswood's face beamed as he paused to examine the contents of the box and then to close it again. He listened while the auctioneer proceeded to rattle off all the items sold at last week's monthly auction—twenty-five hogsheads of sugar, eleven tierces and one hundred and forty-five bags of cocoa, a barrel of indigo and a bale, two bags of cotton and two hundred painted anchors—all from the invasion of North Carolina.

As yet, Spotswood had no idea as to how he would dispose of the proceeds. There had been quite a bit of arguing over the matter, but as of now he had decided to keep the money for himself. In confirmation of his thought, he fastened the strongbox key to a chain around his neck.

"I've no doubt," Spotswood said, taking a pipe from his breast pocket, "that the anchors were particularly difficult to sell. There were quite a goodly number of them." He lit his pipe. Below the chair, Rover opened his mouth to yawn.

The auctioneer, seeing that Spotswood meant to strike up a conversation, settled down. "T'was a quantity at that, sir," he said, taking some chewing tobacco out of his pocket. "Didn't think they'd go at first, sir...to tell the truth, I didn't. But just as the auction was finishing up a seaman steps up and bids on the anchors. He was dressed proper, so I knew he had money...had good manners, too. He had a Bristol sailor's accent and he spoke a seaman's jargon, he did. Only wanted to buy one hundred at first, but I said he'd have to buy the lot."

"And right you were to say so," Spotswood said, standing up. He crossed the length of the room to pour two drinks, one for himself, and the other for the auctioneer and then he returned to his seat. After drinking the king's health the two continued their conversation.

"Well, sir," the auctioneer said. He stuck a fistful of chewing tobacco in his mouth and then rolled it around on his tongue. "He hems and haws a bit, but then he agrees since he needs 'em quick-like...he was in a hurry since his ship sailed that afternoon. He paid on the spot."

Spotswood nodded. He was in good spirits over the sale and he patted Rover gently on the head. The dog's tail wagged quickly back and forth, and he snuggled in closer to Spotswood. "What was the seaman's name?" the governor asked.

The auctioneer paused for a moment. "Damn me, if I can't recollect his name. T'was on the tip of me tongue. But it's of no importance. Do remember the ship's name, though."

"You do." Spotswood exhaled a puff of smoke into the room.

"Aye, sir." The auctioneer looked around for a place to spit his tobacco, but seeing none within any convenient range, he continued to chew. Spotswood did not indulge in the habit of chewing, and he did not make allowances for those who did.

"If I do recollect," the auctioneer said, "the ship's name was the *Ariel* and this captain was from the East India Company. Says he's been looking for some anchors for awhile now for the entire fleet."

"I see," Spotswood said. He reached into his pocket and brought out some coins which he laid on the table. "Here's five guineas for your trouble."

"Thank you, sir." The auctioneer smiled and took the money. He rose to go and was about to place his hat back on his bead when a most puzzled look came over his face. He turned back around to face Spotswood for a moment, continuing the conversation. "You know, Governor, I was thinking, sir..."

"Yes," Spotswood said, casually taking a sip on his drink.

Spotswood directed his attention to Rover and scratched the dog's ear. Rover thumped his tail on the floor.

"Well, it strikes me as most peculiar, sir, that this seafaring person, this man who bought the anchors, had been at sea all his life (he's a man as knows his business, sir) and he's never seen a painted anchor."

"Hm," Spotswood said, only half-listening to the auctioneer.

"Nor I," the auctioneer said, finally putting his hat on his head and then walking across the room to pick up his coat. He put it on, buttoned it and faced the governor again. "It's most peculiar, sir."

Spotswood hooked the leash around Rover's neck again and the dog stood up. "Well, this sea captain did buy the anchors. That's the thing of importance."

"Yes, sir. But you know what that sea captain said to me? He said no one paints anchors. 'Salt eats away a coat of paint,' he said. What do you make of that?"

"I have no idea," Spotswood answered, now putting on his hat and coat also, and following the auctioneer downstairs.

"I was only thinking sir," the auctioneer said, as Spotswood saw the man out, "why would someone paint an anchor? Surely, there's no purpose in it."

"None whatsoever," Spotswood said, his attention on his dog again.

The auctioneer shrugged and Spotswood waved goodbye to him as he walked down the Duke of Gloucester Street. When he had disappeared, Spotswood set out with Rover not far behind, sniffing at the roadside along the way. Walking briskly down the street, Spotswood whistled to himself in pleasure at the thought of the money collected from the sale. He had a good mind to use it toward the building of his new magazine.

The street was noisy that afternoon, filled with the yells of street urchins scrambling between the chaises that clattered along the streets and the scraping of shovels heaving away the animal dung from the walkways. Every now and then Spotswood would pause to tug on Rover's leash and give terse commands to his dog, which were extremely ludicrous for they went unheeded, much the same as Rover's barks and growls went unheeded now that he had lost his teeth.

As he walked, the little key to the strongbox around Spotswood's neck jingled and jangled, and Spotswood's thoughts returned to the anchors. He paused to light his pipe again and then puffed on it, reflectively. Those painted anchors were one of those silly, insubstantial things one just couldn't get out of one's mind. Why would one paint anything, he wondered, if it were not to hide what was underneath? He continued to walk, jerking at Rover's leash, but now more moody than before. His whistling became a little off-key. What did Governor Eden and Blackbeard have to hide, he wondered?

He shook his head. As passers-by continued down the streets of Williamsburg, suddenly Spotswood stopped in his footsteps so quickly that Rover ran headlong into him. Spotswood frowned at the dog. He nervously fiddled with the chain around his neck. And then in one brief moment, a most unusual event occurred that caused people walking in the streets to turn their heads in amazement. In the middle of the street, a rather overweight man leading a dog on a leash was heard to shout in the most horror-stricken voice ever imaginable, "The silver! By God, the Spanish silver!"

Shortly after Blackbeard's effects were sold the king of England received a most unusual letter from Alexander Spotswood of Virginia. The letter informed the king that Blackbeard's effects had been mistakenly sold and that until some agreement was reached with the lords proprietors of North Carolina concerning who the effects rightfully and legally belonged to, Spotswood wished the goods returned to Virginia. The goods, Spotswood said, namely two hundred anchors, were aboard a ship, the *Ariel*, which had loaded out of Virginia. Any expenses incurred by transportation of the anchors would be paid out of Spotswood's pocket.

The king was familiar with the *Ariel*—she was the lead ship of the East India Company—and he gave orders to inform the captain of the mistake. On the 24th of the month when the *Ariel* was scheduled to dock at Bristol harbor, messengers were standing by to give word to the captain. The *Ariel* did not dock at Bristol on the 24th. Nor on the 25th or 26th.

Confronted by this news, the customs authorities merely informed the king that this was usual for weather conditions were not the best at this time of year. They predicted the ship would dock in a week's time.

However, in a week's time when the ship still had not docked, officials began to grow a little uneasy. The earlier composure of unruffled calm was replaced by a growing suspicion that something might have happened to the ship. As time passed and no ship appeared, several of the authorities were of the opinion that an investigation should be completed. In response, small light ships modeled after the Spanish *zabras* were dispatched to the Azores and Canaries to see if the *Ariel* had landed there. When the light craft returned with no word of a landing, the mood of officials became more pessimistic.

In two months' time when she still had not landed, officials began to suspect the worst. There had been a frightful storm at sea just a week after the *Ariel* had set sail. It was assumed by the king that the ship had been caught in this storm and most probably had foundered.

In the absence of any fresh developments, the king eventually posted a letter to Governor Spotswood of Virginia, the lord proprietors of North Carolina and Governor Eden of North Carolina. The *Ariel*, he regretfully said, had never reached port in Bristol—the ship was lost and her goods, he feared, somewhere at the bottom of the sea.

Upon receipt of the letter, the lords proprietors were extremely angry. They commented to an extensive degree on the English colonists lack of culture and hygiene. Lord Carteret was more vociferous, communicating clearly and in detail his unswerving belief in the unnatural American fondness for intimacy with savages. Governor Eden became acutely intoxicated, and Alexander Spotswood suffered from pains in the chest that were said to accompany mild cases of heart failure.

Then All Things
Went Well Again

During the week's time when the silver had been stored in the barn of Tobias Knight, waiting to be melted into anchors, Knight had met Eden alone one afternoon.

"Congratulations," Knight said. "Nothing can go wrong now."

Eden leaned back against the storehouse. "Something can always go wrong," he answered, but he was smiling.

"In only a week?"

"Even in an hour," Eden commented.

Later, at a testimony in a private hearing, Eden was astounded by how prophetic his own words were, for his greatest difficulties lay ahead, and they came from the most unlikely source.

The source was Captain Brand, who upon his return to England wrote a letter to the lord commissioner of admiralty complaining about the conduct of Knight. He accused Knight of constantly assisting pirates and maintaining activities that discouraged the rendition of His Majesty's naval service in those parts. He suggested Knight's behavior be investigated.

This further small development in the alleged conspiracy of Eden's administration and its dealings with pirates was not enough to warrant a trial. Several of Eden's council members suggested it was so slight that it be dismissed entirely. Suspicions were later raised concerning these council members' involvement with Knight and Eden. However, others insisted on a formal hearing for the lord commissioners' sake, although they, too, considered the matter of little importance. So a formal hearing was arranged at the home of Colonel Thomas Pollock, twice acting governor of North Carolina and member of Eden's administration. Those several council members who had objected to the hearing did not attend.

The fact that tea was to be served in an hour from the hearing was an indication of how trivial the council members considered the whole matter. Obviously, they were not expecting any fresh developments.

Five council members and Eden were present. Eden was reported to have been very calm, showing no hint of agitation. Knight was ushered into the room, elegantly set off in pewter candlesticks. He was given a seat in a corner.

A Mr. Sharp, a new lawyer in the colony, had been hired to conduct the hearing. Most agreed it was Sharp's method of interrogation that shed new light on the case. In the first fifteen minutes of questioning, Knight stuck to his old story, professing innocence. Sharp had to admit to himself that the man, coughing and hacking in front of him, presented a particularly difficult case.

Knight was coughing into a handkerchief offered to him by one of the council members when Sharp made a casual remark that turned the hearing. "A nasty cough. Where did you get it, Mr. Knight?"

"I don't rightly know, *wheeze*," Knight said.

Sharp raised his eyebrow. For the first time Sharp saw Knight's hand tremble. It was a good indication he was onto something.

Sharp sighed. "You're lying, Mr. Knight," he said, looking at the man. Everything about Knight—his drooping posture, the way he looked at the floor, admitted deceit. "Try to remember where you got the cough, Mr. Knight."

"There's no blame on me," Knight said. "Lies, all lies, those accusations."

"Shall I help you remember, Mr. Knight?" Sharp said, in sudden pretense of knowing more than he did. "Let me see, now your wife tells me, if I do rightly recall..."

Knight's glance shot across the room to Eden, and then he looked at Sharp. "I believe it was October 15," he interrupted. "Yes sir, it was sir, *wheeze*."

Eden never moved, keeping his hands calmly in his lap as the testimony continued.

"I swear," Knight said, "I didn't do anything. There's no sense to this..." Abruptly he broke off, coughing.

There was a brief silence in the room, punctuated only by the ticking of a clock on the wall that was steady, loud and particularly irritating to Knight at this time.

Sharp's voice was steady. "You were a sick man already, weren't you, Mr. Knight?"

"Yes sir." Knight squirmed in his seat.

"Was that not the night of the gale?" Sharp asked, recalling that October 15 was perhaps the worst weather of the entire year. He looked at Knight in puzzlement. "Well, Mr. Knight?"

Knight stared at the floor. "Yes sir. I do believe so, sir, *wheeze*," he said, softly.

"And yet you ventured forth in a gale!" Sharp said, shocked.

"Yes sir," Knight said, wringing his hands.

"What could have been so important that you would risk your life in a gale?"

"Nothing, sir," Knight said.

"Come now." Sharp glared at Knight over his glasses. "You are a sick man, you know it. You hardly venture forth from your house at all any more. And yet, on October 15, you went into a gale and came back with a hacking cough that will soon be the death of you. I find that quite odd, Mr. Knight."

Knight coughed and looked straight ahead, not meeting Sharp's eyes.

Several of the council members who had been talking quietly among themselves now seemed to show interest in the case, for there was a sudden silence in the room.

"How long have you to live, Mr. Knight?" Sharp asked.

"Not long, sir," Knight said.

"And all for want of staying in bed that one night." Sharp shook his head at the apparent foolishness of the man.

"Yes sir. I'm afraid it's so. The doctors say that."

"Then, why, Mr. Knight, did you go out?"

"Business matters, sir," he finally remarked, shifting his weight in the chair and coughing again.

"What form of business matters?"

"Money," Knight said. "*Wheeze*, I had to accept money for customs."

Sharp whirled around on his heels. "That is a lie," he said, pointing a finger at Knight. "And you know it. Everyone is aware in this town that seamen come to your house to pay you for customs."

Knight wheezed and coughed and blew his nose into his handkerchief. Eden did not say a word.

"It must have been a very important matter to risk your life for," Sharp said. "Tell me what it was."

Knight kept his mouth firmly shut.

Sharp paused and stared at Knight. The man was quite calm now, except for his coughing attacks. He glanced at the council members across the room. It was time for a different approach.

He walked across the room, picked up a piece of paper from a desk and put on his spectacles. "Now then, Mr. Knight. I have here papers from Captain Teach's journal."

"Papers?" Knight asked. This time his puzzlement was genuine.

"Indeed, yes," Sharp said, running his finger across the print on the paper. "Ah, yes, here it is...hm...yes. Tobias Knight...hm...met him the night of October 15...hm...yes...it's all here, Mr. Knight, what you did the night of October 15."

"It's not true," Knight exploded. "There is no journal. Teach had no journal!"

Sharp glared at Knight over his glasses. "It's all here on paper, Mr. Knight," he said, casually walking across the room then and handing the paper to Pollock. "What do you suppose he'll get, Mr. Pollock?" Sharp asked.

Pollock took the paper from Sharp for a moment, glanced over it and then looked up. "Probably imprisonment for life," Pollock said, exchanging a smile with Sharp.

"Hm, yes, that sounds about right," Sharp responded.

"Imprisonment for life!" Knight said in a hushed voice.

There was a murmur throughout the room from the other council members.

"Let me see that paper, Mr. Sharp," Charles Eden interrupted. The council members noticed his face had an expression of alarm on it.

But before Sharp crossed the room, Knight had already begun to talk. "It was all for nothing," he said, putting his head in his hands. "It was all lost at sea." He moaned. "All those murders...all that effort. And for what? Nothing. Nothing at all."

Sharp handed the paper to Eden. It was a notification to the buildings committee to the effect that lots would no longer be sold for less than twenty pounds in the township of Bath. Eden glared at Sharp.

"What was lost at sea?" Sharp asked, turning to face Knight.

Suddenly before all the councilmen, Charles Eden bounded from his chair. "No!" Eden shouted, rising, but it was too late. Knight had already begun to talk.

In the next hour, Tobias Knight told the council members everything he knew about the robbery of the Spanish plate from his collaboration with Eden and Blackbeard to the invasion of North Carolina by

Virginia and the subsequent confiscation of the plate from his property. But what was even more shocking than the robbery was the fact that their governor could have participated in such a crime. As Knight explained how Eden had instigated the entire robbery, several of the council members lost all control, their veins standing out on their foreheads. One, in fact, had to be held down for fear he would beat the governor to a pulp.

"This smacks of treason, sir, and no mistake," Sharp said, turning to face Eden. "I never would have thought you would come to this. The governor in league with a common pirate is beyond my imagining."

"Quite a surprise, is it not?" Eden asked. He stared calmly at Sharp.

Sharp colored. The cheek of this man was beyond all imagining. Unable to contain himself any longer, Sharp raised his voice. "In league with a dastardly villain—a ringleader of a band of sea robbers. You are the worst of your kind—a scoundrel of the most common sort."

"Perhaps," Eden said.

Looking at Eden, Sharp thought the governor appeared to be taking a degree of delight in his actions. "This is shocking," Sharp said, "utterly shocking. You have no scruples. I should have you put away in Newgate. Where are your morals?"

Eden began hammering away at the English government. "Had I killed five hundred Spaniards in Queen Anne's War in the name of the British government, I would have been given an honor."

"You have your nerve!" Eden's comment infuriated Sharp. "The governor of North Carolina—a common criminal. Did you never feel at any time some recognition of impropriety, some sense of misconduct, some moral misgivings at the performance of these criminal acts?"

"I do not understand the question," Eden said flatly.

Sharp was enraged. His eyes fired. "I suspect not," he snapped. "It is written all over your face. Let me rephrase the question. These pirates are beasts of prey with whom no communication ought to be had. Think how many vessels they have taken and pillaged belonging to this place as well as multitudes of others belonging to diverse ports of his majesty's domain, and how many poor men in whose blood they have imbued their hands with the greatest inhumanity imaginable, and how many poor widows and orphans they had made and how many families they have ruined, and how long they have gone on in this abominable wickedness."

Eden shrugged.

Sharp's countenance changed from fury to sudden puzzlement. "But, sir, what was your motivation? Why did you conceive, plan, and execute a conspiracy with Blackbeard?"

"I wanted the money," Eden said simply.

"But you are a well-bred gentleman with more money than anyone in the colony. You are the governor of North Carolina."

"Yes," Eden responded.

"You black-hearted scoundrel!" Sharp shouted. "You are no more than a pirate yourself. Your name ranks as one of the most dastardly villains in the history of mankind."

Eden smiled. "Indeed, that is true, sir."

Odd, thought Sharp. The man actually seemed proud of his misdoings. Angrily, he fired his next statement at the governor. "I expect you to recount what happened to us step by step, leaving out no details. Do you understand?"

"But of course." Eden was most cooperative in recounting the events of the conspiracy. In fact, he took a great pleasure in the privilege of telling the story. He was careful to remind the council members from time to time that he had been in league with one of the cleverest and boldest pirates of all—a pirate that had raised himself above the dignity of a king. Those that watched him recount these events said that he demonstrated extreme enthusiasm for his own cleverness. His greatest delight was in giving detailed accounts of the foibles of people fooled by him, especially the secretary of the lords proprietors whom he referred to as a "puffed-up dandy" and Miss Anne Hassell, who he said was a "twittering old maid."

"You tell us a tale of utmost villainy and greed," Sharp said when Eden had finished. "I will see you strung up at Gallows Road before I'm through with you. You and Knight will both be hanged."

"Hanged?" Knight had been quite quiet up until now.

"Yes, hanged by the neck," Sharp said, turning to face Knight now.

"No!" Knight gasped and wheezed.

"And then you'll be drawn and quartered," Sharp said, taking pleasure in the fact that he was at least making one of them feel uncomfortable.

"No," Knight repeated.

"Next you'll be set in the sun a'drying like any other ill-looked sea dog."

Knight put his hand to his chest in sudden fear.

But Eden, remaining quite calm, stood up. He seemed not in the least concerned with the preceding incidents. He glanced hurriedly at his watch. "Well, gentlemen, this has all been extremely interesting. But until my trial I'll have to go. Will you see me to the door?" he asked, addressing Pollock.

"I'll see you hanged," Pollock said furiously.

"I'll see myself to the door then," Eden replied.

Once it was public knowledge that Governor Eden was to stand trial for one of the largest crimes in the history of the English nation, events of ensuing days followed a certain predictable pattern. Councilmen suspected merchants of being in on the deal; merchants suspected councilmen; councilmen suspected other councilmen and merchants suspected other merchants. If the governor of North Carolina could be in on such a plot, anyone could.

Officials offered rewards for information leading to the arrest of more culprits, and informants from everywhere quickly responded with a dazzling array of tips and rumors.

Theories about the loss of the treasure ship ran rampant—from the most mundane—the crew of the *Ariel* stumbling upon the treasure—to an elaborate plot by the highest officials of the English government engaged in a Machiavellian scheme intended to line their own pockets and to sour relations with Spain.

Nevertheless, the widespread belief in the colonies, and later England, was that it was a plot carried out by only a handful of men, particularly in this case where everything pointed to extreme cooperation between people.

The robbery became a sensational topic in print and conversation. Accounts of Eden were received as far away as London where Daniel Defoe wrote a short history of Eden's connection with the great Blackbeard. It was said there was to be a play written about Eden that would be even greater than "The Successful Pyrate," which was now being enacted on the London stage.

All during the next several months the robbery remained sensational. Since step by step details had not been released to the general public, no one could quite figure out how it had been done. It was questioned whether a man such as Eden could conceive of such a dashing undertaking, not to mention bring it off.

The crime gained such magnitude that when Bath sheriffs found themselves confronted with a scrawny little pirate with a gold ring in his ear, who said he was the mastermind behind the crime, the sheriff turned him away without even so much as a question. He seemed to be, said the marshal, "of that misguided state of mind, wherein a man will seize upon a sensationalized event even if it be unlawful, to gain the attention of the public and thus to satisfy his desire for a place in the limelight."

Newspapers in the colonies and England printed every shred of rumor and hearsay about the piracy. During this time, people's opinions progressed from shock that the governor would steal another nation's money to a sort of admiration for the resourcefulness and daring of English rogues who had plotted and carried out the escapade, however it was done. Eden seemed to have gained a great measure of support, especially from the socially underprivileged who viewed his crime as a sort of heroic act against the standing form of government.

Eager writers conjured up fanciful accounts of the man's appearance, manner and style of living: that Eden lived with three mistresses, that he had been involved in other robberies, that he was the illegitimate son of King William, that he lived with the Indians, that he had previously married a German princess and had murdered her before coming to the colonies in 1706. There was not the least bit of truth in any of these stories, but reports like these whipped public interest to the point of frenzy.

For weeks crowds pressed in front of Eden's house. One well-born woman was apprehended while leaving his house with one of the governor's tiffany whisks. Not in the least embarrassed, she remarked that she only wished a keepsake of the man.

When the trial finally did come to pass, a sizable audience had gathered outside the courtroom. He was brought before the bar for the first time on August 28th, 1719, elegant, handsome, charming, composed, and yet, roguish. While the head of the grand jury read his indictment, Eden seemed to show not the least compunction.

"The jurors of our sovereign lord the king do upon their oath present that Charles Eden, late of Bath, North Carolina, on the 15th day of October in the fifth year of the reign of our sovereign Lord George, by the grace of Great Britain, France and Ireland, king, defender of the faith, by great trickery upon the high seas, in the jurisdiction of the Court of Vice-Admiralty of the province of North Carolina did piratically cause to be wrecked, a certain galleon called the *San Rosario*, commander unknown, and then and there did cause to lose their lives, numerous persons unknown, and within the jurisdiction aforesaid did steal, take and carry away, silver, in bars, coin, and ingots of the value of twelve million pesos, like current money of Spain, against the peace of our now sovereign lord the king, his crown and dignity."

The fact that during his trial Eden did not seem to feel any contrition or remorse for his black deed seemed to strike several of the jury members as quite shocking.

Even more shocking was some of Eden's testimony. One exchange occurred on the third day of his appearance in court. Sharp, who was the attorney-general, directed his questions toward Eden with customary abruptness.

"Do you know a man called Israel Hands?"

"Yes," Eden said.

"Where is he now?"

"I don't know."

"Where is Blackbeard's second mate?"

"I don't know."

"Where is his third mate?"

"I don't know."

"There seems to be a great deal you don't know," Sharp said, studying Eden for a moment.

"Yes."

"Where is Blackbeard's ship, the *Adventure*?" Sharp asked.

"I don't know," Eden said.

"Where is the rest of his treasure buried?"

"Under an oak tree," Eden said.

"What was that?" Sharp asked, whirling around on his heels.

"Under an oak tree beside a tombstone in the Lawson graveyard," Eden said, smiling.

"Why didn't you come forth with this before now?" Sharp asked.

Eden shrugged. "You didn't ask me."

Sharp drummed his fingers on the witness stand for a moment, and then, after discussing the whereabouts of the silver with several people in court, it was agreed two of them should go and check out Eden's statement. Court was dismissed until Eden's story could be substantiated.

In an hour's time the graveyard was located and the oak tree found. Appropriate dispensations were obtained to dig beside the gravestone. Mr. Pollock accompanied by Mr. Sharp found a small chest at two o'clock that day. Surprisingly enough, there was no coffin under the tombstone, neither was there any treasure in the chest. Upon reexamination of the chest it appeared the lock had been recently broken. Mr. Sharp was furious at the discovery and Mr. Pollock was embarrassed. In three hour's time court resumed. Eden, sitting in the chair where the men had left him, was told the news.

"I suppose it was stolen," Eden said with a smile.

There was a short silence. Sharp listened to the ticking of a clock placed directly over the judge's bench. For once it made him more nervous than the defendant. Indeed, Eden appeared remarkably relaxed.

But the most astounding event of all occurred at the end of the trial when the main witness, Tobias Knight, was to make his appearance to testify. It seems the man was so sick that just the slightest excitement of the trial was enough to do him in. He died quite naturally that very morning before his testimony could ever take place. His death occurred as he stepped out of his slippers and nightgown. When the news was broken to the courtroom, the uproar was deafening. When the clamor did finally die down, the judge, rising from his bench made the following announcement.

"Gentlemen of the jury, the prisoner at the bar stands indicted for felony and piracy, committed on a galleon the *San Rosario* belonging to the king of Spain. However, there is no proof that this villainous piracy ever took place."

The excitement in the courtroom was overpowering.

Rapping his gavel on the bench, the judge continued, "First, no one has brought forth a complaint that a robbery ever was committed against him, certainly not the king of Spain. Secondly, our only witness, Tobias Knight, has passed away. Thirdly, there is no evidence. Not one peso of silver has been recovered from the Spanish wreck. And lastly, there is no motivation on the part of the prisoner for committing this heinous crime. I would also like to point out that in all logic the governor's character is not in keeping with this crime. I believe he fabricated the entire story. In the light of these facts, I am dismissing this case."

The fact that Governor Eden's case was thrown out of court was particularly appalling to the governor. He stood for at least a minute with his mouth completely open. Later, he showed reluctance to discuss the dismissal. Instead he preferred to reminisce on the earlier details of his association with Blackbeard. This he would do often with only the slightest inclination of interest from an observer. It is reported that during those times that he recalled his association with Blackbeard, his language became colored with sea jargon and he spoke of himself as a pirate.

There were still times in his life, most notably soon after the trial, when several women made scandalous advances toward him in public. He received also, during those earlier years, stares from visitors to the town of Bath. These slight incidents helped to remind him of his infamy and to lift his spirits.

Soon Eden's connection with Blackbeard was laid to rest. It came to be accepted by the citizens of Bath that this episode in Eden's career was merely a fabrication of the good governor's mind. Many attributed it to the pressure brought on by Governor Spotswood's administration. Of course, Governor Eden continued to reminisce about his connections with the pirate—often speaking of the bold and daring deeds he performed. But others remembered little of this famed episode in the governor's life. He was never again able to enjoy that brief flicker of world-wide renown that he held with the one, the only, the most notorious pirate of them all—the great Blackbeard.

Epilogue

That a respectable, high-born gentleman, a governor of the king of England, should adopt a life of crime was all too shocking for society to take in 1718. Certainly there was nothing in the governor's character that would seem to indicate any inclination to wrongdoing. And certainly, at that time no one was ready to openly admit there was anything wrong with the king's laws. To the English mind, the conspiracy did not make sense.

So having little evidence to back up any accusations made against the governor, all charges were soon dropped against him. In 1726 Daniel Defoe, in his *History Of The Pirates,* retracted his former statements made against the governor.

> Charles Eden, Esqr., which we apprehend by accounts since received, to be without just grounds; therefore, it will be necessary to say something in this place, to take off the calumny thrown on his character, by persons who have misjudged of his conduct by the light things appeared in at that time.
>
> Upon a review of this part of Blackbeard's story, it does not seem, by any matters of fact candidly considered, that the said governor held any private or criminal correspondence with the pirate; and I have been informed since, by very good hands that Mr. Eden always behaved, as far as he had power, in a manner suitable to his post, and bore the character of a good governor and an honest man.

Governor Charles Eden continued to hold public office until his death in 1722 from a lingering yellow fever. Records, although mentioning his association with Blackbeard, do not tarnish his reputation as an able and just governor.

In his will, he bequeathed to John Holloway, William Howard's attorney in Virginia, his gold watch and a Negro slave and referred to Holloway as "my very dear friend." John Lovick, secretary of the colony, was appointed Eden's residuary legatee.

The timely arrival of a commission from England with power to grant a royal pardon to piracies committed before August 18, 1718, saved both William Howard's neck and Israel Hands'. Hands returned to England where he was last seen begging for bread in the streets of London.

On March 30,1722, Pollock became governor of North Carolina. The administration was of short duration for he was now an old man and he died in a few months on August 30, 1722. Then William Reed, next in council, became governor "pro tempore" until the arrival of Governor Burrington.

Anne Hassell became the wife of Edward Moseley.

After Eden's death, Moseley and Moore rapidly gained power and influence in the colony. In 1744 Moseley became chief justice of North Carolina. Moore made a settlement on Cape Fear, founding the town of Brunswick.

The invasion of North Carolina had lasting effects. Ironically, many of the seamen aboard the *Pearl* and the *Lyme* who had been instrumental in the capture of Blackbeard, later went a'pirating themselves. An angry quarrel arose between Captains Brand, Gordon and Maynard about the prize money for Blackbeard's capture and how it should be distributed. To add to this, Captain Brand was threatened with a lawsuit in England for his trespassing on the lord proprietor's property.

As for Governor Spotswood, more and more royal disapproval of his actions forced him from office. Not only had the king looked disapprovingly upon Spotswood's illegal entry into North Carolina, but the lord of Orkney, who had appointed Spotswood with Queen Anne's approval, wrote that great disputes had arisen between the lieutenant governor and his council. In 1721 Byrd and Blair both left for England again with complaints against Spotswood. In 1722 John Holloway was chosen speaker of the house. Finally, on April 29, 1722, Hugh Drysdale presented the board of trade a royal commission, dated April 3, appointing himself lieutenant governor of Virginia.

In Williamsburg, Blackbeard's skull continued to dangle for many years from a high pale on the west side of the mouth of the Hampton River as a warning to seafarers. The place is still known as Blackbeard's Point. It was said that the fascination with this skull was unseemly, even decadent. Some suggested that this fascination reflected some fatal flaw in the character of the English mind.

In time, someone took down the grim souvenir of Blackbeard. It is reputed to have been fashioned into the base of a large punch bowl where it was used as a drinking vessel at the Raleigh Tavern in Williamsburg. Blackbeard would heartily approve. Next to roaming the high seas, Blackbeard enjoyed most the companionship of a well-filled punch bowl.